galloway
publishing

galloway
publishing

This is book is dedicated to Tim

who never let me stop

ℰↄ

and to Mab

who stayed by my side as long as she could

ℰↄ

I am forever grateful

the
DEFORMED

Prologue

ADAIR WATCHES HIM. "Are you going to turn me in?"
Richard looks up, his face pale and full of confusion. "How can you ask me that?"

At fifty-four, Adair is fifteen years older than Richard, and for the first time in his life, he feels every day of those years. The awareness of being closer to the end of life than to the beginning has become so clear and terrifying in these last few hours that it almost seems as if, by taking a life, he has somehow shortened his own.

Everything in this familiar room seems suddenly unfamiliar. He knows that desk, those books, the chair Richard is sitting in with his shoulders hunched, heavy with the weight of what Adair has just confessed to him. He knows all of it, but is so removed from it, so far away. The Adair that was in this room yesterday is not the Adair who stands in it now. And he realizes then, that it's not the room that's unfamiliar—it's him. He's become a stranger to himself. And, of course, to Richard.

"It's the right thing to do," he tells his friend. "To turn me in."

The book on the table beside Richard flies across the room as if thrown by an invisible hand. "Goddammit, Dair!"

"Richard, try to calm down. Please."

Richard jumps from his seat. "You want me to calm down! You want to know if I'm going to turn you in! Why did you do it? He served his time!"

"It wasn't enough."

"*Enough?*" Richard cries, then catches himself, lowers his voice. "Enough for what?"

"Enough for her." Everything settles in Adair's mind as he says these words. Everything rights itself. Because this is the truth, and it makes what he's done, if not right, then at least justified.

"Dair..." Richard shakes his head. "It's not like I didn't want to—"

"You just couldn't. But I could."

Richard stares at him. "You say that like—as if you think... You were wrong, Dair! This is *wrong*. This is all wrong!" He collapses into the chair again. He starts to cry. "We've done so much good here."

Adair puts his hand on Richard's shoulder. "You're a good man, Richard. Better than I am. You'll be all right." He moves away. He can't stay here. He doesn't belong here now.

"Where are you going?" Richard's eyes are wide and afraid.

Adair looks at the book across the room, guides it back to the table with his telekinesis. "I don't know."

"Please..."

But Richard doesn't follow as Adair leaves the room and walks down the hallway. Adair gets his coat and hat, thinks of leaving his breather behind—tired of the charade—but he takes it in the end and loops it over his head.

It's dark now. The gravel driveway is wet and gray. The air is filled with a dirty fog that settles on the mask of his breather. He hears a footstep behind him. He turns. "Liam?"

Liam's red-purple eyes, pale skin, and the scar that cuts diagonally down his face stand out peculiarly under the streetlight. "You leaving, Mr. Holden?"

Adair raises an eyebrow. "That hearing of yours is going to get you into trouble one day. Did you listen to our entire conversation, or just part of it?"

Liam shrugs.

Adair shakes his head, sighing. "Yes, I'm leaving."

"Did you get him?"

Adair shouldn't answer that question. But of all the people he knows, Liam is probably the only one who might understand why he's done what he's done. "Yes."

"Good."

And that's all the boy has to say. It's an acknowledgment, a thank you, and an absolution all in one word. *Good.*

Liam doesn't look at Adair in disbelief; he doesn't shudder or gape or look afraid. He looks at Adair the way he always has: with respect. And it's possible, even likely, that this respect has only increased with Adair's admission.

He feels drops of water on the back of his neck. It's starting to rain again. He walks across the street to his car. The printlock on the door registers his fingerprint, unlocks.

"Can I come with you?" Liam calls after him.

"I don't know where I'm going."

"How about somewhere dry?"

Adair smiles slightly. "You mean leave England?"

"For a start."

Adair looks up at the old house. There are no lights on in the front, but he can make out the shingles and the latticework and the color of the paint and the sign above the porch that reads, "The Shelter for Displaced Dysmorphic People." He knows it all so well; just as he knows that, while this place has saved many lives and will go on to save many more, it will do nothing for Liam. He may only be fifteen, but he's past safe places like this and good people like Richard.

"Come on," Adair says, and Liam walks quickly to the other side of the car.

As they turn out into the street, Adair says, "You'll get in trouble with your probation officer, you know."

"Fuck it." Liam's thick London accent lends itself well to his tone of angry teenage indifference. He opens the Velcro straps of his fingerless leather gloves, yanks down on the ends, tightening them. "I could break her in half." He re-straps the gloves, flexing his fingers.

"I'd prefer it didn't come to that."

Liam tilts his seat back and puts his hands behind his head, his smile pulling that vicious scar in two directions. "You got it, boss."

Chapter 1

SHE REMEMBERS how her ears rang. No, not rang—squealed. A steady, high-pitched, painful squeal. Her eyes were wet, gritty. Her chest hurt. She turned onto her side. A voice said, "Don't move, Dr. Kovich." It sounded far away, underwater. She ignored it.

Hands touched her shoulders. "Stay still, Doctor." She didn't recognize the man's face. He wore a uniform. "We've got you. You're going to be fine. We're taking you to the hospital, okay? Can you hear me? Do you understand what I'm saying?"

He sounded miles away, but he was right there, right above her. She told him that yes, she understood. But she couldn't hear her own voice.

"Great, Doctor," the man said. "You're doing great."

When she woke in the hospital, hours later, Mara was informed by the police that she had survived a bombing.

A bombing? Who would bomb a parking garage? was her question.

The policemen looked at each other, said the bomber wasn't after the garage.

Then what?

Her, the police said. They were after her. The bomb was in her car and it went off prematurely.

Mara remembers that look the two officers gave each other, can see it now, in her mind, but she didn't understand what it meant until the shock diminished and the pain lessened. What kind of a stupid fucking question had that been? "Who would bomb a parking garage?" She's still embarrassed by it. She wishes they had chosen to talk to her when she was more lucid so she could've shown them she's not an idiot; she's not afraid; she's not fragile.

But those thoughts are just as stupid as being surprised that someone would put a bomb in her car.

A few days later, an arrest was made. Kelley Pierce, a low-ranking member of the Dysmorphic Coalition, after rounds of Intensive Questioning, confessed to attempted murder.

"The so-called scientists at Hammond Prison are using people as guinea pigs!" he shouted into a news cam at his arrest. She'll never forget his face, his fierce, leonine eyes, how he yelled and spat at the camera. "They have to be stopped! And we won't stop fighting until they are!"

It got a lot of press. Dysmorphic human rights activists got plenty of face time. Upstate New York and Hammond Prison were back on the radar, and the debate over prisoner experimentation raged again, but only briefly. Mara declined to be interviewed. There was no backlash from DCo leader Alan Bryce after Kelley Pierce was arrested. Security was tightened at the prison and the lab. But Mara refused a personal security team.

It hadn't been all that bad: a few outraged voices on the news, a couple of gradually weakening protests outside the prison. Then a congressman was caught having a threesome, the new season premieres of the most popular Cube shows started, the latest version of World had people sleeping in the streets and lining up around blocks to get it—a hell of a lot more people than had ever shown up at a protest—and it was over.

These memories flash through her mind as she stands in the prison laboratory over the dead body of Rico Martinez, who was serving a three-year sentence for grand theft auto. She ran as fast as she could when Lena told her what Weir was doing, but she's too late.

"Goddammit, Rhys! What did you do?" She slams her fist down on the operating table. "After everything that's just happened—Jaida, Twenty-Five—you pull a stunt like this?"

Weir pulls his gloves off lazily, balls them up in one hand, and lifts his mask off his face with the other. He speaks in his calm, precise way, the barest hint of a Dutch accent coloring his voice. "Mara, if you don't want any of our subjects to die, maybe we should stop experimenting on them."

She glares at him. "You went too far, too fast."

"I wanted to see how much he could handle."

"And now he's dead!"

Weir shrugs. "Mystery solved."

She pulls her mask over her head, throws it on the floor. "This was supposed to be a long-term project."

"It's a ridiculous project, Mara. We already know everything about regeneration that could possibly be known."

"Did you really just say that to me?"

"You can tell them it was my fault."

"It *is* your fault!"

"Then you won't have to lie." He smiles, as if he's just done her a favor.

Mara wants to throw something at him, wants to kill him. She takes a slow breath. "He has family."

"Well, whose oversight was that?"

"He wasn't supposed to die."

"He fingerprinted a waiver."

She rolls her eyes. "In a drug-induced haze."

"It counts."

He's right; it does count. But that won't matter when the Martinez family comes looking for Rico, only to find out that he died during an experiment. Fingerprinted waivers will make a difference in court, if they decide to take it that far, but the media won't care.

Mara watches as Weir methodically disposes of his gloves and mask, fixes his hair, unties his surgical smock. The dead man fills the space between them.

"You know how it will be," he says, dispassionately. "The vultures will come, they'll eat, and then they'll grow bored. Or at least their audiences will. Because the truth is, nobody really cares. Oh, isn't that a shame, they'll say, how awful. And then," he holds an imaginary remote control, "*click*. What else is on?"

She looks down at Rico Martinez's open, dead, lizard-like eyes. His face is already growing pale; his parted lips are blue, revealing slightly pointed teeth.

"Coffee?"

She blinks up at Weir. "What?"

"Coffee. Would you like a cup of coffee?"

Mara's hands tighten. She digs her nails into her palms. "Coffee," she says as calmly as she can.

"Yes."

Rhys Weir is the kind of person who isn't really a person at all. He looks like one. His graying hair and light eyes make him seem friendly, almost fatherly, to anyone who hasn't known him long. But that twinkle in his eye, the friendly curve of his lips, his smile lines—Mara knows that none of those things are real. Or that, if they are, they never mean what you think they do.

There's a strange innocence in his face that doesn't belong on a man his age, a childlike curiosity; the kind of child who would pull all but one of the legs off a spider just to see what would happen, or tie a dog to a pole and put its food and water just out of reach to see how long and how hard the animal would fight the impossible until it gave up in despair, or died trying.

When he asks her if she wants coffee, he's not being funny or ironic or trying to make her feel better; that he's asking her over the body of a dead man—a man he killed in a failed experiment—doesn't strike him as strange. It's that unique ability only children have to look down at the toy they've just broken and say, Oh well, let's do something else.

"Mara?"

"Yes," she snaps. "I'll have a coffee."

He smiles, opens the door for her, and they leave their broken doll behind to find a new game to play.

☙

"Jesus, Vee," Cash says.

Venus tilts her head back, her nose stuffed with cotton. "Fuck," she moans. Her eyes and nose pulsate painfully. "Is it broken?"

"No. I don't think so." He sits on the bed beside her, lightly rubs her back. "The painkiller'll kick in soon."

"Not soon enough." She rights her head, closes her eyes. Even that hurts.

Cassius bites his lip. "We're going to leave now, right?"

"We're not going anywhere."

Cash sighs loudly. "Vee. You just got punched in the face by a neo-Nazi in broad daylight on live Cube!"

"Exactly! I'm not going to leave like I'm scared!"

"*I'm* scared!"

"You can stay in the trailer then and I'll go out there by myself. Somebody's got to cover these protests."

She stands and goes into the little bathroom of their trailer. When she sees herself in the mirror, she feels pity for her reflection, as if she's looking at someone else.

Her light gray lion eyes are surrounded by purple-black bruis-es. Her nose is ugly and swollen. Her already frizzy, mane-like gray hair is even bigger than usual. She wets her hands and runs them down the sides of her head to flatten it. It doesn't do much good. She needs a shower. Looking down at the tops of her hands, she sees blood embedded in the gray fur. She scrubs it away, watches the water drain red.

Cash leans in the doorway. "Venus."

She looks at him in the mirror.

His face is grim, and she already knows what he's going to say, even as he hesitates before saying it. "No one cares about this anymore. You know that."

"*I* care." She turns to him. "You care."

He crosses his arms, looks down at the floor.

She stares open-mouthed at him. "A twelve-year-old dysmor-phic boy gets gunned down by a police officer because the guy thought his 'claws looked like knives'?"

"I know—"

"He gets off without a hitch? He's back on the streets! It was a *head shot*, Cash!"

"I *know*—"

"We've got curfews and tanks on the streets. Riots. People are dying here!"

Cassius looks almost angry now. "You don't have to tell *me*!"

"No. I have to tell the world!"

He points toward the door. "They know, Vee! That's the prob-lem! They know, and they don't *want* to know!"

"Then we just have to keep reminding them!"

"Whether they watch or not?"

His words sting her. She steps past him and into the small kitchen. She takes a soda out of the fridge. When she sips it, her nose twinges. She tries to ignore it.

She thinks of her and Cassius's old job, their "real" news job. That network stopped covering these riots a week ago, and most people have already forgotten about twelve-year-old Michael Eyres, whose murder started it all. If she stops talking about it, he'll disappear completely.

And she can't let him disappear, not after today, not after interviewing his mother and witnessing her powerless grief. She keeps seeing that pic Mrs. Eyres showed her; she can't get it out of her mind.

Venus sees the Cube on the kitchen table. She goes and turns it on. In the 3D vid projected above it, she sees herself sitting with Ellie Eyres. Mrs. Eyres is showing her the pic of Michael projected above a PhotoCube. "He had the most beautiful eyes, don't you think?" the woman says.

Venus watches herself nod, pre-broken nose, and say, "Yes."

"He liked to keep the fur on his head like this." She points. "So the stripes really stood out. See?"

The cam zooms in as, behind the scenes, Cassius focuses his Lens cam on the pic. Michael stands with his clawed thumbs hooked under the straps of his backpack. His head is shaved so close to his skull, the tiger stripes look painted on. Venus was, and still is, awed by the boy's obvious confidence, his self-esteem—encouraged, no doubt, by the loving woman who sits beside her in the vid, who never saw her son as anything but perfect.

Venus wishes she could stop the vid right here, that the story stopped right here, with the picture of this happy, living boy. But she knows what comes next.

"I took this the day he was killed," Mrs. Eyres says.

And Venus's heart breaks all over again.

"He was on his way home from school. He ran into a group of boys from the high school. There's always someone..." Her voice fades. She covers her mouth, shakes her head, reaches toward the pic. Her fingers seem to disappear into the 3D image, the ghost of her son. "I told you never to walk home alone, baby," she whispers. "I told you." She draws her hand back, takes a breath, regains her composure. "I'm sorry."

"Please don't apologize, Mrs. Eyres. I understand."

Venus winces, hearing herself say that. The reply was automatic and thoughtless. How could she possibly understand what Mrs. Eyres was feeling?

But in the vid, Mrs. Eyres gives her a small, grateful smile. "He was a gentle boy, Ms. Carr. He never picked a fight no matter how badly they made fun of him. He told me he was afraid to fight. Because he was so much stronger than... normal people. He was afraid he'd hurt someone."

A child. A pacifist. The more Venus learns about this boy, the more she sees how large a hole he has left in the world.

"So..." Mrs. Eyres goes on. "These boys—they bullied and pushed him and called him names. But he got past them and kept walking. A policeman was nearby. He saw the whole thing, but he followed Michael. He told him to stop and turn around, so Michael did." Her voice quavers and she clenches her fists, not in anger, Venus thinks, but in an attempt to stay in control. "I always told Michael to listen to the police. He did everything he was supposed to do. The policeman told him to put up his hands, and he did, and then he just shot him. He said..." She shakes her head. "He said he thought Michael was holding knives. He said he was afraid Michael would... *attack* him. A little boy." Her eyes are tear-filled now, her hands open, and she looks at Venus with confused pleading, as if she thinks Venus has the answer to this unspeakable evil. "Michael did *everything* he was supposed to do. Everything. And that man just... shot him."

Venus knew all that—she'd seen the vid of the actual event, captured by a traffic cam. Everyone had seen that vid, and still, the officer got away with it.

Venus closes her eyes, tells the Cube to turn off.

Cassius comes up behind her. He puts his hand on her back.

She looks at him. "That should be our tagline."

"What?"

She lowers her voice, movie trailer style. "*Phenomena*: Whether you're watching or not!"

Cassius gives her a small smile. "I like it."

There's a quiet beeping, and he pulls his Lens from his pocket, puts it on. His eye moves rapidly behind the clear eyepiece. She watches him. His smile fades, his frown deepening.

"What is it?"

He takes his Lens off and hands it to her. "Hammond."

Her eyes water at the slight weight of the Lens on the bridge of her nose. She reads quickly. "I guess you get your wish," she says, sighing. "We're going to New York." She removes the Lens. "But this interview goes up tonight. Whatever happens, I'm not going to let this boy die all over again."

Cassius nods, serious and sad. "You got it, Vee."

જ

Layla crosses her legs as she drinks her coffee. After a lifetime of being stared at, she's learned to ignore it. And she's also learned to sit up straight without shame because she knows how beautiful she is. She sets her mug down and stretches her arms out and up. Her bat-like wings expand from her wrists to her waist, the tendons taut, her iridescent skin and colorful feathers glittering under the lights. Some of the diners look away while others become even more fixated.

Adair smiles at her over the dessert menu. "Always showing off, my hummingbird."

"They deserve it."

"No one deserves you." Adair takes her hand and kisses it. He's about to say something else when an argument breaks out near the door of the diner.

A dysmorphic girl, thin and sickly, hangs her head as she's berated by a waiter.

"Give me a moment," Adair says, getting up from the table.

"Dair, no."

Layla hears the word "police," and the girl's head jolts up. She has bright, yellow, slit-pupil eyes and light green skin. Her neck is covered on either side with snake scales, which disappear into her long, glossy black hair. They reappear on either side of her forehead in two separate triangles that curve down through her eyebrows, stopping just above her lidless eyes. The pattern continues just under the eyes, ending in points, like two teardrops. When her lips part, Layla can see fangs. She also sees the intent in the girl's glassy, desperate eyes.

But before the waiter can activate his Lens, before the girl can make her move, Adair steps in. "What's the problem here?"

"No problem," the waiter says. "I'm taking care of it."

"If it's a matter of money, I would be happy to pay for her meal." The girl looks at Adair, at the waiter, at the door. "I'm sure we don't want the police involved."

"This fucking d-form half-n-half thinks she can just walk out of here without paying. I'm blinking the police."

Layla is standing now. Adair leans in, says something to the man, and nods toward a table of college students, too young to be drinking. The waiter follows his gaze, then looks back at Adair, fuming.

Layla hears a soft ping and sees the girl's charges appear with hers and Adair's on the tableface, underneath an ad for PurAir Breathers: "Breathe Better, Breathe Deep." When she looks up, the girl is running out the door.

"My hero," Layla says when Adair returns.

"Don't be angry."

"Can we just get out of here?"

When they exit into the parking lot, the same waiter follows them out.

"Not another problem, I hope," Adair says to him, adjusting his breather.

The man's rat-like smile shows through his own breather mask. "My manager would like me to tell you that you're no longer welcome in this establishment." The smug satisfaction in his voice is blood-boiling.

"I see."

Layla is thinking how much she envies Adair's calmness, but then the waiter says, "You should stick to your own kind, d-form fucker. How much did you have to pay for this half-n-half slut? She looks pretty pricey."

A quick punch, and the man is on the ground clutching his throat and coughing. He doesn't know how lucky he is to be alive. Adair could have broken his windpipe if he'd wanted to. Layla kicks him in the stomach.

"There now, we don't want to kill him." Adair pulls her away because he knows she *does* want to kill him.

Near their car, Layla is surprised to see the girl there, wonders why she's wearing a breather. Adair asks her if she's all right. She says nothing. He asks her name. She shakes her head.

Layla frowns. "You think she could at least say thank you."

"Layla." Adair takes a step toward the girl. She moves back. "My name is Adair Holden. This is Layla Monroe. We're dysmorphic, too. We won't hurt you. Do you need help?"

The girl looks from him to Layla and back again.

Layla sees that the waiter has started to breathe almost normally again. "We need to leave, Dair." She walks to her side of the car and unlocks it.

The girl is nodding. She's crying.

Adair looks at Layla.

"No, Dair. No."

He smiles at her, at what he would call her "hard-heartedness," and opens the back door of the car.

On the way home, Layla keeps looking at the girl in the mirror. She must be in her early twenties, not much younger than Layla is herself, but she's small and thin and pathetic. At one point she looks up at Layla and her eyes widen, as if seeing her for the first time.

"You're so... beautiful." Her voice is barely a whisper.

Adair laughs a little when he sees the expression on Layla's face. "Don't look so sour, hummingbird." He gives the car control, letting it drive itself, leans back, takes Layla's hand. "After all, what she says is true."

ℂ

The sand is warm under his back. The ocean crashes and recedes, crashes and recedes, and the seagulls call. He smells the salt in the air, the sun burning the sand. And the best part is, the light doesn't hurt his eyes. It's the only place where he doesn't have to wear his goggles in the sunshine.

Somewhere in the distance he hears the car pull up the driveway—Holden and Layla back from their trip. The front door opens and closes, and he becomes dimly aware of footsteps in the hall.

"Liam."

He's alone on the beach, half asleep, and he wants to stay that way.

But then Holden speaks again, louder this time. "Liam. Turn that off."

Liam holds back a sigh. "World, off." The beach disappears and he's back on the couch in the living room, fuzzy-headed and barely awake. "Sorry, boss." He sits up, detaches the World from his temple, rubs his eyes. "I was falling asleep. Everything okay?" He looks up and feels a jolt in his chest as he meets the eyes of someone he doesn't know. Holden and Layla are not alone.

"Eden," Holden says to the small, thin girl next to him. "This is Liam."

The girl has a greenish tinge to her skin, with snake scales like intricate tattoos on her neck and face. And her eyes—they're a glowing yellow, with black slit pupils. Liam stares at her, doesn't know what to say.

"Eden will be staying with us. I expect her to be well treated."

I expect you to leave her alone. I expect you not to touch her or even speak to her if you can help it. This is what Holden means, but doesn't say. He's known Liam for most of his life, and knows him too well.

Still, Liam doesn't move. He should say something or nod, but he can't. He's still staring at the girl, and, strangely, she is staring back at him. He's used to people gawking at him because of his eyes and his scar, but they always look away as quickly as they can. They never look into his eyes... like she is.

Holden speaks sharply now. "Liam!"

Liam wakes up, looks away from her. "Yeah, boss. Got it."

The look Holden gives him is louder than a scream.

"I got it," Liam says again. *Don't look at her. Don't touch her.*

Holden holds his gaze for another moment, then looks at Layla. "Would you show Eden to a room? I have some things to do."

"Dair, it's one o'clock in the morning."

"I won't be long." He kisses her cheek and leaves the room.

Layla looks from the girl to Liam. "I'm tired. I'm going to bed. You do it."

Liam nods, looking at the girl again. Her eyes never leave his, and they never blink.

Layla crosses her arms. "You know what 'well treated' means, right?"

He smiles at her. "Sure I do, Layla. I can join you upstairs and give you a quick demonstration, if you like."

"Too quick for me."

He puts his hands up. "I surrender."

When Layla is gone, Liam stands, puts the World into his pocket, looks the girl up and down. Her hands are at her sides, and one of them is holding a breather by its long tube, the mask and clip-on filter dangling close to the floor.

"What are you doing with that?"

She looks at it. "I need it."

"Why?"

She doesn't answer. Her clothes are too big for her. She's so small.

"You leave your kit in the car?"

"My kit?"

"Yeah. Your kit. Your bag. Suitcase, whatever."

"Oh. No. I don't have one."

Her voice gives him a chill. The sound goes right through him. He wonders what she looks like under that big hoodie. He steps up to her, tugs at the sleeve, catches himself and pulls away quickly, stuffs his hands into his pockets. "That isn't yours. Doesn't suit you. Where'd you come from?"

She looks away for a moment, then, "Are you from England, like Mr. Holden?"

"Born and bred. Hail Britannia and all that. Ever been?"

"No. I've never been anywhere."

He sees now that her eyes have no lids. They never close, and this fascinates him. *Don't look at her.* "Right, well. Come on."

The living room opens directly into the hallway, like a stage in a theater, no door. The rug simply stops and the hardwood floor begins. The stairs are to the left, but before he starts to climb them, he points across the hall to the double archways that lead into the kitchen. The light is still on. "You hungry?"

"No. I'm fine. Thank you."

He gestures to the left. "Down that way there's a bathroom and a closet with towels and stuff in it. And the door to the basement. Not much else."

"Okay."

"And the other way," he looks to his right and nods in the direction of the front door, "that door on the left is Holden's office."

He turns back to her. She's already looking at him. His breathing speeds up, so he moves away from her to start up the stairs. "So, yeah. That's that."

Upstairs, she keeps turning her head toward him as they walk down the hall. He can see her out of the corner of his eye.

He undoes the Velcro straps of his fingerless gloves, one at a time, tightening the fit, closing them again. The tearing sound is loud in the silence. He stretches his fingers at his sides. The leather, so broken in by years of daily use, is like a second skin.

They reach an empty room. It's next to his. He knows he's done this on purpose, but lies to himself.

"Here." He opens the door for her.

She steps inside, looks around, then turns back to him. "Thanks."

Now he can't look away. She's caught his eye again and he just can't look away. He has a strange feeling that he knows her somehow, as if they've met before and were friends. But of the few people Liam has ever counted as his friends, she is not one of them and never has been. He knows he's never seen her before. Why does she feel so familiar?

"Eden."

She nods.

"Like the garden." He smiles. "Like Paradise."

"I guess."

Don't look at her. Don't touch her.

But he takes a step forward, pulls his hand out of his pocket. He touches her face, just with his fingertips, then pulls away. She doesn't move. His head is swimming. What the hell is wrong with him? He's tired, he decides. She looks tired, too, and sad. He thinks of doing something nice for her, getting her a cup of tea or... something. But what's the use of that?

"Holden wants me to stay away from you."

"He didn't say that."

"He doesn't have to."

She gives nothing away. All she says is, "Why?"

"Because..." He reaches out again, takes a lock of her long dark hair. It's so soft. "I'm a very dangerous man."

She looks down at her hair weaving through his fingers. "Are you?"

The silken strands move like water over his hand. "You're very pretty. How old are you?"

She's looking into his eyes again, but says nothing.

"Well, doesn't matter." He lets her hair slip away. It falls against her cheek. "Want me to help you make the bed?"

She nods.

He finds sheets and blankets for her in the closet. They look up at each other as they work, down again, up again. They don't talk. When they finish, he can't think of another reason to stay, but he doesn't want to leave. "You need anything else?"

She shakes her head, walks with him to the door.

He steps out, and they're facing each other again. He leans in a little, says quietly, "Personal question? Did I imagine it, or is your tongue forked?"

"You didn't imagine it." And he sees just a quick flick of it as she says this.

He could watch her speak all day. "Bet that comes in handy for all sorts of things."

When she doesn't say anything, he backs away. "Suppose I'll see you in the morning, Paradise. Goodnight, then."

"Goodnight."

His room shares a wall with hers. Lying in bed, he hears her walking around, can tell when she stops and sits on the bed by the creak of the springs. There's a stretch of silence and he thinks she's gone to sleep, but then he hears her crying. It's muffled and quiet, but he hears it. A familiar wave of sadness, which he would usually ignore, washes over him. He wants to go to her. He wants to ask her why she's crying.

He pulls his World out of his pocket, fixes it to the side of his head. "World, on. Beach."

But he can still hear her crying just under the pound of the sea.

಄

"Who the fuck are you?"

The girl drops the egg she's cracking into the pan, spins around and puts her hands up. Damian grabs her by her shirt.

"I came last night... with Layla and Mr. Holden."

"Oh yeah?" He pulls her out of the kitchen to the bottom of the stairs and shouts, "Hey, Layla?"

"What?"

Damian looks at the girl. "Did you bring home a snake last night?"

"*What?*"

"Did you bring—"

"Shit, Grace, you haven't frightened her to death already, have you?" Liam appears on the landing. He jumps down the length of the steps and over the railing to land behind Damian.

"Figured I'd leave that to you."

"Nah, we've met. Old friends by now, ain't that right, Eden?"

The girl smiles slightly. Damian lets her go with a shove. "Someone should have left me a note."

"Don't pretend you know how to read." Liam walks up to Eden, puts his hand on her shoulder. "He's all talk. Don't let those shark eyes and furry white back scare you. It's just a disguise that hides the poetic soul within."

"How do I hate thee. Let me count the ways," Damian says.

"Lovely." Liam tilts his head. "Something burning?"

The girl starts and runs back to the kitchen.

Damian smirks. "She's making breakfast."

In the archway, they watch Eden salvage the meal. She moves smoothly and quickly in the horseshoe-shaped kitchen area—stove on one side, counter opposite, sink straight across the top, facing a small window. The pots hanging above the stove reflect the morning sunlight. Bacon and eggs sizzle in pans on the burners. The coffee pot steams on the counter. It's a disturbingly domestic scene, Damian thinks.

"Now that's what I like to see." Liam crosses his arms, leans against the arch. "A woman in the kitchen where she belongs."

Layla walks between the two of them and smacks Liam on the back of the head.

"What the fuck!"

"For being a misogynistic pig."

He rubs his head. "Jesus, Layla."

Damian watches Layla walk to the refrigerator. "I don't get a hello?"

From inside the fridge, he hears, "Hello," as Layla pulls out the milk. She sets it on the counter and frowns at Eden. "What are you doing?"

Eden turns from the stove to face her. "Making breakfast..."

"We don't need a fucking cook."

"Yes we bloody well do!" Liam steps up to the other side of the counter, between Layla and Eden. "If you stop her, I'll throw you across the room."

"Fuck you. Give me a mug."

Liam gets one from the cabinet, hands it to her, then turns to watch Eden. Her back is to him, and if she's aware of how close he is or that he's undressing her with his eyes, she doesn't show it.

Layla reaches for the coffee pot. She pours, adds the milk, and stirs.

Damian steps up behind her, puts his hands on her shoulders. She always smells good, and he loves her bright, shimmering skin, how it contrasts so completely with the darkness of his own. He loves the feel of her feathers—iridescent layers of pinks, purples, and greens. They trail down the back of her neck in a long line, covering her shoulders and chest, stopping just above her breasts and mid-back. Except for her pointed bat wings, Holden's saccharine pet name for Layla, hummingbird, fits perfectly.

He kisses her cheek, her short hair brushing his face. "I have to agree with Aldrich."

"Get off me," she says quietly. And though he knows she doesn't mean it, he backs away and walks over to the other side of the room to sit at the table.

When they're all seated, the girl finds plates and dishes out eggs, bacon, and toast. She serves them as if she's always been here, always done this. She's small and weak-looking, servile and quiet.

When she puts a cup of coffee in front of Damian, she says, "Your name is Grace?"

Liam nearly chokes, manages to swallow and bursts out laughing. "I think I'm in love!"

Damian gives Eden a long look. Her pale green cheeks blush a pinkish-purple.

Layla doesn't even try to hide her vindictive smile. "*Damian Grace*. It's a pretty name, isn't it?"

"I'm sorry," Eden says to him. "I heard Liam call you Grace."

Before Damian can say anything else, Holden comes in. "I wondered if Layla had tried her hand at cooking again, but I thought, that can't be right, it smells too good." He kisses Layla on the top of her head.

"Ha. Ha." Layla tilts back to look up at him.

He smiles at her. "Only joking, my love." He sits beside Layla, and the girl gets a plate for him as well. "You didn't have to do this, Eden," he says.

"I wanted to thank you."

"Well, I hope you're eternally grateful." Liam's plate is already empty. "Because that was fucking gorgeous. Very much like yourself."

Damian doesn't miss the look that Holden gives Liam or the effect it has on him. Liam goes quiet, turns his attention to his coffee. He rips open the straps across the backs of his gloves, pulls the gloves down tight, closes the straps again—a nervous habit. After a moment, he takes his Lens from his pocket, puts it on, and his gaze focuses on whatever he sees in the clear eyepiece.

"So how's my buddy Gus doing?" Damian chews a piece of bacon.

"A little worn down, I think," Holden says.

Layla lazily stirs her coffee. "He looked like shit."

"He'll be all right."

Damian nods. "What's the game plan?"

"Damian." Layla nods at Eden. "Not now."

"What's she going to do? Blink the police? They're probably looking for her."

"No, I bet Layla's right." Liam smiles at Eden as she pours him another cup of coffee. "You're a spy for the DDAT, aren't you?"

Eden smiles back at him, but says nothing.

Holden looks at Layla. "I don't think we have anything to worry about."

Layla seems ready to argue, but all she says is, "Fine. Whatever."

"You worry too much, hummingbird."

Layla gives Holden a grudging smile. Damian sees her put her hand on his thigh. Ignoring that, he says, "So?"

Holden turns his attention back to Damian. "The rally begins at noon. There are three speakers. When they've finished, I'll take down the south wall."

"Why the south?"

"It's where the cafeteria is. Most of the prisoners are allowed to eat there, so we may get more out than I thought." He accepts Eden's offer of more coffee. "Thank you. August will be able to lower the drug dosages for most of them, so they'll be able to fight and hopefully get away. And he says that all the extra security will be focused on the crowd, not the prison. So they'll have a chance."

August could have blinked and told them all of this, but after the last time they heard from him, Damian and Holden agreed it would be better to see him in person. Damian could tell that August wasn't doing well just by the sound of his voice.

He leans back in his chair, smiles slightly. "This is going to be fun."

Holden takes a breath, his face tensing. "If we start thinking of it that way, we'll lose sight of its importance. It won't be 'fun.' It'll be dangerous. People's lives are at stake. Don't forget that."

"Jesus, Holden. Lighten up."

"Oi!" Liam flips up his Lens's eyepiece. "Show some fucking respect."

"Go back to fantasyland, Aldrich. The adults are talking now."

Liam's chair scrapes the floor as he stands.

"Oh, no," Layla drawls, "the children are fighting again."

Holden picks up his coffee, gets up from the table. "Save your strength, lads. Eden," he turns to the girl, "would you come and speak with me for a moment?"

She nods and follows him.

"And Liam? I need you to check and make sure the house filter is working properly."

Liam frowns. "What for?"

"Just do it."

"Can it wait till the sun goes down?"

Holden shakes his head. "As soon as possible, please."

"Right. Will do, boss."

When the three of them are alone, Layla clinks her nails against the sides of her coffee mug. "So, how do you like our new resident mime?"

"What the fuck?" Damian laughs. "You find her on the side of the road or something?

"Ask Dair about it."

And then he sees it. Of course. He grabs her hand and kisses it. "Don't be jealous. She doesn't hold a candle to you, *hummingbird*."

She yanks her hand back. "Don't call me that."

Liam leans against the counter, pulls out his thick, black goggles from the inside pocket of his jacket. "Fucking house filter. I don't even know where it is."

"Somewhere in the house," Layla says.

"Oh, you're a fucking laugh riot." He cleans the goggles with a corner of his shirt. "What do we need it for?"

"She's got breathing issues or something."

"Jesus!" Damian shakes his head. "You brought home the one the shelter forgot to put down."

Layla laughs and smiles at him.

Liam shrugs. "Well, if it's for her, I don't mind."

"I'll bet you don't."

"Be nice, Damian," Layla says. "I'm actually very proud of Liam. I left Eden all alone with him and she made it through the night."

"Fuck you." Liam loops the goggles around his head and glares at them.

"If only looks could kill, huh, buddy? With those eyes and that face?" Damian points at him, clicks his tongue. "Pow. Like a fucking nanoslug."

"Hey, you never know," Layla's eyes narrow, "she might have a thing for the whole red-eyed albino look."

Damian thinks Liam might throw something, is surprised when he smiles and says, "Anything's possible. Then again, lovely Layla, a sweet little homebound woman in the kitchen might start to look a lot nicer to Holden than a two-timing whore like you. Or is it three-timing now? I can never keep track."

Layla flies to her feet. Liam catches her arm when she tries to slap him, and then the other when she goes to scratch his face. He's laughing. "Keep your claws in, bitch!"

Damian stands, holds Layla back. Liam moves out of reach and pulls the dark, black eyepieces down. "Got to fix the filter. Later, lovers."

"I'm going to fucking kill you, Liam!" Layla screams, but he's gone out the back kitchen door. "Did you just let him talk to me like that?" She turns on Damian, hits his chest with her fist. "Did you?"

"What did you want me to do? Kill him? If I did that, who would fix the house filter for our new friend?"

"I hate you."

"No you don't."

"I hate *him*."

"Yeah, but you love to hate him. You'd miss him if he was gone."

Layla's face is tight with anger. "I wouldn't miss you."

He kisses her forehead. "You couldn't live without me. Now," he pulls out her chair, "sit down and I'll pour you a nice cup of coffee."

"Asshole." But she sits, and he goes to the counter to refill her mug.

He puts the coffee in front of her. "I'll be right back."

"Where are you going?"

"I'm going to punch Liam in the face."

Her eyes widen.

"What? You think I'm going to let him talk to you like that? Come on, Layla. Who the fuck do you think I am?"

೧

Adair sits beside her on the bay window bench in the room he calls his office but is really just a place where he can be alone to think or read. He's the only one of them that spends any time in here, and that suits him.

The bright morning light warms the cool room, lights up the bookshelves opposite the bench. Eden looks all around, but her gaze rests on the books, a look of awe on her face.

"There's quite a lot of them, I know."

The spell breaks, and her eyes come back to his. Then she looks down at her lap. "This is a... beautiful house."

He watches as she nervously twists her hands together. "Thank you. It's been in my family for quite some time."

"But I thought you were from England."

"My mother was American. I was born here."

"Oh," she says softly. "Are you, um, are you very rich?"

He laughs a little. "What makes you say that?"

Her cheeks flush pink. "I don't know. You speak so well. And you have books. And a house."

"Well," he takes a sip of his coffee, "I suppose you could say... I'm reasonably well off."

"Oh."

He waits a moment, but when she doesn't speak again, he says, "Tell me how we can help you."

She looks up. "You saved me. If I'd been arrested—" She stops herself. She's holding back. She's afraid.

"Please tell me what happened to you. If you can. I won't push you."

"You said you're dysmorphic?"

He nods. "Yes. I'm a telekinetic."

"You don't look it. And you use a breather."

"Some of us look like everyone else. The breather is for show. For safety."

"I didn't know... that we could look normal."

"Very few people do."

"You're very lucky." She smiles sadly.

"Eden... whatever's happened, I want to help you."

"You *have* helped me."

"Yes, but..." He takes in her thin face and hands, the circles under her eyes that are lighter today but were like purple bruises last night. He remembers the terror in her face when she was caught leaving the diner and the desperation he saw there when she sought them out in the parking lot. He goes on carefully. "Something terrible has happened to you, hasn't it? Can you talk about it? It's all right if you can't."

She looks everywhere but at him. She wrings her hands. "I..." He hears a catch in her voice. "There was a place... It's, um..." She looks at her lap, then tilts her head back, but without eyelids it's impossible to blink back tears. She takes a deep breath, exhales shakily. "I was in a place, like a hospital. But not a hospital. They did tests on me, experiments, I guess. Other things. I didn't used to need a breather. I used to be... stronger. And..."

She turns her head to the side and pulls her hair back slowly, as if ashamed. There's a wound there, a barely healed hole, maybe an inch wide.

"What happened?"

"I have... venom glands. They put a tube in this one, like an IV, but bigger, and sometimes they'd attach a machine to take my venom. After I got away, I had to pull it out."

Eden has a beautiful face, a perfect, flawless complexion, a graceful neck and lovely hair. But of all these features, the ugly scar and hollow cheeks stand out the most.

He's used to his anger; it's always there, smoldering underneath any other emotions. Love, happiness, fear, once faded, always leave behind that quiet rage. But it's been a long time since it's flared almost past endurance. He looks down so she can't see his eyes. He doesn't want to scare her. "A laboratory. You were in a laboratory."

She doesn't say anything.

He still doesn't look at her until he feels her cold fingers touch his clenched fist. "If I had been arrested, I would've been found and brought back. I know it." She grips his hand. "Can I stay here? Please? I have nowhere else to go. I'll do anything. I'm safe here. Right?"

Adair feels a swell of sadness, of responsibility. "Yes, of course."

Her hand still touches his. "You're... important, aren't you? You're *someone*." Her gaze is shy, but intense.

"I don't know if I'm important, but I'm trying to change things. For people like us."

Her yellow eyes flash. "Let me help. I'll do whatever you say."

"Thank you." He puts his other hand over hers. "I'm glad we found you, Eden."

∽

He's lying on the beach with an icepack on his nose.

"Liam?" The voice rises just above the wind.

"Go away."

"Okay."

"Wait, wait! World off." Liam sits up as the sand vanishes. "I didn't know it was you."

"I can go..." Eden says.

"No. Stay."

"What happened to your nose?"

"Oh, it's nothing. Just broken. I ran into something. Fell. Whatever. It'll be fine in a week." They stare at each other for a moment. "Come sit down." He moves to one side of the couch.

"Thank you for fixing the filter," she says as she sits.

"Yeah, what about that anyway?"

"I just have trouble breathing."

"Oh." He waits for her to explain, but she doesn't. "Right. Sucks."

She looks down at her lap.

He detaches the World from his temple, puts it in his pocket. "So, what do you think of our little cabin in the woods then, eh? The Dacks remote enough for you?"

"The Dacks?"

"Adirondacks? Upstate New York?"

"Is that where I am?"

He frowns. "Where did you think you were?"

"I'm not—I don't know. But this is nice. I like it here."

He could ask her, he thinks. But why should he? If she wanted to tell him, she would. He wants to pull her in, not push her away. So he just shrugs. "It has its charms. I miss the city though."

"You lived in New York?"

"Yeah. Loved it there. It ain't London, but it ain't bad."

She looks around the room, then out the window. "Why did you all come out here?"

Liam picks up the icepack again, presses it to his face. "That's a long story." And he's not sure if he should tell her.

She doesn't ask him, though, just says, "Oh," and leaves it at that.

He lays the icepack down again. "When it's not so bright out, I'll give you the grand tour."

"Bright?"

"Eyes," he says, pointing.

"Does the light hurt you?"

His goggles are on the coffee table. He gives them to her. She looks through the lenses, turns around to see out the window.

"What do you think of the world according to Liam?"

She hands them back to him. "Dark."

He catches her hand before she can draw it back, kisses it, smiles. "You have no idea." He notices she's wearing the same clothes as yesterday, remembers that she brought nothing else. "So, you sticking around then?"

"Mr. Holden says I can stay."

"For how long?"

"Forever, I guess."

His heart feels bigger suddenly. He's so glad. He doesn't even know her, but the fact that she isn't leaving makes him happier than he's been in a very long time. He tries to hide what he's feeling because he knows how ridiculous it is. "Well, in that case, you should raid Layla's closet."

"Why?" She's still holding his hand.

"Got to get you out of that jumper."

She pulls at it. "I don't mind."

"I do. Hang on." He goes to the bottom of the steps. "Oi, Layla!"

"Fuck off, Liam," she calls back.

"Hey, I'm sorry I called you a whore, okay? You know I didn't mean it."

She doesn't answer.

"Damian broke my nose," he offers.

He waits, then hears her walking. She comes down to the landing, arms crossed. "What do you want?"

"Eden needs some clothes."

"So?"

"Come on. She's your size, yeah?"

"I'm taller."

He rolls his eyes. "She can fold up the cuffs."

Layla sighs. "I have some shirts I haven't cut up yet in a bag in the closet. And some old jeans in the bottom drawer. That's it. But I want something first."

"Anything."

She walks down the steps, stands face to face with him, smiles, and flicks her finger against the bridge of his nose.

"Fuck!" He feels the blood start flowing again.

"All yours." She steps around him and goes into the kitchen.

"Goddammit!" He tilts his head back. "I just got it to fucking stop!"

"Here." Eden is beside him with tissues and the icepack.

"Thanks."

"You didn't have to do that."

"No worries. Come on. I'll take you shopping."

He's never been in Layla and Holden's room. It's weird to think of them in that double bed. But Holden is one lucky fucker because whatever else Layla may be, she's the sexiest woman he's ever seen.

Or, at least, she was. He's only seen Eden in an oversized hoodie and jeans that are far too big for her, but there's something about her that attracts him more than Layla ever has.

Going through the closet, he finds the shirts that Layla was talking about, and the jeans are in the bottom drawer of the dresser, like she said. He puts it all on the bed. "There you are."

"I can have these?"

He likes her smile. "Never seen anybody so happy about hand-me-downs. Try them on."

She looks around the room.

"Go behind the closet door. I won't look."

Eden considers this for a moment. "Okay."

"You're very trusting."

She folds the clothes over her arm, pushes her hair behind her ear. "I forgot. You're dangerous, right?"

"Very."

Last night feels like a long time ago. He's already forgotten that he's supposed to leave her alone; well, at least he's chosen to forget it. He can't shake that sensation of familiarity and he wracks his brain trying to figure out if he's met her before, even though he's sure he hasn't. It's the way she looks at him, like she knows something he doesn't.

"You going to try those things on, or what?"

Behind the door, he can hear fabric shuffling. A few moments later, she steps out in a short-sleeve V-neck and jeans. More scales cover the tops of her arms and hands. They look almost painted on, so perfect and smooth. She's like a piece of art.

But the sweatshirt hid more than that. She's gorgeous, but so thin. The shirt clings to her ribs and the pants are just a little too big, and Layla is naturally trim.

She looks embarrassed when he doesn't say anything. "Is it okay?"

He makes sure he doesn't have any blood on his hands before he touches her side. He runs his thumb down her rib cage. "What happened to you?"

She looks away.

He touches her cheek. "Pretty little thing."

She turns her face to him again. "Do the clothes look okay?"

"Hang on." He unbuckles his belt, takes it off. She lets him thread it through the loops of the jeans. He can smell her hair. He feels for the back loop and his fingers brush bare skin. He meets her eyes briefly, then pulls the belt through the rest of the loops. It's too big, so he takes out his pocketknife and makes a new notch in it.

She tightens it, looks up at him.

"Perfect." He nods to the rest of the clothes. "Let's see something else."

Chapter 2

SIERRA WAITS for the woman to stop fussing over her. She feels like she has enough makeup on her face to play a clown at a kid's birthday party. Richard gives her a sidelong glance and a raised eyebrow. He has makeup on, too, though not as much as she does.

The woman flicks the brush over her cheek one last time. "You're beautiful, honey. What are you? Twenty? Twenty-two?"

"Twenty-six."

"Are those your own eyes?"

"Excuse me?"

"I mean the color. Is it natural?"

Sierra resists the impulse to touch her face. "Um, yes."

The woman shakes her head, a wistful look on her face. "Some girls have all the luck." She winks at Richard, turns back to Sierra. "Always wear your breather, stay out of the sun, and you'll never age. Unlike me. That's the best advice I can give you, honey."

"Thanks."

She looks between the two of them. "Father and daughter?"

"Colleagues," Richard says.

"Oh, that's nice." She smiles at him. "Okay, my work is done. You look fabulous. The rest is up to you."

"Thank you. You've been very kind."

When the woman is out of earshot, Sierra sighs. "Do I look ridiculous?"

Richard laughs. "No more so than I." He adjusts his tie. "Are you nervous?"

She takes a deep breath. "A little."

"You'll be fine."

On the set, Kenny Layton stands in front of one of the cameras as someone says, "Five, four, three..."

"Good morning, everyone. I'm Kenny Layton, and welcome to *Get Up and Know*. We've got some very special guests today. Chef Ryan Blake from everybody's favorite cooking show, *Fryin' with Ryan*, will be showing us some delicious recipes just in time for Labor Day. Can't wait for that, huh, folks?"

The audience claps and cheers when the sign tells them to.

"And, very exciting, singer/songwriter Ali Cavanaugh will be joining us to perform a never-before-heard single from her upcoming album, *Undone*."

The audience cheers in earnest now. This is who they're really here to see. Sierra can feel adrenaline pumping through her system. Looking at this audience, she wonders, not for the first time, why she and Richard are here. Publicity is important, but... these people are looking for entertainment, not politics, not a lecture on morality.

Kenny waits for the clapping to stop before he says, "But on a more serious note, I'm talking today with dysmorphic human rights activists Richard Corbin and Sierra Marlowe, about the rally taking place at Hammond Prison at the end of this month. Please welcome our guests."

The polite clapping ends when Kenny sits opposite them. He reintroduces them, describes their credentials, asks them mundane questions about their histories and about why dysmorphic human rights are important to them.

"Our Shelter for Displaced Dysmorphic people in America took in almost a thousand people during its first two years," Richard is saying. "Children, adults, teenagers, single mothers whose families have turned them away because they've given birth to a dysmorphic child—they have nowhere to go and no one to help them. Many of them simply pass through, but others stay for months, occasionally an entire year. Other shelters, more often than not, are afraid to have dysmorphic people in their facilities."

"Why is that?" Kenny asks.

"Well, as you know, dysmorphic people look different from so-called 'normal' humans. And differences can be frightening to those unwilling to look past them."

"But dysmorphic people are also stronger than, as you say, normal people, aren't they?"

Richard nods. "Usually, yes."

"Couldn't this be seen as a kind of threat in a shelter environment to vulnerable people trying to survive?"

"Dysmorphic people are vulnerable as well," Sierra points out.

"In what way?"

"Isn't that what we've been talking about? Why else would we need to have a shelter just for dysmorphic people if they weren't vulnerable?"

Richard steps in. "What Sierra is talking about, Kenny, is the erroneous assumption that, because dysmorphic people have certain advantages physically, they are safer or less vulnerable than the average person. That's incorrect. Dysmorphic people need employment, they need money and shelter and food, just like the rest of us. Currently, many dysmorphic people are finding obstacles in their paths to employment and also to education."

"I assume you're referring to the latest measure in the Senate to overturn the Education Rights Act."

"Yes. If this bill is passed, the difficulties dysmorphic people already face when trying to get into college or graduate schools will increase tenfold."

Kenny looks at Sierra. "Can I play devil's advocate for a minute?"

She shrugs.

"Would it be unfair to suggest that maybe it *should* be more difficult for dysmorphic people to get into schools? Their abilities and talents surpass the average student's in many respects."

Sierra's face feels hot, and she's suddenly glad for the makeup that she hopes hides her red cheeks. "No one would stop a prodigy from entering college, or a football star. Schools would be glad to have them. Why is a dysmorphic person different from any other talented individual?"

"Well—"

She cuts him off. "I'll tell you why. Because they look different. Because they have eyes that are a strange shape or color. Because some of them have fangs or claws. If they looked like everybody else, schools would be falling all over themselves to admit them."

"Are you accusing these schools of racism?"

"Yes—"

"No," Richard speaks over her. "No. We're not saying that at all. We're not accusing anyone of anything. We're merely pointing out a... lack of understanding, if you will, that, if explored and talked about, can be rectified. That's why we're here today, on your show, to explore the issue and talk about it."

But Kenny has latched on to Sierra's anger. "Do you disagree, Ms. Marlowe?"

She holds on to her feelings as tightly as she can. "No. Like Richard just said, we're here to talk to you and to put things into perspective for the American people."

Kenny smiles, but it's predatory, not friendly. "Let's talk about the rally. Let's talk about Rico Martinez. Mr. Corbin, you're expecting thousands of people at the rally. Why has his death sparked such controversy?"

Richard folds his hands. "Rico Martinez was killed in Hammond Prison during an experimental procedure that he should never have been asked to undergo."

"'Killed'?" Kenny repeats. "He was taking part in a medical study. You equate what happened to him with murder?"

"I do. Yes." Richard's voice never rises.

"Well, he fingerprinted a waiver, didn't he? He knew he might die."

Sierra leans forward. "Rico Martinez wasn't fully informed of the nature of the procedure or how risky it was. He was also telepathic, and because of that, he was heavily drugged when he printed the waiver. Telepaths are always heavily drugged to keep them from using their telepathy. They also suggested that his three-year sentence would be reduced if he participated, which wasn't true."

"There's no proof that he was offered a reduced sentence."

"He blinked his family and told them he would get out earlier if he participated in the experiment."

Kenny frowns. "I never heard anything about that."

"Of course you didn't. All blinks in the prison are recorded, but that particular recording was 'lost' somehow. There *is* a record of him making the blink, but conveniently, there isn't any recording of it."

"So how do you know what was said?"

Richard steps in. "His family told us."

"And you believe them?"

Sierra is finding it difficult to smother her anger, which is only heightened by her nervousness at being on live Cube. "Other prisoners were offered similar deals when they participated in experiments. We've talked to many of them. The only difference between their stories and Rico Martinez's is that they survived the procedures and he didn't."

"The prison warden tells a different story."

"He's lying."

Richard looks at Sierra. Be careful, he seems to say.

"Are the doctors and nurses also lying, Ms. Marlowe?"

She takes a short breath. "Why would they admit to conducting an unethical experiment on an uneducated man, whose only thought was to get out of prison a little sooner?"

Kenny leans back. "That's a disturbing allegation."

"A privately owned and operated prison with limited oversight conducting dangerous experiments on desperate people—yes, I think that's the definition of disturbing."

"Isn't this a matter for the DDAT?"

"You mean the Department of Dysmorphic Affairs *and Terrorism*? Just the name of the department tells you exactly how they're dealing with this problem. The DDAT's priority is arresting and detaining dysmorphic people for anything and everything, not making sure they're being treated well in prison."

Layton eyes her for a moment, like a hawk diving for its prey. "Ms. Marlowe, you're a little biased in this matter, aren't you?"

Her heart speeds up. "Excuse me?"

"I mean that you're dysmorphic yourself. Isn't that right?"

Sierra feels the chill of the studio and the heat of the lights. She feels eyes all over her, like crawling bugs, like spiders. She notices how dusty the floor is and that the couch Kenny is sitting on isn't the sparkling white it appears to be on Cube. It's dingy and worn. And Kenny isn't as young as he'd like his audience to believe. The wrinkles around his eyes, his mouth, denote years of fake smiles and forced laughs.

"Ms. Marlowe?"

"Yes," she says, and her voice is louder than she means it to be. "Yes, I am."

"Your full name is Sierra Marlowe Banks, isn't it? That's what it says on your Dysmorphic Registration record. Would you mind telling us what your Dysmorphic Registration ID number is?"

"You have no right to ask me for my RID number."

"Are you ashamed of being dysmorphic?"

"No."

"Then why hide it?"

"I don't hide it—"

"Then why are you wearing contacts today?"

The makeup woman. *Are those your own eyes?* Sierra can barely breathe. "For this exact reason. The fact that you think my being dysmorphic bears any relevance to my credibility."

"I think your lying about being a d-form is what bears relevance to your credibility."

Sierra's blood is pulsing in her ears. She can hear things she shouldn't. She tries to block them, the voices of memory that seep into her mind. She tries to put up the wall, but she can't. Richard sees it. He takes her hand, tries to ground her.

"Mr. Layton," he says, "your cruelty in this moment is what Sierra and I have been fighting against all these years. Your use of that racist term, d-form, reveals the endemic, deliberate ignorance in this country that threatens all dysmorphic humans, and your arrogance does little to hide your idiocy." He stands and helps Sierra up. "We came here today to talk about human decency and compassion. I see now that we'll find none of that here."

As they walk off the set, Layton calls after them. "What about honesty? Did you come to talk about that?"

Sierra is only vaguely aware of walking down the hall and into the dressing room, of the door closing, of Richard speaking to her.

He stands in a room with a beer in his hand. He sips it and stares at a beautiful woman across the bar. She rolls her eyes when he smiles at her and...

"Sierra." She feels Richard's hands on the sides of her face, but she can't see him.

Someone knocks her down. Someone hits her in the face. She strikes back. She bites.

"Help me, help me!" Sierra hears her own voice. It sounds so far away.

"Sierra!"

Her son won't stop crying. He just won't stop crying. She walks back and forth and back and forth. He won't stop crying.

Sierra can't stop crying either. She can't exhale. There are too many people, too many memories flying through her mind like bees, buzzing incessantly, deafening.

"Sierra, look at me. Look at my memory. Take from me. Come on. Focus. You've been here before. You know what to do."

He looks at Sierra Marlowe sitting across the desk from him and he knows that she will be someone great. She will be a better person than he ever was.

A calm settles over her. The visions disappear and she knows where she is again, who she is. "Richard?"

He pulls her to him. "There you are. There you are."

"I ruined everything. I ruined everything."

She feels him kiss her head. "You've done nothing wrong. Nothing. Everything will be fine."

The voices and memories of the audience, of the cameramen, of Kenny Layton fall away, store themselves in the back of her mind, where they'll always be.

Richard lets her go, and she feels like she's floating all alone in the middle of an empty ocean. He puts her coat around her shoulders. "We need to leave now. Let's go home."

"I'm so sorry."

"Dairen will be waiting for you."

Dairen. She needs Dairen. She needs him now. He won't care that she's ruined everything. He'll only want to hold her, only want to make her feel better and safe.

"Richard, I'm so sorry. I'm so sorry."

෴

When they enter the house, Dairen is sitting on the bench by the staircase. He stands up when he sees her, and neither of them moves for a moment. Then he rushes over and hugs her to him.

She cried the whole way home, but now she just breathes, rests against him, exhausted.

"It's all right," he whispers, and she can feel his lips on her forehead. "It's all right."

Sierra is vaguely aware of Richard stepping past them. She pulls away slightly. "I fucked everything up."

Dairen holds her face. "No. Everything's going to be fine. It *is* fine."

"What am I going to do?"

He strokes the side of her face. "We'll figure it out."

"I knew this would happen someday. I knew it. I should never have—"

"It doesn't matter." He takes her hand, leads her down the hall to the kitchen. He's made a pot of her favorite tea, and she almost starts crying again when she sees it.

"Thank you."

"I love you. Sit."

She does, and he pours. They sit in silence for a while. He holds her hand.

"Is my face all splotchy?"

"No." He smiles.

"Liar."

"It's going away. You look fine. Makeup's a bit cakey though."

She touches her face. "Oh God, I forgot about that. I need to wash my face. They put on, like, three inches of foundation."

"It's not that bad." But he's trying not to laugh.

"I hate you." She runs her hands up and down the warm

mug. "I hate that I let Richard down."

"Are you kidding me? Dad was kickass today. The news is focusing more on him and what he said than on you."

Her stomach drops. "The news?"

Dairen grimaces. She can see that he didn't mean to tell her this, not yet anyway. "Yeah."

"It just happened!"

"You know how it is."

"Oh my God..." She hides her face. She can feel new tears forming. "This is a nightmare."

"Sierra." He takes her hand in both of his. "You'll be all right. When people ask why you hid, and they will, just tell them the truth. You were afraid, just like all dysmorphic people are afraid. Doesn't this just... cut right to the heart of what you and other dysmorphic people go through? That you feel you have to hide to be heard, to be taken seriously? You have to tell people that. We're fighting against fear."

"I'm afraid now. I'm afraid right now."

"I know. I know. But you can use this. You've put yourself in the equation. People know you, and now you can tell them who you really are."

"How does that help anything?"

"People know you're smart, they know you're kind and talented, and now they know you're dysmorphic. They'll see that those things aren't mutually exclusive."

"Or it'll just confirm their beliefs that we can't be trusted."

He doesn't have anything to say to that.

Nina walks in, her baby on her hip. "Oh, sorry. I'll come back."

Sierra wipes her eyes. "No, it's okay."

"I heard what happened. I mean, I saw it on Cube. I watched the show. Kenny Layton's a fucktard."

Sierra can't help but laugh. "Thank you."

"Yeah. I think that about sums it up," Dairen says.

"I mean, he's really a fucktard. Supremely."

"Careful," Sierra smiles, "or that's going to be Ben's first real word."

"That would be hilarious. Fucktard, fucktard, fucktard," she says to the baby. He laughs and pats his fat little hand against her lips several times. She looks up at them. "He's punishing Mommy for her filthy mouth."

Nina has an elegant fierceness that Sierra sometimes envies. Her black and orange tiger stripes trail down the sides of her neck, cover her shoulders and the tops of her arms like long, expensive gloves, ending in triangles at her middle knuckles. Her hair is wild, dark black, with streaks of fiery orange.

Sierra takes Ben so Nina can get his food ready. She looks at his small face. He has his mother's tiger eyes and fur, but his stripes start at a point on his forehead, like a widow's peak, then widen over the back of his head and cover his entire back.

He's perfect. He's beautiful.

He will be feared. He will be hated.

He smiles and giggles and pulls at her necklace.

She's afraid for him.

∽

"Poor girl."

Layla sniffs derisively. "Are you serious?"

"Cube, pause." He looks down at her. "You don't feel sorry for her?"

She's lying on the bed, her head on his leg. "Why should I? Now she can join the rest of us in the real world."

Adair runs his fingers over her hair and the silky line of feathers down the back of her neck. "You are harsh and unforgiving, my love."

"And you're too nice. We're the perfect team."

He smiles, then reactivates the Cube.

"And there's Corbin. Master of speechmaking," Layla drones.

Adair watches his long-ago friend. He heard about this on the news and wanted to see the entire interview for himself. Richard looks older, and it reminds Adair of how much time has gone by for both of them.

"Richard is important, Layla. People like him are the face of dysmorphic rights. People like us are the backbone."

"I hate when you say shit like that Dair." She leans up. "You should be the face. You should be the leader. After Hammond, people will look to you, they'll want to follow you, they'll be afraid of you."

"That isn't what I want, Layla. I've told you that."

"But it's what should happen. It has to happen. You can't just... do something like this and then hide."

Layla has the most beautiful face he's ever seen, and that fact doesn't change when she's angry, when her cheeks flush red under her shimmering skin. "Kiss me."

She raises an eyebrow. "You're changing the subject."

"The subject changed itself."

Layla kneels over him. As usual, her clothes leave very little to the imagination after she's cut them up to accommodate her wings. "Aren't you tired?"

"Not anymore."

She kisses him.

"Do I tell you how much I love you enough?" he asks, as she kisses his neck.

"No."

"Cube, off." There's a sudden silence. He cups her chin and lifts her face so he can see her eyes. "I thought I knew what it meant to be in love. And then I met you."

She smirks. "How long have you been putting that one together?"

"I just thought of it now."

"You did not."

"I did too."

"You did not!"

"Well, whether I did or didn't—and I did—it's still true."

Layla has so many walls. But they all come tumbling down when it's just the two of them. She looks sad suddenly, self-conscious. "Why?"

"Why what, hummingbird?"

"Why do you love me?"

He smiles. "Why do you love me?"

She pulls her shirt over her head. He takes in all of her beauty and still can't believe that this gorgeous creature is his; or rather, that he is hers.

"Because you look at me like that," Layla says. She leans in, kisses him softly, sweetly.

He caresses her face. "Because you kiss me like that."

☙

She stands at the sink, wipes a cotton pad across her eyes and cheeks. Without makeup, she looks pale, exhausted. She washes her face, dries it, leaves the water running, looks into the mirror again.

She removes her contacts.

Sierra holds her fake eyes in the palm of her hand. Her disguise. Her lie. Her safety.

Her cowardice.

She turns her hand over and they fall into the sink, get caught in the water's steady stream, and disappear. She panics, puts her fingers into the drain, but they're gone.

"What are you doing, babe?"

She looks up at Dairen standing in the doorway. "They're gone..."

He turns off the water, takes a towel from the rack, and dries her hands. "I'm glad they're gone."

She looks up at him, frowning.

He kisses her. "I love your eyes. I've always loved your eyes. Look at them, Sierra."

She turns back to the mirror. Her real eyes are blue where they should be white. Her irises are a vibrant purple.

Dairen steps behind her, wraps his arms around her waist. "They're like a painting," he says, reaching up to wipe a tear from her cheek. "Look, even when you cry, they're beautiful. They look like the ocean. They're sparkling. Look."

It took more than a week to get used to the thick contacts. They made her eyes feel fat and it hurt to close them. But her mother told her that if she didn't learn to like them, she could kiss her future goodbye.

Her future.

"What's going to happen to me?"

Dairen kisses her neck and rests his head on her shoulder. "I don't know."

"I'm afraid to check my blink messages."

"Don't do it tonight. You know people are going to be angry."

"I don't know what to say to them."

He lets her go, takes her hand, and turns her toward him. "I had a thought about that. Do you want to hear it?"

She closes her eyes. "Can we talk about it tomorrow?"

She feels his hand touch her face. "Yeah. I was thinking the same thing."

Sierra hugs him. "Thank you. I love you."

He holds her close to him. She feels his breath against her hair. "I'm with you, babe."

Chapter 3

BASED ON our studies of dysmorphic subjects Twelve, Fifteen, Eighteen, and Twenty-One, and after extensive animal testing, Regenerall has been proven to speed up the healing process significantly."

"How much is significantly, Dr. Kovich?" asks one of the men at the large, oval conference table. Mara thinks his name is Gabe Martin, but can't be sure and doesn't really care.

She blinks into her Lens and pulls up a pic. It appears on the Cube in the center of the table. The 3D image rotates so that all twelve people can see it. "This rabbit had its leg broken in three places."

The pic of the rabbit is replaced by a series of x-ray images. She zooms in on each one as she speaks. "You can see the fractures here... here... and here. Normally, these breaks would heal in six to eight weeks." She pauses for effect. "With Regenerall, the rabbit healed in a single week with no side effects and minimal scarring."

There's an air of surprise in the room. The men and women at the table look at each other and whisper. Some seem impressed; others skeptical.

She answers their questions before they can ask them. "Experiments conducted on more than two hundred subjects, ranging from rats to chimpanzees, confirmed Regenerall's efficacy. In all of them, the subject healed in less than half the normal period of recovery—broken bones, deep lacerations, severed and reattached fingers and toes, damaged organs, even broken backs." She shows pics of several of the subjects, one after another: before and after shots, x-rays.

"In front of you are file folders containing detailed descriptions of each test and its outcome. But the short version of the story is that Regenerall works, and it's ready to be tested on humans. And we're prepared to start negotiating with standard prisons to secure non-dysmorphic subjects for those tests." She blinks, and the Cube turns off; the 3D images hovering over it vanish. "Thank you for your time."

"Wonderful, Dr. Kovich. You and your team have managed to astonish us yet again." Dennis Donohue claps. The others follow suit, some enthusiastically, some not.

There are several more questions before the meeting ends and the room clears. A few people stop to thank her and shake her hand.

When they're gone, Mara sits down heavily, removes her Lens, kicks off her shoes, rubs her head. Donohue gets up, moves to the other end of the table to sit next to her. "Great presentation," he says.

"Don't patronize me, Den."

"I mean it. Regenerall is going to make Freedom Pharmaceuticals a lot of money."

"That's what I live for." Mara rests her elbows on the arms of the chair.

Donohue gives her a practiced smile. "Tired?"

"No. I just hate presentations."

"You could've had Rhys do it."

She almost laughs. "Have you met Rhys Weir?"

He smirks. "Point taken." He sits back, drums his fingers on the table. "So, how much do I need to worry about this rally?"

"Not one iota," she says. "We have protests outside Hammond all the time. This one will just be bigger and louder. We've got enough additional security to start a war."

"That's not a prediction, is it?"

"You're hilarious."

He gives her arm a playful punch, stands. "Come on. Dinner's on me."

Mara bends down to put her shoes back on.

"Still wearing those, huh?" He gestures to her red heels. "They don't really go with the lab coat."

She stands. "They're comfortable."

"No they're not."

"I don't have to explain myself to you, Dennis."

He puts up his hands. "Mine is not to reason why."

"Yours is but to do or die." Mara smiles thinly.

"So they say. But let's have our dinner first, shall we?"

She ignores his proffered arm, walks past him to the frosted glass door.

"I'll get you, my pretty, and your little dog, too," he says, voice pitched high.

"That's getting old." She holds the door open for him.

"Not to me."

As they walk down the hall, Mara looks at her shoes for a moment. She almost lost them in the bombing, actually made the EMT find them and bring them to her. She had them repaired and cleaned up, almost like new.

She doesn't realize she's slowed down until Dennis says, "Let's get to the car quick before a house falls on you."

∾

Liam's desk is covered with wires and tools, Cubes, Lenses, half-finished projects, World makers, cam collars, and other equipment and junk. This is what he does, who he is: scraps of metal, bits of plastic, scattered and broken, needing to be put together or taken apart.

Eden sits on the edge of his bed, close to the desk. He's pushed his chair back so that he can be next to her. It's evening, so he doesn't have the curtains drawn, and what little light there is catches in her sleek, dark hair like moonlight on water.

"What is it?" she asks him.

Liam holds up the device, showing it to her from all angles. "It's a camera."

Eden frowns. "It's so tiny."

"Complicated little bugger, though. I made this one myself. The other two," he points to the cams still in the small box, "I 3D printed. Cool, yeah?"

"I've never seen a 3D printer."

"It's in the basement. Show you later. Printed these, too." He puts the cam down, picks up a collar.

She reaches for it, stops, looks at him.

"Yeah, go ahead. It's a cam collar."

She looks down at it. "What does it do?"

"You put that on, keeps you from being picked up by cams. Makes your face look all blurry. Beats facial recog every time. But not that one. It's busted. Got to fix it." He takes the collar from her, puts it in a drawer, then faces her again.

It still surprises him, the way Eden meets his eyes so easily and doesn't shy away. "You're really smart," she says.

"Come off it. Ain't that hard, really. I didn't invent the technology. I just know how to make them. This, on the other hand," he goes into a different drawer, takes out another box, opens it, "this was hard. And it's all my own work. What do you think it is?"

"A... bug?"

He laughs. "This is the Fly." He picks up the cam and attaches it to the small, insect-like machine. "She takes the cam to the top of wherever. I control her and attach the camera to whatever. She flies back to me."

"The Fly."

He smirks. "I'm good with gadgets, not so much with words." He points to the cam. "This baby is going on the top of the church spire near Hammond." He takes out his Lens. "The cams will feed into our Lenses. We'll be able to see everything from every angle." He puts it over her head, feels her hair and ears as he adjusts it over her eye. He lingers there longer than he needs to. His face is close to hers. Her lips are a beautiful pink against the green of her skin. They look so soft. "There. Now watch." He points the camera out the window. "You can control it with your eye or your voice. Cam Three, on. Lens on, Cam Three."

Eden jumps.

"You see it?"

She nods.

"You ever use one of these before?"

"Not like this." She touches the Lens. "How can you... focus on anything else with it on?"

"Practice. Want to try and walk around the room?"

"I'll fall over."

He laughs. "Stand up. I'll help you." He puts his arm around her waist, and she holds his hand tightly. And though he'd like to feel all of her hand in his, he's thankful for the gloves that hide everything up to his knuckles. "All right. Walk."

She smiles nervously. "I can't see."

"Use your other eye. Come on." He gives her a little push, and she moves like the floor is made of ice. "Baby steps, love. That's it." He loves the feel of her in his arm. He can tell she's gained weight in the two weeks she's been here, and he's glad. He remembers how thin she was when he first saw her, like she hadn't eaten in ages—still beautiful, but she's even prettier now. "How you doing?"

"Okay. I can kind of see the floor."

"You can talk to the camera, too. Try it."

"What should I say?"

"I don't know. Tell it to turn right or something."

She makes a face and says, "Cam Three... turn right? Oh! Okay. Wow. Now I'm dizzy."

He smiles, squeezes her hand. "You'll get used to it. Don't keep it on too long at first, though. You'll get a bitch of a headache. Lens, off."

Eden falls forward a little. He catches her and spins her around to face him. "That was weird," she says.

He twirls her hair around his finger. "It just takes concentration. Hey, I know. I'll link the cams to a Cube before we go so you can see everything."

Her face falls. "When do you go?"

"Not for a fortnight." He wraps both arms around her waist. "You got gorgeous eyes, you know that?"

She raises her hand and circles her forefinger around the World at his temple. He forgot it was there.

"What's in your World?" Her voice is quiet. She's never touched him before, not like this.

"I can show you. Then I'll make you one of your own and link it with mine."

Eden shakes her head. "No. It's not real."

"Reality sucks. You might like it in my World."

"I already do."

He hooks his thumbs through her belt loops. "Oh, you do, eh?"

She nods.

He tilts his head to the side, tries to read her face. "My Paradise... are you real?"

"Liam."

He lets go of Eden so quickly she loses her balance and stumbles backward a step. Holden stands in his doorway.

"Boss. I was... just showing Eden how to use a Lens."

"I see that."

Liam opens the Velcro straps of his gloves, closes them again. He looks at Eden. "Keep it. I have another one."

"Okay. Thanks." She looks between him and Holden. "I'll go make dinner."

Holden steps aside so she can pass. He gives her a quick smile and thanks her.

When she's gone, Liam turns away and carefully puts the cameras and the Fly back in their boxes. "She's smart. She'll get the hang of it."

"Liam."

"She wanted to know about the cameras. She saw me working on them."

"And while you were showing her, what? She tripped and you caught her?"

"Sort of—"

"She's not a toy, Liam. She's not here for you to play with."

"I know that." He faces Holden. "She's just... different."

"Different how?"

Liam shrugs. "She talks to me."

Holden runs his hand over his face, rubs his eyes, sighing. "Then just talk. Can you do that? For her sake?"

He feels a sinking in the pit of his stomach. "Yeah. All right."

He's lying to Holden, and he's never done that before. Maybe if Eden didn't smile at him, or look him in the eye when she speaks to him... maybe if she hated him, it would be easier to do as Holden says. But she doesn't hate him; she even seems to enjoy his company. Then again, with Layla and Damian as competition for her affection, Liam wins by default. He's lucky August isn't here. That's probably all it is. She doesn't have anyone else to talk to, so she talks to him.

Then just talk. Just listen to Holden.

But how can he just talk to her? How can he just look at her and not touch her? He's not a good man, not a nice man. And he likes Eden too much to just share a wall with her and not wish he was on the other side. He goes to her door a thousand times in his dreams, and more than anything else in the world, he wants to open it.

☙

There's a quiet knock at his door.

"Yes?"

Eden steps in with a mug in her hand. "I made you some tea."

Adair closes the book he's reading. "Thank you."

She sets it down beside him.

"Make one for yourself and join me." She never assumes he'll ask her to stay when she brings him his tea, but he almost always does.

Eden has fit herself into their lives as if she's always been here. She makes their meals, looks after each of them in different, quiet ways. And she brings him his tea. He never asked her to.

She comes back a few minutes later. She sits cross-legged in the other chair, the small table between them, cupping her mug in her hands. "Can I see that?"

"The book? Here."

She sets her tea down and takes the book, runs her fingers over the cover and opens it. "I've never held a real book."

"Hard to find these days, but not impossible. I'm a collector. Or I was. This is nothing compared to what I had back in England." What happened to those books? he wonders, sadly. Did Richard take them? Maybe Emily did. He hopes so.

She hands the book back to him and looks at the shelves behind where she and Adair are sitting. "I've been wanting to ask if I could borrow one."

"Any one you like. I've read them all."

"They're prettier than pics."

"I can't disagree with that." He sips his tea and watches her for a moment. "So, it's been, what? Two weeks now?"

"Yes."

He shakes his head. "I feel like I've known you longer than that. Are you still happy here? I know Layla and Damian can be difficult. But they're good people."

"I know."

He looks into his mug, enjoys the feel of the steam on his face. "And... Liam?" He thinks of how Liam was holding her, the way he was looking at her.

"I like him, too."

He can't tell if she means this or if she's just saying what she thinks he wants to hear. "I've known him since he was a teenager, you know. He's never been very good at—" He pauses. "He doesn't know his limits."

"He's kind to me."

"Well. Just don't let him be too kind."

It's quiet then, but comfortable. Adair starts to relax. It's as if his stress, anxiety, and anger are being taken away from him, put aside for now. When he sits with Eden like this, he feels peaceful, if only for a short while.

"How did you meet Liam?" Eden asks.

"I used to help run a shelter for dysmorphic people back in England. He came there the year before I left."

"And you took him with you?"

Adair thinks back to that night. "I hadn't planned to. He asked if he could come with me." He looks out the window. The moon has risen, illuminating the tops of the trees. "I liked Liam. He was impolite. He always told you exactly what he thought. He never lied. He hasn't changed. And he's loyal, highly intelligent..."

But not good, he wants to tell her. Liam had too much set against him to be good long before their paths ever crossed. Adair taught him discipline when it came to channeling his aptitude for engineering, and tried to teach him a modicum of self-control. He failed at the latter, and Liam's inability to contain his propensity for rage nearly destroyed their friendship once. Adair wants to tell Eden this, but it suddenly seems unfair. Despite everything, his instinct has always been to protect Liam.

So all he says is, "He has his good qualities and his bad."

"Don't we all?"

He looks into those strange, unblinking eyes. "Yes. I suppose we do."

"Is he like a son to you?"

A son. Adair never had children, never wanted any. It's a cruel world to be born into, even if a child is perfectly normal. For children like Liam, it's that much crueler.

It's strange, sometimes, to think back on impulsive choices and see how great an effect they have, often greater than carefully calculated ones. On a rainy night in England twelve years ago, Adair decided on a whim to take Liam with him, with no idea where he was going or what he was going to do when he got there. And that decision has echoed down through the years, to this moment.

"I don't know what it's like to have a son."

She takes a sip of her tea. "Maybe you do."

Chapter 4

DR. WEIR?"

"Mr. Corbin. Delighted to meet you." They shake hands.

"Please, call me Richard."

"Yes. Richard. Then you must call me Rhys." He gestures to a chair and Richard sits. "I suppose I don't have to say 'Welcome to Hammond Prison.' You've been here before."

"Many times."

He smiles. "Yes, of course. I'm sorry we haven't met until now."

Richard doesn't have an answer for that, so he only nods.

This room reminds him of a doctor's office—sterile, lacking any personal touches. The artworks on the walls are common, run-of-the mill prints: Van Gogh's *Starry Night*, Klimpt's *The Kiss*. The furniture is unremarkable. It's more like an example of what an office ought to look like, a department store display, than a place where a unique individual actually works. It's as if, in decorating it, Weir was trying to appear normal.

Weir blinks into his Lens. "Connie, will you bring us some..." He looks to Richard. "Tea? Coffee?"

"Tea, if you don't mind."

"Tea, Connie... Thank you." He blinks off. "Tea is also my preference." Weir's voice is soft, accented, but only slightly. Dutch, perhaps. Or German. His gray eyes observe Richard, almost to the point of discomfort. "I'm sorry Dr. Kovich wasn't able to meet with you. She's very busy, as you might imagine the head of a department would be. But anything we discuss here will be brought to her attention, I assure you. She's given me permission to speak for her. So," he sits across from Richard, "here we are, to talk about your rally."

"I'm not sure what it is you wish to discuss. Unless, of course, Hammond has decided to abandon its experimentation projects."

Weir's mouth lifts in a kind of amused smile, not quite laughing, but not at all serious. "Would you care for some water, Richard? While we wait for our tea?"

"Please."

Weir gets up again, walks to a table with a pitcher and glasses on it. "We have no intention of stopping the project. We're quite within our rights, constitutionally. And I'm sure the Supreme Court will agree with us, if the Martinez family wishes to take it that far." He hands Richard a glass and goes back to his side of the desk.

The glass is cold and wet with condensation. It chills his fingers. "I wasn't aware that human rights violations were permitted by the Constitution."

Weir shakes his head. "No. I wouldn't think so. Not as such."

"Then what are we talking about?"

Weir runs his finger around the rim of his glass, watching Richard. "'Neither slavery nor involuntary servitude, *except as a punishment for crime...* shall exist within the United States.'"

Richard feels a flash of anger. "You're hiding behind the Thirteenth Amendment? Using the abolition of slavery to *defend* slavery?"

Weir shrugs. "I didn't write it. It's a little known but brilliant addition to the amendment, don't you think? And it isn't slavery, Richard. It's involuntary servitude. Let's call things what they are."

"Morally, there's no difference."

"We're not talking about morality."

Connie comes in with the tea, then leaves.

Weir pours. The steam rises from the white mugs. "Or perhaps we are." He passes Richard the milk. "Let me propose a scenario."

Richard forces himself to stir slowly. "I'm listening."

"A man commits murder. He is sent to prison. He must be fed, clothed. The society he committed the crime against pays for his care through taxes; even the family of the victim must participate. Is that moral?"

Richard frowns. "Whatever the citizens of this country are paying for, it's certainly not for the 'care' of the prisoners."

"They are fed, clothed, and sheltered. What more do you want?"

"What more do I want? Education, perhaps? Efforts made toward rehabilitation?"

"These people sit in prison draining resources and contributing nothing for years, sometimes for their entire lives. Richard," he lowers his cup, "I'm sure you would agree that the Dysmorphic Phenomenon has provided opportunities we could never have imagined."

"Dysmorphic people are human beings, not opportunities."

"And here we differ. Why can they not be both? These prisoners, these felons, they can finally give back to the communities they've wronged. Contribute data and material to cure disease, to prolong life. Provide a service... involuntarily or otherwise."

"The pattern of dysmorphic incarceration reveals a disturbing tendency toward maximum sentencing for all crimes. It's almost as if Hammond Prison, and others like it, are being filled with as many test subjects as possible for as long as you need them."

Weir smiles, but something is missing from it, from his eyes, from his light voice, his polite manner. In that moment, it becomes instantly clear to Richard that he will gain nothing from talking to this man. Weir is indulging Richard. This is a game to him.

"'Tendency'? 'Almost as if'? You'll have to do better than that, Richard." He folds his fingers together, rests his hands on the desk. "You don't seem to understand that our work, *my* work, is about bettering the world. Saving it from itself."

"Saving the world? Is that really what you're interested in?"

Weir opens his hands. "What else?" As he pours another cup, he says, "So, I suppose I can't talk you into canceling this rally of yours?"

"No. I suppose not."

"Unfortunate."

Richard stands. There's no reason to remain here with this man, with his dead eyes and his empty smiles. "Thank you for the tea."

"You won't have another cup?"

"No, thank you."

"Then goodbye, Richard. Come again any time. My door will always be open to you."

"Goodbye, Dr. Weir."

Richard has the bizarre feeling that he should run, run as fast as he can from this place, from this man. When he's through the door and out of the building at last, the feeling doesn't go away.

He wants to run... because he's afraid.

❧

"There she is. My little piece of Paradise." Liam turns off the World. The sun and sand blur away. He heard Eden walking past the living room, but she stops when he speaks to her. "What's the rush?"

"I didn't want to bother you."

"Well, what if *I* want you to bother me?" He shakes his head. "Always thinking of yourself. Come here."

He sits up straight, puts his feet on the floor. She sits beside him.

"Where were you off to then?"

"To give Adair back this book. And to see if he needs anything."

He takes it from her hands. "I don't get the book thing." He hands it back to her. "And what about me?"

"Do you need something?"

"As a matter of fact." He twists the ends of her hair in his fingers. "I need you to do something for me."

"What?"

"Stand up and walk very slowly to the other side of the room." He looks into her glowing eyes, wonders if she'll actually do what he's asked or if he's gone too far.

Eden holds his gaze for a long moment before standing. When she reaches the archway, she turns. "Like that?"

"Perfect." He leans back against the couch, hands behind his head. "Better than any World."

He can't tell what she's thinking. She doesn't seem nervous. She looks him in the eye; her hands are still.

There's no one like her in the whole world, he thinks.

"Now walk back."

Never taking her eyes from his, she does as he says and stops in front of him. "Anything else?"

He sits up, puts his hands on her waist, and tilts back to look at her face. "If only I had you all to myself..." He shakes his head, lets go. "Get out of here, girl. Before I do something that'll get me in trouble."

Eden walks toward Holden's office, but stops and turns to him again. "Do you think I'm pretty?"

"Don't ask stupid questions." He turns the World back on. "Now go away. Or I'm not responsible for my actions."

❧

The trees seem to have gone from green to orange overnight.

The sunlight shining on them makes his eyes water, but he doesn't look away, just keeps blinking back the emotionless tears.

He's always liked this small office, with its loveseat under one window, a single chair beside it, where he now sits, shelves against the opposite wall behind his desk, PhotoCubes projecting happy and meaningful parts of his life. People have described it as "cozy." But today, it feels empty and cold.

He's not sure how long he sits there before he hears the front door open and close. Dairen, home from work.

The door is open, so Dairen walks in without knocking. "Hey, Dad."

"Dairen. How was your day?" He hears the tiredness in his own voice and knows it won't go unnoticed by his son.

"Better than yours, I think." He takes off his jacket and drapes it over the arm of the couch, sitting down. "You okay?"

"I'm fine." He shakes his head. "No, I'm... I don't know."

Dairen sits, looks at him, concern in his eyes. He doesn't say anything, waits for his father to explain, or not. His face is so like his mother's, but his hands are identical to his own.

"Sometimes, I'm very glad you're not dysmorphic, Dairen."

"That's a weird thing to say. What's happened?"

"I had a meeting with Dr. Rhys Weir today."

"Oh, right. How did it go?"

He thinks of Weir's eyes. "It was pointless."

Dairen takes a breath. "What did he want?"

"To convince me to cancel the rally." He tells his son everything about their conversation. "What worries me most is that he does have a case. It's immoral. It's evil. But it might not be illegal. And if the Martinez family really does take it to the Supreme Court and loses—it would set us back immeasurably."

"It can't work that way."

"It can, and it does." He rubs his temples. "Ex-convicts—they serve their time, but their punishment goes on and on. They lose the right to vote, and the stigma never goes away. And prisoners are used as cheap labor. Every year you hear about their worsening living conditions, and no one cares. All that matters is that they're out of sight and away from *decent* people. And it's worse for dysmorphic prisoners. Weir knows what he's doing. Very few people will complain about the legal use of prisoners as guinea pigs, especially if it means saving the lives of law-abiding citizens. And they're only d-forms, after all." He can see Dairen is at a loss for words, and he regrets his bitterness. "I'm sorry."

"No, Dad, it's okay."

The house is quiet. In an hour or two, the residents will be sitting around the large dining room table, mostly teens and young adults, home from school, home from work, talking about their days. Richard isn't sure if this will make him feel better or worse—to be among the people he has helped save, while at the same time being reminded of those he hasn't and won't be able to.

"Saving the world..." Richard says quietly.

"What?"

"That's what he said. That his work will save the world from itself."

"Fucking God complex."

"It's more than that. I think... I don't know. There was something about him. Something... wrong. I don't know. But it's not about saving the world, not for him. I think he just... enjoys his work. He *enjoys* it."

Dairen leans forward, puts his hand on top of his father's. The love Richard has for this young man, for his son, is too much to bear at times. He loves him so much he often feels irrationally guilty for helping to bring him into this horrible world. A world where people like Rhys Weir exist.

He looks into his son's normal, perfectly normal eyes, and

is forced to admit to himself that he has always been grateful for Dairen's normality. Not sometimes, but every day.

When his son was born and opened his eyes for the first time, Richard felt such a rush of relief, he started laughing. No one thought anything of it, just another happy father, awed by his first child. And as the years went by and he showed no signs of telepathy or telekinesis, the relief was even greater. But still... there had always been something appealing about the idea of teaching his son how to control any ability he may have been born with. In an ideal world, it would have been a joy to teach a child of his own how to use telekinesis... their shared ability.

But this isn't an ideal world. And Dairen, thank God, is not dysmorphic.

Whatever happens, Dairen will be safe.

His son is safe.

Chapter 5

D ID YOU want to go through the files Ira sent over?" Weir
sits at Mara's desk across from her.

"Oh, right. I almost forgot." Mara searches for and opens the
file on her desk's tableface. "Ira Lenox, my favorite judge," she
mutters. She looks at the first offender's mug shot and description.
She frowns. "Indecent exposure? Is he serious?"

"It does smack of desperation."

"Just a little." She swipes her finger across the screen to bring
up the next file. "How much does he get for each prisoner we
take?"

"More than he deserves. May I?" He taps the edge of his
Lens's eyepiece.

She shares the files with him. "Be my guest."

He smiles. "I love this. It's like getting to pick your own birthday presents."

Mara stares at him for a moment, watches as his eyes light up
when he sees something interesting.

"Here's one." The file he's looking at appears on her tableface. "William Dale. No family. Convicted of..." He blinks into
the Lens, reading, "Bank robbery."

She reads over William Dale's file, considers. He *has* committed a felony. It's perfectly reasonable that he would be sent to
a maximum security facility like Hammond Prison to serve his
sentence. "I don't know. He's so young."

"He's older than Subject Twenty-Six."

"That's true."

"Look at his eyes, Mara. I've never seen anything like them."

Dale has rectangular, goat-like pupils, horizontal, stretched across a solid yellow iris. She's never seen that before either. "Incredible," she whispers. "And he's telekinetic." She nods. "All right. I'll take him."

"Can I have him?"

She gives him a look. "Learn to share, Rhys."

He looks disappointed. But a moment later, his face brightens when he finds another file that intrigues him. "Oh. Very interesting. Maksim Maksimovich Annikov. Chameleon." His eyebrows lift as he smiles.

The file she was reading vanishes as Weir projects Maksim Annikov's file onto her tableface.

She doesn't have to look at it for long. "Oh, yes. This one is mine."

"I found him!"

She ignores Weir. Maksim Annikov has red chameleon eyes with black stripes branching out from the pupils like spokes. He's covered in vibrant scales, has a long, purple tongue, and his skin can blend into any background. She swipes to the next page, does a double take. "He was part of the DCo bust?"

"Does it say that?"

She reads further, shakes her head. "An eWork mixup got him sent to an immigration camp in Arizona. He almost got deported back to Russia."

"Then I guess he's mine."

She shakes her head. "He's already been questioned."

"Not by me."

"Well, if they want you to question him, I'll give him to you."

"You really are being very unfair, Mara."

"Get over it."

It's quiet then, and it looks to Mara as if Weir is pouting. She rolls her eyes, returns her attention to her tableface, flipping from file to file, unimpressed with what she sees.

"I wonder if Annikov was ever a member of the *Schturmovat*," Weir says suddenly. "It doesn't say."

"The what?"

He gives her a look, as though she ought to know what he's talking about. "The *Shturmovat*. The Storm. Russia's version of the DCo."

"I know what the Storm was." She's annoyed at herself for having forgotten the Russian word, but the American media only ever called it the Storm.

Weir focuses on his Lens again. "Although," he says, as if Mara hasn't spoken, "I can't imagine how he would have survived the Purge."

Mara thinks back to a few years ago. High-ranking members of the Storm were lured to the Kremlin by the promise of peace talks. Those who weren't killed outright were imprisoned and tortured until every member of the group had been rooted out and executed. Russian leaders called it justice, but it became known in the dysmorphic world as the Purge.

Mara finds only one more candidate for study, a woman named Keeley Armstrong. No extraordinary abilities, but she has two different kinds of eyes: one normal and blue, the other bright green, round, and reptilian. "Have we ever had a chimeric d-form?"

"No. I would have remembered that. You know how much I like eyes."

Mara tries not to think about any of Weir's obsessions.

A few minutes later, she shuts down her tableface, sighs. It's the end of the day and she's tired. "Tell Ira to stop sending me misdemeanors. It's a waste of my time."

"Yours and mine. I will make sure he gets the message."

Mara slips her feet back into her red heels. "I'm done for the day." She stands.

"Not me. I have to run some tests on the Rosy subjects."

"Why do *you* have to do them?"

He shrugs. "I don't. I just want to."

"Fine. Whatever makes you happy."

"Oh, it has nothing to do with happiness," he says as they leave her office.

She printlocks her door, then looks at him because she can feel him staring at her. He has his hands linked behind his back and a curious expression on his face, like he wants to ask her something. She frowns. "What?"

He smiles slightly. "Nothing. Good night." He turns and goes down the hall to his own office. She's glad he didn't offer to walk her to the door.

A security guard escorts her to the parking lot. He scans every inch of her car, declares it safe. She thanks him.

She nods off on the way home, which is unusual for her. She dreams of Weir and of Maksim Maksimovich Annikov, only in this scenario, Weir is the chameleon and Annikov the scientist, and they're working together, experimenting on her.

ʔ

He makes sure Holden isn't upstairs before he knocks on her door.

She smiles when she sees him. "I thought you left."

"And not say goodbye to you? I'm leaving soon. Come for a walk with me."

Eden turns her head to look out her window. "It's raining."

"Not much. Reminds me of home. Come on." Downstairs, he opens the front door for her. It's gray and drizzling. "Want an umbrella?"

She shakes her head, loops her breather over her mouth and

nose.

"I hate that you have to wear that thing. I can't see your pretty face."

He can't tell if she smiles at this or not. He jumps down the porch steps and enjoys the opportunity to watch her step down after him. They walk in silence along the edge of the wood for a while. The house stands in a clearing surrounded by thick forest. The misty rain feels good on his face, and he loves not having to wear his goggles. Still, even in this dull gray light, his eyes squint.

"Do you miss England?" Eden asks.

"Now and then. Haven't been in years. You like clubs?"

"I've never really been."

He stops and steps in front of her, puts his hands on her hips. "I bet you could dance real good. I know a great place. Back home. I'll take you someday. Informal. You'd love it."

"Informal?"

"Yeah. That's the name of the club. You can always tell a d-form joint. Always got the word 'form' or 'morph' in it."

"Oh." Liam's jacket is open, and Eden takes the edges of it between her fingers, tugs it a little. "You dance?"

"Only when I'm dead drunk. I'm more of a voyeur."

She gives him a slightly playful look. Her hair sparkles with the drops that gather on it. "Would you dance with me?"

"You know I would. And for you, I'd do it sober." He sees goose bumps on her bare arms. "You cold?"

"No. It feels good." She reaches behind her head, takes off her breather. "Hold this?"

He takes it and watches as she stretches her arms out, bends her body and neck back, raises her face to the rain. Some of her hair gets caught up over her shoulders. He pulls it off gently so that it drapes down like a black waterfall. Beads of water drip off the ends.

"How far back can you bend?"

She curves all the way back until her hands touch the grass. Her shirt bunches up around her ribs.

"Flexible."

She keeps bending until her head is between her knees, facing out, her arms around her ankles.

"Now that's just weird. You're a bloody contortionist."

As she rights herself, the clouds open and the rain pelts down in a torrent. They're both soaked in seconds. She starts to laugh, opens her arms, and spins in a circle.

He doesn't think he's ever seen anything so beautiful. He catches her as she comes around. "Dance with me now, Paradise."

She hesitates, then puts her arms around his neck. He holds her around her waist. "Am I doing okay?" she asks after a minute.

"Good enough with no music."

He dips her low and she laughs again, but it turns into a cough, and he pulls her up.

"Shit, put this back on." He helps her with the breather.

"Thank you."

"We better get back. Holden'll kill me if you die of pneumonia." He takes his jacket off and puts it over her. "Hey, look at that. I'm a gentleman."

She slides her arms into the sleeves and he takes her hand, holds it while they walk. It feels strangely natural, as if they've always done this, held hands in the rain.

"Such pretty fingers." He pulls her hand up to his lips to kiss it.

She smiles. "Thank you."

They walk slowly, even though the rain pounds down harder.

Suddenly, she reaches over with her other hand and runs her fingers over his glove. His breath catches. His heart slams in his chest. "I've never seen your hands," she says. Her nail scratches the exposed Velcro. He freezes.

"Stop!" He yanks his hand out of hers.

She looks at him, wide-eyed. "I'm sorry."

He tries to calm down. He shoves his hands into his pockets—to hide them, to keep them still. "Forget it." He starts walking again as fast as he can.

She catches up with him. "I didn't mean to upset you."

He turns on her. "I said forget it! Don't you listen?"

They stand there, staring at each other. He sweeps his wet hair back off his face. Her hair is weighted down with rain; it clings to her cheeks and forehead. Her breather fills and clears rapidly with her quickened breathing. He looks away from her, lost for words, unsure what to do or say. In the end, he says nothing, just keeps walking. He leaves her there, alone in the rain, and he doesn't look back.

He gets to the house quickly, runs up to his room to change, chest tight, head pounding. Back downstairs, he remembers he gave her his jacket, and she's nowhere to be seen. Is she still outside?

But then he sees it on the coatrack by the door. He stares at it for a moment before taking it. He holds it close to his face. It smells like her.

And when he puts it on, he finds that it's still warm on the inside.

Chapter 6

IT'S A QUIET street, almost unnervingly so. The white church spire is topped with a gold cross. The church itself is ancient, made of wood and stone, beautiful in its way, untouched by time. A few cars drive past him, and then nothing. He opens the window and connects his Lens to the Fly, opens his hand and lets it go.

He maneuvers it out the window, up the spire, guides it into a space between two stones. It crawls in and he uses his Lens to see through its eyes, to manipulate the insect arms and place the camera exactly where it needs to be. Then the Fly comes silently back to him, lands in his hand. He boxes it.

The other cameras are in place. All he has left to do now is drop off the big duffel bags, full of clothes and burner Lenses, hopefully enough for all of the prisoners who manage to escape. They'll have a better chance of getting away if they're not wearing prison uniforms and have access to a Lens. It's up to August to tell them the predetermined locations of the bags in the forest surrounding the prison.

"Cam Three, on." In his Lens, he has a perfect view of the south side of the prison. "Turn right." He can see two guards talking to each other, lights in the windows, the guard towers. "Activate night vision." Everything becomes clearer, and he can't help feeling proud of his work.

It doesn't last. He thinks of Eden, showing her the cameras, teaching her how to use the Lens, holding her around the waist... her arms around his neck... drops of water like diamonds in her hair...

Holden was right. He should have left her alone. She's too

close. He can too easily hurt her. But he didn't expect her to be nice. He never expects any woman to be nice to him. Or to want to spend time with him. Or to walk with him in the rain. If she hadn't been so nice, so pretty... but she's nice to Layla and Damian, too, and they hate her. So he's not special. She talks to him because she has no one else. And he always knew that.

Eden is not for him. She distracts him. He doesn't need sweet smiles and gentle touches; doesn't need someone to take care of him or ask him questions. He doesn't need to work so hard to get what he wants. What he needs is to get Eden out of his system. And what he wants, he can find anywhere.

He starts the car, tells it where to go, tilts his seat back, closes his eyes. But open or closed, all he can see is Eden's smile and her black-green hair flying in a circle as she spins around and around in the rain.

⁓

He watches her dress. He's already forgotten her name. His mind is fuzzy with alcohol. And other things.

This pay-by-the-hour motel room is tatty and bleak, the walls dirty, the rug worn down. The bed is far from comfortable, with its rough sheets and its springs poking up here and there. But these kinds of places aren't meant for long stays. And they're not meant for nice things, nice people.

They're meant for people like him.

She had what she called a "pay before you play" policy, so she doesn't want anything else from him, and he wants nothing more to do with her.

"You sure you don't want me to stay, baby?" She has cat eyes, yellow with slit black pupils. But she never seems to stop blinking.

Liam doesn't answer her.

"Just a few hundred more."

"Get out."

Her face changes from seductive to indignant. "Fine." She gets her jacket. Her gaze moves to the coffee table. She picks up the remaining baggie and looks at him, the sultry smile returning.

"Keep it," he says.

"What do you want for it?"

He sits up. His head spins and his stomach flips. "I want you to fucking leave."

She pockets the drugs, an ugly twist to her face. The cat eyes narrow. "You know, you could really use an attitude adjustment." She walks to the door, says over her shoulder, "And some plastic surgery."

He has her pinned against the wall, his hand around her throat before she can touch the handle. There's nothing but fear in her eyes now.

"Say that again."

She chokes, tries to speak.

"Go on. Say it."

She has long, claw-like nails, and she scratches at his hand. He can feel them through his glove.

He smirks. "Cat got your tongue?"

She makes a sound between a gurgle and a wheeze. He squeezes harder until she can make no sound at all. He opens the door with his other hand and throws her out of it.

She kneels on the floor, coughing and gasping. "Freak! You can't—"

"You're still talking? Are you trying to get yourself killed?"

She struggles to her feet. He watches her stumble toward the elevator, then sees she's dropped the drugs.

"Forgot something, you little cunt!" She turns, and he throws the bag at her. He's surprised when she catches it. "Good reflexes.

Could've used those a minute ago."

"Fuck you," she says, and steps quickly into the elevator.

The doors hiss closed, and then there's silence. The hall is as dank as his room, dimly lit to hide the grunginess of it, and it stinks of cigarettes and sweat. He shuts his door, leans into it, presses his forehead against the wood. It's cold and smells of cheap varnish. He feels sick. He starts to shake and can't stop. The rage is gone; all that's left is the emptiness, that dull, vacant ache. He feels like he might cry. He cried when his face was sliced open, and that was the last time. He never thought he'd have need of tears again.

"I want to go home," he whispers into the door. He's never said those words in his life.

He dresses as quickly as he can, grabs what's left of the alcohol, pays his bill through the wallface. The ad that flashes at him when he's finished stops him for a moment. The image is of a business-man in a suit, sitting at his desk, hands behind his head, a World attached to his temple. He's smiling because his desk is on a beach with a tray of margaritas on it and he's surrounded by women in bikinis. The tag line reads:

Worlds: Because Reality Sucks.

He looks around the dingy motel room, at his reality. Then he runs from it, leaps down the ten flights to the parking garage.

He gives the car directions. "Ninety mph."

"This exceeds the legal speed limit," it tells him.

"I don't fucking care. Slow down for cops."

The car barrels out of the garage. It can't move fast enough for him.

 C/3

He stumbles in through the back door. Damian is sitting at

the table, drinking a beer, looking into his Lens. Liam loses his balance as he walks past the counter toward the arch.

Damian tilts his eyepiece up, sits back. "Bring any back with you or is it all up your nose?"

"What? No. I don't have anything." Liam can see his own reflection in Damian's solid black eyes, like two glass marbles.

"Selfish prick." He smirks. "You know, I think you might have a problem. I'm concerned."

Liam ignores him, leans through the archway to look down the hall and into the living room.

"Your girlfriend's upstairs."

"She's not my girlfriend."

"Oh, right. Your future rape victim is upstairs."

"Fuck you."

But he doesn't really care what Damian says. He runs up the steps to her door. It's open. She's watching a silent Cube, Bolts in her ears; he can't tell what program. The 3D image projected above it is a confusing mess of colors to his bloodshot eyes.

He feels the panic ebb away as he watches her. She sits cross-legged, her elbows on her knees, her head on her hands, the Cube on the bed in front of her. She doesn't notice him. It's so quiet. He feels his mind slow down. He doesn't want to disturb her. He just wants to look at her, be near her.

Then she sees him, and that smile, that small, sad smile, cuts into him like a razor. She's so beautiful it hurts.

She doesn't say anything as he steps into her room, as he sits on the edge of her bed. He doesn't look at her, but out of the corner of his eye he sees her remove the Bolts from her ears, and the sound of whatever she's watching comes from the Cube's speakers now. She touches his hand, just above where the leather of the glove ends.

He can't look at her, so he looks at her fingers—long, elegant, like they were meant to play the piano. Her nails are clean, rounded, and underneath them, instead of light pink, he sees lavender. He runs his forefinger from her wrist, down the back of her hand, to the tip of her finger, feels the delicate bones, the soft hairs, her cool, smooth skin and silken scales.

She touches his face. He closes his eyes, and she lets him lower his head onto her shoulder. He feels her hand on the back of his neck, the other caressing the side of his face. He wishes he wasn't high, wasn't drunk, wasn't spent; but he is all of those things and she knows it.

She gets up, closes the door, helps him take his jacket off. His eyes grow heavier and heavier. And then he's not sitting up anymore, he's lying down on his side. He should take his shoes off, he thinks, but he can't remember how. And he can't stay awake a second longer. He should really take his shoes off...

Her fingers move through his hair... cold raindrops running smoothly, gently, down his face as he dances with her...

He looks up at her, eyes burning, barely open. "Eden? Am I home?"

She nods.

He falls asleep with his head in her lap.

She never says a word.

〇〇

When he wakes, it's morning and he's not in his own bed. He sits up too quickly and blood rushes to his head. The drugs and alcohol have left him blurry-eyed and shaky.

He's in Eden's bed, but she's not here. The smell of breakfast makes him feel nauseous.

Did he sleep here all night? Did she? Has he been in her bed all this time and not known?

"Fuck me."

Downstairs, he walks unsteadily into the kitchen to get coffee, sees that it's still brewing. The light coming in through the window is horrible.

"Looks like somebody had fun last night," Layla says. "What was her name?"

He rubs his eyes hard. "Whose name?"

Damian laughs.

"He never remembers their names," Layla says as Eden dishes out her breakfast.

Damian nods. "Probably the drugs. I think it's time for an intervention."

Eden doesn't say anything, and she doesn't look at Liam. She keeps her back to him, setting the pan on the stovetop. His heart sinks.

He thinks of her cold, delicate fingers running through his hair, of the woman's claws scratching at his hand. He leans his elbows on the counter, presses his head against his fists, and hates Layla and Damian for the game they're playing.

"Hey." Damian points his fork at Layla. "Who was it at Formz? The one who drugged his drink just to get him to leave her alone."

"Nakita," Layla says. "You remember Nakita, don't you, Liam? Not enough money in the world could get her to fuck you."

Their voices are like knives. "Leave me alone."

"You're being stalked by a real ladies' man, Eden," Damian says.

Liam pushes away from the counter. The coffee's done, but he doesn't care now. He feels sick.

He goes back upstairs, slams the door to his room. He stands there, looking at nothing. Then his eyes move to his desk. He's there in two quick steps, and without stopping to think, he sweeps his arm across it. What doesn't clatter to the floor, he throws against the far wall, and when there's nothing left to throw, he kicks the chair over, loses his balance, falls back onto his bed. He swings his fist, stops short of slamming it into the wall. He just presses his knuckles against it as hard as he can, and again, that feeling that he might start crying creeps through him. "Fuck, fuck, fuck."

There's a knock at his door. He's afraid it might be Holden, so he doesn't move. He doesn't want Holden to see him like this. The knock comes again, and he realizes it's too soft to be Holden, and Damian or Layla wouldn't bother knocking.

He opens the door. Eden is there with a cup of coffee and two plain pieces of toast. He stares at her, takes them slowly. He doesn't know what to say. He wants to explain himself to her. He wants to apologize for who he is. He wants to kiss her. But all he can think to do is lie, and he never lies—except, it seems, when it comes to her. "Those two are full of shit, you know."

"I don't care."

He looks at the toast and the coffee. "Thanks for this. And for—"

For what? For letting him pass out, drunk and high, in her bed? For letting him stay there all night? For even speaking to him after what she's just heard?

"Just... thanks."

"I can bring you more later. If you want."

"This is fine."

"Hey," Damian's voice carries loudly up the stairs, "do I have to pour myself a second cup?"

He hates Damian, but Eden just gives him a little smile. "Get some rest. You'll feel better." She closes the door for him. He listens until he can't hear her footsteps anymore.

He turns around, looks at the mess he's made. But instead of being angry, he feels lighter and in less pain. It's like the sadness has been pulled out of him. He thinks of Eden's eyes. He thinks of tomorrow and feels a rush of adrenaline.

And then he remembers Holden telling him that he'll be taking Layla to lunch somewhere special this afternoon. And Damian will be going on a supply run. He'll finally have Eden all to himself.

She let him sleep in her room last night, in her bed. She doesn't care about what Layla and Damian said. She brought him breakfast. She danced with him. She held his hand.

She likes him. She doesn't have to love him—he thinks that might be nice, but he's not an idiot. She likes him though. She looks him in the eye. She smiles at him. Isn't that enough?

He thinks of her bed and the smell of her on the blanket, her beautiful thigh under his head as he fell asleep, her soft, sweet fingers like a light breeze through his hair.

He puts the coffee and toast on the desk, walks over to the wall they share, presses his hand against it, and smiles.

Then he waits for everyone to leave.

❧

She stands in the doorway to his room. Damian's beautiful polar bear fur, covering his muscular upper back and the back of his bald head, glitters against his dark skin. He pulls a plain black hoodie over his head and turns around.

"Oh, Jesus!" Layla cries, covering her eyes, her heart hammering.

"What?"

"God! I hate when you wear those! They freak me out!"

His solid black, opaque eyes are hidden behind contacts—normal-looking, with eye whites and dark brown irises. She looks down at the floor.

He laughs. "You're probably the only person in the fucking world freaked out by normal eyes."

"No. Just on you. They don't look right."

He walks up to her, takes her chin between his fingers to tilt her head up.

"Ew! No! I'm not looking!" She closes her eyes. "Couldn't you have waited until you got in the car?"

"I might've forgotten."

She opens her eyes slightly, cringes. "They're so creepy, Damian."

He smiles, lets her go. He walks back to the bed, grabs the two empty duffel bags lying there, turns. "You heading out?"

She nods, focusing on his chest rather than his face.

"Come on." He walks past her and she follows him down the hall. He turns around at the top of the stairs, smiling slightly. "Hey." He flips his hood up. "What's more dangerous? Being a d-form or a black guy in a hoodie?"

She raises an eyebrow. "Being a d-form black guy in a hoodie. That joke is so old."

"Cracks me up every time, hummingbird."

"Don't call me that."

On the first floor, he leaves her side, walks to the front door and opens it. "Bring me back something," he says, without turning. Then he's gone. She stands there listening until she hears the gravel and dirt crunching under the wheels of his car.

She rubs her arms up and down, chilly suddenly.

Damian is going on a food run. She and Dair are going to lunch. They're still normal people doing normal things. That will all change tomorrow.

"Are you all right, hummingbird?"

She looks behind her. Dair stands above her on the landing. He looks so handsome in his blue shirt and gray slacks. "I'm fine.

I'm hungry."

He walks down to her. "Shall we go?"

Without thinking, she pulls him to her, kisses him, presses her body against his.

When she breaks the kiss, she can see the sudden desire in his eyes, and behind that, ever present, the love he has for her.

"What was that for?" he asks.

"Nothing." She shrugs. "Everything."

He takes her hand, kisses it. "I love you." He cups the side of her face. "Everything will be all right, you know."

She leans into his hand, loving his touch as she always has. "Are you sure?"

"I'm sure."

And she believes him.

❧

"Just you and me today then, eh? How'd I get so lucky?" Liam watches her as she walks down the stairs.

"How are you feeling?"

"Fanbloodytastic." He twists a lock of her hair around his finger. "So, how are we going to spend the afternoon?"

"I was going to make lunch."

He touches her cheek. "Can I show you something first?" He takes her hand without waiting for an answer, pulls her to the couch. He gets the World out of his pocket, puts it in her hand. "Told you I'd make you one."

She half smiles, half frowns. "These scare me a little."

"Nothing to be scared of, love. Turn around. I'll put it on." She hesitates, then turns her back to him. He puts one hand on the side of her face, pushes the World into her temple with the other. She flinches at the slight pinch. "World, on. Beach."

She gasps. "Oh…" She breathes a little laugh, reaches out into the air.

"No, no." He pulls her arms to her sides. "The trick is to move in your mind. Just think about moving, without actually doing it."

He watches her face as she concentrates, her chest as she breathes faster and then laughs. "I can feel the sand!"

He moves her hair to one side so that he can see her neck, leans in close to her ear. "Can you hear the ocean?"

"Yes! And I can smell the flowers!"

"This is my favorite World."

"But the sun…"

He smiles. "It don't bother me in there. Not real, remember?"

"It feels real. And you sound like you're far away."

"I'm right here, Paradise."

She focuses on the World and he focuses on her. She smells like fresh water and some kind of flower, a rose maybe, something clean and new. He traces his fingers down her neck. She shivers.

"World, off," she whispers. She looks at him over her shoulder. Their faces almost touch. She's not smiling now. He can't tell what she's feeling.

"Do I frighten you?" he asks.

"Do you want me to be frightened of you?"

He runs his thumb over her lips. "Well, a guy like me doesn't get what he wants by being nice."

"What do you want, Liam?"

"I want to kiss your neck."

He can hear the rapid beating of her heart. Her lips part, but she doesn't say anything.

Her skin under his lips is cold and soft. He waits for her to pull away, but she doesn't. He rests his hand on her hip, slides higher. But when he feels her tense, he breaks away.

"I'm sorry." He puts his hands up. "I'm sorry." Why is he apologizing? He's wanted her since the first time he saw her. And a day like this couldn't be more perfect. And she didn't say no. So what the fuck is he doing?

She turns to face him. "It's okay." She takes his hand, and he lowers his arms.

He could push her down on this couch right now or up against the wall or pull her onto the floor. No one will be home for hours. "Are you going to tell Holden?"

"No." She's still holding his hand.

"I'm keyed up about tomorrow. Got a lot of energy, you know?"

"It's okay. Come for a walk with me. It's still raining."

And just like that, he knows; knows it like he knows the inside of a World or a Cube; understands all her kindnesses and smiles, her gentleness, the way she looks at him, touches him: she's not afraid of him, but she doesn't want him either.

He stands up, wrenches his hand free. "You bitch! I don't need you feeling sorry for me!"

"Liam—"

"I'd rather pay for it than get a pity fuck!"

He yanks the World from her temple, crushes it between his fingers, flings the broken pieces at her. She holds up her hands to shield her face, then raises her eyes and meets his so calmly he wants to hit her.

"Keep your fucking head down, Eden. Look at me again and see what happens."

And still, she looks.

He's so angry, he's shaking. He thinks of Holden and digs his nails into his palms to still his hands.

He can feel her eyes on his back as he goes out into the rain, slamming the door behind him.

Chapter 7

IN THE KITCHEN, Eden dishes out a stew. Holden compliments her; the other two say nothing. Liam grips his fork as tightly as he can when she serves him. He has to be careful with Holden at the table.

They talk around him. It's all hollow noise. He hears Layla laugh at something Holden says, looks up to see what the joke is. He never finds out. When he lifts his head, he meets Eden's eyes. She's looking at him again. He glares at her, wraps his hand around the knife beside his plate.

But her yellow eyes are so warm. Her mouth lifts in a small smile meant just for him to see. He feels his anger start to slip away like smoke, leaving behind a breathlessness inside him, a pull in his chest. He wants her so much, and he feels sadness, just sadness. That look—he can't stand it. Hatred is less painful than pity.

Liam stands. Holden glances up, but no one stops him as he leaves the room.

☙

He looks at himself in the mirror, something he rarely does. His eyes stand out more than his other features. They're red and purple. He always thinks of a lab rat when he sees them.

His jet black hair makes his white skin seem even paler. And, of course, there's his scar. He follows the line with his finger, starting just above his split eyebrow, over his cheekbone, through his lips and chin. He looks at his hand in the mirror as it traces the scar. He hates his hands the most.

A knock on his door startles him. He pulls his gloves on, walks over. "What?"

"Liam?"

He freezes, his hand on the doorknob. "Eden?" He thinks of his reflection. "What do you want?"

"Can I come in?"

"Why?"

"Please?"

He grits his teeth, opens the door.

She stands quietly. She's looking at him like before, her yellow eyes fixed on his, but there's something more in them now, something he can't place.

He can hear the old house creak in the cold silence. The last crickets of the season call out weakly to each other. "What do you want?"

She steps up to him, puts her hand on his chest, and he can't breathe. "Liam. I'm not afraid of you. And I don't feel sorry for you."

She kisses him. He closes his eyes. Her lips are so warm. She tastes so good. He pulls her through the door, takes her head in his hands, pushes her away. He looks into her face. "What is this?"

"Don't you want me to kiss you?"

"Yes." Staring into her eyes, he sees it again, knows it now, and it doesn't make sense—she's looking at him the way he always looks at her. "Yes. I want you to kiss me."

He moves his hand behind her head, her hair tangling in his fingers. She kisses him again. He pushes the door closed, walks her to the bed. He feels her forked tongue in his mouth, her hands in his hair. He pushes her down onto the mattress. He takes off his jacket. "You don't know what you're doing, girl." He takes off his shirt.

Sitting on the edge of the bed, she looks up at him, puts her hands on his hips, and starts to examine each scar. Her fingers are freezing, but her lips are warm and wet as she kisses the one between his ribs.

"Stop," he says.

She doesn't, moves on to the long line of perfect pale pink circles that winds its way around his side to his lower back. She kisses each one, like they're something special, like they mean something. They mean nothing to him. He doesn't want them to mean anything. He doesn't want her to see them. She could at least pretend she doesn't see them; could at least pretend that some part of him isn't flawed or scarred or fucked up. "Stop."

"Why?"

"Just stop."

She stands, touches the one on his chest, looks into his eyes for a moment, then runs her tongue over the scar. And it's like fire. He remembers how much that one bled, and he doesn't want to.

He grabs her arms, lifts her, shoves her down onto the mattress. He kneels over her, undoes his belt. "I told you to stop."

"I know."

He pushes her shirt up to kiss her stomach and ribs, her beautiful, soft, perfect skin—no scars here, no permanent marks of things and people best forgotten. "Everything they said this morning is true, you know. The whores, the drugs, everything."

"I know."

He unzips her jeans. "Fucked a girl just last night. Didn't know her name, didn't care. Just some cunt I'll never see again. Fucked her well and good."

"I know."

"Pretty little thing. Had eyes like yours." He slides his hand between her legs. "I'm a bad person, Eden."

"I know, I know," she gasps, tilts her head back, twists the blanket in her hands.

"You don't know anything." He watches her face change, how her mouth opens as she breathes faster. "You want this, Paradise?"

"Yes..." Her knuckles are white.

"You want me?"

"Yes, *yes*..."

He doesn't know what to think of a woman who wants a man like him. Doesn't she hear what he's saying? Doesn't she understand?

He kisses the curve between her neck and shoulder, licks her throat and along her jaw. He whispers into her ear, "You going to come for me, Paradise?"

He looks into her eyes and he sees pain there and surprise and absolute pleasure, and he knows, but he doesn't want anyone else to hear.

He kisses her, feels her moan against his mouth, feels her fangs. He pulls away. "Shh. Keep your voice down, Paradise. No screaming." He kneels upright. "And I *will* make you want to scream, Eden. That was nothing."

"Liam—"

"Take off your shirt."

Her skin is softer than anything he's ever touched, and her body is more sensitive than any woman he's ever been with. She shivers under his hands, under his lips, under his tongue. He holds his hand over her mouth or kisses her when he can tell she wants to scream. Holden would kill him if he knew.

When he can't wait anymore and kneels between her legs, she puts her hand on his thigh, shakes her head.

"Everything," she says.

He doesn't know what she means until he feels her tug on the strap of one of his gloves. He pulls his hand away, but she holds on.

"No," he says.

"I want all of you."

He doesn't know why he lets her. He doesn't have to; there's no bargaining here. She'd never get away from him; it's too late for that. But he lets her pull off both gloves, and she holds his bare hands.

They're like alien things in hers, ugly, a part of himself he can always hide—until now, because Eden won't let him. He looks for disgust in her face, or pity, or morbid fascination. But it's like before. She looks at them like they're something beautiful. But they're not. They can't be.

She laces her fingers through his, strokes the veined webbing stretched between them. She touches the burn scars on the backs of his hands, the raised messes of random pink-white lines, like raw, chewed-up meat. She kisses these scars too, gently, and so sweetly. Her lips are the same color as the scars. How can one color be so awful and so beautiful?

When she looks into his eyes and runs her tongue along the wide web between his thumb and forefinger, a chill runs through him. This is all wrong. It doesn't make sense.

"Stop!" He pulls free, grasps both of her wrists, pins them above her head. "You don't know me! You don't want to know me!"

"I know you, Liam."

He kisses her just to quiet her, moves to kiss her neck. He feels her pulse against his lips, her breath against his ear, hears her sudden, sharp gasp, feels her stomach against his when she arches her back. And the faster he moves, the faster she breathes. He digs his nails into her wrist and she moans.

"I want to see you," she begs. "I want to see your eyes."

She wants to see his eyes.

And it is this, more than anything, that finishes him, that takes away his control and leaves him blind to everything but her. He can't keep hold of her wrists. She takes his face in her hands, won't let him look away. This will kill him.

He's never cried out before; he's never needed to. But the pleasure and the grief and the release are so great, he has to turn his head and press his mouth against her arm to stifle the scream he can't hold back.

When it's over, she has tears in her eyes. And he knows why, because he feels the same way.

❧

He's never seen her sleep.

It's strange because her eyes don't close. He spent the better part of an hour lying face to face with her, just looking at her eyes, knowing she didn't see him. Now he's leaning up on his elbow, looking down at her, her black-green hair spread across the pillow, her bare shoulder uncovered. Several times he's reached out to pull the sheet up in case she's cold, but he doesn't want to wake her.

He isn't thinking clearly. He can't latch on to any of the thoughts that flit through his mind. He keeps hearing her say, *I want to see you. I want to see your eyes.*

"Liam?" Her eyes focus as she wakes. "Are you okay?"

"Can I touch you?"

"You don't have to ask."

He puts his hand on her shoulder, lies back down. She kisses him, and he closes his eyes. He feels her touch his scar. She does what he did hours ago, traces it from beginning to end. "Don't," he says.

"Why not?" Her fingers touch his lips.

"I don't want you to."

She rises slightly. He lies back on the pillow, looking up at her. She kisses the top of the scar, kisses his eyelid, his cheek, his lips. "You're beautiful."

"You're crazy."

"I have scars, too."

He frowns. "Where?"

She pulls her hair back, turns her head. There's a perfect, raised, light green circle under her ear, at least an inch wide. He can't believe he's never noticed it before.

He touches it. "Did someone hurt you?"

"Yes."

"I'll kill them." There's a tightness in his throat and a fire in his heart. "I'll kill them for you."

Keeping her eyes on his, Eden leans up, kneels over him. The sheet falls away. "You would, wouldn't you?"

"Yes." He puts his hands on her hips as she lowers her body onto his. He feels the curve of her bones. "Do you want me to?"

"Yes."

It's as if he's belonged inside of her all his life, and not just in this way, but in all ways. He knows, suddenly, that if he were separated from her and couldn't return to her, he would die. He doesn't know how he's lived so long without her. "Would you watch me do it?"

"Yes." She moves like a snake, like her bones are made of water. He's never let a woman do this to him. Never. But this is right; this is what he wants. He's not in control, and he feels free.

"Fast or slow?" He tightens his grip on her hips.

"Slow."

"I'll make them suffer," he says, clenching his teeth. "I'm going to scream, Eden."

"I want you to."

"Kiss me or I'll wake up the whole fucking house."

She does, pushes her fingers through his hair. He pulls her down against him, feels her spine, her muscles moving beneath his hands—his bare, gloveless hands. She breaks the kiss, runs her tongue up his chest, over his throat, back to his lips. And he doesn't need anything else in the world. There *is* nothing else in the world. Just her. Just now. Just this.

Then everything slows and she's looking into his eyes again. He can't speak, can only stare at her. There's a light sheen of sweat on her skin that makes her glow. She tries to catch her breath, kisses him softly. Her hair drapes around their faces like a curtain. He runs his fingers through it.

Her hair is so soft; her skin is so soft. Her eyes are brighter and deeper than any sun or ocean he's ever created in any of his Worlds. He touches her face. "Eden. Who are you?"

"I'm yours."

❧

Damian hits the top of the stairs just as Liam walks out of his room. They both stop mid-step. Liam doesn't know what gives him away, but only a second goes by, and Damian is laughing.

"You're too fucking much, you know that?" He walks up to Liam. "So, how'd you like not having to pay for it?"

Liam smiles. "I don't know. How do you like having to share?"

Damian is fast, but Liam is faster and ducks under his swinging fist. He kicks the back of Damian's knee and it buckles, sending him to the floor, but Damian flings his heavy arm back, and it catches Liam's shin. Pain shoots up his leg. He backs away as Damian gets to his feet, and they stand, facing each other, on either side of the wide hallway.

"I've got a list of shit as long as my fucking arm that I could tell her about you." The white fur that covers Damian's upper back and the back of his bald head, and those glassy obsidian eyes, make him look like an ancient tribesman wearing a prized pelt. He seems simple to Liam suddenly, ignorant.

"You tell her anything you want."

Damian isn't expecting this reply, Liam can tell, but he recovers quickly. He folds his arms in front of him. "So, how long has she got?"

"What?"

"That tiny little bitch down there making my breakfast. How long before you lose it and break her face?"

Liam can hear Eden talking to Holden downstairs, can see her in his mind pouring him coffee, a smile on her face. And he imagines that other smile, the one that's just for him, the one that no one else sees. "I'd never hurt her."

"Yeah. You'll never hurt her." He walks past Liam to his room, claps a hand on his shoulder. "Except that one time, right? I'd warn her if I cared. But it's always more fun to sit back and watch."

Liam thinks of yesterday afternoon, how he ripped the World off her temple and threw it at her. Nothing gets past Damian.

"Already started, huh?" He squeezes Liam's shoulder. "Well, here's hoping she likes it rough." He lets go.

Liam bites down, focuses on a crack in the wall by the stairs. He should fix that. Holden might have even asked him to and he forgot. He cuts his eyes back to Damian. "Jealousy doesn't look good on you, Grace. Clashes with your fur."

"If you think I'm jealous over that pathetic little housemaid, you're out of your fucking mind."

Liam nods, walks to the stairs, turns and shrugs. "At least she's all mine."

"Keep her, Aldrich. Keep her till you fucking kill her."

The steps creak under Liam's feet. He gets to the first floor, sees her by the stove through the arch.

Damian is wrong.

He will never, ever hurt her.

He won't. He *won't.*

He's too anxious to eat, so he walks out the front door. He sits on the steps, watches his breath cloud and disappear in the cold morning air. He takes his gloves off, looks down at his hands.

The room grew so cold last night, it woke him. He was naked and half out of the covers. He pulled them around himself, turned onto his side, saw her shivering. When he put his arm around her, she stopped and sighed. He fell back to sleep holding her, keeping her warm.

In the morning, he felt her turn and face him. The blue light of dawn made her eyes a greenish-gold. He untangled his hand from under the blankets to stroke her face, and stopped. He'd forgotten that she'd made him take his gloves off. She took his hand when he tried to slip it back under the sheets.

"Don't," she whispered.

"Where are my gloves?"

She smiled. "Under here somewhere, or on the floor with all the other clothes."

She was lying. "Did you hide them?"

"No."

He tickled her under the covers. "Did you?"

"No!" She pushed him away, laughing.

"Give them back, you naughty girl! Or I won't stop. "

"Okay, okay!" She reached under her pillow and handed them to him. "But don't wear them here, with me. Please."

He looked at them, crumpled them into a ball, and tossed them over her onto the floor. "Deal."

"Thank you." She traced her finger around his face, under his eyes, along his jaw, before resting her hand on his cheek.

For a while, they just looked at each other. He had his arm around her, idly running his fingers up and down her back. The more light that entered the room, the sadder he became. He could see it in her eyes, too.

"You have to go," she said.

"I don't want to." He cupped the back of her neck and kissed her. "We should have done this sooner."

"I know," she said. "I was afraid."

"Of me?"

"No. Of me."

"Why?"

"I didn't want to ruin everything."

He didn't know what she meant. "You were perfect." He kissed her again and again, stroked her hair. "You *are* perfect."

"I'm not."

"You are." He kissed her once more, laughed quietly. "You are. The way you walk. The way you move. Your voice. Your eyes. God, your fucking eyes. Everything about you. You couldn't be anything but perfect. From day one. No doubt in my mind." He ran his hand down her leg under the covers. "And what about me, then, eh? I don't look like much."

"I told you. You're beautiful."

"You need glasses."

She touched his face again and her eyes grew so serious, she looked almost angry. "Liam. There's no one more beautiful than you. No one."

He didn't know what to say. She meant it.

Her thumb brushed his scar. "What did this?"

He closed his eyes. A heat spread inside him: shame, anger, fear, other things he didn't understand and didn't want to. "Piece of glass." He didn't speak above a whisper, as if by saying it as quietly as possible, she might not hear him, he might not hear himself, might not have to remember.

She kissed his closed eye, pulled the sheet down. The cold air in the room was like ice water on his skin. The daylight frightened him. She'd seen him in the dim glow of a small lamp last night. Everything is different in the day.

"This one?" She ran her finger down the one on his chest.

"Knife."

She kissed it. His eyes felt hot, his throat tight. He was so afraid. He looked up at the ceiling, at the cracks in the plaster. Everything became blurry.

"This?" The one between his ribs.

"Screwdriver," he whispered. All the blood, all the pain—what kind of life had he led?

"These?" The line of perfect circles.

"Cigarettes." Two tears, warm as blood, fell from the outside corners of his eyes, over his temples, over his ears.

She took his hand, stroked the back of it. "And these?"

"Hot iron." He was ashamed of the tremble in his voice, of the tears. She kissed and kissed and kissed his hand, held it against her face, the scarred side pressed to her cheek. He couldn't look at her. "Jesus, Eden. What are you doing here?"

"Oh, Liam," she whispered. "Don't you know?"

She kissed his lips. He tasted salt; she was crying too. She held his hand to her chest. He felt her heart beating under his palm, looked up at her.

"This is where my other scars are."

The fear disappeared then, and everything he'd felt last night came back to him, filled him with a fire so unlike hate and fear, he couldn't name it. He kissed her there, swore to her that he would kill whoever had caused her pain. If it took his whole life, he would do it.

He gripped her waist. "You're mine, aren't you?"

"Yes."

The light came in through the curtains and the house woke—voices, the shower, footsteps on the stairs. He should have been out of bed, dressed by then. She should have been downstairs making breakfast. But none of that mattered; none of it existed.

How could he have left without having her one more time?

Liam's thoughts are broken into by the sound of the door opening behind him. Eden sits next to him on the steps. She slips her hand into his. He holds it tightly. "When I get back tonight, I expect all your stuff to be in my room and you in my bed. Got it?"

"Yes."

"Good." He looks out at the morning mist. "Cube's all set up for you."

"I know." She puts her arm through his, rests her head against his shoulder.

"So..." He pauses, takes a breath. "Do you love me?"

"Yes."

Liam nods. "Okay."

He hears footsteps coming from around the other side of the house. It's Holden. "Time to go, Liam."

Eden stands, lets his hand go. She steps in front of him, looks into his eyes, and kisses him. Then she walks down to Holden and hugs him. She doesn't see the look he gives Liam over her shoulder. He says something to her as she steps back, and she nods.

"Let's go," he says to Liam.

☙

An hour or more passes in silence. They're alone. Layla and Damian are in the other car. Liam heard Holden breathing tightly when he first got in, but he's calmed somewhat, enough that Liam feels he can speak.

"I'm sorry, boss."

He sees Holden clench and release his fists around the armrests. The car turns itself around a bend before he replies, "You're sorry."

Liam is not sorry and Holden knows it. "I didn't hurt her, boss. She came to me. I swear to God."

"You swear to God." Holden takes his Lens from his pocket and cleans it with the end of his shirt as he speaks. "Does she know, Liam? Did you tell her? Did you tell her about any of it?"

Liam closes his eyes, rubs his temples. "I wouldn't hurt her."

Holden puts his Lens away. "You can't promise that. That's why I told you to stay away from her."

"She said she loves me."

"Did she?" Holden stares out at the road. "What will she say when you lose your temper? When she does something you don't like?"

"Boss—"

"I need you, Liam. I need you thinking clearly."

"I'm here, boss."

The car adjusts to the speed limit as it turns onto the highway. Liam lowers his window halfway. It lets in the cool breeze, but the sounds of the highway do little to fill the gaping silence in the car. He pulls his gloves down tightly, unstraps and re-straps them, stretches his fingers. It's strange, but for the first time since he started wearing them, the gloves feel... uncomfortable. They've been a part of him for so long, but then he let Eden take them off, and he felt all of her hand in his, and there was freedom in that, a weird joy in having nothing to hide.

"She's not strong, Liam," Holden says. "She's vulnerable."

Vulnerable. *She doesn't love you. She doesn't know what she's doing. She's not in her right mind.* Liam always knows what Holden is really saying. But this time, he's almost sure that Holden is wrong. "What happened to her?"

Holden leans back and sighs.

"She has a scar on her neck. She said someone hurt her."

"She didn't tell you?"

"No."

Holden closes his eyes. "She was experimented on in a laboratory."

Liam can feel the weight of the gun inside his jacket, his nails digging into his gloves. "Hammond?"

"No."

"Where, then?"

"She doesn't know. When she got the chance, she just ran. And then we found her."

Liam thinks of that first night, of how pale she was, how thin.

Holden's hand is on his arm. "After this is over, we will find that lab—"

"And tear it to the ground." Liam looks up at him.

Holden nods slowly.

The rest of the trip is spent in silence, until they're nearly at their destination.

"Do you love her?" Holden asks.

She wanted to see his eyes last night when he came. She wanted to see his face. *His* face. She held his hands. She kissed his scars. She told him that he was beautiful. And she cried because she was happy. He made her happy. *I'm yours,* she said. His Eden. His Paradise. "Yeah." He looks at Holden. "I love her."

Holden gives him the chance to look away, to take it back. When he doesn't, Holden says, "Well, that's the first time you've ever said that."

"First time I've ever felt it."

"Hope for us all, then."

Liam smiles. "Suppose so."

Holden takes a small box from his shirt pocket. He opens it, then looks into the rearview mirror as he puts the contacts in. He blinks repeatedly, adjusting to them. He turns to Liam. "How do

I look?"

The contacts have changed Holden's eyes from normal to reptilian. "You look d-form."

"Well, that's the idea."

"It's kind of weird."

Holden looks into the mirror again. He touches his face just under his eye. "Yes. Such a simple thing. But it really does change everything." He stares a moment longer, then he switches the car to manual control, takes the wheel. As he turns off the highway, he says, "You know I trust you with my life, Liam." And he's asking if he can trust him with Eden's.

"I'm with you, boss."

Holden nods. "All right, then."

Chapter 8

HAMMOND PRISON for Dysmorphic Offenders is a huge, maximum security facility. Sierra has been here too many times. It's one of several prisons in the United States, maximum and minimum security, built to hold only dysmorphic prisoners. The men and women inside are kept in check by drugs that repress their strength and speed. Telepaths and telekinetics are given stronger, mind-altering drugs—some so powerful they leave many of the prisoners in nearly catatonic states. The building itself is surrounded by three layers of fences, electrified and barbed at the top. It's bordered on all sides by flat, football-sized fields, three of which lead into a thick forest. The field at the front of the building is crowded with the people attending the rally; with them is a significant police presence, and even National Guardsmen.

It is a place that reeks of despair.

Richard's speech was well received by the crowd, as she knew it would be. They clap and cheer, even as he walks off the stage and is no longer in their sight.

But when she steps up to the podium, the crowd goes quiet. They don't cheer; they don't boo. She wishes they would do something, anything. The silence is worse than what she imagined this would be like. She keeps her sunglasses on, makes sure her Lens is connected to the speaker system, then calls up her speech. She grips the sides of the stand. When Dairen told her his idea, she hated it; it terrified her. And that's how she knew it was the right thing to do.

"My name is Sierra Marlowe. I'm a counselor at the Shelter for Displaced Dysmorphic People. I'm sure most of you recognize me."

She focuses on the space above the crowd, on a streak of gold that a passing jet has left in its wake. She doesn't see the plane.

"And I know you're all wondering the same thing: Why did I hide? Why didn't I tell people that I was dysmorphic? I'm ashamed of the answer. I hid because it was easier. Easier to get into school. Easier to get a job. Easier to make friends. And it was safer, too. Safer to walk down the street. To go to a bar. To stand at a tram stop. No one ever asked me for my RID number, or yelled at me in the street. Because I wore contacts and a breather. Because I don't have wings or feathers or claws or fangs. Because I looked *normal.* I hid because I could. Because I was scared. And I think that's the point of all this. Why we're all here today. We're afraid. We're not safe. Things aren't easy for us—ever."

She feels like two people. One of her is speaking; the other is watching it all happen and wondering if this was the right thing to do.

"People think we're lucky. We shouldn't complain. They resent us because we're stronger and faster. We don't get sick as easily. We don't need breathers and we don't have to filter our water."

She's not used to saying "we" and "us." It's always been "they," "them." She practiced with Dairen a thousand times so she wouldn't slip, but each time she sees the word "we" on her eyepiece, it still looks wrong and she almost changes it.

"But I don't know one dysmorphic person who hasn't wished they could trade their strength for a chance to get into a good college, or their speed to be able to walk down a street and not be afraid; who wouldn't rather put on a breather and be accepted than be an outcast in their own family."

Sierra can feel the passive memories of sorrow and pain that her words call up in the crowd—moments of fear in the lives of the people in front of her. They flit around her like lightning bugs, flashing brightly, then disappearing. She absorbs them all. Her next words are not in her speech.

"You're all so brave. So much braver than I've ever been. I don't belong up here. You do."

She looks down. There are a thousand faces in her mind, a thousand disapproving glances and angry stares, a thousand stories more important than her own. But here she is. She has to join their struggle now as one of them, and be as hated and feared as they are, and this is where it really starts. With the end of this speech.

"I hid because I could. But most of us can't. And we shouldn't have to."

Her hands are shaking. She tilts her eyepiece up.

"So let me start again. My name is Sierra Marlowe. I'm a telepathic dysmorphic woman. I'm sorry for my hypocrisy. I'm sorry I've been hiding for so long."

The part of Sierra that is watching herself huddles in a corner and closes her eyes. The part of her that is actually here takes off her sunglasses with trembling hands, looks up at the crowd and into the cameras.

"This is who I really am."

❧

"Liam?"

He freezes at the sound of Corbin's voice. In a crowd of thousands, how can he possibly have singled him out?

He turns. "Mr. Corbin. Good speech you gave."

Corbin smiles, his eyes wide with surprise. He reaches out to shake Liam's hand with both of his. "It *is* you! I don't believe it. How are you? I never expected to see you again. This is incredible!"

Liam tries to focus. "Thought I'd check out the rally. You know, heard a lot about it on the Cube. See you on it all the time."

"You should have come to see me. Well, I suppose you're busy. But this is really fantastic. I always hoped you were all right. I had no idea you'd gone to the States. Do you live nearby?"

"No. Bit of a ways away. When did you come to America?" Where is Holden? He can't let Corbin see Holden. He uses his eye to switch his Lens's view from camera to camera, sees that Holden is some distance behind Corbin, and Damian is close to him.

"About six years ago. We wanted to open a branch of the shelter here, so," he shrugs, "here we are. God, it's been twelve years, hasn't it?"

"About that, yeah."

"I don't suppose you know—" He looks down, then back at Liam. "You did go with Adair, didn't you?"

"I did, yeah."

"Do you know what happened to him? It's been a long time, I know, but... I haven't seen or heard from him since that night."

"I'm sorry, Mr. Corbin. I haven't seen him in years."

Corbin looks disappointed. He nods sadly. "Well, I just thought I'd ask." His smile returns. He puts his hand out again and Liam takes it. "Will you come and see me after the rally?"

"Sure, Mr. Corbin. I'd like that."

Corbin nods, shakes Liam's hand, lets go. "Really wonderful to see you again, Liam. And please call me Richard."

"Good to see you, too." Liam smiles back, tries to think of something to say to keep Corbin from turning around.

There's a crack and a rolling scream, a wave of panicking voices. The wall is coming down. Corbin looks at the cascading stone, then turns sharply to Liam. There's a moment that lasts a lifetime between them, where neither of them speaks, but both know exactly what the other is thinking. Liam tries to rush him, but he can't move. He can't even speak. Corbin is holding him there. Running against a telekinetic hold is like trying to walk through a brick wall with your arms tied behind you and your legs bound together.

Corbin looks around and his eyes land on Holden, whose gaze is focused on the prison. Corbin runs to him, pushing past the frantic crowd.

And there is nothing Liam can do.

&

"Adair!"

Adair looks over his shoulder.

Richard is running toward him, stops breathlessly in front of him. "What are you doing?"

"Get out of here, Richard!" He feels the wall in his mind—the coarse concrete, the steel frame—as he takes it apart. Damian runs to him from the right, but Richard holds him back, freezes him mid-stride. A young man and Sierra Marlowe rush to Richard's side.

"What's happening?" The young man looks from Richard to Adair. The air is filling with fine white dust.

Richard grabs Adair's arm tightly, and it feels as if a hand is pushing against his brain.

"Richard! Stop!"

Richard locks eyes with him. "I can't let you do this! It won't help us! You'll ruin everything!" He's so focused on Adair that his mental grip on Damian starts to fail.

"Let go, Richard!"

Adair forces Richard's mind to release Damian, and when he's free, Damian charges. Marlowe steps in front of Richard, takes Damian on herself. The young man joins her. Adair sees a spray of blood.

Some people are running in panic; others are frozen in fear. An empty circle has formed around Richard and Adair as if people know, somehow, that whatever's happening is being controlled from here.

"Richard! Let go!" Richard's fingers are digging into Adair's arm painfully, but the worst pain is in his head, where Richard's mind is trying to wrench away his control of the wall. Adair pushes back with everything he has, sees Richard's face tighten as he does. He puts his hand on Richard's shoulder. "Please try to understand."

Richard's face falls. He looks at Adair's hand on his shoulder, his eyes filled with sadness and hurt and pain. "Dair…"

Layla dives out of the sky and knocks Richard to the ground. They tumble over each other, her wings and feathers flashing. She punches him in the face. It's enough to free Adair's mind from Richard's grasp; he's too focused on defending himself from Layla to maintain it. The wall thunders to the ground. People scream and run.

Damian has knocked Marlowe off her feet. She tries to get up. He kicks her under her chin and she stops moving. The young man is already unconscious nearby. Adair tears down what remains of the wall, and with a final push, he flattens the fences surrounding the prison. The dust is like a heavy fog. He can't see if anyone has escaped.

"Boss!"

Liam is running to him. His path is blocked by the surging mob. He raises his weapon, fires it into the air. People drop down and Liam leaps over them. He throws himself in front of Adair, shoving him to the ground.

And that's when Adair hears the shots.

For a moment, it's as though nothing has happened. Liam is still standing, cupping the side of his neck. Then he turns, looks down at Adair, down at his own chest. He weaves, falls onto his side.

"Liam!" Adair crawls to him, turns him over. His neck is bleeding where a bullet grazed him, his cam collar almost severed. There's blood on his coat and a hole in his chest. He's not moving.

Adair pulls up the goggles. Liam's eyes are wide and blank. To think that he's known Liam for thirteen years and will never know how he got that scar.

Is he like a son to you?

Another shot strikes the ground too close to him.

Damian is there suddenly, helping him up, pushing him along, shielding him with his own body. Layla is just ahead. As Adair steps over Sierra Marlowe, she opens her eyes and starts to sit up. He slips from Damian's grasp as he tumbles over her, hits the ground hard. The pain in his head blinds him.

And then...

Everything stills and disappears.

He's in a cold room—metal tables, metal drawers. A faceless man with old hands pulls back a sheet, and he sees her...

༄

"Holden!" In the moment between when he loses his grip on Holden and turns around to get him up again, a team of armed men pushes him back and they're separated.

Damian links to Cam One so that he can see above the crowd blocking his view. He zooms in. Holden isn't moving. And there's no way he can get to him and not get shot. The cops have already pinned down Corbin and restrained him. Holden will be next.

He doesn't see Layla, calls to her in his Lens.

"Is Dair with you?" she asks, her voice frantic.

He tells her what's happened.

"We have to go back!" she cries.

"We can't get to him! You want to get shot?"

She doesn't say anything.

"Where are you?"

Silence.

"Layla!"

"I'm closest to Dair's car."

"Wait for me!"

"Get the other car!"

"You fucking wait for me, Layla!"

He looks through all the cams to find the best way to her, but what he sees are National Guardsmen moving through the crowd and along the perimeter in open jeeps, guns drawn. They're herding everyone to the center like sheepdogs in a panicked flock. If he doesn't move now, he'll be trapped, along with any other d-form who isn't fast enough to get away.

So Damian runs. He disappears into the crowd, and he runs.

Chapter 9

THE HOUSE is dark.

Damian slams the car door shut, leaps up the steps. Inside he sees a flickering faint gray light coming from the living room. Eden sits on the floor, hugging her knees, staring at the Cube, the camera feed from the prison still live.

He tells the lights to turn on. She drops her head at the sudden brightness.

"What the hell?"

She doesn't look up.

"Cube, off." The images vanish. "What are you doing? Is Layla here?"

She shakes her head slowly.

He feels a sinking in his stomach. He hasn't heard from her since he was on the field, where he had no choice but to run to the other car to meet up with her on the road. He's blinked her a thousand times.

Eden looks up at him. Her yellow eyes are bloodshot. "Your arm..."

He doesn't remember getting it, but there's a deep gash on his left arm.

"I'll get you some bandages." She stands up shakily.

He grabs her arm as she walks past him. "Don't fall apart, you hear me?" She doesn't look at him, and he shakes her. "Do you hear me?" He digs his fingers into her arm. "No one's going to care if you cry. If you can't keep it together, get the fuck out."

She looks up at him slowly and he's surprised by what he sees in her eyes, how it makes him feel.

He lets her go. "Forget the fucking bandages. Just get me something to eat."

When she's gone, he sits on the couch. His arm aches. Driving brought mindless focus. He kept the car on manual the whole way. Home now, all of his thoughts crash down on him like a wave. What the fuck happened? And where is Layla? Where the fuck is Layla? "Cube, on. Rewind, four hours."

Eden comes back. He takes the plate and sandwich, suddenly ravenous. She sits beside him, touches his arm.

"I said forget it. I'll take care of it later." He keeps his eyes on the Cube. The rally is underway, people chanting, projecting signs. He sees Holden among them, himself nearby. He can't see Layla. "Cam Two, same time." The angle changes. Layla is behind Holden, twenty feet or more. Liam is to his left.

"Cube, forward... Play." The wall is falling. Richard Corbin runs to Holden, grabs his arm. Damian remembers not being able to move, trying to run against the invisible hold on his body. It was like a nightmare.

"Cube, forward... Play." Layla comes out of nowhere, tackles Corbin. He watches the police close in. He sees Liam break through the crowd. Liam saw what the others didn't—a sniper on the roof. He leaps in front of Holden, takes the bullets.

Damian looks at Eden. She's watching the footage. She doesn't look away when Liam is killed. She has no reaction at all.

He watches himself yank Holden to his feet, watches Holden trip over Marlowe as she sits up. The police push between him and Holden, and he sees himself talk to Layla for the last time, then run away.

He can't slow his heart down. His mind runs over every possibility. "Cube, live, news."

"Let me take care of your arm, Damian."

"Jesus Christ." But he gives in. She gently applies disinfectant, paints on skinseal. The wound is deep. It will probably scar.

Damian sees his own face projected from the Cube. The 3D image is his Registration pic from ten years ago. "... were wearing cam collars, but witnesses were able to describe them. Damian Grace is wanted for murder in the state of New York," says a voice. "The victim, Simon Alvarez, was the owner of a dysmorphic brothel in Manhattan called Formz of Pleazure. He himself was not dysmorphic—"

"Cube, change."

Another news anchor is speaking. "It is also believed that this woman, Layla Monroe, was involved in the plot." Layla's mug shot appears. "Monroe has been charged with prostitution in the past and is known to have worked at the same brothel—"

"Cube, change."

The Cube jumps to *Phenomena*. Venus Carr is talking about Holden, his image appearing next to hers. "... that Mr. Holden is in stable condition. He has no criminal record."

"Cube, change."

"... including solicitation and rape. Aldrich served a four-year sentence at Hammond Prison for assaulting a prostitute. He was declared dead at the scene," says a male reporter, standing outside a hospital. Liam's mug shot is to his right.

"Cube, change."

"... not heroes, not freedom fighters. They're terrorists. Plain and simple. They're a threat to America, to freedom." A group of three men and two women sit around a half-moon table. "Now, I'm not saying that all dysmorphic people are terrorists. But in the last ten or so years, all terrorists have been dysmorphic. That's just a fact."

"Cube, change."

Damian recognizes the Reverend Emery Tibbot-Robinson, the apocalyptic evangelist. "We have ignored the signs," Tibbot-Robinson exclaims in his thick Southern drawl. "The Anti-christ is among us, brothers and sisters. And he is not alone."

Holden as the Antichrist. Under any other circumstances, Damian would find that hilarious.

"Cube, off." He squeezes his eyes shut, rubs his head. The news hasn't changed since the last time he checked it. Layla hasn't been caught—not that the media is aware of, at least. But where is she? Where is she?

Eden wraps his arm, secures it, rests her fingers on it. His eyes start to feel heavy; his heart slows. Why is he calming down? He shouldn't be calming down.

He becomes intensely aware of Eden's touch suddenly and turns his head quickly to look at her. She draws back, but holds his gaze. They stay like that, looking at each other, for a long moment. Then, just to get her to turn away, he says, "Get me some water."

She comes back with a glass, puts two painkillers in his hand.

He stares at them, weirdly grateful and tired enough to feel some pity for her. Looking up, he says, "The rape charge was bull-shit, if you were wondering."

She meets his eyes but doesn't say anything.

There's a voice in his ear. "I'm ten minutes away."

He jumps up, drops the water and the pills. "Where the fuck have you been?"

She doesn't answer.

He yanks his Lens off, throws it on the couch. "Goddammit, Layla."

❦

When her car pulls up, he doesn't go out to meet it. When she walks through the door, he doesn't get up.

She's pale. There's a cut on her face and a bruise on her jaw.

She looks at him, then sits and stares down at nothing.

He leaves the room, grabs an icepack from the freezer, comes back, and slams it into her hand. She throws it on the floor.

"Your face is purple."

"I don't care."

He looks at Eden. "Fix her up."

Layla smacks Eden's hand away from her face.

"Please, Layla," she says quietly. "You're bleeding."

Layla is breathing hard. She glares at Eden, about to lose it altogether. But when Eden doesn't shy away from her anger, her shoulders slump and she nods, the fire gone from her eyes.

When Eden's finished, she picks up the icepack from the floor, hands it to Layla. A moment goes by, and Layla takes it, holds it to her face, too tired to fight.

Damian's waited long enough. "Where were you?"

"Have you heard from August?"

"Where the fuck *were* you?"

She meets his eyes. "I followed the ambulance."

He can't speak for a moment, then, "What the fuck were you thinking?"

"I was thinking of Dair!"

"Jesus Christ. And I thought *she'd* be too emotional." He nods at Eden. Her face is a mask.

Layla rubs her forehead. She doesn't seem to have heard Damian at all, speaks more to herself than to him. "He didn't even see Dair. He didn't even see him. He recognized Liam."

"What?"

"Corbin. I saw it. Liam tried to distract him, but when the wall started to come down..." She shakes her head.

"Jesus Christ."

The silence between them is heavy. The heat doesn't seem to be working, and Damian's first thought is to tell Liam to fix it.

He saw Liam's eyes when he grabbed Holden, only for a second; saw that frozen look of blank surprise. He's seen dead eyes before, but this was different somehow. He wonders what his own eyes will look like when he dies. Will he be surprised?

He looks over at Eden. She senses him staring, turns to him. And he sees again what he saw in her eyes as he held her arm: nothing. Calm, cold nothing. His whole body tenses, because right now, looking into her eyes is like looking into his own.

"Did you hear from August?"

Damian turns from Eden to Layla. "No."

"What the fuck is he waiting for?"

Damian stares at her for a moment, then says, "Give me your Lens."

She frowns. "Why?"

He walks over to her, puts his hand out. "Give it to me."

"What? You think I want him to get caught, too? I'm not stupid. I'm not going to blink him."

"Now, Layla."

She glares up at him, then pulls the folded Lens from her pocket and slaps it into his hand.

"Now we wait."

Layla adjusts the icepack, winces, and nods.

Damian crouches down in front of her. He touches the underside of her chin to tip her head up. He'll kill Richard Corbin one day for putting that bruise and that cut on her perfect face.

Layla stares at him with glassy eyes. "It wasn't supposed to be like this, Damian."

He moves his hand to stroke the feathers on the back of her neck.

She closes her eyes. "It wasn't supposed to be like this."

He can't sleep. Every time he nods off, he thinks Layla is dead and he jolts awake. It takes a few agonizing seconds for him to remember that she's fine; she's just down the hall. He gives up, sits on the edge of the bed, holds his head in his hands.

He jumps when he hears a scream come from somewhere in the woods. It sounds like an animal, but he knows almost immediately that it's not. He goes downstairs, opens the front door, and listens. He hears it again—long, loud, full of pain. But not as strong as the first cry. It grows weaker each time, cuts right through him like a thin, sharp wire, splits him in two: the part of him that wants to ignore it and the part of him that can't.

Damian stays on the porch until she stops, until his body aches from standing stiff and still for so long. When he goes back in, he sees she's left her breather behind, so he waits in the dark to make sure she comes back. He'll go looking for her if she doesn't.

When she walks inside, she's breathing hard, wheezing. She can't see him, can't see in the dark like he can. She takes the stairs slowly.

He stays in the living room long after she's gone, falls asleep on the couch and doesn't dream about Layla again.

In the morning, he makes his own coffee.

Chapter 10

THE ROOM IS like a refrigerator. The floor is tiled and has drains in it, small dips leading into them. There are metal counters, metal drawers, metal tables. It smells damp, but sterile. He doesn't hear anything.

A faceless man beckons him to a table with a body on it, covered in a white sheet. The man's voice is muffled, but he knows what's being asked and he nods. The man's old, liver-spotted hands pull back the sheet to just below the tops of the shoulders.

"Yes," he says. "Yes. That's her."

That's her. Her eyes are closed. Her dark skin is pale with death. He can see where the pathologist made his cuts during the autopsy, the beginnings of a crisscross starting at each shoulder. Her face is bruised, her lip cut, her eye battered, but her hair is strangely untouched—those beautiful spiral curls, black and caramel, pillowing her head on the slab.

Oh, my girl…

The too-clean smell of the room is becoming intolerable. He keeps waiting for something else to happen, but this is it. There is nothing else. He's done what he came here to do.

He has a sudden memory of being at the beach as a child. He was pulled into the water, dragged across the sharp shells along the shore. He righted himself, but was knocked down by another wave. It pulled him deeper. Another and another crashed down on him until he couldn't breathe and his feet couldn't find the seafloor. He was saved eventually, but as he was drawn deeper and deeper into that huge, cold emptiness, he was aware of being at once weightless and heavy as lead, floating and drowning and, more than anything else, powerless.

And he's a child again. He's in that ocean now... drowning, dying, yet still alive, and more powerless than ever.

Who will save him this time?

He stumbles out of the morgue, trips, catches himself against a wall, slides down to the floor, and screams.

Sierra wakes with a start, her heart slamming in her chest. She sits up, touches her face. There are bandages there, wet with tears and sweat. She's sitting in a chair by Dairen's bedside. She fell asleep, resting her head on the mattress, holding his hand.

He's still asleep. His face is a mess. His right hand is broken and he has a few cracked ribs.

She pushes her sweat-dampened hair back, sees the dead girl's beautiful curls in her mind, shudders. And then her eyes are hot and her throat is thick with grief over someone she's never met. She doesn't even know the girl's name. The memory isn't hers. It's Adair Holden's.

It came into her mind so suddenly and strongly, she didn't have a chance to try to block it. All his sadness and pain poured into her for the briefest moment before he fell unconscious. It was like being struck blind. She couldn't think after that, couldn't move. She wasn't hurt badly, not as badly as Dairen, but she was on the ground long enough that the paramedics started to lift her onto a stretcher before she was able to tell them she could walk to the ambulance.

The man who attacked her—she's never seen anyone that fast. He was like an animal—his dark skin, darker eyes, and white fur flashing around her in a violent blur. After the Kenny Layton show, Sierra had, almost unconsciously, started to carry around her father's old vintage pocketknife; she got the man once with the knife, but that only made him angrier and move even faster, and he hit her in the face so hard she thought he'd punched her head inside out. Then there was his boot coming toward her face when she tried to get up, and she blacked out.

She thinks the gunshots must have brought her around. She vaguely remembers hearing two sharp cracks, seeing the dark-eyed man lifting Adair Holden to his feet and pulling him forward; seeing the body of the dead man they left behind. Everything snapped back into focus then, and she tried to get up again. Holden tripped over her... He fell... And then...

The memory.

"Hey... don't cry, babe."

"Oh, Dairen!" She takes his hand and kisses it over and over. "Oh my God! Are you okay?"

He cups her face, then looks down at his broken right hand, sadness in his eyes. "I'll never bowl again."

There are only the sounds of the machines and the hospital digicom for a moment, and then Sierra can't help laughing. It hurts her nose and eyes, and Dairen looks in pain too as he laughs with her. She holds his wrist, and her tears fall onto his hand as he strokes her cheek with his thumb. She stands, leans down to kiss him.

"Am I as much of a mess as I think I am?" he asks.

She sits again, holds his hand. "Probably."

He looks up at the ceiling. "God, who was that guy? That was like getting hit by a car. By a bloody tank." He frowns, looks back at her. "Is that a dysmorphic thing? Are *you* that strong?"

"No. I mean, I am strong, but not like that." She sees him again in her mind, a swirl of black and white... those furious, opaque eyes flashing as he kicked her in the face. She runs her hand over the bruise under her chin, winces.

"Where's Dad?"

She grimaces. "He's being questioned."

Dairen sits up. "Questioned? For what?"

"He knew that man. Adair Holden. They knew each other, and your dad tried to stop him. They want to know everything he knows and make sure that..." She trails off.

"That Dad didn't have anything to do with it." He falls back against the pillow. "Wait. What was that name?"

"Adair Holden."

Dairen frowns. "I know that name..."

"Maybe Richard mentioned him to you once?"

He shakes his head. "I don't think so. Maybe. I'll ask him about it. Hey, when can we get out of here?"

"Oh! I'm supposed to tell them when you wake up."

"Well hurry, before I fall asleep again." He smiles, and she kisses him.

"I'll be right back."

She gets up, pulls the curtain back, turns to close it again, and the dead girl is lying in the bed in Dairen's place.

And then she's gone and Dairen is staring at her. "Sierra? You okay?"

She can feel blood pulsing in her throat. "Yeah... I'll be right back."

She walks down the hall looking for the doctor, wraps her arms around her stomach, tries to breathe slowly. It wasn't real. She's tired. It will go away like all the other memories. It will retreat to the back of her mind and she'll hardly ever think about it again. Memories are always hard the first time she sees them—confusing, disorienting. But she'll be fine.

She'll be fine.

♋

Adair dreams of the table, only she isn't on it. He is, and she's looking down at him with dead eyes. He's strapped to the cold metal. He can't move.

He opens his eyes to find that it isn't a dream. The light above him is blinding; he can't see anything around him, but he can sense other people nearby.

"Where am I?" Speaking sends a shudder of pain into his already aching head, like a razor through his brain.

No one answers him. Then he feels a hand on his arm. He looks away from the light, sees a woman in a surgical mask holding a needle above the inside of his elbow.

"What are you doing?"

The needle goes in. "Welcome to Hammond Prison, Mr. Holden. I'm Dr. Mara Kovich." She pulls the needle out. He watches it slide out from under his skin, feels his muscles start to relax. "How are you feeling?"

He's sure there are more people in here, but where are they? "My... my head hurts."

"Of course it does," Kovich says. "That's bound to happen when you overuse telekinesis. Kind of like pulling a muscle."

"Who are you?" His lips and tongue feel fat. He's not sure if he's speaking clearly.

"You fooled us all with those contacts, you know," the woman says. "But you're not really like the rest of them, are you? Good thing the press doesn't know that yet. People would be tearing each other apart out there if they knew some of the deformed weren't so deformed after all."

What is she saying? Where is he? Where are Damian and Layla and Liam? When did his bed become so uncomfortable? And what is this strange, masked creature doing in his bedroom? His vision starts to blur. "What... What am I...?"

The masked being stands over him and pats his hand with its leathery, inhuman one. "Go back to sleep, Mr. Holden. We'll talk later."

How can he sleep with this pain... with this...

"Where am I...?" He struggles to speak. "Where...?"

"Don't worry, boss," Liam says. "Everything's fine."

Adair looks at him. "How did you get that hole in your chest, Liam?"

Liam looks down at himself, surprised. "Damn." Blood pours out of the hole. "This is my favorite jacket."

"I'll get you a new one."

Liam shrugs. "Don't bother. I'm dead."

Icy cold dread fills Adair's body and heart as, just before he slips back into unconsciousness, he remembers everything.

❧

"All right, Mr. Corbin. Let's go over this again."

Richard's eyes are burning. His throat is dry. He has no idea how much time has gone by, but it feels like he's lost days.

"How do you know Adair Holden?"

"I've told you everything I know."

Special Agent Jamie Wynne, Department of Dysmorphic Affairs and Terrorism, shakes his head. "I don't think you have, Richard. I just don't think you have. Maybe you left something out."

"I haven't."

"Humor me."

"Could I have some water?"

"How do you know Adair Holden?"

The table is greasy. The air in the room is stale and too warm. "We met in England twenty years ago."

"How?"

He is so thirsty. He doesn't think he's ever been this thirsty in his life. Every word is an effort. "Through a mutual friend."

"What was your friend's name?"

He's lost count of how many times he's answered these exact questions. "Reynard Finlay."

"How did you know him?"

He rests his head on his fists, feels the bandages on his face, the swelling around his eye. He looks down at the streaked table. "We were both involved in dysmorphic human rights organizations. Adair worked with him. That's how we met."

"Then what happened?"

"Please, I've already told you so many times."

"Tell me again."

He squeezes his eyes shut. "We opened a shelter in London. We ran it together. It was my idea. He put up most of the money. Reynard and I covered the rest."

"Did you know Adair Holden was dysmorphic?"

"Yes."

"You didn't think that was odd? No deformities? No, what do you call them, AFs?"

Richard looks up at the man. The lights are oppressively bright. "I didn't care."

"But did you think it was odd?"

It occurs to Richard, not for the first time, that if he wanted to, he could open that door behind the agent and leave. He could do exactly what Adair did—knock down a wall. Escape. "Yes," he says quietly, "it was odd, I suppose."

"You didn't think you should tell someone?"

"Who would I tell? And why?"

"That was pretty clever of him to wear contacts today, don't you think? So he looked like the rest of them. Like your friend Ms. Marlowe."

"Don't bring Sierra into this."

"Just pointing out a little irony. She wears contacts to make herself look normal; he wears them to make himself look dysmorphic. It's kind of funny, don't you think?"

"I hope you'll understand if I don't."

Wynne smiles. He flips his eyepiece down, stands, focuses on his Lens. "Now, you said that until today, you hadn't seen Adair Holden for twelve years? Is that right?"

"Yes."

"Why?"

"We had a falling out."

"Over what?"

"It was a personal matter."

"What kind of personal matter?"

"A personal one."

Wynne's eyes move rapidly as he looks into his eyepiece. "Money problems?"

Richard doesn't know what he wants more: a glass of water, or to put his head down and fall asleep. "No."

"Lovers' quarrel?"

"No."

"Love triangle?"

Richard lowers his hands to the table. "Please, Agent Wynne. I would like a glass of water."

"And I'd like a straight answer, Richard."

"What does any of this have to do with today's events?"

The agent sits. "Call it context." He takes a Cube out of his jacket pocket. "See, I have a theory." He sets it on the table. "You want to hear it?"

Richard doesn't answer. What would be the point? He watches the agent's eyes as he uses his Lens to control the output of the Cube. All his thoughts of sleep and thirst disappear when Wynne calls up a pic of a young, dark woman with wolf eyes and beautiful caramel curls. She's smiling. Richard presses his fingers into the table, afraid he'll fall off his chair.

"Recognize her?"

He stares at the image. It's so clear; it seems as though she'll speak at any moment. She's *smiling...*

"Richard?"

"Why...?"

"I did a little research in between our chats. I'm thorough like that. And here's the funny thing. Eleven years ago, this young lady here, a resident at your shelter in England, attacked a guy, tried to mug him. He killed her in self-defense. He was tried, sentenced to a year in prison for involuntary manslaughter. Gets out nine months later, good behavior. Then he ends up dead under mysterious circumstances. And right afterward, Adair Holden just..." he opens his hand, "disappears. You did say it's been twelve years since you've seen Holden?"

His vision blurs. "Yes," he manages to say. "Yes, I said that."

"So, here's what I think. You knew Holden did it. And you helped him get away."

"No."

"You knew he killed the guy. He's your friend; you helped him escape."

"No."

"What was it? He was in love with this girl?"

Richard stares at Wynne, wide-eyed. "She was nineteen years old. Adair was in his fifties."

Wynne shrugs. "Fine. He was banging this girl?"

He wants to scream. He wants to throw this man into the wall for saying these things, for his vulgar assumptions. "Agent Wynne," he says slowly, "whatever Adair has done, he always treated our residents kindly and with respect. He took care of them, helped them find employment or get into school." He looks into the girl's wild, beautiful, gentle eyes. "We all loved this young woman. And her death—" His voice catches. He shakes his head. "You have no right to say these things."

Wynne slams his fist down on the table as he stands. Richard jumps back. "I can get you deported right now, Richard, right now. Send you back to England and see that you're charged, at the very least, with impeding a criminal investigation; at the most, aiding and abetting a murderer."

"You can't do that. I'm a naturalized citizen."

"Are you and Holden part of the DCo?"

"What?"

"The Dysmorphic Coalition, Richard. Are you a member?"

Richard looks down, covers his face with his hands. "No."

"And this guy. You know him too, right? Look up, Richard, come on. Don't fall asleep on me."

The image of the girl has been replaced with a pic of Liam.

"I knew him as a boy. He came to our shelter when he was fifteen."

Wynne plays a muted vid of Richard talking to Liam on the field, shaking hands with him, smiling. Liam's face is obscured by the cam collar he's wearing. "Can you explain this?"

Richard's heart feels like it's being squeezed through his throat. "I recognized him as I was going through the crowd. He has a very distinctive scar on his face. I hadn't seen him in years. I said hello."

"Did you know he was working with Holden?"

"No."

"Do you know he's dead?"

The warm air is thick, smothering. His head is swimming. "What?"

"He took a bullet for your buddy Holden. Two, actually. Generous guy." The vid moves forward, slows. Liam jumps in front of Adair, saves his life. Richard feels sick seeing how Liam's body jerks when the bullets hit him; how, with his collar damaged, his face becomes visible, and he looks down at the wound in his chest before falling to the ground.

The first day Richard met Liam, he'd had to meet with his probation officer first. She'd warned him about Liam's explosive personality, his problems with rage. "We don't know how long he'll last in your shelter, Mr. Corbin," she'd said, "but hopefully a little longer than in the previous one."

"You look pretty upset, Richard. Guy's got quite a rap sheet. Solicitation, assault, drugs, rape."

Richard turns his head up sharply.

"Yeah, you heard me. Want me to put the list up on the Cube?"

"No." His hands are sweating. His neck is hot.

"You know either of these people?"

Pics of the woman and man who came to Adair's defense hover in front of Richard. "I've never seen them before."

"Pretty unsavory characters your pal associates with. A rapist, a prostitute, a murderer."

Richard clenches his fists. "He's not my 'pal,' Agent Wynne. I don't know his 'associates.' I've never seen either of these people in my life. I saw what Adair was doing. I tried to stop him. They attacked me. And my son, Dairen. And Sierra. And no one will tell me where they are or if they're all right."

"Do you know Alan Bryce?"

Richard eyes Wynne. "I know *of* him."

"I mean, do you know him personally?"

His breathing is short now. The heat, the thirst... and he's so angry; it's choking him. "No. I don't."

"Does Holden know him?"

"You should ask him that question, not me."

"Calm down, Richard." The agent raises his hands. "No need to get upset. I'm only asking because Bryce and the DCo are taking credit for Hammond. You don't know anything about that, do you?"

"No." But it doesn't ring true, and he can tell that Wynne doesn't think so either. The DCo are random, guerilla-like, unthinking. Richard can't imagine Adair associating himself with them. Adair is a careful thinker. Hammond was carefully planned. It would have succeeded, and no one would have known who was responsible—if Richard hadn't recognized Liam. That ruined everything.

And like that night twelve years ago, Richard finds himself torn between being glad about what Adair has done and being disgusted by it. He wishes that he hadn't seen Liam, hadn't seen Adair. He would be home now, with his son and Sierra. They wouldn't have been hurt, and he wouldn't be locked in an airless room with this maniac special agent.

"Am I under arrest, Mr. Wynne?"

The agent watches him for a moment, slowly sits down, leans back with a sigh. "How about some water?" He blinks into his Lens. Richard hears a tinny voice come from the earpiece. "Yeah, a pitcher for our friend Richard here. Thanks." He blinks off. "I don't know about you, but I'm parched."

Richard glares at him.

"So, just relax, have a glass." He stands up, goes to the door. "And when I come back, we can start again. How's that sound?"

❧

"Dad!" Dairen runs to him, throws his arms around him. "Dad, are you okay?"

"Just get me home, please."

They haven't seen Richard in more than twenty-four hours.

His face is ashen, tired, and bruised. There's swelling around one of his bloodshot eyes. Sierra takes his arm, looks back at the agent as he watches them leave. He has a curious expression on his face, a small smile. She hates him.

In the car, Richard doesn't speak. Dairen keeps looking over at him. Sierra touches his shoulder from the back seat. "Richard? Are you all right?"

He seems surprised to hear her voice, as if he thought he was alone in the car. It snaps him out of his silence. "Oh my God. I should be asking *you* that question. Look at your faces."

"We're all right, Dad. Just banged up. What happened to you? Did they hurt you?"

"No, they just questioned me. Over and over. The same questions. It was maddening." Sierra sees tears in his reddened eyes. "They wouldn't tell me anything. They wouldn't tell me if you were all right. I didn't know anything... The last I saw of both of you—" He shakes his head.

Dairen is crying too. He holds his father's arm tightly. "We're okay, Dad. We're okay. They wouldn't tell us anything either."

Richard wipes his eyes, then suddenly looks panicked. "Is everyone all right at home?"

Dairen starts to speak, but can't.

Richard looks at both of them. "What is it?"

Sierra doesn't want to tell him. She just wants him to be able to go home in peace, to rest and recover. "Richard," she says quietly, "the press is waiting for you. They've been waiting. They're all over the place."

Richard puts his head in his hand.

"You just walk through, Dad," Dairen says. "We did."

"They'll stay out there until they have answers." Richard speaks with a certainty that makes Sierra think he's done all this before. "Do they know about Adair Holden? The police know he doesn't have any AFs, but does the public?"

"No." Sierra glances at Dairen, who looks as confused as she is. "He doesn't have AFs? He's like you? No one's talking about that."

Richard squeezes his temples between his thumb and forefinger. "Thank God. That's all we need."

He doesn't say anything else about it, so Sierra doesn't ask. She takes his hand. "Richard, there are some protestors too. And someone broke a window last night."

"*What?*"

"Everyone's fine," she says quickly. "Just scared. We told them all to stay inside for a while, or if they have to go out, to take someone with them."

Richard goes silent again. Dairen and Sierra look at each other. They wait for him to speak, but he doesn't until they pull up to the shelter. She watches his face as he takes in the mob of reporters, ready to pounce the second he steps out.

He shakes his head, speaks so quietly she's not sure they're meant to hear his words. "Goddammit, Dair."

And then he seems to transform in front of her. Exhaustion hides behind resolution; fear turns into calm. The man they picked up from the police station has put on a mask.

"All right," he says, but he's not speaking to them, and he's not speaking to himself.

It's like a challenge to the world.

He opens his door.

∾

"Who is she?"

The girl lies still on the slab.

The faceless man tilts his head. "Don't you know?"

"I'm supposed to."

"So sad," he says, "so sad."

"I wish I knew her name."

He clicks his tongue. "So sad. So sad."

Sierra reaches out to touch the girl's face. Her eyes flash open, wild and ice blue like a wolf's, full of tears, but dead, *dead*, open and seeing nothing. "So sad," she whispers, with a voice like tearing paper, "so sad."

"Sierra!" Dairen shakes her. "Sierra!"

She's cold with sweat, shivering. "Oh God, oh God!"

"It was a nightmare. You were dreaming. It's okay."

She's crying. "Oh God, God..." Her heart feels like it's in a vise; it aches.

Dairen holds her. She clings to him. "Dairen!" she cries.

"It wasn't real, baby. You're okay. It wasn't real."

"Are you sure? Are you sure?"

"I'm sure."

But she knows. She knows he's wrong.

☙

"Well, you are one interesting son of a bitch, you know that Holden?"

He looks up at Agent Wynne. "Am I?"

"You don't think so? A dysmorphic human with no AFs? What's up with that?"

Adair says nothing.

"How many more of you are there?"

"None that I'm aware of."

"Who are these people?"

Pics of Layla and Damian appear on the Cube.

He almost closes his eyes with relief. Almost. He couldn't ask about them, had no way of finding out what happened to them. But now he knows. Thank God.

They got away.

Damian will take care of Layla; Adair knows it. And as much as they'd like to believe in their own heartless apathy, he knows they won't abandon Eden.

"I don't know them."

"Layla Monroe, prostitute. Damian Grace, murderer. Liam Aldrich, rapist." The pic changes to one of Liam on the field being zipped into a body bag. "DOA. And your nephew, apparently. Sorry for your loss."

Adair is momentarily confused, but then, of course, Liam *is* his nephew, at least on eWork—otherwise Adair could never have brought him into the country as his legal guardian. Adair had American citizenship; Liam didn't—until he faked the eWork. It was the first time Adair realized exactly how intelligent Liam was.

Was...

Liam *was*.

The shot... the blood... "He saved my life."

"Yes, he did. Why would he do that? Are you just, like, the best uncle ever, or what?"

The dead eyes... "I don't know." And he doesn't. He took Liam in, took care of him, but... what else? He did nothing for Liam that deserved that kind of sacrifice in return. What should he have done? Was he supposed to have been a father to him? Should he have tried? What does it even mean to be a father? There must have been something... He should have done more for him. He should have. "I don't know." His mind clears of grief suddenly, as anger wakes him up. He can't save Liam, but he can at least defend him. "He wasn't a rapist."

"Never served time for it."

Adair tightens his hands. "Liam was not a rapist. He was

found not guilty."

"Oh, right. Of course. I forgot that part. Just remember the pics, I guess." A woman's face that Adair knows all too well floats above the Cube—swollen, battered, bloody. "Don't try to tell me he didn't do that."

"This isn't what we're here to discuss, is it, Agent Wynne?"

"You know, you're right. It's not. What was I thinking?" The pics of Layla and Damian reappear. "I get sidetracked sometimes. I was asking you about these people you don't know."

"I still don't know them."

"They're just random people who came to your defense?"

"The world is full of Good Samaritans."

"Good Samaritans who just happened to be wearing cam collars? If it wasn't for eyewitness accounts, we'd have no idea who these people are."

"I still don't know who they are."

Wynne smiles. "You know, I like you Holden. I really do. You're a hard man to break. But we've got a guy..." He leans forward, speaks conspiratorially. "He can get anything out of anybody. Don't ask me how. I don't want to spoil the surprise."

"You're talking about torture."

"Oh. Are we calling it torture again? I was going to go with Intensive Questioning. Well, in any case, this guy is going to question you very intensively if you don't tell me what you know now. Save yourself a lot of trouble."

"Liam and I worked on our own. I'm grateful to those two for their help, whoever they are, but I don't know them."

Wynne stares at him. "God! I almost believe you!" He smiles. "You're good." He snaps his fingers, points at Adair, and winks. "Our guy's better."

"That remains to be seen."

"Why don't you just tell me the truth?"

"Do you want me to lie to you and tell you that I know these people? I can do that."

"Let's talk about your other partner in crime."

"And who might that be?"

"Richard Corbin. Now, don't pretend you don't know who he is."

"Richard had nothing to do with this."

"And yet..." He activates the Cube; there's Richard, holding his arm. "There he is."

"He was trying to stop me."

"Really?"

Adair looks away from the images, up at Wynne. "Yes."

"Is he like you? Is he dysmorphic?"

"If he is, he kept it to himself all the time we were friends."

"Friends? You'd call him a friend?"

He remembers the day Reynard Finlay introduced him to Richard, called him "that cocky, beautiful boy," said, "He's a relentless optimist, Dair. Doesn't that just make you ill?"

They were attending a charity benefit to raise scholarship money for dysmorphic students. Adair shook Richard's hand. "Not ill, perhaps, but skeptical."

Richard smiled. "Reynard's right, I'm afraid. I tend to look on the bright side."

"Well," Reynard gave Adair an amused, knowing glance, "we'll soon cure you of that."

But they didn't. Instead, Richard cured them. When they opened the shelter and Adair saw how much good they could do—if not on a grand scale, then at least on some level—he started to think that maybe, just maybe, he and Richard and Emily and Reynard were raising a new generation.

And then...

"I called him a friend," Adair says to Wynne. "A long time

ago."

"How's Alan Bryce doing these days?"

"What?" The agent's rapid changes of subject are starting to make Adair dizzy. The Neutralizer sends strange pulses into the back of his neck; he's not sure if they're real or imagined. He wants to reach up, scratch the skin around the circular device that's been embedded in his flesh, thinks that might help, but his hands are cuffed and locked to the table.

He woke up with the device already in his neck, at the base of his skull. When he asked what it was, he couldn't believe the doctor's answer. Scientists have been trying to make a Neutralizer for years—a machine that could cut off a telepath or telekinetic from their abilities without the use of drugs. The successful creation of a working model has only ever been rumor or speculation. There's never been any proof—until now. And the inability to use his telekinesis is making him sick. He tries not to think about it.

"Bryce. Alan Bryce. Dysmorphic Coalition—"

"I know *who* he is. Why would I know *how* he is?"

"He's taking credit for your little stunt, my friend."

This almost makes Adair laugh. "Is he?"

"He is. Must piss you off. After all your hard work."

"It wasn't all that hard, Agent Wynne."

The agent gives him a lazy smile. "Want to show me how you did it?" He points to the back of his own neck. "Bet that Neutralizer would make it kind of hard to do a demonstration, huh?"

"I'm sure we'll have another opportunity."

Wynne takes off his Lens, taps it on the table for a moment. "I'm hungry. You hungry?"

"I could eat."

"You like burgers?"

"I'm handcuffed to a table. I'm hardly in a position to be picky."

The agent puts the Lens on again. "You know, you remind me

of a teacher I once had. Cool guy. Sharp as a tack."

"Thank you."

The agent's eyes move rapidly. Adair assumes he's placing an order for food, but he could be doing anything. "Guy turned out to be a kiddie rapist, though. You believe that shit?" He squints, finishes whatever he's doing, takes the Lens off again, rubs his eyes. "People are full of surprises."

Surprises. He knows he will never forget the look of surprise in Liam's fixed, dead eyes; knows it will haunt him for the rest of his life.

They didn't talk much during the first hour of their trip twelve years ago, he and Liam. It was late. Adair was more tired than he'd ever been, was trying not to think about anything at all.

"Can I watch Cube?" Liam asked suddenly.

"Do you have Bolts?"

"No."

Adair sighed. "What do you want to watch?"

"Don't know. Don't care. You can pick."

"Find something you like and I'll give it a yes or no vote. Fair enough?"

Liam smiled. "Yeah, all right."

He doesn't remember what they watched, but halfway through it, Liam said, "Thanks for taking me with you. I was going mad in there."

"What makes you think you won't go mad in this car with me?"

"Nah. You're all right, boss."

You're all right. Was being "all right" worth Liam's life? Adair doesn't think so. But Liam did.

"What—" He concentrates on controlling his voice. "What will happen to Liam's body? Will you bury him?"

"That's not up to me." Wynne sits back. "But I think he may

have inadvertently donated his body to science."

They'll cut him up. They'll *study* him, take him apart. "No...
You can't just—"

"Oh, yes, we can. With the right eWork and a wink and a
nod from a friendly judge, you'll find that we 'can just' do just
about anything we like. But cheer up." He does a drumroll on the
table. "Food's here in five."

Chapter 11

"JESUS, LAYLA! It's me!"

Layla glares at him over her gun. "August? What the fuck is wrong with you?"

"Besides almost getting *shot*? Not much! Can I put my hands down now?"

"You blinked two hours ago and said you were an hour away!"

"I got hungry! Please take your finger off that trigger! And put some lights on! I can barely see you!"

"*Hungry?* Are you shitting me?"

"Layla—"

And then it hits her. "You stopped for a drink."

"Layla—"

She aims the gun between his eyes. "You stopped for a fucking drink!"

"Okay! Yes! I stopped for a drink! Now either shoot me or put it down!"

She thinks about it, but only for a second, then lowers the weapon.

"Hey! I saw that!" August cries.

"I'm allowed to fantasize." She turns on the light.

"Christ. I'm safer at Hammond." August steps inside, turns to close the door, and jumps. "Jesus, Damian!"

Damian has been standing behind him the entire time, his gun pointed at August's back. When August didn't arrive after an hour, they shut off the lights and waited. Damian's hearing is almost as good as Liam's was, and when he heard a car coming up the road, he went around the back of the house while Layla watched the front door. Damian was indistinguishable from the darkness outside until she turned the light back on.

"Welcome back, Gus."

"How long have you been standing there?" August turns to Layla. "You could've told me he was there!"

"What? And miss that face? That's the funniest thing I've seen in weeks."

August looks back and forth between them, rubs his hands up and down his arms. "Jesus, Layla, I get the gun, but you didn't have to sic the dog on me."

Damian tucks the gun into his waistband, steps inside. "You say you're an hour away and show up two hours later? Pull that shit again and I'll shoot you on principle."

August shakes his head. "I need a drink."

In the kitchen, Eden is by the sink, holding a gun.

"It's fine," Layla tells her.

"Oh," August says, "did we finally get a cleaning lady?"

"That's Eden." Layla sits at the table. "What do you want?"

He takes his hat off, shoves it into the pocket of his coat, then removes the coat and drapes it over the back of a chair. He sits down heavily. He runs his fingers quickly through his wavy, neck-length blond hair in an attempt to unflatten it. "I'd love a beer."

Layla nods to Eden and watches August watch her.

"Even better." He raises an eyebrow. "A slave."

She shrugs. "We all have our place."

Eden puts a beer in front of him. He looks up at her. "So, Eden, what's a pretty girl like you doing in a shithole like this?" August's amber eyes glow a little, a mix between whatever he drank on the way home and the usual charm he turns on for any woman he meets.

"I was in trouble, and Layla and Adair brought me here."

"Oh. That was nice of them."

Eden gives him a small smile, then turns to Damian, who's leaning against the counter. She has a beer ready for him, too.

"Why doesn't anybody tell me these things?" August looks to Layla.

"Because it wasn't important."

August takes a deep drink of his beer, and Layla taps her fingers on the table, clenching and unclenching the gun she still holds in her other hand.

"You seen him?" Damian asks.

"Yeah."

"Is he all right?" Layla can't hide her fear. She remembers the things Liam told her once, when he'd had too much to drink, about what they'd done to him in Hammond.

August hasn't been able to blink long enough to give them many details. The prison guards have been pulling double shifts since the wall went down. When he blinked a few days ago, he said it would be better to see them all in person, so they could decide what to do.

August shrugs. "He's okay." He looks at his beer, rolls the bottle back and forth on the table.

"What is it?" Layla breathes slowly, shallowly.

August keeps his eyes down. "They're not drugging him. They're using a Neutralizer."

No one moves. "Those aren't real..." Layla whispers.

August lifts the bottle, takes another swig. "It's real. And it works. It's a prototype." He finally looks at her. "And you can't just take it off like a World or something. It goes too deep."

Layla sees Adair in her mind, alone, on a cold bed in a windowless room. "You have to get it off him!"

"I can't. You need this... special tool. I've seen it once, but I don't have access to it. And I can't *get* access to it. I've spent all this time making sure everyone thinks I'm John Leonard, your friendly neighborhood prison guard. I'd have to start all over again to make them think I'm a lab tech. New name. New ID. New record. Everything. And who's going to fake all that for me, huh? Liam?"

He's right. Liam was the one who'd done all that—turned August Wright into John Leonard, created a past for him, an ID number.

August goes on. "The most I could do, maybe, is get someone to give me the codes that bypass the retina scan to get into the lab. But I can't get someone to give me their fingerprint, and that's how you get into the fucking box that has the fucking Neutralizer in it."

"Make someone get it *for* you!"

"And then what? Someone would notice it was missing. Or see me with it. Or see someone else take it and wonder why. And we won't get a second chance. They'll lock it up even tighter. The whole thing is too unpredictable, and I can't risk being exposed. I need help. Someone to go in and get it, someone to watch my back. Someone to disable the cameras long enough to make sure we're not seen, but not so long that it would seem suspicious. They know he's d-form now. They won't be able to keep it from the press much longer. So they've hired all this extra security. And there's DDAT agents all over the place. They're expecting something like this. It needs to be big and fast and confusing. It needs to be fucking perfect. I can't do it by myself."

"How would we get in?"

"I don't know." The silence is heavy and smothering. "We could forget the Neutralizer, just get him out and find a way to remove it later. He's himself otherwise—he just can't use his telekinesis."

"We can't get him out without his help! The three of us? Are you kidding me?"

"There's four of us. What can she do?" August nods to Eden.

"Nothing. She's useless." Layla rubs her temples; her head is splitting open. She stands up too fast, leans on the table to keep her balance. "I... I have to think."

Eden hands her a glass of water. Layla wants to shove it back at her or throw it across the room. But she takes it.

"I have to think," she says again.

∾

August finds Layla on the porch in the dark. He leans against the doorframe, looking at her. He's on his fifth beer and finally starting to feel the illusion of calm.

The low light coming from the house is just enough to see her profile, and he can hear her clinking her nails on her glass.

"You look like someone who needs to relax," he says.

"Don't even start."

"Yeah, I know," he smiles, "you only have eyes for Holden... most of the time, anyway."

"Go away."

"Don't be like that." He sits in the chair beside her. "You know, you look so gorgeous right now."

"It's dark."

"Doesn't matter." He taps the side of his head. "I can see you in my mind."

"You're drunk."

"I find that remark insulting." He takes a long pull on his beer, looks at her. "You know, for a second tonight, I thought you were really going to shoot me."

"So did I."

"That is so hot."

"What is *wrong* with you?"

"So many things." He raises the bottle. It's empty. He throws it off the porch into the yard.

"What the hell? This isn't a fucking trailer park!"

"I'm decorating."

"Oh my God..." She presses her fingers into her temples. "Could you please go the fuck away?"

He ignores her, leans in closer. "Hey, what about your slave? Who does she have eyes for?"

This makes Layla laugh. "Believe me, you're not her type."

"What's wrong with me?"

"You're too good-looking for a start."

"Thank you. Wait. What?" He thinks for a moment, frowns. "Come on."

Layla nods.

"Seriously? Liam?"

She looks up at the ceiling. "May he rest in peace."

"Shit..." he says, then shrugs. "Hey, well, good for him." He leans back, puts his hands behind his head. "Good for him." But he doesn't want to think about Liam, not now... not at all. "You think she needs a shoulder to cry on?"

"You really want Liam's leftovers?"

He pretends to find this funny. "Well, *you* just spurned my advances, so it's either her or Damian. And I don't think Damian's that into me."

Layla turns to him. "I've got a great idea. Why don't you start saying crazy things and slapping her around a little? Maybe that'll win her over."

He stares at her. "Jesus, Layla."

She's very still for a moment, then looks away from him. The silence between them is heavy with all the things they're not saying, all the emotions they're trying not to feel. August knows Layla well enough to see through her coldness; he knows that, whatever tensions there were between her and Liam, his death means more to her than she'll ever admit.

August leans his elbows on his knees, bows his head and ruffles his hair. It's not long before he can't stand the quiet anymore. "So. Where'd she come from anyway? Eden."

Layla sighs. "We found her after our last trip to see you. We were at a diner. She was there. She needed help." Layla shrugs, looks into her glass. "Dair felt sorry for her."

"So, what? You guys just brought her home?"

"Yeah."

"What's her story?"

Layla's quiet for a moment, then, "She escaped a lab."

The night seems louder and colder. And he's suddenly too aware of the effects of beer on an empty stomach. "What did they do to her?"

"She never said. Not to me anyway. But it made her weak. That's why she's our little housekeeper."

"What's your issue with her?"

"I don't have an issue with her." Layla shifts in her chair. "She's just... I don't know. She hardly speaks. I don't know anything about her. She's just weird, okay? Honestly, her and Liam were perfect for each other." She takes a sip. "Eden's not even her real name. Dair gave it to her because she wouldn't tell us."

"That was very poetic of him."

"Don't get me started."

August sits a moment longer, then gets up to go inside. He bends down, kisses the top of Layla's head, thinks better of it, kisses her lips. "Don't worry, babe." He holds her chin, kisses her again. "Holden's only got eyes for you, too. Like me."

"Liar."

He opens the door. "But, hey, if you change your mind—"

"I'm this close to changing my mind about not shooting you."

"I'm gone." But he stops before he steps inside. "Hey."

"What?" she snaps.

His eyes have adjusted to the dark and he can see her face more clearly. "You okay?"

"I'm fine." Her voice is quiet, all traces of acerbity gone. And she's lying; he can tell.

"You need anything?"

"No."

He nods, says, "Okay," and goes inside.

Upstairs, he sees a light on in Liam's room. He frowns, goes over to the door, knocks lightly. There's no answer. He opens it part way. Eden is lying on her stomach on Liam's bed, watching Cube, Bolts in her ears.

He takes in her curves, her face, her pretty green skin and scales. He's met beautiful women who've had features similar to Eden's, but he's never really been into the reptile look. Something about her is attractive, though, and he finds he wants to touch her skin to see what it feels like. The pattern of scales on her forehead is beautiful, like a painting or a tribal tattoo.

When she doesn't notice him, he steps all the way into the room.

She jumps, takes out the Bolts. "Cube, off." The image disappears. "Do you need something?" She starts to stand. Her feet are bare, her hair loose.

"Relax," August says. "I just saw the light on."

She sits on the edge of the bed, looks away from him. "This is my room now. I mean... it was supposed to be ours."

Ours. That word and the sorrow contained in it pull at him, threaten to break down the already weak walls he's built around his heart. He just manages to say, "I'm sorry," and feels stupid for saying it.

Still averting her eyes, she nods. "Thank you."

He's never been in this room. He doesn't know what he expected, but it's bare and nondescript, almost as if no one has ever occupied it.

He's desperate to fill the silence. "Kind of empty in here."

"I put some of Liam's things in a box. To keep them safe. And I don't have much."

"Oh." He looks around the room again, back at her. He chances walking forward and sitting beside her on the bed. She doesn't seem to mind, but she still keeps her eyes down. "So, what's on Cube tonight? Anything good?"

"I was watching a vid file."

"What file?"

She hesitates. "The footage from the rally."

He frowns. "Why were you watching that? Isn't it kind of—" She looks up. Her yellow slit-pupil eyes are stunning, but a little unnerving, like they see more than he wants to show. "—morbid?" he finishes.

She reaches behind him, picks up the Cube, stands. He watches how she walks, fluidly and smoothly and without a sound. It's dizzying.

He squeezes his eyes shut. "This beer is getting to my head."

She puts the Cube on the desk. "I'll make you something to eat."

"You don't have to." But she's already halfway out the door.

Downstairs, she heats up leftover sauce, boils water for spaghetti. They don't speak again until after she's set it down in front of him and he's eaten more than half of it.

"This is really good. Thanks."

"You're welcome."

He looks up at her. "God, your eyes are like the sun or something."

She doesn't say anything, but he can see a faint blush on her cheeks.

He props his elbow on the table, leans his head on his fist. "So, Eden, who are you?"

She smiles. "I'm the slave."

"Come on. Seriously."

She looks away, smoothes her shirt. "Do you want any more?"

"I wouldn't say no." She brings the pot over. He watches her dish it out. "Okay. I get it. You don't know me. I don't know you. Why should you share your secrets with me? Right?"

"Something like that."

She puts the pot in the sink, starts to wash it. The sound of the running water is soothing. Drinking his umpteenth beer, he watches the movement of her back. She stops suddenly, turns off the water. "Is he really all right?" She faces him.

August looks down at his plate, spins the spaghetti with his fork. "Yeah. I mean... they questioned him for days, you know. He was a little out of it. I didn't want to tell Layla..." She nods, and he knows that she won't tell Layla either.

She's quiet for a moment, then, "What is a Neutralizer? I mean, how does it work?"

"Kind of like a World. Same size and shape." He turns so he can show her the back of his neck, bows his head a little, points to the base of his skull. "It goes in here." He turns back. "It doesn't really *do* anything. It creates an illusion, like a World does, except, instead of seeing something, you feel something. Or, actually, you don't feel something. It makes you *think* you can't use your tele-kinesis or your telepathy. They give him drugs to make him weak, but they don't want him catatonic. They want him awake so they can question him and stuff."

Eden cups the back of her neck. "Does it... hurt?"

He looks down, shakes his head. "I don't know. He doesn't

look like he's hurting. But he's tough, you know?"

She nods.

"I got it into all the guards' heads to leave him alone. So he's safe for now. But I can't do anything about that fucking Neutralizer."

"How do you do that?"

"What?"

"Get it into their heads."

He smiles. "I use the Force, Luke."

She gives him a look. "How do you do it?"

He waves his fingers in a half circle. "This is not the prisoner you're looking for."

"That's a terrible impression."

"Everybody's a critic." He leans back. "Okay. You know how sometimes if you hear something enough, you start to believe it?"

Any trace of a smile leaves her face. It's like a cloud passes over her. "Yes, I know what that's like."

He thinks of what Layla said about the lab. He wants to ask her about it, but stops himself and goes on. "Okay, so, I can tap into that part of the brain and convince someone of something, put a thought in their heads."

"Is it hard?"

"Sometimes. This prison thing's been a bitch. So many minds to change, to make them believe I work there. Once it's done though, it can't be undone unless I change it myself. That's easier to do. To erase the thought."

"Why?"

"I don't know. It just is."

She tilts her head. "Can you convince them to just let him go?"

"I'd have to convince the whole world. I could get him out of the building, but not past the press, not past the cams, not past every person watching Cube. And there's the Neutralizer. A breakout is better. Something big and confusing that you can't pin on just one person. I can't do it myself. I need to keep a low profile. If my face gets out in the world, like Layla's and Damian's," he spreads his hands, "I'm useless. They can't do what I can do. And they look d-form. I don't. Layla doesn't get it. It's not like in the fucking movies where you can just control people's minds and make them do anything you want. Like crowds of people all at once. That's impossible. The mind is like... a fucking maze, you know? It's complicated. It's... you know, fucking complicated. And I can just affect this one part. And every person's different. I've been in that prison for two fucking months. Changing minds, getting people to trust me. And they've got to trust me, you know? Because I can't just disappear when this is over. If I do, they'll suspect me. And maybe my face ends up all over the news. The last thing I fucking need is someone thinking I'm an inside man. I've got to be sure that when the DDAT asks my boss, 'How's that John Leonard guy?', he'll say what a great, trustworthy employee I am. When shit starts to calm down, *then* I can leave and make everybody forget about me. I'm fucking exhausted!" He realizes he's rambling. "Jesus, am I making any sense?"

Eden looks at him for a long moment, sits at the table again, puts her hand on his. "Yes."

August stares down at her hand, feels the pain in his chest that he's been trying to ignore. It rises in his throat and comes out in a shaky sigh. His eyes feel hot. "Fuck..."

"It's okay."

He shakes his head. "You know, when I met Holden, I was nobody. Nothing. I still am, I guess, but he... believes in me. And now I can't even..." He runs his hand over his face, tries to hide the fact that he has tears in his eyes. "And without him, me and Layla and Damian and Liam—" He catches himself. "Goddammit." He blinks up at the ceiling.

Eden's fingers are cold, but soft. She has a gentle grip. "It'll be okay, August." And for some reason, he believes her. Maybe it's the way she says his name, like it's something special.

He wipes his hand under his nose, realizes what he's just done. "Oh, fuck, sorry. That's gross." He gets up to wash his hands, splashes water on his face, as cold as he can make it. He leans on the sink, lets the water drip down his face instead of his tears. "You never think anyone's going to die, you know? Even when you think it, you don't think it."

Eden is beside him suddenly, turning off the water, handing him a towel.

"Thanks." He dries his face, looks down at his bare wrist. "Hey, look at that. Time for another beer."

She smiles. "I'll get it." She goes to the fridge, pauses, turns back to him. "We have ice cream."

August laughs. "Do beer and ice cream go well together?"

"I don't know."

"Hey, I'll try anything once. But only if you'll have some with me."

On the couch, they pass the carton between them and watch some inane movie on Cube.

"See, now that would never happen."

Eden shrugs. "Anything's possible."

"Nope." He takes the carton. "No way."

"You can switch it if you want."

"It's too late. Now I have to see how it ends." He takes a big scoop. "You know this shit used to be two-dimensional? Flat. Like a painting."

"Ice cream?"

"No, movies and shit."

"I know," she says. "I was joking."

He turns to her. "You are so damn cute." He hands her the carton. "Layla's a bitch, you know. Don't let her boss you around.

But Damian, I can tell you from personal experience, is, in fact, a homicidal maniac. So continue to fear him."

She licks her spoon, and he sees that her tongue is forked.

"Whoa! Nice tongue."

"Thanks." She gives him back the ice cream. "Layla's not a bitch. She's got a lot going on. And she loves Adair."

He raises his eyebrow. "I could tell you stories."

She shakes her head. "No. Her stories are her own. And I'm not scared of Damian."

"Oh, no?"

She lifts her upper lip slightly, points to a fang. "Venom."

"No shit?"

They both look up when Layla's voice comes from upstairs. She's shouting. Damian says something. Layla just gets louder.

August looks at Eden. "What the fuck's that about?"

"I don't know."

It stops after a minute. Heavy footsteps stomp across the floor and two doors slam.

He takes another spoonful of ice cream. "Troubles in paradise."

Eden gets up, goes to the bottom of the stairs. She listens, comes back and sits down. He offers her the carton, puts it on the table when she shakes her head.

"I wouldn't worry about it," he says. "Their freakish relationship goes back way before I ever knew them." But Eden is quiet, and keeps looking up at the ceiling. "Hey, can I ask you something?"

She nods.

"Why were you watching that vid?"

She opens her mouth like she's going to answer, but closes it again, looks away.

He's a fucking idiot. "Hey, I'm sorry. Never mind. It's none of my business."

"No. It's..." She pulls all her hair over one shoulder, twists and untwists it around her hands. "I just... I keep thinking... maybe it's a mistake. That he'll just... show up, you know? He'll come home. All this week, every door opening, every footstep on the stairs—they're all him. Until they're not. I even thought that maybe you'd bring him home; that he's been with you this whole time and you couldn't tell us. And that's ridiculous and I know that. So I watch that vid to remind myself. I know it's weird."

"No... I mean, maybe. But... no, it's okay."

She goes on quietly. "The worst part is, no matter how many times I watch it, there's no way for me to tell the exact moment... The cam collar gets severed by the first bullet and I can see his face, but I can't see his eyes until Adair pulls off the goggles. And it's too late; he's already gone. I don't know exactly when he died... I don't know why that's important to me."

The movie dialogue fills the quiet. The wind beats against the windows. What was he thinking, asking her that? She doesn't look at him. He's afraid she won't speak again.

But then, very quietly, she says, "He's not coming home."

He wishes he could tell her otherwise, just to get her to smile again. "No."

She nods. "No." She picks up the carton, points to the Cube with her spoon. "You're right, that would never happen."

He stares at her. Layla called her weak.

He digs his spoon into the ice cream while she's still holding it. "Told you."

They watch the movie, don't talk for a while. Then he sees Eden turn away from the Cube and look at him.

"What?" He faces her.

She smiles. "I like you."

"I like you, too." He clinks his spoon against hers. "Cheers."

✧

August watches Eden make the breakfast. She's quiet, and he wonders what she's thinking while she stands at the stove, while she pours their coffee.

"Thanks," he says when his cup is filled. She smiles. Layla and Damian don't even look at her. They're not looking at each other either. He can tell Layla hasn't slept; she looks ready to kill.

He hesitates before asking, "So? Any ideas?"

"You're the one in that fucking prison every day, August," Layla says.

He rubs his head. "Did you hear anything I said last night? Extra security? Neutralizer?" He looks up at her. She stares into her coffee, tapping the sides of the cup.

"Fuck me," Damian mumbles. "Just when you need Aldrich, he's dead."

"Hey." August nods toward Eden.

"Oh, she doesn't mind." Damian smiles. "Do you?"

She shakes her head.

"What'd I tell you?"

August glares at Damian. "You're a real shithead, you know that?"

"You haven't been around much lately, Gus. Eden and I have developed a rapport." He lifts his mug, and she comes over with the coffee pot. "See? I don't even need to say anything. She just reads my fucking mind."

Layla slaps her hands down on the table. "Both of you, shut the fuck up!"

Damian takes a slow sip of his coffee, lowers the mug. "Calm down, *hummingbird*. You're going to start molting if you're not careful."

"Don't call me that, Damian, and don't you fucking tell me

to calm down! If it wasn't for you, Dair would be here! If you hadn't left him behind—" She stops herself, but it's too late.

The crackling of the hot oil in the frying pan is the only sound in the room. Damian's eyes are like cold black glass, staring at Layla. His face doesn't change, even as he backhands his mug off the table and it shatters on the floor.

"Damian—"

He gets up, leaves through the back kitchen door, shaking the house as he slams it behind him.

Layla's shoulders slump. Her hand goes to her mouth. August barely hears her whisper, "Fuck..."

"Jesus, Layla."

"Don't. Just... don't." She looks toward the door, but when she leaves the table, she doesn't follow Damian.

Eden kneels on the floor, picking up the broken pieces, wiping up the spill with a towel.

"Let me help you." August gets down beside her.

When they're nearly finished, Eden stops, looks up at him. "There's a 3D printer in the basement."

"What?"

"We have a 3D printer."

"I know. So what?"

She gets up, throws the glass shards into the garbage, turns to him again. "What if you got as many doctors as you could to touch something, like a cup? We could lift their prints, scan them into the printer, and print them on... latex or something."

He stands, stares at her.

"Am I crazy?"

He opens his mouth, closes it again, shakes his head. He rubs the back of his neck. "Jesus Christ, that's fucking genius." He starts to smile. "You're fucking brilliant! I mean, it's still risky, getting in and out, but..."

She's smiling. "No, I thought of that. Is there a filter system in the prison?"

"Yeah. For the guards."

"Can you get a map of it?"

He shakes his head. "I know what you're thinking. It's too small to crawl through. Even for you."

"Can you get a map?"

"What would be the point?"

She grabs his hand, pulls him to the staircase. She doesn't say anything, just kicks off her shoes, curves her body sideways, and slips her head through the impossibly small space between the first two balusters. She pulls her whole body through, weaves up the length of the railing, in and out, twisting around the balusters effortlessly, bending and turning as if her body is boneless. Slithering...

"Holy shit..."

"Are the ducts smaller than that?" Eden looks down at him from the landing.

He shakes his head slowly. "I think they're a little bigger, actually." She seems so solid, as if she didn't just squeeze her body, even her skull, through a space less than a foot wide.

"Can you get a map?"

"Did you really just do that?"

"Can you?"

A thought comes to him then, and he starts laughing. "Their cars!"

"What?"

"I can get their thumbprints from their cars! The fucking locks!"

She starts to speak.

"And yes, I can get you a map!" He grins. "I will get you a fucking map!"

❧

Damian sits on the grassy slope that dips down toward the forest. She watches him from Dair's office window. The sun is bright, and he's like a dark shadow on the grass, except for his white fur. It glitters like ice-glazed snow.

He lights cigarette after cigarette as he stares out at nothing. He never looks back at the house, but she's sure he knows she's watching him.

Layla goes out the front door, stands on the porch. She watches the clouds of smoke drift up and away from him. It takes her a long time to walk down the steps. She sits on the ground beside him. He doesn't look at her. She breathes in his smoke. He's so quiet, it's as if she's out here all alone. The ground is cold. The wind crackles over the dead, dried leaves that cover the ground. The branches of the woods have been stripped bare.

Without looking at her, Damian tilts the pack in her direction. She pulls out a cigarette.

He takes a long drag. As he breathes out, he extends his arm. She holds his wrist, lights her cigarette off his.

When he's down to the filter, he puts his out, pressing it into the grass. She offers him hers. He takes it, passes it back. They sit together in silence until she's shivering. Damian stands. He gives her his hand; she takes it. He pulls her up and she follows him back to the house.

They find August and Eden in the kitchen, looking at a Cube. Layla's seen these images before. He's showing her the inside of Hammond Prison. They're both smiling.

August looks up. "If you guys are finally finished with your soap opera audition, we've got something to show you."

"I hope you're not talking to me, Gus."

"What is it?" Layla asks.

August has a smug smile on his face. "The useless one has come up with a fantastic idea." He nods to Eden. "Show them that thing you did."

Chapter 12

"WE HAVE TO release Holden into gen pop."

"What? Why?" Weir sits up in his chair at the round glass table in the lounge area.

She leans back against the counter, waiting for the coffee to brew. "We'll get him back when the frenzy dies down, but for now, he needs to be seen. If he isn't, people will get suspicious. We want the reporters to go away, not find something else to blink home about."

"But... I want to talk to him."

"You'll get to talk to him. They want you to talk to him. But it'll have to wait."

"Mara." Weir is actually whining. "This isn't fair."

"Stop acting like a child." She pushes away from the counter. "This is what's happening. Get over it." She turns to pour herself some coffee.

Weir drums his fingers on the glass. "How long do you think we'll have to wait?"

With a fresh, steaming mug in her hand, she sits one seat over from Weir. "A few weeks?"

He sighs. "I hate red tape."

"It'll be over soon." She stirs her coffee before sipping it. Weir watches her long enough to make her uncomfortable. "What?"

"Are you happy in your work, Mara?"

She shrugs. "I've given up everything for it."

"But are you happy?"

"What difference does that make?"

"It's just a question."

Mara has a feeling, a familiar feeling: that Weir thinks of her in the same way he thinks of his subjects—like a project, a puzzle to solve, a toy to take apart and reassemble. "What about you? Are you happy?"

He thinks for a moment. "I don't know. But, happy or not, I was born for this."

"Why do you care if I'm happy?"

He smiles. "Like I said, just a question."

"I'm fine." She gets up again. "I'll be in my office."

"I'll be in mine."

༄

It's the first day he's being allowed to join the general prison population. They've had to turn the long, large space between the walls of cells into a temporary eating place. It's quiet, more like a church than a cafeteria. Adair picks up a tray, takes his place in the food line. It shuffles forward slowly. People mumble softly among themselves. The guards are all tall, muscular men and women, all of them resting their hands on the tops of their zProds, waiting for any prisoner to make a false move. A nervousness fills the room like an energy field; it reminds Adair of the way the air feels right before a thunderstorm.

He's not paying attention and bumps lightly into the man in front of him. The man turns, seems startled when he sees Adair. Adair's first thought is to prepare himself for trouble, but the man stands aside, gestures for Adair to take his place in the line. Adair shakes his head, but the man insists, then nudges the woman in line ahead of him. She turns, sees Adair, steps aside as well. Before he knows it, every prisoner has moved to allow Adair to go to the head of the line. He doesn't know what to do. He looks back at the man who moved first. The man smiles, nods, encouraging

Adair to move forward. He does, slowly. Every man and woman gives him a small smile or a nod as he passes.

The servers are also prisoners. They give him extra food and two cups of coffee. He leaves the line, goes to find a place to sit. As he walks past the tables, the people sitting at them stand until the whole room is on their feet.

"Sit down!" a guard yells. "Everybody sit the fuck down!"

They don't.

The guards pull out their prods.

The same guard shouts, "I said sit down!" and prods the man closest to her. The man doubles over, clutches his side, but rights himself. She prods him again, and this time, he can't help but collapse into his seat.

Each guard prods the person nearest them, but the rest of the prisoners don't sit down until Adair does. The guards start to pace between the tables.

Three men and one woman sit with him.

"Hey, Mr. Holden," the man closest to him says in a low voice. He has red eyes, similar to Liam's, but not as disconcerting, and mottled yellow and brown skin. "Here." He reaches out quickly, drops something onto Adair's tray—toothpaste. "It's not much, but the stuff they give you in here is basically hydrochloric acid in a tube."

Adair picks up the toothpaste, hides it up his sleeve. "Thank you."

"Figure you don't have anybody on the outside to send you money for the commissary."

Adair smiles. "No. Unfortunately, all of my friends are fugitives."

The man laughs. "Well, if you need anything, you just say the word. I'm Kaieem. This is Ramon, Valerie, and James." They nod to him and smile. "You can ask us, or anybody in here. We've got your back."

"Thank you."

"No thanks necessary." Kaieem takes a bite of his sandwich. "You're our hero, man."

❧

The next morning, a guard orders him back into his cell when it's time for breakfast.

"You'll be eating in here from now on, Holden," he says.

"Why?"

The guard jabs his prod into Adair's stomach. A fire lights in his belly and spreads through his whole body, down his legs, across his chest and arms, into his head. He falls to his knees.

"Any more questions?"

Adair manages to shake his head.

He watches his cell door close.

❧

"Nina?"

Sierra is walking down the hall. Nina's door is open partway, and Sierra sees her on the floor, back against her bed, her arms around her knees. She looks up. Her face is pale, sad.

Sierra walks in. "What's wrong?"

Ben is asleep in his crib. He looks so peaceful and warm. Sierra envies him.

"Nothing really," Nina says. "It's... I'm just thinking about something."

Sierra sits beside her. "You want to talk about it?"

Nina looks toward the window. It faces the building next door, but the clouds are visible just above the roof. Sierra doesn't expect her to answer, is surprised when she says, "I know that woman. Well, I knew her."

"What woman?"

"Layla Monroe."

Sierra's eyes widen. "How do you know her?"

Nina turns to her, gives her a look, and she understands immediately.

"Oh."

"Yeah." Nina leans her head back against the mattress. "I was on the track, you know, a..." She looks away. "A streetwalker or whatever. Layla worked at Formz of Pleazure, this really nice... brothel, I guess you'd say. We called it a club. I know that doesn't sound right to you, but you don't know what it's like being on the street. The club was, like, the best thing that ever happened to me, I thought. I know better now..." She pauses for a moment. "But I was on the track since I was, like, thirteen, and once you're there, you're there, you know? You're stuck. There were women who'd been there for ten years. But one day, Layla saw me, and she told me I was too good for the streets. She said if I wasn't addicted to drugs, I should apply to Formz and she'd, like, vouch for me or whatever. So I did. I wasn't addicted to anything." She says this defensively, proudly. "Most of the girls were. I wasn't."

Sierra waits while Nina gathers herself. Seeing her like this is strange. Nina always seems so together, never rattled or bothered by anything, despite being a young, single mother, living in a shelter. She declined Sierra's offer of counseling from the beginning and has never changed her mind about it. All Sierra knows about her past is that she worked in a dysmorphic brothel, one of many in the United States that cater mostly to non-dysmorphic humans who have a desire for the strange and exotic.

"I knew Damian, too," she says. "And that guy who died, Liam? They were both... I don't know. Damian was like a bodyguard, kind of scary, and he and Layla had a thing. And Liam was a... client. He was... I don't know. I heard he could be a little rough with the other girls. They didn't like him. He was nice enough to me, but he was never my client. Anyway," she goes on, slowly, evenly, "when I got pregnant with Ben, I kept some of the money I made, more than I should have—you had to give some to the club, you know? Like, a percentage or whatever. But I kept what I owed the club so I could go to an OB. When Simon, the club owner, found out I'd stolen it, he came to my room—I lived at Formz—and he beat me up. I thought he was a cool guy, but he just lost it. When I told him why I'd stolen it, he told me I had to get an abortion or he'd kill me. Then he started to rape me." She waves her hand dismissively before continuing. "Then Layla came in and she just went crazy. She jumped him. She scratched up his face. She screamed at me to run." Her eyes become glassy, but there are no tears. "The last I saw of her, Simon was beating her with a lamp...."

She looks at Sierra. "I wanted to help her," she says this like she's looking for forgiveness, "but... she just kept telling me to run. So I did." She shakes her head. "All this time, I thought she must be dead. That he killed her. There was so much blood."

"Nina—"

"No, don't... Don't look at me like that. Don't feel sorry for me. I left Layla to die to save myself."

"And Ben," Sierra says. "And she wanted you to leave. She wanted to save you. That's why she did what she did."

"Since I saw the news, I have this impossible desire to find Layla and show her Ben. To show her who she saved. Now that I know she's alive. But I don't know how she could have lived through that." She stands up, goes to the crib, strokes Ben's tiny fingers. "When I went to the OB, she knew what I was right away. She told me about this place." Ben's hand closes reflexively around his mother's finger. "I just wish she knew. I don't care what she did at Hammond, and I know she hurt Mr. Corbin, but... she saved us. I'll forgive her anything."

She looks down at Sierra. "If they catch her, do you think I could be, like, a character witness or something? People should know she wasn't just some hooker. She's a good person."

Sierra remembers how Layla Monroe dove out of the sky like a bird of prey, how she knocked Richard down and scratched his face. But as with Nina, she was trying to save someone, defend another person. Defend Adair Holden.

There aren't any villains in this story, she thinks.

And then, just then, when she looks up at Nina's face, she sees the dead girl's wolf eyes staring back at her. She gasps and falls back onto her hands.

Nina is startled, looks behind her. "What happened? Are you okay?"

"No, it's nothing... I thought," her heart is thudding painfully in her chest, "I thought I saw someone on the roof for a second... It was just a shadow."

Nina walks to the window, looks out. "Are you sure? It could have been one of those paparazzi fucks."

"No, I'm sure. It was nothing. I'm just tired. Sorry." It's not a lie. She is tired, achingly tired. She can't sleep without seeing bits and pieces of that memory in her dreams.

Nina looks back and forth along the roofline. "So, do you think I could do that?"

"Do what?"

"You know, be a character witness for Layla?"

"Maybe. I don't know. But I don't think we should ask about it just yet. They'll want to question you if they find out you knew her. They were so awful to Richard. I don't want them to come anywhere near you."

"Okay. Yeah. And she might not even get caught, right?"

"Right."

Nina turns around. Sierra forces herself not to look away from her; she's so afraid to see those eyes again. But they're gone now; Nina's eyes are her own. "I don't see anybody," Nina says.

Of course Nina doesn't see anyone. There isn't anyone to see; just a dead woman in Sierra's mind from someone else's past who won't leave her alone. "Yeah. It was just my imagination. This whole thing's got me on edge."

"Me too."

Sierra stands, tries to hide her shakiness, and she and Nina look at each other for moment. "Nina, you didn't do anything wrong. You know that, right?"

Nina crosses her arms in front of her, looks down at the floor. "I thought she was dead because I ran away. I thought she was dead, Sierra. All this time."

"She wanted you to be safe."

"I know." She shifts her weight from one foot to the other, rubs her arms up and down. "I don't..." She pauses. "I don't want them to catch her."

Sierra walks to Nina, touches her arm lightly, then moves away. Nina doesn't like to be touched, but when she starts to cry, and her arms fall to her sides, Sierra is hugging her suddenly and Nina is crying into her shoulder like a child.

"I don't want them to catch her. They'll put her in that place. They'll experiment on her. They're just like the pimps and runners, using us. They're all pimps and runners, those fucking doctors, the whole fucking system, and I don't want them to put Layla in that place. She doesn't deserve it."

Sierra nods, strokes Nina's hair. "I don't want them to either." And she's surprised to realize that she means this. "Maybe they won't. She seems like a survivor."

Nina pulls away, looks up, smiles sadly. "Yeah, she was—is. Maybe we'll meet again one day, you know? And I can show her Ben."

"Yeah, maybe. I hope so." But they both know this will probably never happen.

Nina wipes her eyes. "If they do find her, would you take me to the prison to see her?"

"Oh, Nina... I don't know if that's..." She trails off.

"I know. I know." Nina shakes her head. "I was just... Never mind."

A shock goes through Sierra. The prison. Of course. It's simple, so terrifyingly simple. "No, you know what? Yes. I will. I promise."

"Seriously?"

"Yeah. Seriously."

Nina looks relieved. "Thanks." She looks past Sierra for a moment. "You're not going to tell Dairen or Mr. Corbin any of this, are you?"

"No, of course not." She bites her lip. "Look, I, uh, I was on my way out. Are you going to be okay? I mean, it's not that important. I'll stay with you if you need me."

"No, go, go. I'm fine."

"Are you sure?"

Nina nods. "Go ahead. I feel a lot better."

"Nina, you can talk to me any time. I mean it. And just as friends, you know? Not a counseling thing, okay?"

"Okay."

Sierra walks to the door, turns around. "You're sure you're okay?"

"Yeah. I'll see you when you get back."

"I won't be long."

Downstairs, she grabs her bag, steps outside, plows through the gaggle of reporters without even looking at them, barely registers their presence at all. She walks to her car as fast as she can, gets in, gives it directions and figures she has just enough time between here and there to change her mind and come back.

❧

Damian runs downstairs, goes straight for the living room.

"What's wrong?" Layla follows him from the kitchen. Eden's on the couch watching Cube.

"Cube, live, news," Damian says. "Take those out!"

Eden pulls out the Bolts.

Layla's heart is racing. "Is it Dair?" She sits on the couch beside Eden. Damian stays standing. He doesn't answer her, just stares at the Cube.

An interviewer is questioning a scientist named Dr. Kathleen Schwartz.

"Until now," Schwartz is saying, "we believed the Dysmorphia Phenomenon began about thirty years ago. We started seeing children being born with exaggerated or non-human features. At first, we called these features 'deformities'—that's where the slur 'd-form' originated—but when it became clear that we were dealing with a worldwide phenomenon, we started referring to them as Atypical Features, or AFs. Along with having AFs, dysmorphic people are stronger than the average human, in some cases incredibly so. They're faster and healthier. Their immune systems are better; they rarely get sick, if at all. They can process the toxins in our atmosphere. They don't need to wear breathers. They can drink unfiltered water. Many of them have special abilities, like telepathy and telekinesis."

Layla wrings her hands.

"We already know all this, Dr. Schwartz," the interviewer interrupts.

The doctor looks annoyed. "Yes, well, my point is that Adair Holden is the first dysmorphic human, that we know of, to be born *without* AFs. He is a sixty-six-year-old telekinetic with the same strength and resilience as registered dysmorphic people."

"Is there any way to tell him apart from normal people?"

"No. The scientific community has learned a lot about Dysmorphia in the last decade or so, but what causes it hasn't been discovered yet. There are no telltale genetic markers that we've been able to find."

It gives Layla a moment's satisfaction to see how nervous the interviewer looks suddenly, how frightened he is at the idea of unidentifiable dysmorphic people. He's trying to hide it, to be the stalwart, dispassionate reporter he thinks he is, but she knows better. "Dr. Schwartz, I think the question on everyone's mind is: Could there be more?"

"I'm a scientist. I don't speculate."

"But you can infer."

 Schwartz sighs. "It is possible, yes."

"Cube, change," Layla says.

"... government's known all this time and has just been hiding it from the American people," says a pundit, sitting on a couch with two other people. "He can't be the only normal-looking dysmorphic out there."

"Why would the government do that?" a woman beside him asks.

"To keep people from panicking."

"Well," the woman responds, "maybe they were right to. Because that's exactly what's happening."

"Cube, change."

"Already in many states, police are being authorized to stop anyone they suspect is dysmorphic." A reporter on location somewhere in Manhattan is in view of a police checkpoint, cars lined up, officers looking into each of them. "If they are and don't have a Dysmorphic Registration ID number, or it's expired, they're being told to arrest them."

The anchor back in the studio shakes his head. "'Suspect'? How can you suspect someone if they don't have AFs? What are they using as criteria?"

"According to the order," the reporter says, "police are to look for 'typical dysmorphic behavior.' Outside without a breather, exhibiting unusual strength and speed, et cetera."

"Sounds like a witch hunt to me."

"Cube, off."

The three of them sit in silence. Damian leans on the arm of the couch, eyes down. Eden looks back and forth between them.

"Will August be okay?" she asks.

"When he gets in tonight, you can ask him."

"Might make things harder," Damian says. "People freaking out. Mobs storming the castle and shit. They'll tighten security even more."

"Thank you, Sherlock."

"It doesn't make any difference to me. I'll get the Neutralizer," Eden says.

Layla holds her head in her hands. "God, I can't believe this whole fucking plan depends on you."

"I'll get it. They're not going to put security guards in the vents."

Damian huffs a laugh. "She's got a point."

"Yeah... well, you've got to get through the fences first."

"I'll do it."

Layla looks up at her. "If you fuck up... that's it. You know that, right? That's it."

"No pressure."

"Shut up, Damian."

Eden's golden eyes are steady as she looks into Layla's. "I will get through the fences. I will get into the vents. I will get the Neutralizer. And I will get Adair out. I won't fuck up."

Layla breaks eye contact first, rubs her forehead. "Goddammit," she whispers before she gets up and leaves the room.

⁊

They're not showing this on the news. Until she reaches the prison, she didn't know how many people were protesting outside its walls, or even that there was anyone protesting at all. Perhaps a thousand dysmorphic and non-dysmorphic people alike are shouting and projecting signs from Cubes attached to their Lenses that say things like "FREE ADAIR HOLDEN" and "INJUSTICE ANYWHERE IS A THREAT TO JUSTICE EVERYWHERE" and "WE ARE PEOPLE NOT EXPERIMENTS."

People are sitting in front of the entryway to the prison, trying to prevent a bus full of new convicts from being brought in. She feels her stomach drop when she sees helmeted and bulletproof vest-clad policemen line up in front of them, zProds in hand, pointing cans of pepper spray at their faces.

She stops her car in the middle of pulling into the parking lot, frozen by the sight. Another heavily armed and armored policeman steps up to her window and blocks her view of what she knows is coming next. He taps her window with his knuckle. She jumps. He gestures with his gun toward the lot. "Keep moving."

As she does, she hears the collective cry of surprise and pain.

Before, when no one knew she was dysmorphic, Sierra only had to turn in her bag and walk through a full-body scanner when she visited the prison. Now she has to tell her RID number to five different guards. Each of them searches her more thoroughly than the last, even after she's gone through the scanner. It feels like hours before she's allowed into the visiting area, a long bank of seats separated by thick dividers. She sits in a cracked plastic chair, and once she does, it's too late to turn back. He's already on the other side of the plexiglass. She picks up the old phone receiver.

"Miss Marlowe," he says. "I believe I have you to thank for my sitting on this side of the glass."

Adair Holden seemed tall and terrible on the field. Now she sees him for what he is: a man in his sixties, average height and build. His eyes and face are firm, but there's a kindness there that would surprise her if she didn't have the memory. Still, she's not sure if the real Holden is less frightening or more in his normality.

"Well," she says, "you did telekinetically pull down a wall of a prison. That might have something to do with it, too."

Holden smiles, seems mildly impressed. "Yes. There was that, I suppose."

The murmurings of other visitors, the muffled replies of the men and women on the other side, fill the room. The old phone feels waxy and strange in her hand; the table she leans on is dirty, worn from years of elbows pressing down on it.

"I have limited time, Miss Marlowe."

"Yes." Sierra moves the phone to her other ear. "I'm sorry to take up your time, Mr. Holden."

He sits back. "Well, I shouldn't complain. I don't get many visitors. DDAT agents, mostly."

Her heart shudders, beating too fast. "I need to ask you something, if it's okay."

"I may not answer."

"I wouldn't blame you." Now that she's here, her practiced words seem ridiculous, silly.

"Well?"

She squeezes the phone handle. "I'm telepathic."

"Yes, I heard your speech. It was very good."

She feels herself blush. "Thank you." She swallows. "Um... I don't read minds, though, or change thoughts or anything." She looks up at him. "I see... memories."

Holden's face pales. They stare at each other. "I understand..." he says, his voice strained.

"I'm sorry. I can't always control it. And it was so strong—"

He hangs up the phone, starts to stand. She jumps up, puts her hand on the window. "No, please!"

His face is dark with anger, hands clenched, white-knuckled. He glares at her, then slowly picks up the receiver. She can hear him breathing. They both sit down again.

She's embarrassed by the tears that heat her eyes. She hasn't thought about what she'll do if he doesn't answer her, and she loses all pretense of calm and self-possessiveness. All her fear, everything she's been hiding from Richard and Dairen, spills out of her in desperate words spoken too quickly. "I dream about it every night. I see it over and over. Even when I'm awake. And I don't just see memories, I experience them, I feel them. I feel... what you felt. And I can't—" She tries to steady her voice and fails. "I can't stand it. It's too much."

He stares at her.

"Please tell me who she is. Please."

⁕

Please.

Sierra Marlowe grows more frantic with each passing moment. Adair can see it in her body movements, in her face. Her eyes are tired, her skin pale. A cruel part of him is glad she's suffering, wants to keep her in this state of panic that his past has put her in. She's seen something she shouldn't have, taken something precious and terrible; a part of him he's never even shared with Layla.

But he looks into her eyes and sees something beyond the desperation. There's more to her question than just a desire to understand a single incident, to put to rest a nagging problem. He saw it on the Kenny Layton show, heard it in her speech. She wants answers to questions she can't put into words yet, wants to resolve doubts she's only just beginning to acknowledge. She's wrong if she thinks his next words will ease her mind for long.

"Her name was Tanya. Tanya Riggs."

Sierra stills; her shoulders fall; she closes her eyes. "Tanya." He hears relief in her voice. "What happened to her?"

"She was murdered."

He sees her tears, sees the way she holds on to the phone with both hands. "I thought so."

He ignores the swelling in his throat, the burning in his eyes. "The man who killed her claimed it was self-defense. He said she attacked him after he refused to give her his Lens. It was a lie, of course. Tanya wasn't violent. He was a member of an anti-dysmorphic group; he pulled her into an alley and beat her to death. She simply walked down the wrong street at the wrong time. I think they call that a 'crime of opportunity.'"

Sierra shakes her head. There are more tears.

"He was convicted of involuntary manslaughter and sentenced to one year in prison. One year."

"Why?"

He shrugs. "She was dysmorphic. She'd been accused of violence in the past. No record, but what do facts matter when fear and hatred come into play?"

Sierra puts a hand on her chest. She struggles to get her next words out. "I can see her eyes…"

"Yes."

The door buzzes as another prisoner is let into the visiting room. She exhales a slow, trembling breath, hesitates. Then she meets his eyes. "What did you do?"

When he doesn't answer, she knows. She knew before she asked. He doesn't need to tell her.

After a moment, he says, "So. Does that bring you peace of mind? Will you be able to sleep now?"

She shakes her head slowly. The tears fall onto the table.

"Good. None of us should sleep." Adair nods to the guard at the door.

"Can I come and see you again?"

"Why?" he asks. The guard looks on impatiently. "Haven't you learned everything you wanted to know?"

"Please."

"Come on, Holden," the guard says. Adair looks up at him, then back at Sierra.

"Please," she says again.

He sighs. He was right. But does he want to answer all her questions? To guide her through her doubts? He laughs to himself silently. What else does he have to do? "If you like," he says, and she thanks him.

The guard takes his arm and leads him back inside.

❧

When she comes home, Dairen calls to her. "Have you seen this?"

"Seen what?" She steps into the living room.

He's frowning, leaning forward on the couch, elbows on his knees. She sits beside him, looks at the Cube.

"Dr. Schwartz, I think the question on everyone's mind is, could there be more?"

"I'm a scientist. I don't speculate."

"But you can infer."

Schwartz sighs. "It is possible, yes."

"Cube, mute." Dairen looks at her. "It's started."

"When?"

"The news broke about an hour ago." He leans back against the cushions, crosses his arms. "They couldn't keep it secret forever. We knew that."

She watches the muted reporters and scientists weigh in silently. She doesn't need to hear what they're saying. It's enough that they know and that the world knows.

"There's going to be a panic," she says.

"There already is. People are getting pulled over, stopped in the streets if they so much as seem dysmorphic. If they pick up a box that looks too heavy for a normal person or are walking faster than usual."

"Oh my God..."

"And no one's mad at the police or the government. They're mad at dysmorphic people for making their lives harder."

Sierra wants to tell him about the protestors outside the prison, about the signs and chants and the pepper spray. But he'd want to know what she was doing there, and she's not ready to tell him that.

"What are we going to do?" she asks.

"I don't know. Dad's in his office. I don't want to bother him."

Sierra leans back against him. He puts his arm around her and she rests her head on his chest, listens to his heartbeat. He's angry. He's scared.

"I've been thinking about something," he says.

"What?"

"You remember how I said Adair Holden sounded familiar to me?"

"Yeah."

"I think I might have known him. I mean, obviously Dad

knows him. The more I think about it, the more his name feels familiar. It feels like…"

"Like what?"

"Well, like he's a family member I can't recall all that well, but I know I liked him. Like some uncle who died when I was a kid or something."

She thinks of Holden's eyes, the way he smiles. "You must have known him. Maybe he was different back then."

He moves his arm, sits up straight to look at her. "Have you ever noticed how my name is spelled?"

"I've never thought about it."

"It's unusual. Most people spell it D-A-R-R. Mine's D-A-*I*-R. It gets messed up on eForms all the time."

She understands immediately. "You think you're named after him."

"You heard Dad in the car. He called him Dair."

She looks away from him, at the Cube again. An image of Adair Holden's mug shot is rotating between the scientist and the reporter. Dr. Schwartz is nodding and gesturing to it as she speaks.

"You should talk to your dad about it."

Dairen is quiet for a long moment, then looks over at her. "I think he's really hurting, Sierra. I don't know what to do."

She takes his hand. "Just talk to him."

❧

"Hey, there you are." August steps out onto the porch. "I've been looking for you."

He can see her smile under the breather. "Sorry. I was out walking. I didn't want to go inside yet. When did you get in?"

"Hour ago." He sits next to her on the steps. The sun is setting; an inky blue light shadows the woods and lawn. "You want a beer?" He offers her his own.

"No, I'm all right. I don't drink much."

"Yeah, me neither." He takes a swig. "You want company?"

She nods.

The breather covers the lower half of her face, but he can see her eyes clearly. The blue light has turned them a kind of moss green. Her hair is like black silk. He finds himself drawn to the tattoo-like scales; the pattern is hypnotizing.

She turns to him, and he looks away quickly. "Sorry. I didn't mean to stare. I'm drunk. You're pretty. It happens." He shakes his head. "And I love embarrassing myself."

"Thank you. For saying I'm pretty. It's nice."

"This has got to be the first time a girl has ever thanked me for ogling her."

She laughs. It makes her mask cloud up.

"How long did you say you can go without that?" He points at the breather.

"Ten, maybe fifteen minutes, more or less."

"So you'll be all right on the field?"

She nods. "I'll be fine. And once I'm in the vents, the air will be clean again."

He passes the beer from hand to hand. The light is fading fast. "Figure you got to run the length of a football field, a little more."

"I guessed that from the pics. I've been practicing."

"Good."

She's quiet for a moment, then says, "I'm glad you're here."

He smiles. "What? Damian and Layla not being their usual, cheerful selves?"

"Not lately."

He bumps her shoulder with his own. "I'm here for you, kid."

She looks over at him. "I was worried about you. The news

and everything."

"Oh, don't worry about that. I'm fine. Thanks, though." He stretches his legs out, crosses his ankles over the next step. "It's nice to be thought of once in a while."

"I do think about you. I wish we could blink you."

"I could blink more often. How about at the end of the day? I'll blink you to say goodnight and then you'll know I'm okay."

"Would you?"

"Yeah."

"That would make me feel better."

"Then I will." It would make him feel better, too, he thinks, to hear her voice before he goes to sleep. He swallows the last of his beer, sets the empty bottle down. "You doing okay?"

Eden looks out into the darkness. Strands of her hair lift in the light, chilly breeze. "I don't know."

It's almost dark now. He listens to the wind in the trees. It sounds like loneliness and desolation, like an echo of her voice. He wishes he'd brought another beer for himself. "You know... we were friends. Me and Liam. Like, good friends, you know? I don't think I told you."

"You didn't."

"Well, we were. I mean, we didn't do sleepovers or anything, but..."

She tears up suddenly, hides her face in her hands.

"Hey." Without thinking, he touches her back. He feels her tense, so he pulls his hand away. "I didn't mean to make you sad."

She laughs a little. "I'm already sad."

"Right. Yeah." He looks out at the woods, back at her. "I'm sorry."

She slides her fingers under her eyes. "No. Finish what you were saying. Please."

August runs his hands through his hair, wishes he hadn't said anything. "I was just going to say... Look, all the time I knew him, Liam was an angry motherfucker. I mean, really angry. But we'd talk sometimes, you know, over drinks and stuff? 'In vino, veritas' and all that shit. And I think he was... really sad, you know? More sad than angry. Or maybe angry about being sad. I don't know. But, I'm thinking that if he loved you and you loved him back... that must've made him happy. And if he was happy even for just a little while... that's something, right? And especially at the end and everything... I mean... Oh, fuck." He shakes his head, looks up at the sky. "Shut up, August, you're not helping."

She's quiet, and he thinks he's done more harm than good. But then, in a small, sad voice, she says, "He loved the rain." He looks at her again. Her eyes are shining. "He was going to take me to England someday because he wanted to bring me to a club in London. And he loved my hair."

August believes all of this. Liam was always honest. If he said he would take her to England, then he would have. It makes him smile just for a second, thinking of the lengths to which Liam would have gone to get them there, just for a chance to dance with her at his favorite club. But then she's crying, and it's breaking his heart. He instinctively goes to touch her again, but stops, asks, "Is it okay if I put my arm around you? I mean, not in a creepy way or anything. Okay, I just made it sound creepy. Jesus. Somebody cut me off right now."

"August." Her soft voice quiets him. "It's okay."

So he does, and she rests her head against his shoulder.

He joked with Layla about Eden needing a shoulder to cry on. He didn't defend her when Layla called her "Liam's leftovers."

He's ashamed of himself. Besides Holden, he was Liam's only real friend, and whatever else Liam may have been, August always knew he could depend on him for anything. He could trust him.

He's never thought the same of Layla or Damian, doubts he

ever will.

A memory comes to him. He was sitting at a bar with Liam, maybe two or three years ago. He doesn't remember what they were talking about, but for some reason, August said, "Love's a bitch, ain't it?"

Liam stared into his drink, smiled sadly. "I wouldn't know, mate."

Chapter 13

DAIREN STEPS into his father's office. "Dad?" He sees his father is focused on his tableface, Bolts in. He mouths, "Sorry."

Richard nods to him, holds up a hand. "Yes, I understand—yes, of course—thank you. I will—goodbye." He removes the Bolts, rubs his eyes.

Dairen sits in the chair on the other side of the desk. "Everything all right?"

"They've canceled the fundraiser."

"What? Why?"

He leans back in his chair. "They feel my connection with Adair Holden would make people uncomfortable."

Dairen sees lines on his father's face that weren't there two weeks ago. "It'll pass, Dad."

"I wonder."

He waits a moment, shifts in his chair. "This might be a bad time, but I need to ask you something."

"The answer is yes."

Dairen frowns. "You don't even know the question."

"I do. And yes. You are named after Adair Holden."

Dairen doesn't speak for a moment, then, "So, what? You're telepathic now?"

Richard laughs a little. "No. I overheard you talking to Sierra."

"I hate your super hearing."

"I was in the kitchen."

Dairen raises an eyebrow. "Eavesdropping, Dad?"

His father smiles. "I was listening to the report, and, well, it took a very long time for me to make my sandwich. I couldn't help but overhear."

Dairen looks around the office. It's a small space, with one large window. The desk is wooden, fitted with an average sized tableface. A few shelves hold books, as well as several PhotoCubes showing images of him and his father, him and Sierra, his father shaking hands with people at various fundraisers. There's one of all three of them. Other photos show men and women who've passed through the shelters, here and in England—people who have gone on to better things. Lives his father helped change.

There's no evidence of Adair Holden in this room. Yet his father named Dairen after him, and you don't name your first and only child after a person who's just a casual acquaintance.

"Dad, what happened between you and him?"

The smile fades. "It's not something I can talk about. We had a falling out."

"Why can't you talk about it?"

"Dairen, please trust me when I tell you this. It's a very personal matter."

If his father thinks those words will satisfy Dairen, he's wrong. It's too important. If he's going to carry around the name of a man who's been deemed a terrorist, he needs to know why.

When Richard sees that Dairen won't let him get away with his usual obfuscation, he sighs. "He was my best friend. He was older than I was, a sort of... mentor for me. We were both telekinetic. He helped me learn to focus and control my ability. He put up more than half the funds to open the shelter in England. He helped me run it. We were a good team." He smiles a little. "When I told him I wanted to name you after him, he wouldn't let me. He said it was silly. So I found a way around it. Adair's closest friends always called him Dair. So your mother and I decided to name you Dairen—and, as a result, unwittingly doomed you to having your name consistently misspelled for the rest of your life."

"Yeah, thanks for that." Dairen smiles. "Mum liked him, too?"

Richard nods. "Dair introduced me to your mother. He taught literature at Cambridge, and she was one of his best students. That book your mother has? The printed copy of *Wuthering Heights*? He gave that to her. Ask her to show it to you next time you see her."

"Dad, I wish you'd told me about him."

Richard rubs his temples. "I should have, but it's a painful subject for me."

"I'm sorry."

The tableface dims, casting his father in shadow.

"Did I know him?" Dairen asks.

"Yes. He left just after your eleventh birthday."

"I thought I might have. He seemed familiar. But I don't remember him, not really."

"Well, he spent most of his time teaching. He visited often. He tutored many of the residents for free. But I'm not surprised you don't have any vivid memories of him. They might come back to you though, now that we've talked. He was very fond of you." Richard turns off the tableface. "I know why you're asking these questions, Dairen. I can't tell you everything, but I will tell you this. Dair was a good man when I knew him. He probably still is. But he made a choice twelve years ago that I couldn't accept. And we parted ways."

"Is that why you and Mum split up?" Dairen is hurting his father; he can see it. He doesn't want to, but this is his life, too.

Richard sits back, looks away from his son. "She couldn't understand why he'd left, why we'd quarreled, and I couldn't tell her. I *couldn't* tell her, Dairen." His eyes are pleading. "It would have put her in danger. And it would have broken her heart. I loved your mother. I still love her."

Whatever his father is hiding must be a terrible weight to bear,

Dairen thinks. And while he's frustrated that his father won't share it with him, he's beginning to understand that it's not out of a misguided attempt to protect him from something unpleasant. He's protecting him from something real, just as he protected his mother. If what he knows would have put her in danger, it would put Dairen in danger as well. "I'm sorry, Dad."

"No, you're right to ask these things. I'm sorry I've kept them from you."

Dairen looks away for a moment, then gets up. "Tea?"

Richard nods. "Please."

Dairen is nearly out the door when his father calls him back. He opens a drawer, takes out a PhotoCube, hands it to him. "Here. Take this."

Dairen turns it on. It projects a 3D image of his mother, his father, and Adair Holden. Dairen is in it, too, a baby in his mother's arms. They're all smiling, standing outside the house Dairen grew up in.

"It's the day we brought you home."

They all look so happy. "Can I keep it?"

Richard nods. "I've wanted to show it to you for a long time. I just—"

Dairen turns it off, puts it in his pocket. "It's okay, Dad. Thank you. Can I show Sierra? Can I tell her all this?"

"Of course."

He pauses for a moment, then, "Dad? This isn't going to be one of those things where I find out later that Adair Holden is my real father, is it?"

Richard's eyes widen. He looks offended. But when he sees the expression on his son's face, he shakes his head, gives him a sardonic smile.

"Sorry, Dad, I couldn't help it. I'll be back with the tea."

In the kitchen, waiting for the water to boil, he sits at the table, stares at the image, and wonders what could have gone so wrong that it tore them all apart.

☙

August watches Eden walk around the room as she practices focusing on her Lens and her surroundings at the same time.

"I've thought about it," he says. "Kovich's is the only print you'll need."

"Who's Kovich?" Her concentration breaks when she looks up at him, and she bumps into the archway. "Ow."

He tries not to laugh. "You okay?"

"Lens, off." She rubs her head. "I suck at this."

"'Suck' is such a strong word."

"You're laughing at me."

He puts a hand on his chest. "Me? Never!"

"You're mean."

"I'm the nicest guy you know."

"That's not hard."

He smiles. "Come here." He pulls a chair out for her; she sits. "Don't worry about it. You've got time. And you're definitely getting better, running into walls aside."

She sticks out her forked tongue.

"Cute," he says. "Very mature."

She bares her fangs.

"Okay. Now we've moved on to scary."

Eden smiles, but it quickly fades. She leans her elbows on the table, rubs her temples. "I don't want to fuck up, August."

"It'll be fine. Damian's got the map. He'll be with you the whole way."

Damian is studying the map in the other room. He'll being wearing a World when they go, linked to Eden's Lens, real time.

He'll see everything from Eden's perspective, as if he were in the vents too. In the meantime, Layla will be keeping an eye on the prison with Liam's cameras.

August stands, gets Eden a glass of water. "Don't do any more today. Your headache'll just get worse."

"Thanks." She takes the Lens off, picks up the water. "Who's Kovich?"

"Head of the department. Dr. Mara Kovich. She'll definitely have access to the Neutralizer. I got others, but I don't think we'll need them."

"Okay. I'll print them out tonight."

"How do you know how to work that thing?"

"Liam showed me."

He meets her eyes for a moment. She looks away.

"I'm done with this fucking map." Damian comes into the kitchen, a World attached to his temple. He taps Eden's arm with his knuckle as he passes her. "Get me a beer."

"Get your own goddamn beer, man," August says.

But Eden is already up.

Damian sits at the table. "How many times do we need to go over this, Gus?" Eden brings him a bottle and the opener. He looks up at her. "I have to open it myself?"

"Jesus Christ." August watches Eden pop the top and set the bottle in front of Damian again.

"No glass?"

August glares at him. "Since when do you drink from a glass?"

Damian links his hands behind his head, leans back. "I feel like being civilized today."

"You're just doing this to piss me off, aren't you?"

"Is it working?"

Eden goes to the cabinet, brings him a glass. Damian stares at it, looks up at her, waits.

"Oh, for Christ's sake!" August grabs the glass and pours the bottle into it.

"Gus," Damian shakes his head in mock dismay, "that's what the slave is for. Get one for him, too, slave." He takes a long sip.

August starts to stand. "I'll get it."

Eden puts her hand on his shoulder. "It's okay."

"See? I told you, Gus. Rapport."

"Jesus Christ."

Damian takes the World off. "I hate these things. Never got Aldrich's obsession with them."

"He liked the beach," Eden says quietly as she sits back down. She passes August his beer.

"The beach, huh?" Damian spins the World on the table like a coin. "I would've thought a portable strip club."

"Christ, Damian, what is your problem?"

Damian looks at Eden. "Aw. Too soon?"

"Have some respect, man," August says.

"Yeah." Damian smiles. He spins the World again, watches it go around and around. "He had a lot of respect for you, didn't he, Eden? Following you everywhere like a dog? All sunshine and roses with good old Liam, right? Here's a question: Did he at least let you wear a blindfold?"

"What the fuck?" August stands.

"It's fine." Eden touches his arm, but looks at Damian. "It doesn't matter. He doesn't understand."

"Understand what?" Damian's lips turn up in a cruel half smile.

"Who Liam was."

"I knew him a lot longer than you did. Believe me, you're better off."

"You knew him longer. But you didn't know him at all."

The World slows its spin, wobbles, falls onto its side with a quiet click.

Damian and Eden stare at each other across the table. There's no anger in either of their eyes, just a steady coldness. August doesn't know what to think of it.

"You see that, Gus?" Damian points at her, their eyes still locked. "When she looks at me like that, it makes me wonder what she was like before that lab fucked her up. I bet you were something."

"I was." Eden stands. "I still am." August watches her leave, listens to her climb the stairs.

He looks down at Damian. "What the fuck is wrong with you, man?"

Damian has a strange expression on his face. He doesn't look at August, stares straight ahead, as if he's still watching Eden leave the room. "Come on, Gus," he finally says, downing the rest of his beer in one long swig. "We both know the best thing Aldrich ever did for her was die."

August shakes his head. "I don't know how you can—how you can look at her and talk to her like that. Why do you have to be like that?"

"Nature of the beast, my friend." Damian gets up, goes to the fridge. "You want another beer?"

August gapes at him. "You are un-fucking-believable." He picks up the half-full bottle he already has, leaves the kitchen, goes upstairs.

He knocks on Liam's door—*Eden's* door. "Eden? Can I come in?" When she doesn't answer, he opens it. "Eden?"

She's sitting on the bed, staring out the window, her arms around her knees. The sun is lowering in the sky; a gold-orange light pours into the room.

He closes the door behind him, sits on the edge of the bed. She gazes past him at the light.

"You shouldn't have to put up with that shit."

She doesn't say anything or look at him.

"I should've—" He shakes his head. "You want me to go hit him or something?" When she still doesn't respond, he stands. "Sorry. I'll leave you alone."

He's a step away from the door.

"It was because of the sun." Her voice is quiet, far away.

He turns back.

"He liked Worlds because he could be in the sun and it didn't hurt. The beach was his favorite."

August thinks of Liam's red eyes, the goggles he wore, how he wouldn't go out during the day if he could help it. "I never thought of that."

She rests her chin on her knees. "He showed me once. It was beautiful. It felt real."

He doesn't know what to say, isn't sure if he should go to her or leave.

She looks at him then, and there's such a sadness in her eyes. But it's strangely beautiful because of the obvious, honest love he sees there as well—uninhibited. She hides nothing, not like the rest of them. "Do you want to see it?"

It's more than a question, more than a simple offer. It's a kind of gift, he thinks, a gift of trust—*her* trust. And he so badly wants to have that. "Yeah."

She opens the drawer of the nightstand while he walks over to sit on the bed. When she finds it, she moves to sit behind him. She puts a hand on one side of his face, presses the World into his opposite temple with the other. She speaks quietly. "World, on. Beach."

And he's facing the sea now. The water laps over his bare feet. He looks behind him at the dunes and the beach grass, swaying in the breeze, at the huge cliffs that reach up into a cloudless sky. He looks up and down the empty, glowing beach. The air is perfectly warm, and it smells of the ocean.

"Do you see it?" Eden's voice is soft and distant.

"Yeah..." He's never been in a World like this. The surreality is so complete, it's almost indistinguishable from reality.

"Isn't it beautiful?"

"I've never seen anything like it," he breathes, awed by Liam's creation. He's afraid, suddenly, that he might tear up as it occurs to him that this is all that's left of his friend—this unreal perfection, a place that will never change, never age, never be anything but what it is.

It's the forced perfection that real life can never be. "World, off." And his voice is shaky. He turns to Eden.

"That's him," she says. "That's Liam. Did you see?"

He nods. "Yeah. I saw."

She smiles, then raises her hand and gently wipes his tears away.

℘

As August paces the block, he passes Holden's cell, catches his eye quickly. He has time to put just one thought in his mind: *We have a plan.* Holden doesn't react. If it were August, he'd want to know what the plan was, when they were going to enact it, and how. He wishes he could tell Holden everything, but it would take too long. He'll have to give him the details in bits and pieces.

It's not until he's past the cell that he realizes he's being watched. One of the prisoners is leaning against his cell door, arms stretched idly through the bars. He's shirtless, probably because of his huge brown wings, which are, at the moment, tightly bound to his body by thick metal bands that wrap around his torso. If Layla has trouble fitting clothes around her wings, his must make it nearly impossible. His face resembles a bird of prey: orange-yellow eyes, hooked nose. He has tan skin, shoulder-length black hair, and talons for toes. His feet are shackled together. If he were able to lift his leg high enough to kick someone, those talons could easily rip through flesh and muscle, maybe even bone. He smiles as August passes him.

"What are you looking at, morph?"

"I'm looking at you, Mr. Leonard." He has a thick Middle Eastern accent and a knowing smile that puts August on alert.

He rests his hand on the prod hooked to his belt, makes sure the prisoner sees him do it. If it scares the man, he doesn't show it. "You got something to say, half-n-half?"

"I had a question, but I think you just answered it." There's something in his eyes. He's taunting August. He thinks he knows something, and whatever it is, August doesn't like it.

He reaches into the man's mind, wants to put it in his head that he should be frightened of August, should leave him alone. He searches for that place, that center of suggestion, where a simple idea can become a reality. He finds nothing. Nothing at all.

The man winks one of his orange, predatory eyes at him. "That won't work on me, Mr. Leonard."

August jabs the man in the stomach with the prod. The blue electric jolt pushes him back from the bars. He doubles over, gasping. "Does *that* work on you, morph?"

The gasping becomes a wheezy sort of laugh. "Oh, Mr. Leonard," he says, and looks him right in the eye. "If it weren't for these drugs—the things I could do. The things I could tell you." It's quiet in the cellblock, cold and gray. The man's mind is blank—no, it's black; it's hidden. August can't see it, can't touch it. The man smiles knowingly at him, but his eyes are serious, so clear and open. It's as if he's speaking through them.

And August thinks he understands. "You'd like that, wouldn't you, morph?"

"Very much." The man steps up to the bars again.

August shoves the prod into his belly a second time. He cries out and falls to his knees.

"From now on, morph, you call me 'sir.' Anything else and I'll accidentally hold on too long next time. Got it?"

The man coughs, winces, clutches his stomach. "Yes... sir. Got it."

"Good. You need a doctor, you pathetic little bitch?" For the people in Hammond Prison, the threat of having a doctor come to their cell in the middle of the night is more frightening than the prod.

"No, sir." The man looks up. He's smiling again.

The next morning, when August accompanies the doctor on her rounds, he makes sure she gives the man only half his usual drug dose.

ভ

"You really came back. I didn't think you would."

Sierra holds the ancient phone to her ear. "I had to."

"I'm glad you did." And he means it. In his cell, he has too much time to think; too much time to be angry, to grieve... to miss Layla. If life has taught him anything, it's to take solace where he can find it. Talking to Sierra is better than being trapped in his own head, talking to no one but himself.

But it isn't just that. He was angry at first, but now he finds a strange comfort in knowing that she feels the pain of his worst memory as keenly as he did... and still does. He didn't realize until yesterday just how lonely he's been, carrying that ache around and never telling anyone about it. Except for that brief conversation in front of the shelter in England, twelve long years ago, he and

Liam never spoke about Tanya. Liam only wanted to know one thing: did Adair "get" the man who'd killed her. That Adair had was enough for him.

It has never been enough for Adair.

Sierra pushes her hair back nervously. "Do you mind if I ask you something?"

"That's why you're here, isn't it?"

She nods. "When I see her, Tanya, I feel so..." Her hand tightens around the phone. "I'm so angry... and I'm so sad. Who was she? What was she like? Why was she so special to you?"

He wants to tell her, but there aren't words. "It's... very hard for me to talk about." He looks pointedly at her.

After a moment, understanding appears in Sierra's eyes. She's smart enough not to say anything, or give any indication that Adair's words have a deeper meaning. She focuses intently on his eyes.

It feels like someone is opening a drawer in his mind. Inside it is a memory, carefully locked away. His instinct is to close the drawer, to cut her off; this is no one's business but his.

Sierra needs to see it, though. And more than that, he wants her to.

Tanya sits in his office on the couch. Her wolf-like eyes are clouded over with sadness. "They let me hold her."

"I'm so sorry."

She wipes away her tears. "Can I still stay here?"

"Of course you can."

"I don't know where else to go."

"You can make this your home as long as you like."

"Thank you."

Adair hesitates before saying, "Richard has arranged... a burial service."

Tanya wraps her arms around herself. "Do they make..." She swallows, shakes her head. "Do they make coffins that small?"

He can't be strong anymore. How could anyone? "Yes," he manages to say.

"Don't cry, Mr. Holden. She weren't in any pain."

"But you are. How can I help you? What can I do?"

"I don't..." Her throat catches and she can't speak.

He can't either. He wants words. But there aren't any. He sits beside her, and she lets him hold her while she cries. And how she cries. Loud, long, painful cries, slowing time, breaking his heart.

"What am I going to do? I don't know what to do now. She was my hope," Tanya says. "My reason."

"No, no. No, my girl, you are *your hope. You were* her *hope. You would have been a wonderful mother. You* are *a wonderful mother. That can't change because she died. Do you understand me?" He pulls away, holds her arms, looks into her eyes. "You are here. You're here. And you'll survive and love her all your life. And I'll help you, I swear. I'll stand with you until you can stand on your own. And you will. You're the same woman who carried that little girl. You're still that woman. You're strong, Tanya. Do you understand me?"*

"I'm not."

"Not today. Today you'll cry. And you'll cry when we put her in the ground—"

"Oh, God..." If he wasn't holding her arms, she would collapse.

"But the next day, you'll get out of bed and cry less. And on and on until you hardly cry at all."

"I'm going to die."

He hugs her. "No, you're not. You'll want to. But you won't. It goes on, Tanya. You'll see."

Sierra hides her face behind her hand. Her shoulders shake.

"She wasn't special in any extraordinary sense," Adair says. "She was a drug addict who got pregnant, came to us, and cleaned up. Two weeks from her due date, the baby died. Strangled by her umbilical cord. It happens." He can see the baby's face in his mind. "But Tanya was special to me because…" He can't finish; he can't say the words.

But Sierra already knows them. She's been inside his mind. "You loved her."

He wonders if Tanya's daughter would have had hair like hers; she had the same eyes. "Yes. For no reason at all. And…" He runs his hand over his face, rubs his eyes. "I'm sorry. It's been a long time since I've thought of… No, that's a lie. I think about her every day."

"Were you in love with her? It doesn't feel that way."

"No. I wasn't. But I cared for her so deeply. I wanted her to… find some peace in her life, some happiness. She deserved that. She was beautiful and kind to everyone. She wanted to be a good mother. She wanted to change her life. And she did. And then she was murdered. And that's all. That was her life."

Sierra wipes her eyes. "You were thinking about her at the rally. That's why I saw that memory. Was it because of… the man who died? Aldrich? The man who saved you?"

Liam, still standing after being shot through the chest, weaving and falling, the sound of his body hitting the earth… his dead eyes.

"I'm sorry," Sierra says, having seen that memory, too. "I don't have any right to ask you these things."

"His name was Liam," he says quickly.

Saying Tanya's name brings pain. Saying Liam's, Adair feels the hollow ache of failure. Liam died, and he died for nothing. "I can tell you about him another time. They'll take me back inside in a moment."

"I can come again?"

He sees the guard walking toward him. "If you don't mind."

"No. No, I don't." She holds on to the phone like a lifeline. "Thank you."

He nods, hangs up on his side. She doesn't, not until the guard comes and takes him away.

❧

Do I still have to call you sir? a voice echoes in his mind. August was right. The man is telepathic.

For now, he answers. It feels strange to speak without opening his mouth. *What do you want?*

What everybody here wants. To get out.

I can't help you.

Bullshit. The voice sounds amused. *You think I'm an idiot?*

I don't know what I think. Who are you? August passes the man's cell but doesn't look at him.

Just call me Hawk.

He can't help smirking. *Seriously?*

If I told you my name, you wouldn't be able to pronounce it. August hears a note of indignation in the man's tone.

Try me.

It's just Hawk.

Fine, Hawk, *or whatever your name really is, I still can't help you.*

Bullshit, John Leonard, or whatever your *name really is. If anyone can help me, it's you. You're a telepathic d-form who's convinced everyone you're a guard in a d-form prison.*

August feels for the prod at his belt, tightens his hand around it. *Except for you. Why is that?*

Good fortune. Telepathy, the kind that changes minds, doesn't work on me, like I said. The funny thing is, I didn't even know that part of my brain was still working until I felt you messing around in my head. It was nice to know the drugs didn't block everything.

August listens to the sound of his own shoes on the concrete.

It echoes through the silent cellblock. *So, what now? You're black-mailing me? If I don't do what you want, you'll tell someone and get me thrown in here with you?*

Why would I do that? I want to help you.

Help me?

You're here for Holden. I want to help.

This is dangerous. Too dangerous. Tomorrow, he'll convince medical to raise Hawk's dosage, put him out completely. He can't know these things. They could take him to the lab at any time and get him to tell them everything if they weaken him enough.

You raise my drugs, Leonard, and I'll start screaming right now.

You son of a bitch.

It's not like that. I don't want that. All I want is for you to do what you set out to do in the first place. When you break Holden out, get the rest of us out, too. I want to come with you. I want to help Holden. Like you. I swear that's all I want.

Jesus Christ.

Tell me what to do and I'll do it.

You can shut the fuck up, for starters, and let me think.

He feels a silence inside himself, like the volume in his head has been turned down. Hawk has left his mind for the moment. Alarm bells should be going off all over his brain. But he has a feeling he can trust this man. When he saw him in the cafeteria earlier today, he noticed the long lines of raw skin where the metal bands rub against him every time he takes a step, and likewise around his ankles where those medieval shackles bind his taloned feet. There were two bruises on his stomach where August stabbed him with the prod.

Hawk's deformities are so extreme that it won't be long before he ends up on a table in the lab. What could he possibly gain by exposing August? Why would he want to prevent Holden from escaping? Holden is his only way out.

And that's when August realizes that they can do it. They can finish it. Everything August has done in this prison, all the work he's put into it, all the people he's had to hurt to fulfill his role as a guard—it doesn't have to be for nothing.

Liam's death doesn't have to be for nothing.

They can do it. He knows they can.

He also knows that Layla is going to throw a fit.

Can you hear me? August asks.

Loud and clear.

I have to talk to my people. I can't give you an answer now.

All right, he says. *You won't forget about me, now, will you, Leonard?*

Not a chance.

❧

"Are you *insane?*"

"Layla—"

"Are you drunk? If you're drunk, I'll kill you right now!"

"Layla—!"

"Right now, August!"

"Layla," Damian says, "if he's drunk, *I'll* kill him. Sit the fuck down and let him talk."

Layla glares at Damian, but she sits.

Damian stands behind her chair, holds the back of it. His smiles are always scarier than his frowns. "All right, Gus. Talk."

August looks over at Eden, who sits serenely at the other end of the table. She gives him a small smile. He turns back to Damian and Layla. "It'll work. It's the same plan, just from the inside out, and at night. Think about it. The amount of chaos it'll cause, the amount of people we'll get out—it'll be better than what we originally planned."

"I guess it's a good thing Dair got thrown in prison then!"

"I didn't mean it like that, Layla."

Damian puts a hand on her shoulder, squeezes lightly. He doesn't say anything, but it quiets her.

August leans forward a little. "And this guy, Hawk, all he wants to do is help us. And he's not the only one. They say they keep Holden in his cell at mealtime because they're afraid some DCo member will assassinate him to make him a martyr for their cause. And they *are* afraid, but that's not why. They're afraid because, when he's around, everyone looks at him like he's God or something. He's a hero. That's what scares the guards."

Layla's eyes light up, but not with anger. He's almost sure she's holding back a smile.

"If we finish what we started, they will tear that place apart. And if I ask Hawk to make sure Holden gets out alive, he will. I'm sure of it. He'll watch his back the whole way. You should see this guy. He's a total freak. These huge fucking wings. He's got talons on his feet! He looks like some kind of Arab superhero or something."

"Aw, somebody's got a crush."

"Jesus Christ, Layla! Are you listening to me?"

"I think it's a good idea," Eden says quietly.

"No one gives a fuck what you think," Layla snaps.

"I give a fuck," August says. "And she's right."

Layla rolls her eyes. "You're so obvious, August. It's pathetic. Coming up here every chance you get. You could've just blinked."

"Are we really talking about this right now?"

"It's what Adair wanted," Eden breaks in. "Isn't it?"

"I don't need you to tell me what Dair wants." Layla leans her elbow on the table, her head on her hand. "All I want is him out of that place and safe. And your new boyfriend, he can make sure that happens?"

August smiles. "Yes. My new boyfriend will make sure that happens."

Layla looks up at Damian. He shrugs.

She stands, goes to the fridge, comes back with a beer and a bottle opener, hands it to August. "Okay."

☙

"How did he get that scar?" Sierra's face hurts just thinking about the wound that must've caused it.

"I don't know. He had it when I met him and wouldn't talk about it." Holden looks down for a moment. "I don't suppose I'll ever know now."

"I'm so sorry."

He's quiet for some time, then says, "He was only twenty-eight. He had a hard life before I ever knew him. I did what I could for him, but I don't know if he was ever happy. Well, that is—I suppose he was happy this last month."

"Why?"

He breathes a short, quiet laugh. "He fell in love." He shakes his head. "You can imagine it would be difficult for someone like Liam to catch a woman's interest."

She's embarrassed because she had the exact same thought. "Well..."

"You don't have to be kind."

She bites her lip, hesitates. "On the news, they said he was wanted for... a lot of things. And that he'd been in prison for assaulting a... prostitute."

He looks coolly at her. "It's true." He leans forward a little. "We're terrorists, remember?"

She feels a thrill of fear in her stomach and chest. She forgot for a moment whom she was speaking to. He feels like a friend.

Even now, as he reminds her of who he is and why he's here, that sense of familiarity remains. She no longer simply wants answers from him; she cares about him.

"But he didn't rape her, if that's what concerns you."

She didn't realize how tightly she was squeezing the phone until she loosens her grip.

"But everything else?" He shrugs. "We all have our weaknesses."

She laughs nervously. "Mine's chocolate."

"I favor ice cream myself."

They look at each other for a long moment. Holden leans back, seems to consider his next words carefully.

"Liam wasn't a good person, Sierra. And neither am I. You understand that, don't you? It's important that you do."

She feels sad suddenly. "I don't think you're a bad person. And I didn't know Liam."

He smiles wryly. "Murder? Assault? Domestic terrorism?"

It's too much to think about. She knows that what he's saying is true; she knows what he is. But she doesn't know what that makes her.

"Sierra." Holden is looking closely at her. "This is what I've come to understand: peace is an outcome, not a solution. Change comes first, and change can be violent. That's where people like me come in. The consequences of change—that's Richard's department and other good people like him. They take destruction and build upon it. They unite people. But before peace, there is always war. People like me bring war. People like Richard fix everything when all hope seems lost."

Peace is an outcome, not a solution. The words repeat themselves in her mind over and over.

Holden goes on. "I said Liam and I weren't good people. But... good and evil? Morality and immorality? Those are easy words for the self-righteous to bandy about. But we know better."

He says "we," not "I." He says "we" because she knows something about him that he keeps secret, an action he took more than a decade ago that determined the course of his life. An immoral action, most people would say.

But we know better.

There is no good and evil, Sierra thinks, only pain and the things we do to make it go away.

She saw the body of Tanya through his eyes; grieved like he did when she lost her baby; is enraged that someone murdered her and would have gotten away with it had it not been for Holden.

And that was it. That was her life.

Sierra thought she understood pain. She knows nothing.

"Who was she?" The question surprises her. She didn't realize she wanted to ask it until the words left her mouth.

He looks questioningly at her.

"The woman Liam fell in love with."

"You know I can't tell you that."

She nods. "But—did she love him, too? Did he at least have that?" She doesn't know why this matters, but it's suddenly more important than anything.

His grief seems to bleed through the old phone line, into her mind, and right to her heart. "Yes. She did."

Relief fills her, then a heaviness. "I'm sorry for her."

Holden's face hardens. "Her life has been miserable enough, the little I know of it. Liam's as well. It's unkind to say, but I couldn't understand why she loved him. And knowing him like I do—*did*—" The self-correction, present tense to past, seems to startle him, but a look of resignation quickly follows. "Knowing him like I did, I tried to discourage him. I didn't think he was capable of loving her the way she deserved to be." He rubs his hand down his face. "But I was wrong. They needed each other. The last time we talked, he told me that he loved her, and I believed him. I hope she was his last thought." He pauses. "And I hope that she—" He sighs, shakes his head. "Life is so very cruel sometimes."

She wishes she could say something, anything, to comfort him. But everything that comes to mind sounds stupid, inadequate. The plexiglass window separating them is streaked with years of desperate fingerprints on both sides, traces of people longing to simply touch someone. She adds her own as she presses her hand against it.

He looks at her for a long moment, at her hand, then lightly touches the glass with his fingertips. The guard surprises them both, and neither of them has a chance to say goodbye.

❧

August comes into the living room with two blankets in one arm, two beers tucked in the other. "Get a jacket. Come outside."

Eden takes off her Lens and follows him. In the clearing surrounding the house, he flips one of the blankets out onto the grass. She adjusts her breather, tightening the strap around the back of her head.

"Look up," he says.

She does, and her eyes widen. She grows very still. "It's beautiful."

"It's not usually this clear. I thought you'd like to see it."

He sits on the blanket, hands a beer up to her. "Have one with me. Just one."

She raises an eyebrow. "All right."

"Thanks. Drinking alone makes me feel like an alcoholic."

After their bottles are empty, they lie on the blanket, staring up at the stars. "You don't know the constellations, do you?" August asks her.

"Just the usual ones."

"I get the spoons—the dippers or whatever—but the others I don't see."

Eden points. "That's Orion's belt."

"Yeah. But where the fuck is Orion? There's supposed to be a bull, too, right?"

"I think so."

August closes one eye, tries to connect the dots with his finger. "Nope. I got nothing."

"You could use your Lens to make them out."

"Where's the fun in that?" He puts one arm behind his head and closes his eyes for a moment, tired suddenly. He feels Eden sit up, watches her get the other blanket and pull it over them. "This is cozy."

"I'm cold."

He turns his head in her direction. "You ready for tomorrow?"

"Yes," she says without hesitation.

He can barely see her in the dark. But he can feel that her shoulder is almost touching his. He slides his hand over slowly until it brushes hers. She pulls away. He pretends it's an accident, doesn't try again.

His eyes feel heavy. He's thinking of going inside to get another beer, when suddenly she takes his hand. He laces his fingers through hers. His heart beats faster. He leans up on his elbow, looks down at her. He lifts the mask off her face, lowers his head to kiss her. She turns away.

He's surprised. He shouldn't be. He slumps back down on the blanket, lets go of her hand. "Fuck. I'm sorry."

She doesn't say anything, just replaces the mask.

He stares up at the sky, not seeing anything, hating himself. A lead-gray, endless cloud rolls over the tree line, moving fast—a cold front coming in. It brings an icy breeze with it. The blanket shifts, and he's sure she's getting up to go back to the house. But she moves closer, curls against him, rests her head on his shoulder.

He's afraid to move. "You okay?"

"I'm cold."

He takes a breath, pulls her closer. She doesn't resist. He kisses the top of her head, and she hugs him.

"Are you okay?" she asks.

"Yeah."

It grows darker and colder.

"Thank you for the stars."

"Thanks for not leaving."

"Why would I?"

He watches as the dark front covers Orion's belt. She shivers. "You want to go inside?" he asks.

He feels her shake her head. "Not yet."

He never wants to go inside. This is perfect. He starts to feel sleepy, hears a song in his head. *Everything is perfect / but nothing is quite right / I'd stay out here forever / but I don't think I'd last the night.*

"I'm sorry," Eden says suddenly.

He smiles. "Don't be sorry, baby," he sings, half-drunk, half-asleep. "Don't forget I hurt you first. When the day is finally over, I'm the one who'll come off worst."

"What song is that?"

He laughs. "It's that Ali Cavanaugh song. 'Undone.' They play it everywhere. I hate it."

"Sing the rest of it."

"Come on."

She leans up, looks down at him. "Please?"

"Are you serious?"

"Yes."

"Okay." He sighs. "Everything is perfect, but nothing is quite right." It's amazing how bright her eyes are, even in the dark. "I'd stay out here forever, but I don't think I'd last the night. You said you wouldn't leave me, but you lied to everyone. I'm standing here alone tonight, you've made me come undone. If I had words..." His breath catches, and he stops.

She frowns. "Is that the end of the song?"

"No." Her long, dark hair spills onto his chest. He can feel it on his neck. He knows he shouldn't, but he reaches up, runs his fingers through it, finishes the song. "If I had words I'd say the words and tell you what I feel. But I can't remember who you are, or if we were ever real." He holds his hand against the side of her face.

She leans into his palm. "You're so warm."

"You're so cold." He rubs his thumb lightly along her cheekbone. "We should go in."

She nods. "I really am sorry, August."

"Don't be sorry, baby," he whispers. "Don't ever be sorry."

Chapter 14

DAMIAN AND Layla are parked near the church. Layla's Lens is connected to Liam's cams. Damian is in a World tapped into Eden's Lens, seeing everything from her perspective. And hating every second of it.

She belly-crawls through the grass, lies on the ground outside the entrance to the fence, watching the clock on her Lens.

The guard who should be on duty in this spot isn't. August gave him the idea that he'd swapped shifts with someone, so he went home.

But to be safe, Layla watches Eden's progress through one of the cams. "You're clear, Eden." The World makes Layla's voice sound like she's talking from across a room, not sitting beside him in the passenger seat.

At the right moment, when Eden knows the prison's cams have rotated away from her position, she squeezes through the small gap between the gate and the fence. The gate is locked and bolted a thousand times over, but whoever designed the prison never imagined that someone trying to break in would have a collapsible skeleton.

When she's past the fences, she stays in the shadows, moves along the wall until she's just under the vent.

"She's there."

"I see her," Layla says. "You're clear, Eden."

She unscrews the grate from the wall, climbs inside, replaces it.

"Looks good," Layla says.

He's not used to Worlds. And this one is made all the worse by the fact that he has no power in it. He's just along for the ride, trapped in Eden's eyes. He feels claustrophobic, squeezed into a space too small for any normal person. He stretches his arms out to remind his body that he's not in that space, Eden is. But it feels too real. "I'm never doing this again."

Eden calls up the map on her eyepiece. She's been practicing using the Lens, but it's easier for him to follow it and tell her where to go, rather than hope she doesn't make a mistake. "Go straight," he tells her, focusing on the map rather than on his—*her*—surroundings. She makes no sound as she moves, sliding along faster than he would have thought possible.

"How close is she?" He can hear Layla tapping her fingers on the dashboard, like the sound of distant drums.

"Minute and a half. Climb up that next duct." His stomach flips as the angle changes; his skin is crawling in the confined space. "I'm going to need therapy after this."

"You're such a baby."

"That's your floor. Get into that vent." He's relieved when Eden is horizontal again. "Go straight." He waits, watches. "Turn right."

"How close is she now?"

"Christ, Layla, thirty seconds."

There's a faint light coming up from the grate in front of Eden. "That's it," he tells her.

She peers through it.

He can't see anyone. "She's there."

Layla zooms in on the windows of that part of the medical wing. "There's nobody in there. You're clear," she says; then, to August, "She's there."

With that, August shuts the power down to the medical wing and the light coming up from the grate disappears.

"Two minutes, Eden." Now he's seeing in greens and blacks—night vision.

She doesn't speak, drops soundlessly from the ceiling into the lab. He sees long tables, desks, cabinets, wallfaces, tablefaces. She moves quickly, turning from side to side.

"There." Damian sees it first. "On your left."

She turns to it, takes the printed latex glove out of her pocket, puts it on. It has five different thumbprints etched into it, on the off chance that Kovich's doesn't work.

Eden presses her thumb against the rectangular lock on top of the steel box. A small sign lights up, reading "Dr. Mara Kovich," and the box pops open. She lifts the lid, pulls out a six-inch steel cylindrical tool, tapered at the end like an overlarge pen. She turns it in her hand. There's one button, and it, too, requires a fingerprint. Damian shakes his head. Even if he'd managed to steal it, August would never have been able to operate the damn thing.

"Thirty seconds. Move it."

She closes the box, locks it, walks back and jumps, pulling herself up into the duct. He watches her fiddle with the grate. The lights flash back on as she turns the last screw. Two doctors come rushing in, a woman and a man. He can see their faces clearly when they step under the grate. He looks at the timer on Eden's Lens. Seconds are ticking by and she isn't moving.

"What the fuck are you doing? Get out of there."

She doesn't move. Her breathing gets louder, faster. Something is wrong.

"What is she doing?" Layla asks, panic in her voice.

"I don't know. She just froze up."

She thumps her fist on the dash. "Eden, goddammit, we don't have time for your fucking PTSD! Move!"

Another few seconds, and Eden's slithering away, moving even faster than before. "She's moving."

"Is she fucking crazy?" Layla screams.

"Shut up." He feels for Layla's arm, holds it tightly. "Eden, you're going to make a right... now." She does. "Keep going for another minute."

Layla yanks out of Damian's hold. He finds her shoulder, squeezes the back of her neck. "Lens, mute." She tries to pull away, but he won't let her. "Calm the fuck down. Don't do that again."

She struggles once more, then stops. He feels her nod tightly. He loosens his hold, moves his thumb up and down the side of her neck for a moment. "Easy does it, hummingbird."

"Don't call me that."

He knows she hates this—that it's Eden in there and not her. Layla wants to be the one to save Holden. But Damian, though he'd never admit it, is glad it's Eden. He wants Layla safe, but that's not the only reason. Eden may have taken on the role of housekeeper and cook, but he's seen a coldness in her that none of the others have noticed.

He gives his full attention back to the World, unmutes his Lens. "Next left."

Layla thinks Eden is weak. He thought so, too, once, but not anymore. He felt it when Liam died; when he found her on the floor and made her get up; when he gripped her arm and all he could see in her tearless eyes was hatred.

Layla hates, but with fire and rage, and he wouldn't have her any other way. But Eden's hatred is like his: still, quiet, cold. Hatred is only useful if you can detach yourself from it. And that's why he's glad it's her; because even if she doesn't make it, he knows that Holden will.

Eden will make sure of it.

☙

Adair is awake, waiting. August passed his cell early in the evening and put one thought into his head, one single word: *Tonight.*

When the lights go out, he knows it's time, but he's still surprised when a hand closes over his mouth. He doesn't make a sound, but adrenaline speeds up his heart. He turns his head and sees bright yellow snake eyes looking back at him.

He wants to embrace her, ask her a thousand questions, but they can't speak. She motions for him to turn around. He does, and a moment later, he feels pressure on the back his neck, painful but short. He knows immediately that the Neutralizer has been deactivated. The whole world seems to hum. He can *feel* again. There's a sensation like strings being pulled out of his neck; then, nothing.

He turns back to Eden. She smiles, then jumps up and disappears into the vent. He reaches up to touch the base of his skull. The Neutralizer is gone, sticky blood in its place.

It all happens so fast, it feels like a dream. Nothing has changed. The lights come back on. He can hear the quiet snoring of his fellow inmates. One guard says to another, "What's with the lights?" He receives no answer. No one knows that anything has happened.

Adair focuses his mind on the wall at the end of the block. He can feel the concrete, the beams holding it together. He takes a slow, deep breath, and he pulls the wall down like a curtain of cement and steel.

Everyone wakes at the deafening sound of the tearing and the crashing and the screaming of the guards. Alarms go off, the doors to the cellblock open, and a dozen more armed guards appear, all wearing breathers. But they weren't expecting this.

Adair's cell opens on its own, along with every cell in the block, every cell in the prison. The prisoners rush the guards, run for the opening. There's more screaming, the sounds of guns fired aimlessly as the dust rises like a thick fog, making it impossible to see clearly. But he only needs to feel the fresh air to know where the opening is. Once he's outside, he tears apart the fences.

Lights and spotlights illuminate the field around the prison and the trees that border it. There is yelling, orders being given, weapons being drawn and fired, guards giving chase. But there are too many on the run. And they're all dysmorphic—faster, smarter, stronger.

Adair's not a young man, but he's faster than any of the guards. He runs across the field toward the trees.

༝

Leonard lowered everyone's drugs, but he cut Hawk's off completely. As soon as his door opens, he uses all his strength to break apart the bands around his body and tear off the ankle cuffs. He's in the air a moment later, swooping through the opening in the wall to freedom.

He flies high, looks below him, sees Adair Holden running across the field. Just before he disappears into the trees, an open jeep with four guards in it catches sight of him, spins around to follow.

Hawk dives. The jeep is on manual control, so he goes for the driver, digs his talons into the man's shoulders, lifts him bodily from the seat, tosses him aside. Before the other guards have a chance to either fire at him or command the jeep to drive itself, it crashes into a tree and Hawk is a thousand feet in the air.

He finds Holden again, follows his path as he runs through the woods. On the other side, a car waits for him in front of the white church. Holden jumps inside.

Hawk is mildly amused. "That was easy."

༝

The back door opens just before he gets to it and closes as he rushes inside. Layla reaches for him from the front seat and he takes her hand and kisses it over and over. He claps a hand on Damian's shoulder, but Damian doesn't respond. And Layla won't look him in the eye.

Adair looks to his right. He sees the breather on the seat beside him. "Where's Eden?"

"She's still in there," Damian says.

Adair can't speak.

Layla looks at him finally. "She said they were pumping gas into the vents. Then we lost her."

"You *lost* her?"

"August is looking for her." Layla's voice is barely audible. "But he can't..."

Adair lets her hand go and the realness of it all crashes down on him like that wall he just destroyed. Until this moment, it's been like a fantasy... all of it, like a good dream. He felt young for a moment, running to freedom like that. And now he feels ancient. He grabs the breather. "Why doesn't she have this?"

"She said it would restrict her movements in the vents. She said she'd be fine without it for a little while."

"Well, she's *not* fine, is she?" He's shouting at Layla. He never has before, but he can't stop himself. "I should never have allowed this! She shouldn't be here! Why did you involve her in this?"

Layla has tears in her eyes. "It was the only way! You know that!"

"We have to go," Damian says.

"We're not going anywhere!"

"If we don't leave now, we're dead."

"We're not leaving her behind!"

Damian starts the car, tries to move it. Adair holds it still. "Holden! Let go!"

"No."

"Let go of the fucking car!"

"Dair, please!"

"No!" He's being irrational, stupid; he knows it. But she saved him. Eden saved him. He won't leave her behind.

"Holden!"

"Dair!" Layla screams.

He's not expecting it, doesn't know what Damian means to do until it's too late. Damian leans over the back of his seat and hits Adair's head so hard, he falls to the side and loses his grip on the car. Layla commands it to move.

"No…" He fights for control, but Damian hits him again.

He hears Layla sobbing quietly before he passes out.

ᥴᣣ

Hawk flies back to the prison to see if there's anyone else he can help. It's chaos down there. He sees bodies on the field, some d-form, but mostly guards, he's happy to note.

Leonard told him where to meet him tomorrow if he still wants in. If he doesn't show up, he'll never get the chance again. But unless he has an unfortunate accident with a plane, there's no way he won't be there.

He circles around the prison one last time. He's a mile in the air; no one on the ground can see him. There's a thin stream of green gas escaping the vents on the sides of the building, a last attempt to stop the escapees, to knock out as many remaining d-forms as possible. He saw that all the guards who answered the first alarm were wearing breathers, even before they knew the wall had been destroyed. It makes sense now. They had to protect themselves from the gas.

He's about to pull away, to put this place behind him forever, when he sees one of the vent grates being pushed out from the inside, close to the ground. A girl crawls out of it, barefoot, stumbling and coughing. She collapses. Hawk swoops down. A guard sees the girl, runs to her. Before he gets there, Hawk is on top of him, flinging him aside, and scooping the girl into his arms. He's seen by another guard and fired at. But he's too fast. He climbs higher and higher until he's invisible. He hears the helicopters before he sees them. It's time to go.

The girl is conscious, but barely. She's not a prisoner. He doesn't recognize her. "Hey. Girl." He shakes her gently. "Girl? Are you all right?"

"August…" she wheezes. "August." Her eyes don't close, but her pupils are dilating and contracting madly. She's drugged, poisoned by the gas. She turns her head, sees the drop below her, starts to struggle in his arms, terrified.

"Hey! Don't do that! Do you *want* to fall?" He holds her tightly and presses her head into his chest so she can't see. "You're drugged, okay? You're drugged. I'll get you out of here."

He hears a whisper in his ear. It's a man's voice. "Eden? Come on."

The voice comes from the Lens she's wearing. It's awkward with her in his arms, but he takes it off her and puts it on. The screen is blank. "Hello?"

There's a tense pause. "Who the fuck is this?"

"Leonard? Is that you? It's Hawk. I found this girl. She's with you?"

"Hawk?"

"Leonard! I've got your girl!"

"Is she all right?"

He listens to her wheeze, feels her chest expand against him as she tries to take a deep breath. "She's not breathing right. Probably the gas."

"Jesus. She needs a breather. She needs one right now."

"She's d-form."

"Just find her one! I've got to go."

He looks at the girl. "You need a breather?"

"Help me..." He can barely hear her.

"Lens." He thinks for a moment. "Blink... someone."

"Who do you wish to blink?" it asks him.

"Read me my list of contacts."

"Damian, Layla, August."

He chooses the first name and blinks. "Eden? Where the fuck are you?" a deep, angry voice says. He should have chosen the woman's name.

"My name is Hawk. I'm a friend of Leonard's. I've got... Eden with me."

The connection breaks. The girl's breathing is getting worse. He blinks again. The answering voice is different—older, groggy and a little slurred. "Who is this?"

Hawk knows it's Holden. "My name is Hawk. I escaped Hammond and I found this girl. Eden. Leonard says she needs a breather." He looks down at her; she's barely conscious.

He hears two other voices arguing. Holden quiets them, sounding stronger now. "Hawk. I remember you."

He thinks he's been cut off again, but then he hears a woman's voice telling Holden to blink off.

"No! Don't! Listen to her!" Hawk lowers his face close to the girl's mouth. It's painful to hear the high, scratchy rasp as she fights for each breath.

Finally, Holden asks him where he is, tells him to meet them off an exit a mile away. Hawk can hear the woman shouting, but Holden speaks over her. "Tell me she'll last that long."

"She will."

After he blinks off, the girl's eyes focus on his. "Adair?"

"One more mile. Can you make it?"

She nods and slips into unconsciousness.

∾

The tall man with huge brown wings steps into the glare of the headlights. He's carrying Eden. Adair is out of the car before it stops, hears Damian curse. He runs with the breather, loops it over her face before he says a word to the man who's rescued her. "Eden? Can you hear me?"

Her eyes focus on his. She gives him a weak smile. "You made it…"

He strokes her forehead, feels the smooth, delicate scales. "Oh, my girl. You've saved my life."

She shakes her head.

"Will she be all right?" Hawk asks.

Adair listens to her breathe. Damian appears at his side. "Yes, I think so. Damian, will you take her?" Hawk hands Eden over to Damian, who takes her roughly, walks back to the car. "Hawk?"

"Yes." Hawk extends his hand.

Adair takes it. "I saw you once before in the prison. I don't know how to thank you."

"I do." He smiles. "Let me come with you. I'm fast, strong, smart. I can help you."

He's momentarily amused by the man's candor and confidence. "Why do you want to come with us?"

"If it weren't for you, I would have been a rat in a lab, or worse, sent back to Afghanistan. Is that enough of a reason?"

Adair looks back at the car. The headlights make it impossible to see Damian or Layla. "I don't know what my next move is." He turns back to Hawk.

"But you will know. And I want to be there." The man's eyes

are orange and fierce, but a smile plays on his lips. He already knows what Adair will say.

"Come with us then."

Hawk gives him a quick nod. "I'll follow you."

"You can see the car from up there?"

His wings expand. "Of course." He takes off, and the pressure from the beat of his wings pushes Adair back a step. He watches Hawk's ascent for a moment, then hurries to the car.

He sits in the back with Eden's head on his leg. Her eyes are unfocused, glazed. She's still wheezing, but it lessens with every breath. Layla keeps looking behind her, but he won't meet her eyes.

"Is she okay?" she finally asks.

"She will be."

Layla faces forward. "Dair—"

"Don't tell me you're sorry."

He sees Damian give Layla a quick glance, clench his fists around the wheel. Layla's breathing quickens. "I'm not sorry."

He looks at her.

She turns to face him again, eyes glowing with anger. "I'm not fucking sorry, Adair. Did you think we were going to leave you in there? Did you think we wouldn't do everything we could to get you out?" Her voice catches. "If I thought slitting her throat would have helped, I would have done it."

"Layla—"

"No." She shakes her head. "No."

The car is cold, silent. He thinks of Hawk up there, watching them. He thinks of Layla, who won't even look at him now. He thinks of Eden, of Liam. And then of Tanya.

"Layla, I'm sorry," he whispers.

She says nothing.

Damian leans back, stretching. "Well, as long as we're all on the apology train, I guess I'd better say sorry for giving you that bump I'm sure you have on your head, Holden."

"Yes, well, I was being irrational."

"Yes, you were being fucking irrational," Layla mutters.

"Get over it, Layla." Damian tilts his seat back and yawns. "It all worked out. We're going home. No snake left behind. Plus, we got a new friend. Fucking Birdman of Alcatraz up there."

Layla crosses her arms. "So, we're just going to trust that guy?"

Adair looks at Eden, asleep on his knee, eyes open, looking at nothing. "He's given us every reason to."

"Of course. He saved your favorite pet, so that makes him completely trustworthy."

"Layla, don't do this to me."

She curls her legs underneath her, stares out of her window. When they reach home, she gets out of the car as soon as it stops and walks quickly into the house.

❧

"She won't wake for a while. Not until tomorrow, I think," Hawk says. "What's wrong with her? Why does she need a breather?"

"It's a long story," Adair says. "She'll tell you herself if she wants you to know."

"Fair enough."

Hawk seems like a giant in this house. He's over six feet tall, but the wings make him seem even taller. They're standing in the hallway and he looks around—at the living room, the kitchen, the stairs—his taloned toes clicking against the wood floor as he moves.

"There are bedrooms upstairs. You're welcome to any one of them."

"Thank you." He turns. The smile on his face is contagious. "But I think I'll go out and stretch my wings for a while. Maybe watch the sun rise."

Adair nods. "I understand completely." He points. "You'll need to treat those sores, though."

Hawk looks down at his torso. "These? They're nothing. But yes, when I come back, if you have some skinseal?"

"I'll leave it out for you on the kitchen table."

Hawk nods. His smile fades, and his face grows serious. Adair sees some part of his past shining through his orange-gold eyes, a long history of pain. It's a look he knows too well, and one he doesn't think Hawk readily shows to anyone. "Thank you, Mr. Holden."

"Don't thank me yet."

Hawk steps up to him. "I'm not in a prison. I'm not on a plane back to Afghanistan. I'm not being tortured and pulled apart in a lab or hung from a scaffold in the street." He laughs a little. "I'm going outside." He extends his hand. "Thank you, Mr. Holden."

"Well, when you put it that way..." Adair takes his hand.

ဆ

The room is dark. He can just see her in the faint moonlight, a shadow curled up on the bed. She knows he's there. He steps in, closes the door, stands for a long time—waiting, watching.

"Layla. What do I need to do?" he asks.

The wind blows hard against this side of the house. He thinks of Hawk, riding on that breeze thousands of feet in the air, is jealous of him. He walks to the bed, to her side of it, kneels on the floor. He can't tell if her eyes are open or not.

"Please, Layla."

She takes a breath. "Just tell me..." She's been crying; he can hear it in her voice. "Tell me you would care as much… if it were me."

"I would care more! Layla!" She couldn't have hurt him more if she'd stabbed him in the heart. Adair touches her face, feels tears there. "I would care more! You're my life, Layla. You're my *life*!" He runs his fingers over the line of feathers on the back of her neck, kisses her forehead. He wipes away her tears, smiles through his own, whispers, "'I cannot live without my life. I cannot live without my soul.'"

"What's that from?"

"It doesn't matter."

She sits up, slides her legs over the bed in front of him. He rests his hands on her knees. "You and your books," she says. She tugs at the collar of his prison uniform. "Why are you still wearing this? Take it off and we'll burn it."

"Oh, Layla…"

She grips the collar tightly, pulls hard at it, looks down to hide her tears. Her voice shakes. "I *missed* you…"

Adair pulls her into his arms.

She clings to him. "Please don't leave me again," she cries. "Please."

"Never, never, my love. Never." He holds her tighter. "Whatever happens to us, I'll never leave you. I love you, Layla. I love you. You know that, don't you?"

"Dair…"

"You know it, don't you, my love?"

She nods, crying freely now. He can feel her fingers pressing into his back.

"You don't know how lonely I am without you, hummingbird."

She pulls back, kisses him. "Yes, I do."

Chapter 15

I T'S EARLY, gray dawn, too early for either of them to be up.
"Dairen?"

It was the Cube that woke her. He sits on the end of the bed, watching. She leans up, rubs her eyes, freezes when she sees the words:

Adair Holden Escapes Hammond Prison.

"More than one hundred other inmates are said to have escaped the prison," the news anchor says. "The exact number is not yet known."

"What happened?"

Dairen turns to her. "He did it."

Sierra wants to smile, wants to cheer. Dairen misinterprets her rapid breathing for fear. He moves back to his side of the bed, holds her in his arms.

"How?" She fights to keep the joy out of her voice.

She can feel him shake his head. "Somehow, he tore down a wall in his block."

He can't see her face, so she risks a smile, takes a slow breath. "Does Richard know?"

"Probably. But I don't want to wake him. He'll know eventually. My Lens went off fifteen minutes ago with a blink alert. You slept through it."

She kisses his arm where it crosses over her chest. "It'll be okay."

Dairen is quiet for a moment. "Do you think they'll come after Dad again?"

This thought sobers her. "They'll probably want to ask him

more questions."

"God, this is getting fucking crazy."

She turns in his arms, hugs him. "It'll be okay," she says again.

They watch the news until it starts to repeat itself. Yellow light begins to peek through the curtains. Sierra feels herself falling asleep again, more relaxed than she's been in weeks. She's vaguely aware of Dairen moving slowly, lowering her to her pillow, covering her with the quilt. She hears the door click shut, and Tanya looks over at her from the driver's seat. Sierra can't look into her eyes—fixed and dead, but awake and aware.

"What now?" Tanya licks the ice cream in the sugar cone she holds.

"I don't know." Sierra's ice cream is vanilla with rainbow sprinkles. It's melting onto her hand. "Where are we going?"

The desert outside the window speeds by in a blur of browns and golds, but the car doesn't feel like it's moving. "I was going to ask you the same thing." Tanya's voice is as gentle and melodic as in Holden's memory, with just a hint of sadness. She doesn't sound dead, but her eyes, her unnaturally pale brown skin, and the thick stitches that poke out just above the top of her shirt are a constant reminder.

"Did those hurt? The stitches?"

"No." She takes a bite out of her cone, speaks around it. "I guess they would have if I'd been alive." She smiles, catches Sierra's eye. Sierra doesn't mean to flinch, but she can't help it.

"Sorry." Tanya looks away. "I keep forgetting."

Sierra is embarrassed, concentrates on her ice cream. She hears a faint beeping, doesn't know where it's coming from. "Tanya," she says after a moment, "I'm sorry you were murdered."

"Me too."

Sierra takes a breath, turns, makes herself look into the dead, vacant eyes. "I would've liked to have known you."

Tanya looks confused. "You do know me."

In a way, that's true, Sierra supposes. "What do I do now?"

"I think you know."

The beeping gets louder.

"No. I don't."

"You should answer that."

Sierra looks around, tries to find the source of the beeping. "Where is it?"

"There." Tanya points to Sierra's nightstand, and Sierra is in her bed, awake, looking at her Lens as it flashes and beeps. It only does that if she's receiving an emergency blink. She starts, grabs the Lens too quickly, knocks it onto the floor.

"Goddammit." She reaches for it, puts it on.

The message is from an unknown source. She opens it. It's an address and a time, nothing else, no preceding message, no signature. She reads it over twice.

It vanishes.

She searches for it in deleted blinks, sent blinks, every folder, does a general search of her Lens. But it's nowhere.

Her heartbeat picks up. She sees the address clearly in her mind, calls up a map. It's a small shopping center between here and Hammond. She waits for more.

Nothing.

She flips her eyepiece up, looks around the room. A sense of being watched creeps over her.

She lies back on the pillow, stares at the ceiling. She can ignore the message, forget it, curl up and hide under the sheets. Go back to sleep.

None of us should sleep.

She turns the covers back, puts her feet on the floor. There's a chill in the room that moves right through her. She wraps her arms around herself.

The door opens. Dairen is holding a mug of coffee. "Hey, I was just coming to wake you."

She smiles, stands. "I'm awake."

∾

"This is a nice place. A little quiet though." Hawk takes a bite out of the apple in his hand.

"It *was* quiet." Damian gets up from the table for another cup of coffee. Layla notices the way Hawk's eyes follow him, how his mouth turns up into an appraising smile as he looks him up and down. When Hawk sees that Layla is watching him, he winks at her, then turns his eyes back to Damian.

"So, Damian Grace, where are you from?" He says Damian's name with a flourish, like he's talking about a piece of art or someone famous.

"About a mile away from none of your goddamn business."

"Beautiful country, I hear. And you, Layla?"

"We're from the same neighborhood."

Hawk shrugs, takes another bite, speaks around it. "I see. Very insular people. I'm from Afghanistan. Hellish little place. Heard of it?"

Neither of them answers. Damian sits back down, watching Hawk with a dark stare.

"Better get used to the silent treatment, Hawk. That's the M.O. around here." August comes into the kitchen, pours himself a mug of coffee.

"I've noticed."

"When did you get here?" Layla asks, surprised to see him.

"Hour ago."

"You drove all night? Why?"

August shrugs. "I wanted to make sure everyone was okay."

"Yeah, Layla." Damian sets his mug down, his dark eyes seeming to glitter with amusement. "He wanted to make sure *everyone* was okay. Gus is considerate like that."

"Oh, God," Layla drones, "are you serious?"

"What?" August says. "I can't care that Eden almost died? She's my friend. I give a damn. There. That's my deep, dark secret, Layla. You finally got it out of me."

"Aw, August has a friend. That's so sweet."

Hawk looks at him. "You must be exhausted, Leonard."

August leans against the counter. "I'm fine. And you know my name's August, right?"

Hawk waves away this comment. "So tell me. How long have you all been in the terrorist business?"

"We're pretty new to it, actually." August takes a sip of his coffee. "Hammond was our first gig."

"And not the last, I hope. What's next?"

Layla is wondering that herself. Hammond has been at the forefront of all their minds for so long that thinking about what they'll do afterward hasn't been a priority.

"Not sure," August says.

Layla looks up at him. "Dair will know what to do."

Hawk's eyebrows rise, and he smiles at her. "Dair? That's lovely. May I call him that?"

She glares at him. "No."

Hawk's smile doesn't fade. He looks back at August. "I presume you've been up to see Eden. How is she?"

August looks down into his mug. "Still asleep."

"She'll be fine. Don't worry. I slept for a day and a half when they tested that stuff on me."

He says this so casually that it takes Layla a moment to realize its significance. She lowers her fork, looks up at him. "They tested it on you?"

He chews a bit of apple, swallows. "Sure. Things like that, you always pick the strongest people. If it brings us down, it's bound to get the weaker ones, too."

It's hard for her to imagine Hawk being brought down by anything. Despite the wounds on his torso, he has one of those impossibly perfect bodies that most people can only achieve through surgery. He's Damian's height, but looks taller because of his wings; they seem to fill the entire room. And of all his physical perfections, it's those wings that fascinate her the most.

"Stop staring, hummingbird. You're embarrassing yourself."

She gives Damian a look. "Stop pouting because we've met someone bigger than you."

"I like these two, Leonard. They're adorable."

August laughs. "I've heard them called a lot of things. Adorable is definitely not one of them."

"This is like one of those reality shows, you know?" Hawk continues. "A bunch of people trapped in a house, trying to live together. You should film it. Set up a Cube channel for yourselves."

"Yeah, I'll get right on that," August says.

Layla feels a buzzing in her brain, something tumbling and clicking into place. Damian sees the look on her face, frowns questioningly.

"Well," Hawk says, "you think it would be okay if I went up and talked with my savior?"

"Go ahead. Tell me if she wakes up."

Layla barely hears them.

When Hawk is gone, Damian looks at her. "What?"

"A Cube channel."

"What are you talking about?" August sits next to her.

"A Cube channel. For Dair."

Damian looks at her like she's crazy.

"He needs to be seen or people will just forget about him. He needs to be heard."

"Does he also need to be traced back here and get us all arrested?"

"Don't be stupid. You know our Cubes don't get traced, or our Lenses." Liam had made sure of that. Whatever else he may have been, he was a genius with all things technological.

"No, wait a second. Wait a second." August sets his coffee down. "What about that girl? That reporter. Venus Carr. He could record something and we can send it to her. She's already got an audience. I mean, it's not huge or anything, but..."

Layla's heart speeds up. "That's perfect!"

"What the hell do you want him to say?" Damian asks.

She stands up. "Whatever he wants to. Whatever he needs to. People want to know who he is, why he's doing what he's doing. You've seen the news. They want to hear him and see him."

"He's not Jesus fucking Christ, Layla."

She looks down at him, shakes her head. "You're a real fucking idiot sometimes, Damian." She turns, leaves the room to find Dair.

☙

There you are, my sleeping beauty, Hawk pathspeaks softly into her mind, sitting in the chair by her bedside. Her eyes are open and still. The scales that decorate her face are like delicate black webs. He can hear the hissing of the breather in the quiet of the room. Like most people, she's smaller than he is, and seems even more so wrapped up in the covers.

He shakes his head. *You're a brave girl.* He watches her for a moment. *I saw that scar on your neck, you know. And that look you have. We're from the same hell, you and I. I can tell.* He reaches out, touches her covered arm lightly. *I want to make a promise to you.*

I will always do whatever I can to keep you from suffering any more than you already have.

He feels a stirring in his mind, hears her voice as if from a distance. *Am I dreaming?*

No. You're asleep, but I can hear your thoughts.

He feels her think, come to a conclusion. *You're Hawk.*

I am.

You saved me.

He smiles. *It's the other away around, I think.*

He feels her start to fade, then come back. *I'm so tired.*

He squeezes her arm. *Go back. Let yourself rest.*

Is... August all right...?

He's here, safe and sound. A barely formed thought flits by him. She hardly registers it. He sees it, pretends not to. It's not for him to know or mention. *Rest now, okay? He'll be here when you wake up.*

Okay... she says, faintly. *Thank you...*

She slips into deep sleep again, and her thoughts become muddled and strange, going off in different directions, into confusing loops and dream tangents. He sees a woman's face, brown hair, dull green eyes, red shoes... not a dream; a memory that her unconscious self keeps visiting again and again. He wonders what it means, if she'll remember it when she wakes. Then he stands, leaves her mind, kisses the top of her head, whispers, "See you soon."

∾

She leans against his desk. He looks up at her from the chair, shakes his head. "But what would it accomplish, my love?"

She puts her hand on his chest. "People want to hear you. They *need* to hear you."

He covers her hand with his. "Hummingbird, I'm not like Richard. I'm not a speechmaker."

"Good! No one wants to hear speeches! They want the truth. I've told you a thousand times: Corbin is nothing. He's a hypocrite. It's you, Dair."

"Layla, where is this coming from?"

She pushes his chair away from the desk so she can sit on his lap, facing him, her arms wrapped around his neck.

"Layla—"

"I watched you on the field, Dair." Her voice is low. "I could feel how powerful you are. I never knew..." She kisses him. Her lips are warm. She tastes of coffee and something uniquely her. Her kisses never fail to surprise him. Layla never fails to surprise him.

She breaks away, rests her head against his. "I would kill for you, Dair. I would die for you."

"Layla—"

"And when other people hear you, they'll feel the same way. It's you, Dair." She kisses him again. "It's you." She starts to unbutton his shirt.

He laughs quietly, watching her quick fingers. "Did you even lock the door?"

She doesn't answer, and it isn't long before he stops caring.

⁓

Her eyes flit back and forth as she wakes. His heartbeat picks up. He leans forward. "Eden?"

"Liam?" she whispers.

He looks down at the floor. "No, baby, it's just me." It's ridiculous to be jealous of a dead man.

Her eyes widen then, and he sees terror. She sits up, looks

around the room like she doesn't know where she is.

"Eden?"

She turns when she hears his voice. "August!" She throws her arms around him. She's shaking.

"Hey, hey. It's okay."

She pulls away, clutches his shirt in her fingers. "Who is she?"

He wonders if the drugs are still in her system, holds her wrists as she clings to his shirt. "Who's who?"

"The woman in the lab. Brown hair, green eyes. She was wearing red shoes."

"Kovich?"

"Kovich." She repeats the name like a prayer. Her grip loosens. "Kovich." She lets go. Her hands fall into her lap. She stares at them.

He puts his hands in hers. She doesn't react. "What is it? What's wrong?" She won't answer. "Eden." He takes her chin gently, tilts her head up. She still won't look into his eyes. "Tell me."

"I killed her," she mumbles.

"What?"

"I killed her."

He leans back. "No, you didn't. Don't get me wrong. I wish she was dead. But she's not. You must have dreamed it."

She grips his hands tightly now, looks him in the eye with clarity and fierceness. "I *killed* her at the lab."

She's scaring him now. "Eden... what are you talking about?"

"*My* lab."

His heart is beating so hard it hurts. He feels it in his throat.

"I was running. She tried to stop me..." Eden looks over his shoulder at nothing. "She grabbed me. I got away. I *bit* her." She touches her lip where it covers her fangs. "I broke her skin. I tasted her blood. I gave her all the venom I had. She fell. I *killed her*!"

He thinks of lying in the grass, drunk, singing to her under the stars. He thinks of her, starving and desperate, sinking her teeth into someone to save herself... killing them.

"Please tell me you believe me!"

He speaks without thinking. "I believe you." And he does. He has to. "Eden. I believe you."

"I'm not crazy!"

He wraps his arms around her. "You're not crazy." She holds him tightly, but she doesn't cry. "I believe you." He kisses her hair. "I believe you. I mean, it's a lab, right? You don't know what happened after you ran. They could've had an antidote. You don't know."

She sighs with relief. "Thank you." He can feel the warmth of her breath against his shoulder as she speaks. "Thank you. Thank you."

He runs his hand down her hair again and again. She saw Kovich in the lab and kept going. She saw a ghost—a ghost who'd held her captive and tortured her—and she kept moving. She saved Holden, almost died doing it. "Jesus, Eden. You're the bravest fucking person I know."

It's a strange moment for him to realize that he's never loved anyone, not really; a strange feeling to be more angry about someone else's pain than about his own; to want to cry, not because he is hurting, but because someone else is—because she is; to feel so responsible for another's happiness, so desperate to take away their pain, and knowing that he can do nothing.

This is love, he thinks. And it's awful.

ல

He stayed with Eden until she had something to eat and went to sleep again. When he left her room, his chest felt hollow, his skin raw like it had been burnt and scraped with a bristle brush. He searched through every cabinet in the kitchen until he found it. Before he even opened it, he felt the fist around his heart start to ease its grip. He grabbed a tumbler, sat at the table. It was around eleven p.m. After the third glass, he stopped looking at the clock.

He stares down at the table now. It's scratched in places. There's a long, deep groove near the middle. He runs his fingernail up and down it, wonders what caused it. The slip of a sharp knife? No, it looks deliberate. He sips the whiskey.

"You've got that look, Gus." Damian is at the counter, opening a beer. When did he come in?

"What look?"

He points at him. "*That* look. You've had enough."

"Who the fuck're you? My mom?"

"If I was your mom, I'd beat the shit out of you with a belt."

"That's very true." August raises his glass. "To Mom." He drinks, hisses through his teeth at the sharp burn.

Damian sits at the table, takes the half-empty bottle, puts it out of August's reach.

"Hey!"

"How much have you had?"

"Oh, fuck you, Damian." He reaches across the table. His fingers touch the bottle's neck. Damian brings his fist down on the inside of his elbow. "Jesus fucking Christ!"

"How much, Gus?"

He tries to move, but Damian presses down so hard, August's fingertips start to tingle.

"How. Much."

He clenches his teeth. "Bottle was full."

Damian lets him go. August yanks his arm away, rubs life back into his hand. They stare at each other. If Damian's eyes are the windows to his soul, it explains a lot, August thinks. Black like crude oil, inscrutable. He feels like he's looking into nothing, so he looks away.

He thinks of getting up, leaving. He doesn't need Damian's shit and he doesn't need that bottle. He'll get up and leave. Go check on Eden, go to bed...

Damian tips the bottle from side to side. "You want it back?"

A heaviness, like a lead blanket, presses down on him. August nods slowly.

"Ice?"

"Neat."

Damian picks up August's tumbler, pours, sets it in front of him again. August just stares at it.

"Drink it."

His hand moves with a will of its own, raises the glass. It's cold and smooth on his lips. The whiskey burns over his tongue, down his throat, a slow, searing fire—a joy so strong it can only leave abject misery behind when it's gone. He closes his eyes. Only a few seconds left before it disappears.

"Don't know how you drink that shit, Gus."

And it's gone. "It's easy. Just tip the glass and swallow."

Damian drinks his beer and waits.

August knows he could sit there all night. He sighs. "It's Kovich."

"The doctor?"

He swirls his drink around in the glass. "Eden knows her. That lab she escaped? Kovich was there. Eden saw her when she was in the vents."

Damian stops mid-swig, lowers the bottle slowly. "That's why she froze."

"Yeah." August looks at the wall, back at Damian. "Can I have my bottle back?"

"Give me a reason."

"I just gave you one."

Damian shakes his head.

"Just give it to me, man."

He pushes the bottle farther away.

"Jesus Christ." August swallows back the rest of what's in the tumbler, too much, too fast. He holds back a cough, puts his head in his hands. His eyes are burning. "Back in the city, we never saw any of this shit. Fucking prisons, fucking labs. We knew about it, but... And that girl up there? What the fuck, man? What kind of a life is that? How long was she in that lab? Why her? And then Liam fucking dies? What is that shit?"

"So, you're getting fucked up because she's fucked up."

"I'm getting fucked up because *I'm* fucked up." He taps his empty glass on the table. "Come on, man."

Damian pours for him again.

Before August drinks, he looks up into those empty eyes again. "What the fuck are we doing here, Damian?"

Damian picks up his beer and shrugs. "I'm just here to get laid."

August stares at him, furious, opens his mouth to scream and curse at him. But he bursts out laughing and can't stop. He laughs until he tears up, has to wipe his eyes. "God, I fucking hate you."

"Hey. Words can hurt, Gus."

August laughs again, until he can't remember what was funny. The scratches on the table bend and blur, seem to writhe along the surface like worms. He rests his chin on his arm, touches the deep groove again; it reminds him of Liam's scar. "How did this get here?"

"How the fuck should I know?"

He circles his finger around it over and over, is vaguely aware of Damian pouring him another drink. The sound of the liquid filling the glass is so loud, like ice breaking over a frozen lake—one misstep, too much weight in the wrong place, and crack, you're drowning. August shivers.

"You tell Holden?"

He shakes his head. He thinks of how heavy his clothes would be, soaked in ice water, how much more easily he'd drown with dead weights pulling him down faster than he could take them off.

Damian snaps his fingers in front of August's face. He jumps, sits up. The movement makes him dizzy. It feels like his head is disconnected from his body. He was falling asleep.

Damian slides the tumbler in front of him. "Last one. Go to bed. Tell Holden tomorrow."

"Go to bed. Tell Holden tomorrow." Thank God, he thinks, thank God for this fiery joy.

As he drinks it, he remembers hearing somewhere that if you're freezing to death, alcohol will only kill you faster, make you think you're warm when you're not. Makes sense. It makes him think he's happy when he's not. So he decides, then and there, that if he's ever freezing to death, he'll drink until he blacks out. Better to die warm and happy, feeling like he'll live forever, than the alternative. "What is the fucking point?" He thinks he says this out loud, but isn't sure.

Damian looks at him, shakes his head. He stands, grips August's shoulder tightly. "Come on."

August leans down heavily on the table, pushes himself up. Damian catches his elbow when he trips backward. August looks up at him. "You're a good friend, man."

"Get up the fucking steps."

He doesn't feel the floor under his feet. It's more like he's walking on a waterbed. And then he's at the top of the steps and can't remember climbing them. Now he's in front of a door, reaching for the knob.

"Wrong room, Gus. One more."

August shakes his head. "I want to check on Eden." He looks at Damian. "Am I allowed?"

Damian puts his hands up. "This is where I get off."

August salutes him. "Thank you for your service, sir. Have an excellent day."

"Jesus fucking Christ..." Damian turns, walks toward his room.

August falls against the door as he opens it, stumbles inside, closes it too loudly. He looks over at Eden in the bed, walks with one hand on the wall for support. He hits the floor hard when he kneels, knows that'll hurt like hell tomorrow, but feels nothing now. He rests his head on the mattress. "Sorry. Did I wake you?"

"It's okay," she says.

He closes his eyes. His brain spins in circles, around and around. It's cold and damp on the floor... he's slipping and sliding on the ice...

"August?"

He jolts awake. "Oh, Jesus. Was I asleep?"

"Yes." She pulls back the covers, moves over.

He raises himself up just enough to roll into the bed. "Hey, this is comfier than mine."

"You can stay."

He can feel the mattress hugging every part of his body. "You don't want me to stay."

"I don't mind."

He turns onto his side, has that waterbed feeling again. "I'm not *entirely* in control of my actions, you know."

"I trust you."

"You do, don't you? That's nice." He smiles, is only just aware of reaching out to push a few stray strands of hair off her face. His hand looks weird, not his, apart... "You're so pretty, it's ridiculous." He takes his hand back. "Sorry. I'm a little drunk."

"It's okay."

He lies on his back again, smiling stupidly, because somehow, that joy is staying with him this time. He's so happy, so relaxed, like nothing is wrong in the whole world. Maybe nothing *is* wrong in the whole world. Maybe *this* is the whole world and all that other horrible shit is just some nightmare he keeps having.

"Hey," he says, louder than he means to, "did you know if you're freezing to death, you shouldn't drink?"

"No."

"Well, you shouldn't. So don't, okay?"

"Okay."

He turns his head to her. "Seriously. Don't."

"I won't."

"You promise?"

"I promise."

"Okay. Good."

The house is so quiet, he only hears the ringing of his blood in his ears, that high-pitched whine. He wonders what actual silence sounds like, then laughs to himself. How can silence sound like anything?

He opens his eyes, doesn't remember closing them. She's still looking at him, eyes glowing like the whiskey in the bottle. "Sorry I woke you."

"I don't mind."

"Me neither. I mean, I'm actually not sorry I woke you. I lied. I wanted to talk to you."

"About what?"

He laughs. "I don't know." He's at war with his eyelids; he doesn't want to sleep. "Damian took my bottle."

"Why?"

"So I wouldn't drink all of it. He's always doing that."

"Why?"

"Because he knows me." His eyelids are winning.

"How long have you known Damian?"

"Ages..." He tries not to slur his words. "Hundreds and hundreds of years."

He doesn't realize he's fallen asleep again until he wakes up and she's not there. She's at the end of the bed, untying his shoes. "What are you doing?"

She doesn't answer.

"I should go to my room..." But he can't move. He feels the light weight of the covers as she pulls them up over him. She lies down again. "Do you sleep with your eyes open?" he asks.

"Yes."

"Are you asleep now?"

She smiles. "No."

He's warm despite the cold, wrapped in the covers, next to her. He tries to move closer... but he slips, loses his balance. He can see right through it, all the way down to where there's no light and no life. It's so dark down there... so cold... lonely. There's a small crack starting under his feet...

"I don't want to fall through the ice, Eden."

"You won't," he thinks she says, thinks she holds his hand. "I'll save you."

Chapter 16

"HOW?"

"It's obvious, isn't it?" Weir leans his head on his fist, watching her with his unwavering, unperturbed gaze.

"Is it?"

"We have a d-form in the ranks, Mara."

"In the prison? Are you serious?"

He shrugs. "That or a sympathizer."

She's not paying attention to what she's doing, and the coffee she's pouring overfills the cup. "Goddammit!" She puts the pot down, shakes her hand, sucks the finger she's burned.

Weir stands, gets a towel, starts to wipe up the mess for her. "Put it under cold water."

She does, and as the water pours over her burn, she says, "Everyone in here has been scrutinized and vetted by our people, Rhys, *our* people."

"We're not perfect. Are you all right?"

"I'm fine." She dries her hand. "Okay, let's say you're right."

"I am right."

She glares at him. "How did they get into the lab? How did they open the box?"

"Well, according to the records, Dr. Mara Kovich opened the box." Weir pulls a chair out for her and she sits. He takes the one next to her.

"We both know that didn't happen," Mara says. She sips her coffee. "No one went into the lab—"

"No one went in through the *door*," Weir corrects.

She rolls her eyes. "And no one went in through the window,

either."

"No."

"So, what then? Someone walked through a wall? We're living in strange times, Rhys, but they're not that strange."

His smiles unnerve her; they always have. "The vents."

"No one could fit into the vents."

"Not one of us." He gestures to the empty room, the large oval table and unoccupied chairs. "But we both knew someone who could have."

Mara almost drops the cup, is just barely able to set it down without spilling it. "That's impossible."

"Is it?"

A chill moves through her. "How could she have survived?"

"Oh, I don't know..." He waves his hand in the air. "Maybe some kindly older gentleman found her in dire straits, took her in, nursed her back to health..."

"That would be incredible. Unbelievable."

"As you said, strange times." He leans forward. "If I'm right, then you're in more danger than any of us. I know you've been refusing the security detail, but don't be stupid. Even at her weakest, look how strong my girl still is."

"Your girl?" Mara holds back a shiver of revulsion.

"And no one else's." He sits back, a look in his eye that she's become familiar with, but not at all comfortable: a possessive, predatory gleam, like a leashed animal in view of its prey, pulling at its restraints, knowing that if it could just get free, it could tear that rabbit apart, enjoy its screams and the taste of its blood.

She pretends to be annoyed rather than show how disturbed she is by him. "I never understood your obsession with her. She was important, but by the time she escaped, she'd almost outlived her usefulness."

"Not quite. There was something more in her. I would have

found it, eventually."

"You would have killed her, eventually."

"No, not her. Come on, Mara. She was special. You know she was."

There are very few people so completely dysmorphic as to be almost non-human. She was one of them—the green skin, the lidless eyes, the collapsible skeleton, the teeth, the venom glands, her ability to heal, how long she could go without oxygen... She was a prize.

And Weir pulled her apart. She's never seen him more committed to any project in all the time she's known him.

"Yes... she was special. But you left her with nothing. Even if she's alive, she couldn't have..." Mara's voice trails off. She cups the side of her neck without thinking.

"I never asked. Is there a scar?"

She thinks of the girl's eyes, alive and conscious, and so much more incredible for that; remembers how weak and thin she was; how simple Mara thought it would be to subdue her when she tried to escape; how easily she slipped from Mara's grasp, leapt onto her back, sank her fangs into her neck.

Mara knows she would be dead if they hadn't drained so much of her venom the day before. As it was, she only passed out, got a concussion from hitting the corner of a counter and a scar on her neck for her trouble.

It isn't the bite itself that she recalls with any kind of fear; it's the girl's eyes before she did it. She doesn't think she'll ever forget that animal fierceness, that cold, hateful fire.

"Yes. There's a scar," Mara says quietly.

"May I see it?"

She snaps back to the here and now, glares at him. "No. You may not."

He lifts his hands in front of him, palms up. "I'm sorry."

She feels silly for her spark of anger, especially in front of Weir. "What's going on with Thirty-One?"

"Thirty-One?" Weir shrugs. "Nothing unusual."

"McFadden told me you had her remove one of his eyes."

He gives her a playful half-smile. "Tattletale."

"She said she could've saved it."

"I didn't want to save it. And besides, it's much easier to study an eyeball outside the socket than in it. What difference does it make to you? He's my project."

It makes no difference at all. She doesn't know why she asked in the first place. She stands, dumps her coffee into the sink. "I don't want you mentioning your... *theory* to the agents."

"Of course not."

As she leaves the lounge, Weir calls her back. "Mara. The security detail?"

She sighs. "Fine. But tell them I'll choose my own people."

"They won't like that."

"I choose my own people," she says again, slowly this time, trying to keep her anger in check.

Weir opens his hands, gives her conciliatory nod. "You choose your own people."

Later, when she's back in the main lab, she stands at the counter where the Neutralizer's box once sat. It's in a crime lab now, somewhere, being taken apart, examined from every angle. The Neutralizer itself is gone. She slides her gaze slowly to the left, and then at the ceiling. She walks over, looks up into the small grate above her head. She stood here that night after the lights came back on; she remembers very clearly. If the girl had been in the vent at that moment—

She touches her neck again, feels the two soft bumps, barely visible to anyone else. She sees them every day, the second she looks in the mirror.

"Dr. Kovich?"

Mara blinks, lowers her hand. One of the technicians stands near her. "What? Yes?"

"Sorry to bother you, but would you mind having a look at something?"

"No, of course not."

"Just over here." The technician—she thinks his name is Ezra—gestures to the left.

Mara takes one more quick glance at the grate, then follows him.

❧

August has a terrible headache. It's like an axe is being hacked right between his eyes over and over. It only gets worse the more he thinks about what he has to do.

"I know this was supposed to end here," Holden said when he told him about Kovich.

But it's not going to end. Holden needs August to stay at the prison. Eden needs him to stay. Because it isn't just about Kovich.

Eden was never at Hammond. And that can mean only one thing: the lab that held her is somewhere near Hammond and Kovich is their link to it.

August could have refused. The prison is a hell on earth. All that was keeping him going was knowing that when Holden got out, he could start to make himself disappear; pull out the thoughts he'd planted in people's minds about "John Leonard," make it so that he never existed. It would've taken some time, but at least he would have been well on his way to getting out of that place for good.

He could have refused.

But there's no one else who can do what he can.

"August?"

He opens one eye, smiles, doesn't put much effort into it. "Hey."

Eden sits on the floor next to the couch.

"I can move." He starts to sit up.

"No, stay." She pushes down lightly on his chest.

"Oh, thank you," he sighs. "I really can't move."

Her smile is like sunshine... God, what a cheesy thought. He's glad he didn't say it out loud. He closes his eyes again.

"Can I get you anything?" she asks.

"A new brain."

He hears her stand.

"Pick your head up," she tells him.

He does, and she sits. He lays his head down on her leg. "Mmm," he says. "You're way better than a pillow." He feels her cold fingers on his forehead, moving in pressured circles, slowly, gently. "That feels good."

"Good."

He gets lost in the feel of her hands, the firm but tender movements of her fingers. Circles, lines... circles, lines... "Eden, that's amazing. What are you doing?"

She says nothing, just goes on. The pain eases out of his head, seems to slide up her fingers with each caress. His anxiety, like a vise around his chest, drifts away. A dream-image comes to his mind: this August—hung over, angry, frightened—is separating itself from a better version of August, floating up into the air like a ghost.

"Hey. I hope I didn't freak you out last night."

"You didn't."

He smiles. "You're very tolerant."

After a few silent minutes, Eden says quietly, "I know you don't want to go back. I'm sorry."

"If you do this for me every time I get fucked up, we can call it even."

"I'm..." Her hands stop.

He opens his eyes. "What is it, baby?"

"I'm grateful."

August reaches up, touches her face. "We're going to get the bitch, I promise."

She takes his hand. "You're so good."

"No, I'm not."

She kisses his hand. "You are." She kisses it again. "You are."

Her lips on his skin are like cold flower petals. He imagines what it would be like to kiss her, pushes the thought away. "Subject change," he says, and she goes back to rubbing his forehead. "What do you think of our new roommate?"

"I think Damian might kill him."

"I love when something makes him uncomfortable." August smiles. Her fingers are like feathers. "It's like he's actually human."

She's quiet for a long time. He gets drowsy, focused on the pattern her fingers make across his head.

Then she asks, "What time do you have to leave tomorrow?"

He's glad to hear a little sadness in her voice. "Afternoon. Holden wants me to meet with Sierra Marlowe around six or something."

"I like her."

"You don't know her."

"I'd like to."

August takes her hand from his head, kisses her beautiful fingers, puts it back. "Maybe you will. That's the idea, I guess."

He's just starting to doze off when Eden says his name. "August?"

"Hmm?"

"Can you sing that stupid song again?"

He opens his eyes. "Seriously?"

"Yes."

He sighs. "Get us a couple of beers first?"

"Are you kidding?"

"Don't look at me like that. My headache's gone. Let's celebrate." He lifts up his head to free her legs. "Pretty please?"

Eden shakes her head, but stands. "Now you have to sing it twice."

He watches her leave the room, hears the fridge open. "Hey," he calls, "two songs, two beers!"

∾

Layla looks up from the Cube. Hawk leans against the doorframe, smiling, arms crossed.

"Are you just out of shirts or are you protesting the textile industry?"

He laughs. "Not all of us can cut our clothes to shreds and still look sexy in them, like you."

She sniffs, looks back at the Cube. He sits beside her.

"What are we watching?"

"*I'm* watching a movie. I don't know what you're watching. Hint?"

Hawk sighs. "Let's get out of here. All you people do is sit around all day and stare at Cubes."

"If you want to go, I have no problem with that."

"Come on, fly a few miles with me. It's a beautiful day. Leonard's gone and I'm sad. Cheer me up."

"I'm fine right here."

Eden comes downstairs.

"Ah," Hawk says. "You'll come with me, won't you?"

"Where?"

He points up. "Ever seen the view from up there?"

Her eyes widen. "Oh. I don't know—"

"Come on. I can carry you on my back."

"Don't drop her," Layla says, "or there won't be any dinner tonight."

"Such lovely people you live with." Hawk holds out his hand and Eden takes it. "Last chance, Layla."

"Oh gosh. I'm having such a crisis of indecision here." She crosses her arms.

Hawk's smile is unfailing. "Until our return then, Miss Monroe."

She rolls her eyes, but when they turn around, she watches him walk away and almost regrets not taking him up on his offer. She's sure she's never seen anything so beautiful as Hawk's wings.

◌

The man has a playful smile on his lips. "Marlowe, right?"

"Sierra."

"John Leonard." He puts his hands in his pockets. "So, how can I be of service, Marlowe?"

He leans against her car. She looks closely at him.

"You're not going to find anything."

Sierra turns away, embarrassed.

"I'm like the guy you work for." He winks.

Like Richard. Like Adair Holden. Dysmorphic, but with no AFs. John's eyes only stand out because they're beautiful—a soft, amber brown. "Sorry."

"No worries. You're welcome to take in the sights."

He's waiting for her to speak. She bites her lip, then, "Is he all right?"

"He's fine. I'll let him know you were asking." He waits again. When she doesn't speak, he says, "Anything else, Marlowe?"

Her breath catches. That's all she really needs to know, isn't it? She can walk away now, can't she? Go home. Go back to her life...

"I want to help." She says it, but her lips feel numb.

"He'll be glad to hear that." He pushes off of her car.

"So what do I do?"

"I'm going to tell you without telling you, okay?"

"What?" But suddenly, she knows. She knows where she has to go next, the name of the person she's going to meet. It's in her mind, like a blink message appearing on her Lens.

John is telepathic.

"You got it?" he asks.

"Yeah..."

"Oh, here." He goes into his front pocket, pulls out a thin piece of metal, like a flatter version of an old flash drive. "Put this under your steering wheel. Whenever you come to meet with us, turn it on. Do not forget."

"What is it?"

"Tracker-blocker."

She stares at it. She's never seen one before. "These are... expensive. Really expensive."

He winks again, hands it to her. "Don't lose it."

She holds on to it so tightly the corners dig into her palm.

"And don't lose this either." He takes a cam collar from his other pocket.

"I won't," she says as he puts it in her hand.

"Or this." He holds a Lens out to her. "Burner Lens. One-way. Only use it if you need to set up a meeting, okay? Then we'll hit you back on your real Lens."

"Okay."

"We used to have a guy. He could make your Lens untraceable, but..."

She thinks for a moment. "Liam Aldrich."

He puts his hands in his pockets again, nods. "Yeah."

"I'm so sorry. I really am."

"Thanks." It's quiet for a long moment between them, then John says, "Okay. The next thing you're not going to like."

"What do you mean?"

"When you get in your car you're not going to remember me, not my face, not my name. You'll know that you met someone, that you can trust them and that they told you what to do next. But that's it."

"Why?" She's frightened now, takes a step back, as if she can protect herself from his telepathy by widening the distance between them.

"I don't know you, Marlowe. You might go home and change your mind. I've got to protect myself."

"I won't tell anyone."

"I don't know that." He sighs. "Look, I'm going to do it whether you want me to or not. It just makes it easier for me if you don't fight it."

Everything he's saying makes sense. He's right to do it.

She nods. "Okay."

"You won't really feel anything."

"Okay." She opens the car door, turns back to him. "If everything works out—if you guys, you know, decide to trust me or whatever—can I have it back?"

John steps up to her, extends his hand. His grip is strong, but gentle at the same time. "I'll even tell you my real name."

"Your real—" She feels like an idiot. Of course John Leonard isn't his name. "Right. Okay. Thanks."

"See you, Marlowe."

He closes her door for her. The first thing to disappear is the sound of his voice, then his name, then his smiling face. And he's gone.

"Who's gone?" she asks out loud. All she knows is that she met with someone she can't remember, but trusts for some reason, and that he or she has told her what she has to do next.

Whether she does it or not is entirely up to her.

༄

When Richard opens the door, his first impulse is to close it in the man's face. He resists it. "Agent Wynne."

"Hi, Richard." The agent smiles. "You're looking a lot better since the last time we saw each other."

"How can I help you, Mr. Wynne?"

"You could invite me in."

"Yes, I could." Richard doesn't move.

Wynne nods. "All right, I don't mind it here. It's a nice day."

"What do you want?" He tries to control his heart rate, his breathing. He doesn't want this man to see how much his presence is affecting him.

"I'm here to talk to Sierra Marlowe."

"Dad, who is it?" When Dairen sees the agent, his face darkens. "What the hell do you want?"

Agent Wynne gives Richard an approving nod. "Nice kid."

"What do you want with Sierra?" Richard asks.

"Sierra?" Dairen steps closer to the door. "Unless you've got some kind of warrant or something, you're not talking to any of us. Dad, just close the door."

Richard gives his son a warning look. But Agent Wynne steps in. "No, he's right, Richard. I just thought I'd give Sierra the opportunity to explain herself without getting too official about it." He extends his hand. "As a courtesy to you, Richard."

He's thinking of that small, warm room. That feeling of being trapped clamps down like a fist squeezing his heart. It's degrading to feel like this in his own home, to feel so small. And to think, if he wanted to—and a part of him does—he could literally throw Agent Wynne into the street without lifting a finger. "I think you should leave, Mr. Wynne."

"Can I at least get a glass of water before I go?" He clears his throat. "I'm feeling kind of parched."

The pain in his chest, that buildup of furious anger, is almost intolerable. "Dairen," he says, without looking away from Wynne, "please get the agent a glass of water."

"Dad—"

"Please." As Dairen walks away, Richard sees Sierra's car pull up the street.

℃

Sierra feels sick when she sees the agent, almost drops her bag as she walks up the path to the house.

"Miss Marlowe." Wynne greets her warmly, holds out his hand. "Just the person I was looking for. Jamie Wynne, Department of Dysmorphic Affairs and Terrorism."

Her sickness gives way to the hate she had for this man the first time she saw him. She looks at his hand like it's a poisonous snake. "What's he doing here?" she says to Richard, but keeps her eyes on Wynne.

"He wants to talk to you, Sierra."

"About what?"

The agent gives her that same mocking smile he did at the station. "I think you know. So, if you don't mind coming with me to answer a few questions...?"

"I do mind." Sierra walks past him, past Richard, into the house. Dairen is there, a glass of water in his hand. She stands beside him. "I don't have anything to say to you."

"I think you do," Wynne says.

"And I think you have your answer, Mr. Wynne. Now, please," Richard takes the glass from Dairen, "drink your water and leave my home."

Wynne takes the water, sips it. "It wouldn't take long, Sierra. I just want to ask you a few questions about Adair Holden."

"Sierra doesn't know anything about Adair Holden," Dairen says.

"Then why has she been visiting him in prison?" The agent drinks calmly, looks at Sierra. "What was it? Three or four times?"

"What the hell are you talking about?" Dairen is almost shouting now.

Wynne ignores him. "I wonder what the two of you had to discuss."

Richard turns. "Sierra?"

She's been dreading the moment they would find out about her visits with Holden. But now that it's happened, she doesn't care. It doesn't matter. She walks up to the agent. He's still smiling. "First of all, it's none of your business what I talk about with anyone. And second, do you really think I didn't know I was being recorded the whole time? If you'd heard anything incriminating, I would be under arrest. And I'm not under arrest, am I, Agent Wynne?"

"No, you're not, Miss Marlowe."

"Then you should leave. Now."

He looks at Richard. "She's good. But I'm better." His eye focuses on his Lens, moves rapidly. "If you all don't mind putting your Lenses on? I've just forwarded you a warrant for the arrest of Nina Harrison. I believe she's a resident here?"

"*What?*" Richard cries.

"You can't do that!" Sierra says at the same time.

He tilts his head. "No, I'm pretty sure I can."

Sierra flips her eyepiece down, sees the warrant.

Wynne turns, waves his hand. Two people in tailored suits exit a car and start up the path. "Those are some friends of mine from social services. If you'll excuse me?"

He pushes past her. Sierra chases him up the stairs. "No, stop!"

Dairen and Richard are right behind her. Before they reach the top of the stairs, they hear Nina scream and Ben start to cry. Agent Wynne walks out of Nina's room, the baby wailing in his arms, Nina clawing at the back of his jacket. "Ben! Ben!"

"You can't do this!" Richard reaches for the baby.

Wynne shoulders him aside, starts down the steps. One of the social workers takes Ben. Nina screams again, pushes past Agent Wynne with all her strength. He grabs her arms. She struggles against him, frees herself, punches him in the face.

"Nina! No!" Sierra yells to her, but Nina is blind and deaf to everyone but Ben.

Before any of them realize what he's doing, Wynne unhooks his prod and jabs it hard into Nina's back. She cries out, turns on the agent, her teeth bared, eyes wild. He prods her again. She collapses. He rolls her onto her stomach, pins her down, straddles her, restrains her hands.

"Nina Harrison, you are under arrest for endangering the welfare of a minor. And I guess we can add assaulting a DDAT agent to the charges. You have the right to remain—"

"Endangering the welfare of a minor?" Richard cries. "What are you talking about?"

"Got a few parolees living here, don't you, Richard? That's not too good for the moral welfare of a child, is it?"

"Are you *insane*?"

"I'll go!" Sierra shouts. "I'll go with you! I'll go with you! Please, Agent Wynne, I'll go with you!"

"No, Sierra, this is fucking crazy!" Dairen holds her wrist.

She pulls out of his grip, kneels on the floor in front of the agent. "I'll go with you. I'll do whatever you want. Please!" Nina is starting to hyperventilate. She's panicking. Sierra hears a distant scream in her head; it's Nina from the past, a horrible memory.

He bends her over the bed, yanks up her skirt. She hears him undo his belt, unzip his pants. He presses her hard into the mattress. She's smothered by the covers. She can't breathe...

"Get off her!" Sierra begs. "Get off! Please!"

The agent looks from her to Nina.

"Please!" she says again. "Look at her! Please! I'll do whatever you say!"

He waits a moment longer before uncuffing Nina and nodding to the social workers. He stands. Nina pushes herself to her feet. She limps over to Ben, who is red-faced, reaching for his mother. She grabs him, holds him tight to her, kneels in a far corner of the hallway and cries and cries. But behind the tears, there's a feral look in her shining, terrified eyes that Sierra's never seen before.

"Agent Wynne, this kind of coercion can't be legal!" Richard says.

The agent gets to his feet, brushes off the knees of his pants. "Morally reprehensible, maybe, but not illegal. Nice try though. Miss Marlowe?" He looks to Sierra. "Shall we?"

Sierra stares at the man. He took a baby from his mother's arms just to prove a point. And no one will ever know. "You're so cruel," she says quietly, looking into his blue eyes, in awe of his cheerful callousness. "You're so cruel..."

She expects the smile, but it doesn't come. Wynne's gaze hardens at the word "cruel." She sees his eyes flit to Nina, curled up in the corner, silent now, that same wildness in her stance and eyes. "Let's go." He nods to the door.

"We're right behind you, Sierra," Dairen says as she passes.

She gives him a small smile. He is no more reassured by it than she is.

☙

Agent Wynne lowers his window, looks over at Sierra sitting next to him. He taps the steering wheel, sighs, finally says, "None of that would've happened if you'd just cooperated, you know."

"You don't have to explain. I understand." Sierra is thinking of Adair Holden, of his calmness even when speaking of the most horrible things; remembers his steady eyes, his controlled fury. *What do facts matter when fear and hatred come into play?* She feels a strange stillness now, can't explain it, but it's there, as if he is here in the car with her. "How long will this take?"

"That depends on you."

"I'll answer any questions you have. I don't have anything to hide." She lies so easily. She's fearless, suddenly, and more than that, she's completely unfazed by what's happening. Wasn't it only two months ago that she sat on a couch with Richard, lost control of herself as Kenny Layton attacked her, exposed her secret on national television? She was never more frightened in her life than on that day. How much worse is it to be in a car with a DDAT agent on her way to discuss her conversations with an escaped terrorist? And yet, she feels nothing.

At the station, they put her in a small room with a metal table and an uncomfortable chair. Probably the same one Richard was put in. It's unpleasantly warm, so she removes her jacket, lays it across her lap. Wynne takes a Cube out of his pocket, calls up a vid file.

"Why did you visit Adair Holden?"

"I had to ask him a question."

"About what?"

"We can just watch the vid."

"I want you to tell me."

She takes a breath. "My telepathy allows me to see other people's memories. I can't always control it. At Hammond, during the fight, I saw a small part of one of Mr. Holden's memories. It was disturbing and I wanted to know more about it."

"What was the memory?"

"A death. A woman he knew named Tanya Riggs."

Wynne sits across from her, leans back lazily. "Are you aware that Adair Holden is wanted in the UK for questioning regarding the murder of Francis Harold, the man convicted of the murder of Tanya Riggs?"

"No."

"He didn't tell you?"

"You know he didn't."

"Did you ask him?"

"I asked him what he did after Tanya died. He didn't answer."

"Do you think he had anything to with Mr. Harold's death?"

"I have no idea."

Wynne raises an eyebrow. "It must have crossed your mind."

"It didn't." All she can think about is going home, seeing Nina, holding Ben. But she won't let herself be upset. She knows they could keep her here for hours, like they did Richard; ask her the same questions over and over again. But what the agent doesn't know is how strong his heartlessness has made her; it's inspired her in a way. She can tell he's a little put off. He didn't expect her to be as detached as he is himself.

Wynne turns the Cube on and lets it play.

"*Who was she?*" Sierra listens to herself ask. "*What was she like? Why was she so special to you?*"

"*It's... very hard for me to talk about,*" Holden says.

She watches Holden and herself stare at each other as he gives her the memory of Tanya in his office after her baby died. In the vid, nothing appears to happen, just a long silence between the two of them. Then Sierra is watching herself cry.

"What happened here?" Wynne says.

"Nothing more than what you just saw."

"Why are you crying?"

She shrugs. "I was upset."

"About what?"

"The memory affected me badly. It's why I came back to see him again."

He eyes her. He's trying to intimidate her. She feels nothing. "Cube, forward," he says.

"But did she love him, too? Did he at least have that?" she is asking Holden.

"Cube, pause. Do you remember this conversation?"

"Yes. It was about Liam Aldrich."

"Why did you want to know about him?"

She folds her hands on the table, tries to get more comfortable in the chair. It's impossible. "Memories come up usually because the situation you're in reminds you of something. I wanted to know why the memory of Tanya came up at the rally."

"Why?"

"Curiosity. Context."

"You seemed upset by the end of the conversation."

"I was. I felt sorry for Liam Aldrich and for Mr. Holden."

He has a glint in his eye, like he thinks he's getting to something important, something to justify his suspicions about her. "You felt sorry for a terrorist and a rapist."

"Yes. I'm capable of empathy. No one is born a terrorist or a rapist."

"That's debatable."

"It's not, actually. And being emotional, as far as I know, isn't a crime."

"Helping a felon escape from prison is."

"I would hope so."

He raises an eyebrow, taps his finger on the table twice. "Cube, rewind... Play."

"Good and evil? Morality and immorality?" Holden is saying. *"Those are easy words for the self-righteous to bandy about. But we know better."*

Wynne pauses the vid. "What's he talking about?"

"Francis Harold was convicted of involuntary manslaughter, not murder. He said that he defended himself when Tanya Riggs attacked him. But Mr. Holden believed that Tanya's death was intentional murder and not an act of self-defense."

"And you agreed with him?"

"Yes."

"Why?"

"After he told me about it, I looked up more information on the case. I found articles and a transcript of the trial. There was so much evidence against Francis Harold, and it was pretty obvious that the jury's verdict was just a reflection of their own prejudice. It was disgusting."

"You know what?" Wynne leans forward, crosses his arms on the table. "I don't think that's what he's talking about. I think you're lying to me."

"If I lied about anything, you'd know it. It's all on the vid. Every word we said to each other."

"But you're telepathic. He could have told you something without speaking to you."

"I don't pathspeak. I see memories."

"Right. Seems like kind of a... useless ability to me."

She says nothing.

Wynne's hands are red and rough. They make her wonder what else he is, besides a DDAT agent. A husband? A father? Does he work outside? Does he keep the lawns and gardens around his house neat and tidy? Does he play with his kids on the swing set he built for them in the back yard?

He tells the Cube to fast forward.

"Liam wasn't a good person, Sierra," Holden says. *"And neither am I. You understand that, don't you? It's important that you do."*

"I don't think you're a bad person. And I didn't know Liam."

"Cube, pause. You don't think Adair Holden is a bad person?"

She looks into his eyes. She should be so afraid of him, but she isn't. "No, I don't. What he did may have been wrong, but he did it for the right reasons. He feels the same way about Hammond as I do."

"You know, Ms. Marlowe, I appreciate your honesty, but you do realize you're digging yourself into a hole here, right?"

The metal table is warm and greasy. She remembers the window that separated her from Adair Holden, all those lonely fingerprints. "Here's what I know, Agent Wynne. This country is fucked up, and it gets more fucked up by the day, but until someone decides otherwise, my freedom to think and feel isn't a crime. If there was anything on this vid that proved I helped Adair Holden escape, I would be in Hammond Prison myself right now."

She has him and he knows it. There's just enough emotion in his eyes to tell her how confused and angry he is by her demeanor, by his inability to intimidate her, and she's glad.

When she's finally allowed to leave, he tells her that he has his eyes on her and warns her not to leave the state.

Holden comes to mind again, and she's gladder than ever that he escaped, that he got away from men like Agent Jamie Wynne. She's not sure what makes her do it, but she pauses before she exits, turns to him, extends her hand and says, "Have a good night,

Agent Wynne."

His mouth opens in surprise. He doesn't move for a moment, then he takes her hand. There's a look of grudging admiration in his eyes. "I won't say it's been a pleasure."

"No. But I'm sure we'll see each other again."

He nods. "Count on it."

એ

"Nina?"

She's sitting on her bed, back against the wall, cross-legged, cradling a sleeping Ben in her arms. Her face is expressionless, but her eyes are glazed and red. Dairen told Sierra that she won't let anyone near Ben, hasn't put him down since Sierra left.

"You're back." Her tone is flat.

Sierra sits on the edge of the bed. "What can I do for you?" She touches her knee.

Nina won't look at Sierra.

They sit in silence for what feels like a long time, then Nina takes a deep, trembling breath. Fresh tears come to her eyes. "They could do it, couldn't they?"

"Do what?"

"Take him from me."

She wants to say no, wants to tell her that that will never happen. "We would fight it every step of the way."

"Am I an unfit mother?"

"No!" She tries not to cry herself. She thinks of Tanya, can't imagine the grief, the pain of losing a child. "No. You're the best mother... I've never known anyone who took better care—Nina, I'm so sorry."

Nina looks at her at last, her tiger eyes narrowed. She speaks slowly, every word sharp and clear. "I will kill anyone—*every-*

one—that tries to take him from me. I will *kill* them, Sierra."

Sierra nods. Nina's eyes burn right through her heart. "I know."

"He's *mine*. He's *my* son."

"I won't let anything happen to him, either. I promise."

The fire goes out of Nina's eyes and they widen suddenly, as if she's just remembered something important. "Oh my God! They could've hurt you! They could've put you in prison!"

Sierra shakes her head. "I didn't care."

"They could've hurt you! Like Layla…"

"I'm okay. No one hurt me. And no one is going to hurt you or Ben."

Nina shakes the tears from her eyes, blinking them away. "I want to put something in digi. An official eForm, witnessed and… whatever. If anything happens to me, you take Ben. You and Mr. Corbin and Dairen. Can we do that? Tomorrow?"

Sierra wants to believe that what she's just told Nina is the truth—that no one will ever hurt her or Ben. Adair Holden's words echo in her mind: *But we know better.* The rally, Kenny Layton, Tanya's murder, Richard's interrogation and her own, Rico Martinez—anything could happen. To any one of them. To all of them.

"Okay," she says. "We'll go to Richard's lawyer tomorrow."

"You promise?"

"Yes."

"Okay." Nina's eyes soften; her shoulders relax. She leans her head against the wall behind her. "Okay."

Sierra pushes herself farther back on the mattress to sit next to Nina. "Will you let me hold him? Your arms must be killing you."

Nina looks down at Ben, then up at her, bites her lip and nods. "I can't feel them anymore." She laughs a little, but when more tears spill down her cheeks, Sierra starts crying too.

As she takes Ben from Nina, his eyes flutter open briefly, but he doesn't wake. And again, she finds herself envying him. Safe in his own ignorance. She would keep him that way forever if she could.

When was the last time she felt safe? Has she ever?

And there again is Adair Holden's voice: *None of us should sleep.*

❧

He tells her that she should have come to him, that he could have answered her questions.

She tries to explain that he couldn't have answered her questions even if he knew the answers. Richard isn't telepathic, can no more imagine the intricacies of the human mind than she can lift a chair without touching it. The same muscle, perhaps, the brain, but two separate parts that are complete mysteries to each other.

She needed to hear Adair Holden's story from Adair Holden, she tells him. Because a story, a memory, isn't just the facts involved, but the emotions. Hearing about Tanya from Richard would have been secondhand, and she needed the original.

"Why did you keep going back?" he asks her.

"I just... had to."

He can't get any more out of her than that, not yet anyway. She needs to think, needs to be quiet.

"Please don't be angry, Richard."

"I'm not. I'm not." He sighs. "I'm just trying to understand."

"I don't understand it myself, for the most part. But..." She looks at him, into his eyes. "I'm different. This memory... it's changed me. I feel..."

"Sierra, you know the memories often have that effect. It'll wear away in time."

"No, there's something... more. I can't explain it. I *feel*... different."

Richard folds his hands on his lap. "I'm worried for you now, Sierra. Truly worried. Agent Wynne is a bloodhound."

She shakes her head. "He's amazing, isn't he?"

"Wynne? How do you mean?"

"I mean... isn't it amazing that someone can be that cruel and just..." she opens her hands, "walk around every day? Go to work? Eat lunch? Be... human."

"I suppose it is, yes."

"He doesn't scare me, Richard."

"He should."

Suddenly, Sierra sees blue and red lights in her mind, flashing through a curtain from some other place and time, sees them through eyes that aren't hers. She's in Richard's mind now, in a room, looking out a window at British police vehicles as they pull up and park in front of the house.

"You've done all this already," she says, still in the memory. "Suffered because of his choices."

"Yes, I have." The Richard from long ago looks through the curtains at the flashing lights in a memory twelve years old, and Sierra can feel his fear and sadness.

The memory fades away. "You could have told the police, back in England; you could have told them what you knew."

"No, I couldn't." He looks into her eyes. "He was my friend. My best friend. And..." He pauses, looks away, says slowly, "I didn't want him to be punished for doing..." When he turns his gaze back to Sierra, he has tears in his eyes. "For doing what I couldn't."

His sadness is still inside her, still echoing down the paths of her mind. She puts her hand on his arm.

"Francis Harold should have been put in prison for life," he says. "He would have killed again. I know that. I knew it then. I was afraid for all our residents. Dair..." He swallows, quickly wipes his eyes. "Dair did a terrible thing, against his own nature, to save us. And I... Well, you saw him, Sierra. You spoke with him. You've looked inside his mind. He's not... evil."

"He thinks he's a bad person."

Richard's eyes fill again.

"He told me that there are bad people like him and good people like you. He said that, when the fighting is over, and everything seems hopeless... people like you will save us."

Richard's hands come up to cover his face. "Oh, God."

And now she's sitting in a plush chair, looking up at a younger Adair Holden.

"Where are you going?" Richard asks, full of fear.

"I don't know," Adair tells him.

"Please..."

The Richard in this memory won't see Adair Holden for another twelve years, can't fathom that the next time they meet will be infinitely worse than this.

She never knew. Sierra never knew that Richard was carrying so much pain.

"Richard..." She puts her arm around his shaking shoulders, takes his hand. "I'm sorry. I'm so sorry."

Chapter 17

ADAIR STARES at the Cube. He feels ridiculous. He asked Layla to leave; he couldn't stand having an audience. She protested, but finally gave in, kissing him, saying, "Hurry up. I'm waiting for you upstairs."

"You don't have to wait, hummingbird," he said to her.

She smiled, shook her head. "This is the right thing to do, Dair." She kissed him again, said, "I'm waiting for you," and left the room.

He locked the door behind her, sat at his desk, has been staring at the Cube for twenty minutes. He wrote down what he wanted to say, finding it easier, as always, to get his thoughts and feelings out with pen and paper.

He wrote Layla a love letter once. She laughed when he gave it to her, said, "You're so twentieth century, Dair!" But he knows she keeps it in her bedside drawer and reads it at night sometimes when she thinks he's asleep.

She's waiting for him upstairs.

He waited for her all his life.

He'll do this, he decides, for her, because she wants him to and because it's possible that she's right. Maybe people do need to hear what he has to say. Maybe he does need to tell them.

Adrenaline makes his legs tremble. Somehow, this is more difficult than tearing down a concrete wall. He takes a deep breath.

"Cube, record."

Venus's hands start to shake. She hears Cash's voice as if from a distance.

"I like this." He holds up a shirt. "What do you think?"

The sounds of the mall become muted, drowned out by the noise inside her head. She stares into her Lens at the vid she's just downloaded. The message it came in has vanished completely, but she's not thinking about that now.

"Vee. Are you paying attention? Hello?"

"Shut up!"

"Hey!" He lowers the shirt. "You're the one who said I needed new clothes."

"Shut up!" She stands. "Shut up shut up shut up!" She jams her Lens onto his face, loops it over his ears.

"What the hell, Vee?"

"Shut up! Lens! Play vid!"

"What—" He freezes. He listens. His eyes widen. He reaches out blindly for her, and she grabs his hand. He squeezes it painfully, but she's squeezing his just as hard, her other hand covering her mouth. She bounces on the balls of her feet, waiting for him to finish watching. It takes forever.

Finally, his eyes focus on her. "Is this real?"

She nods rapidly.

"Oh my God..."

She clutches his arm.

"Oh my God!" he shouts.

She can't hold back anymore. She screams into her hand. Cash lets out a loud, laughing cry and they're jumping up and down and then hugging each other.

"Is there a problem here?" A uniformed security guard approaches them. He looks disdainfully at Venus, then at Cassius. "Is she bothering you, sir?"

Cash is still smiling. "What? No. We're fine."

The guard raises an eyebrow, a suspicious look on his face.

"It's okay." Cash's smile is fading. "We're friends."

The guard looks back and forth between them. Venus feels a hot anger replace all the excitement she was feeling only moments ago as she watches the man's face fill with disgust.

"I'm going to have to ask you both to leave," he says.

Her mouth drops. "What? Why? We didn't do anything!"

His gaze hardens and she sees his hand hovering over his zProd. "I'm not going to ask you again."

Venus is too furious to be afraid. "What the fuck—"

Cash puts his arm around her shoulders suddenly and directs her past the guard. "We're leaving. We're leaving." He hurries her out the door and down the walkway until they're well past the store.

Venus shrugs roughly out of his hold. "What the hell, Cash? I'm not a kid!"

"Don't fight me, Vee," he says, his face unusually serious. "We just got the best story of our lives. Let's just stay with that, okay?"

Venus crosses her arms, looks away from him, her eyes taking in the passersby and the obnoxious, myriad stores. But the sounds and sights around her fade, replaced by a painful memory.

She and Cash were interviewing Miles Quinn, a well-known pro bono lawyer and dysmorphic human rights activist. Quinn was a short man with glasses, a slight paunch, and a round, earnest face. He wasn't dysmorphic himself, but he'd been working hard for dysmorphic people most of his career.

They were discussing the issue of discrimination.

"Well, the truth is, it's not illegal," Quinn said.

"Discriminating against dysmorphic people is legal?" Venus asked.

"In a sense. It's a tidy loophole that we're trying to close."

"Can you explain the loophole?"

"It's simple, really. When it comes to things like school, jobs, or housing, the law states that a person can't be discriminated against based on race, orientation, or disability."

"Right."

"Well, dysmorphic people aren't a race or an orientation. And dysmorphia can hardly be called a disability." He opened his hands, shrugged. "And there's your loophole. As a result, dysmorphic people end up in the poorest schools and mostly low-level jobs. And because of housing discrimination, most dysmorphic people are forced to live in..." She remembers how he hesitated there, but that the uncertain look on his face was brief, fading into a resolute one. "They're forced to live in ghettos."

Venus always admired Miles Quinn, but worried for him. It was that type of declaration that brought on the numerous death threats he received every day. "You're a very brave man, Mr. Quinn," she said.

"Oh, no, Ms. Carr. No. I'm not." There was no false modesty in that statement. He gestured to her and Cassius in turn. "That distinction goes to you and Mr. Belle."

She was embarrassed by his words, coming from a man who'd dedicated his life to helping people like her, and more often than not at the expense of his own safety.

He saved her from having to reply. "We're reliving history here, Ms. Carr, as I'm afraid we're doomed to do in every generation. That said," he smiled; she'll always remember that smile, "the generation of women's rights saw women get the vote; the generation of civil rights saw the end of segregation; the gay rights generation saw the legal marriage of gay couples. My hope is that this generation will see the acceptance of dysmorphic people as fellow human beings."

And for a brief moment, Venus was filled with an unfamiliar sense of hope. She wanted to believe him, wanted what he said to be true.

But she didn't believe him. She was afraid to—afraid to be drowned in despair when all the hopes that had left her vulnerable were destroyed by the reality of life. She's always believed that it's safer to build walls against hope, to instead keep going without the expectation of results, so as not to be crushed by what actually happens.

And three days after the interview, she was glad for her walls. Because three days later, she and Cash were on site outside Miles Quinn's office, where he'd been shot and killed only an hour before.

Her thoughts are broken into by Cassius's excited, but very low voice. "Vee. We just got contacted by Adair fucking Holden!"

She looks up at him. "Do you remember Miles Quinn?"

Cash's eyes lose all their vibrancy. "Yeah. Of course I do."

Venus can see the bloodstain on the pavement outside Quinn's office as clearly as she can see Cassius now.

And Cassius, as always, sees right through her. He pulls her into a hug. "We don't have to hope," he says. "We've just got to keep going."

She wraps her arms tightly around him. "He said we were brave. You remember?"

"Yeah."

"I don't feel brave."

She feels Cassius shrug. "Hey. Fake it till you make it, right?"

☙

"What was he like?"

Sierra rests against Dairen's shoulder. He wraps his arm around her, kisses the top of her head. "He was... strong."

"Strong?"

"Yes. He wasn't afraid. He talked to me like we were... sitting together in a restaurant or something. He was... dignified. And honest. But sad." She tilts her head to see his face. "Everything he said made me wonder if... maybe he did the right thing, Dairen. He saved people's lives."

"Some people died."

"People die in wars."

"Are we talking about war now?"

She sighs. "I don't know."

Dairen rubs her arm up and down. They sit quietly. The muted Cube projects a news program.

"Dairen—don't you think wars have been fought for lesser reasons than what's happening now? People enslaved and experimented on? Being forced to register themselves if they're dysmorphic? Institutionalized racism?"

"Hey." He sits up suddenly. "Cube, unmute."

Sierra turns, sees Adair Holden's face.

A news anchor talks over the image. "—speech aired earlier today on a dysmorphic Cube channel known as *Phenomena*. In it, Mr. Holden refers to humanity as a 'virus' and himself as a 'superior human.'"

A still image of Holden fills the Cube, accompanied by his voice. "Humanity is a virus on this planet. I am a dysmorphic human. I am a superior human. I have adapted to the willful mistakes of my own species. I can breathe our filthy air, drink our vile water, fight the diseases that should be killing me."

The anchor reappears. "Mr. Holden went on to describe Hammond Prison as a 'blight upon this nation' and he encouraged dysmorphic people to let their Registration ID numbers expire and to resist police."

Again, Holden's pic is there. "Diplomacy is too slow. Fight for yourselves. Resist arrest. Let your Registration Identification numbers expire. I will fight for all of you in every way that I can. I swear it."

It all sounds wrong. It's aggressive and threatening, and she can't imagine that Adair Holden would call himself a "superior human."

Dairen looks confused, and it's as if he's read her mind. "There's something wrong with this," he says. "Why aren't they showing the vid? I mean, it must be a vid, right? Why would he do a voiceover?"

"And I'm sure it's been edited. It doesn't sound like him. It's got to be out of context."

"Cube, change, *Phenomena*, vid file archives," Dairen says. Among the vid file selections on Venus Carr's Cube channel is a piece called "Adair Holden Speaks Out." Dairen chooses it.

Venus Carr appears at her desk, an image of Holden beside her. She introduces herself and briefly describes the speech they're about to hear. "It was enclosed in a message we received today from an unknown source and it is the first time we'll be hearing from Mr. Holden directly. Here is the speech in its entirety."

The vid begins, showing Holden sitting at a desk, a shelf of books behind him. Sierra watches as he takes a breath, then:

"It has been said, perhaps too often and without a true understanding of its meaning, that we are a free people.

"And what have we done? We have used our freedom to destroy our environment, pollute its air and waters, its soil. Humanity is a virus on this planet and, like a virus, we are killing our host.

"And yet, despite this, nature has decided that humanity is worth at least a chance to survive. Dysmorphic people are that chance.

"Mutation is random and often cruel, but in this case, it seems that nature is throwing every possible mutation at our species in an attempt to save it.

"And what have we done? We have sneered at it, aborted it, fought it. We are afraid of it.

"I am a dysmorphic human. I am not a superior human. I have merely adapted to the willful mistakes of my own species. I can breathe our filthy air, drink our vile water, fight the diseases that should be killing me.

"We are a foolish species, ignorant of our *selves*, of our place in the world. How many species of insect, animal, and plant have gone extinct as a direct result of our ignorance? How much damage have we done to this world, to ourselves? We have thought ourselves superior to our fellow creatures. And now nature, in its infinite irony, has given us wings, fur, cat eyes, snake eyes, fangs, talons, and paws, as if to remind us that we are not separate, as if to forcibly pull us back into itself, and make us one with it again.

"And what have we done? We have laughed at it, beaten it, experimented on it, abused it, killed it. We have fought against our own chance at survival.

"It has been said that none of us are free until all of us are equal. And if this is true, then we are not a free people. We are an enslaved people. Enslaved by our hate and our ignorance.

"It has also been said that freedom is not free. Freedom is bought by blood and war. Hammond Prison, and places like it, are a blight upon this nation, where men and women are treated like animals, experimented on like animals.

"I am not a superior human. I am not a violent man. I freed the prisoners from Hammond to save them from ending up like Rico Martinez. I freed them because diplomacy is too slow. I freed them to show the world that I will not stand back and witness the abuse of fellow dysmorphic people and neither should any one of us.

"Fight for yourselves. Fight for each other. Defend your friends and strangers alike. Resist arrest. Let your Registration Identification numbers expire. They will threaten you. They will hurt you. But do not let them take away your dignity and your right to be free.

"And I swear that I will fight for all of you in every way that I can.

"I swear it."

The vid ends. Carr starts talking again, but Sierra isn't paying attention. Her eyes are hot and her throat feels full. Tears fall down her face. She sees Adair Holden's hand touching hers against the glass...

But it's Dairen's hand that touches hers now. "Sierra?"

She looks at him. "He's right, Dairen. He's right about everything."

♋

"It's Leonard, isn't it?" a voice calls.

August is just about to get into his car to leave for the day. He turns and sees Dr. Kovich leaning against the wall by the door, tapping a cigarette pack against her wrist. "Yes, ma'am."

She beckons him with a gesture.

As he walks up to her, his gaze drifts down to her shoes. The red heels are so incongruous with her austere, dark clothes, white jacket and tightly pulled back hair.

She sees him looking. "I know. They're ridiculous."

"No, ma'am." He smiles, moving to stand next to her. "I like them. They stand out."

She draws a cigarette from the pack. "They help me remember that I'm not just," she gestures to her lab coat, "this. Sometimes I don't go home for days and I forget." She lights the cigarette between her lips, inhales deeply, closes her eyes. "Sometimes I think I'll quit." The smoke trails from her mouth as she speaks. "But I figure by the time it starts to be a real problem for me, we'll have the solution."

"From the d-form studies?"

She wags her finger at him. "Careful. The PC police could be watching."

He looks away. "Sorry, ma'am."

"I won't tell a soul." She offers him the pack. He takes one. She lends him her lighter.

"Thanks."

They smoke in silence for a bit, then, "I saw the vids from the breakout."

He tenses. His brain runs quickly over everything he can remember from that night. Did he make a mistake? Give himself away somehow? He takes a deep drag on his cigarette.

"You really handled yourself well."

His relief escapes in a long, smoky exhalation. "Just doing my job."

She shakes her head. "No. I watched you. You never panicked. Most of them did."

"I don't know about that."

"I do." She flicks the cigarette onto the ground, stamps it out with her bright, ostentatious shoe. It would be kind of sexy if she were any other woman, but when he looks at Kovich, all he can think of are Eden's panicked eyes.

He feels sick to his stomach when he's anywhere near this woman. Even this cigarette is making him feel ill, knowing it came from her pack, that she may have touched it. He forces himself to keep smoking it.

"How would you like another job, Leonard? What's your first name?"

"John. What kind of job?"

"Security," she says. "Better pay, better benefits. Interested?"

August's heart beats faster. "Very." He's been catching her eye every chance he gets, not speaking to her, just letting her know that he's there, putting into her mind that he's interesting; he might be someone she'd like to talk to. That she's offering him a job is a better outcome than he was aiming for.

She smiles, puts her hands in her pockets. "I'll pull your records, see if you'd be a good fit."

August taps into her brain to plant the thought that he would be the perfect fit for whatever she has in mind.

"You may or may not have noticed that I'm not the most popular person in the dysmorphic world."

He blows out a small laugh with his smoke. "I can imagine, ma'am."

"Well, it may be funny to you..."

He shakes his head. "No, ma'am. I—it was the way you worded it—I didn't mean—"

"Relax, Leonard. Give me a hit off your cigarette and I'll forgive you."

When he hands it to her, her fingers brush his. A crawling sensation creeps up his spine. Her lips leave a light pink mark at the top of the cigarette. She passes it back.

"You can finish it, Doctor."

"No, I just wanted one more puff."

His instinct is to throw it as far away from himself as possible. He puts it between his own lips, tries not to think about those pink stains.

"Anyway," Kovich goes on, "I'm used to death threats. But lately..." She crosses her arms in front of herself. "I need protection. The powers that be insist. Especially after Holden's little holier-than-thou broadcast." She sniffs derisively, shaking her head.

"They want you to have bodyguards?"

She nods. "I insisted on picking my own people, though. They loved that. And I lied, by the way. I've already pulled your records." She looks at him. "So?"

August finishes the cigarette, exhales, crushes it under the toe of his boot. "When do I start?"

༄

"Ms. Carr."

The DDAT agent sits across from her at the nondescript metal table. Venus's hands are cuffed to the surface. They arrested her only a few hours after the broadcast. She's not sure exactly how they found her and Cash—she disabled the trailer's built-in tracker ages ago—but they're no strangers to the authorities and it's more likely than not a local cop saw their trailer and followed them discreetly until the DDAT agents could catch up.

"I'm Agent Jamie Wynne, Department of Dysmorphic Affairs and Terrorism. Sorry to keep you waiting." He gives her an insincere smile. "Busy day. You know how it is."

She remains silent.

"You've been pretty busy yourself these days, huh?"

Agent Wynne is a stocky man with brown eyes and hair. He has a ruddiness to his not-unhandsome face. It's the face of someone who's seen a lot and done a lot. He has a few small scars and one large one on the back of his hand. She wonders if he was in the military at some point. She wouldn't be surprised.

"Look," Wynne says. "I get it. You don't want to speak. You want to protect your source or... whatever. But we've got your Lens, your Cubes, your tableface. Everything. What are we going to find in them? It would be better for you if you told me now, and it would save us a hell of a lot of time."

"Do you have a warrant to take my things? To invade my

privacy?"

"Mmm." He tips his hand from side to side. "Sort of."

"Sort of? You either have one or you don't."

"Well, things are little different in the DDAT. We've got... I guess you could call it a warrant to get a warrant."

Anger wells up in her. "That's bullshit!"

"Whoa. Language, please."

"Fuck you."

He smiles again. One point, Agent Wynne, she thinks, ashamed of herself for losing control of her emotions.

"Back to my question. What are we going to find in your devices?"

"Porn."

He looks amused. "Is that right?"

"Yeah. Lots of it. The really kinky kind."

"Well, that ought to keep the boys in the lab entertained for a while." When she doesn't respond, he goes on. "Where'd you get the vid? Who sent it to you?"

"I don't know."

"Where did you get the vid?" he repeats slowly.

"I don't know."

"Who sent it to you?"

"I don't know."

In a split second, Wynne switches from lazily indifferent to intimidating. His whole demeanor changes—the way he's sitting, the look in his eyes, all traces of amusement gone. There's a sudden tension in his hands and arms. "Where did you get the vid? Who sent it to you?"

"I—"

He slams his hand down on the table. She flinches back and hates herself for it. "Say 'I don't know' again! Say it!"

She bites down, her jaw stiff, heart racing.

"Come on! Say it!"

Cash's voice comes into her mind. *Don't be proud, Vee. Pride cometh before the fall and all that shit.* "An anonymous message showed up on my Lens. I opened it. The vid was in it."

"That's an obsolete term, Ms. Carr. Anonymity doesn't exist anymore."

"I'm telling the truth. It was there, and as soon as I download-ed the vid, the message disappeared. You won't find any trace of it in any of my devices. I checked, and I know as much about IT as anyone in your department."

"That a fact?"

"Yes."

Wynne relaxes again. He folds his hands together, rests them on the table. He eyes her closely. "Are you telepathic? Telekinetic?"

"No."

"Seems kind of unfair."

She frowns. "Why?"

"Well, you know." He gestures to her, hand open. "All those AFs and no superpowers?"

She takes a small breath before answering. "I'm fine with who I am."

"And who are you, Ms. Carr?"

"I'm a reporter."

"Mm-hm." He drums his fingers on the table for a moment. "Pro-Holden? Anti-Holden?"

"Pro-information."

He nods admiringly. "Good answer. Me too." His voice is soft and even now. "What kind of information are we going to find on your devices?"

"Nothing you'd be interested in."

He's quiet for a long moment, then, "Do you have any idea what that broadcast has done? The trouble you've caused? Adair

Holden is a terrorist. He's the bad guy. And because of that little speech of his, the speech *you* broadcasted, we've got people all over the country protesting, rioting, hurting people, getting hurt themselves. That's on you, Ms. Carr."

"If people fighting for what's right is on me, I'm okay with that."

"So you're an activist now? What happened to objectivity? What happened to being pro-information?"

Venus feels like he's laying a trap for her, so she doesn't answer.

"Ms. Carr," he says calmly, conversationally, "do you know what I can do to you in the interest of getting information?"

Her stomach twists. "Yes."

"I don't even need to ask for permission. Did you know that?"

She's dedicated entire programs to the issue of Intensive Questioning, particularly regarding dysmorphic people, but this is the first time she's ever been threatened with it personally. "Yes."

"We could start right now, even." He says this like he's offering her a drink.

He'd probably start with sleep deprivation and heat. He might attach a World to her temple to confuse her as she gets more exhausted and dehydrated. He might bombard the room with discordant music or disturbing sounds next. And he'd keep her hands cuffed to the table; she thinks that might drive her crazier than anything. The last thing he'll do is inflict pain.

Or, it suddenly occurs to her, he might start with physical pain in an effort to get information out of her as quickly and efficiently as possible.

You won't do anybody any good if you get locked up, Vee. Or fucked up. You know that. Cash's voice again, speaking reasonably, rationally. "Okay."

"Okay what, Ms. Carr?"

"I'll make it easy on your tech guys."

"How exactly?"

"I'll give them all my passcodes. They can tear into my devices as much as they want and you'll see I'm telling the truth."

He thinks about this, then nods. "It's good start." He takes his Lens out of his jacket pocket, puts it on. "Go ahead. I'm listening."

ᔓ

"*Another* drink, my friend?"

Hawk's claws tip-tap across the porch as he emerges from the shadows at the other end. August didn't know he was out here, or he would've gone around to the back of the house to drink his whiskey alone. "What else have I got to do?"

Hawk smiles. "Eden is sitting in the living room... all by herself."

August nods. "Yes, she is."

Hawk leans his back against the porch railing, crosses his arms. "Not interested?"

"Didn't say that." August takes a slow sip of the whiskey.

"Leonard—"

"August."

He ignores the correction. "What the hell did you come home for, if not to see her?"

"To tell you guys about Kovich and the bodyguard thing."

He raises an eyebrow. "You could've blinked."

August rests the tumbler on the railing. "Can I just have a nightcap without the interrogation?"

"What are you afraid of?"

He wants to deflect, pretend he doesn't know what Hawk is talking about. But Hawk can read his mind, and even though he claims he won't do it without permission, August has his doubts. He sighs. "Look, man. Eden already met the love of her life. And he died. Okay?"

"Yes. Damian was kind enough to tell me about that. Something about how it was the best thing that could've ever happened to her?"

"Prick."

Hawk smiles. "I like him more by the day."

"You better watch yourself. He's not as big as you, but he's fucking fast."

He shrugs. "I'll take my chances." He watches August drink, then says, "There's room for more than one love in a life. And Eden's life isn't over."

August huffs a joyless laugh. "Jesus, man, that sounds like some kind of motivational ePoster."

"You know I'm right."

He doesn't answer, just drains his drink. Hawk steps forward, puts his hands on August's shoulders, and kisses him.

August blinks, stares at Hawk. "Dude. I don't swing that way."

"I know." He pats the side of August's face. "You're just so cute." He steps away, opens the front door.

"You got nice lips, though. I'll say that."

Hawk laughs. "You *should* swing my way, Leonard. I'd blow your mind."

"Sorry. I'm afraid I'm stuck on the lonely hetero side of the field."

"Your loss." Before he steps inside, he says, "You can do this, you know. This thing with Kovich. I have faith in you."

"You don't even know me, man."

"I think I just hinted that I'd like to get to know you."

"Hinted?"

Hawk smiles, says, "Subtlety isn't my strong suit," and goes inside.

August stares at the closed door for a moment, then laughs to himself. "I don't get any action for months and then I get kissed by a dude." He shakes his head. "Jesus Christ, August."

☙

"Turn right, here." Kovich points.

August does as she says, frowning. "We're not going to the prison?"

"Not today."

His heartbeat picks up and a thousand thoughts enter his mind, the most frightening that he's been found out, that Kovich is directing him into a trap, right to the DDAT. He gives the rear-view mirror a quick glance to make sure his face isn't giving away his apprehension.

Kovich isn't looking at him. "I'm going to be spending less and less time at Hammond, more at our second location."

"Second location?"

A small smile appears on her face as she nods. She turns to him. "It's much quieter. I think you'll like it."

It's only a half hour or so before she tells him to turn into a driveway. The building is small, unassuming, made of red brick with a flat top. It looks more like a warehouse than anything else. Like Hammond, it's separated from its nearby town by forestry and fields on three sides. Unlike Hammond, there's only one fence surrounding it and no guard towers. The sign at the foot of the driveway reads, in a cheerful blue font: *Freedom Laboratories*.

"Any relation to Freedom Pharmaceuticals?"

"Go to the head of the class," she says.

She tells him where to park. He opens her door for her, follows her to the entrance. Their IDs and bags are checked by security guards after they walk through two full-body scanners. The inside of the building doesn't match its outside. Past the entrance and the scanners is a large desk in the center of a wide, white lobby. Huge skylights let in the morning light, giving the building a bright, airy feel. Two sets of shining metallic staircases on either side of the lobby wind up to a second floor. It's early, but already the place is active.

The guard at the desk nods to her. "Morning, Dr. Kovich."

"Hey, Pete." She steps up to the desk, gestures to August. "This is John Leonard, my new tote bag."

The guard gives her a confused smile.

"Bodyguard," she clarifies. "Where I go, he goes."

Pete laughs. "Got it. Pleasure is mine, Mr. Leonard." They shake hands. "Peter Krill."

"Nice to meet you, Mr. Krill."

"Just Pete."

August nods.

"Okay, John," Pete says. "First things first. There are no Lenses, Worlds, Cubes, or holowatches allowed past this point, so..." He puts out his hand.

August gives him his Lens.

"I'll keep it safe." Pete smiles, then looks at Kovich. "You want me to show him the cameras, Doctor?"

"Please." She gestures for August to join Pete on the other side of the security station.

On Pete's desk is a MultiCube showing footage from all the cameras inside and outside the building. "They can be accessed from any wall- or tableface, if you've got the code. Which is..." He writes the security code onto his own tableface. "Can you memorize that?"

August nods. "I got it."

Pete erases the series of numbers and letters, then goes on to explain what each camera is looking at in more detail. August sees nothing remarkable in any of them: the entrance, the perimeter of the building, offices, hallways.

His confusion must show on his face, because Kovich touches his arm and says, "These don't show the fun stuff."

"Nope. That's a different department altogether," Pete says. "Any questions, John?"

He shakes his head. "No. It looks like you've got a pretty good setup here."

"We do. But we've got backup, too, in case anything goes wrong."

"Backup?"

Pete points to a black button at the right of the desk. "That's the FMB, the five-minute button. If that button isn't pushed every five minutes, the cavalry will be here in five minutes flat. I'm talking police, fire department, *and* military."

"Why not just have a military presence here at the lab?"

"We don't want to draw attention to ourselves," Kovich says. "Do we, Pete?"

Pete smiles. "No, ma'am."

"Well, if that's everything, me and my shadow need to head downstairs."

Pete shakes his hand again, and August thanks him.

The "fun stuff" is one floor down. On the elevator Kovich presses her thumb into a printlock to give them access.

"There aren't any cameras down here," she says as they descend, "not one. And we don't store anything digitally."

August frowns. "Nothing at all?"

"Nope. Good old-fashioned paper is the name of the game down here. We're very retro."

Ironic, August thinks, remembering the notebook Holden had him give Sierra Marlowe. "Paper can be destroyed," Holden said when August asked him about it. "But digi is forever."

Kovich puts her hand on his arm, whispers playfully, "We

even have a filing cabinet. Several, actually."

He ignores the way his stomach flips when she touches him, smiles. "This I've got to see."

The elevator opens, revealing another security station, and the screening process starts all over again: body scanner, ID inspection, bag search. Then they have to pass through a heavy metal door, maybe five inches thick, print- and retinalocked. Overkill, August thinks.

"Is it like this on every floor?" he asks as they walk down a short hallway.

"No, just ours. We added the extra scanner and the door after Hammond." She stops suddenly. "Although, when it comes to someone like Adair Holden, scanners are useless. Still," she keeps walking, "the law of averages states that there can only be so many Adair Holdens in the world. We're more worried about the DCo and their penchant for IEDs if this place ever gets on the public radar."

August frowns. "I thought Adair Holden was one of a kind. That's what they said on the news and at the prison."

The final door is also print- and retinalocked. "There's a reason you had to fingerprint all those eForms, John. We've known about NormForms for awhile now."

This amuses August, but confuses his alterego. "NormForms?"

The printlock confirms that Kovich is who she claims to be. She leans in close to the retinalock next. "That's our fun little name for Typically Featured Dysmorphic People."

"I like it." And he really does. He can't wait to tell Eden that he's a NormForm.

The retinalock identifies Kovich and the door slides open. August's amusement disappears in an instant. He forgot where he was for a moment, what he's doing here. He follows close behind Kovich into a huge open room, much like the lobby, but with no natural light since it's underground. People mill about in white coats, carrying clipboards and file folders. It's like stepping back in time, or walking into an old movie. There are computer banks in the center of the room, and a group of five long tables, one behind the other, with three to four computers on each one, but he's sure they're not linked to the Internet and maybe not even to each other. There are no table- or wallfaces or Cubes. No one is wearing a Lens or holowatch. It's as if the twenty-first century somehow skipped over Freedom Laboratories.

Lining the walls on both sides are separate, locked rooms, the interiors visible through thick sliding glass doors; a dozen in all, varying in size. In one of the larger rooms, a man lies on a slab, unconscious, hooked up to myriad machines, with tubes attached to his arms, neck, and leg, and fluids pumping in and out. Other people are in the smaller cells, like the ones at Hammond, furnished with a cot, a toilet, and sink. One of them is being examined by a scientist. He's taking some kind of skin sample while two others observe.

"You don't have a problem with blood, do you, Leonard? I guess I should've asked you that before hiring you."

Her voice is a distant echo, like someone calling out to him through a nightmare, trying to wake him. No... someone *in* a nightmare, trying to drag him back into sleep. "No, ma'am. No problem."

"Good. Oh, that reminds me." She reaches into her jacket pocket, takes out a small box, and hands it to him. "Present for you. Welcome to Freedom Labs."

He opens it. "HushPlugs?" He picks up one of the conical ear devices. "I thought you said it would be quiet here."

"Generally speaking, it is. But every now and then, it doesn't serve our purposes to anesthetize a subject." She shrugs. "Nothing a little noise cancellation can't take care of."

Screaming. She's talking about screaming. And how a "little noise cancellation" can block it out if it distracts the scientists from their work. As a d-form, August is strong enough to crush the HushPlug between his fingers, has to stop himself from doing it.

He puts the Plug back into its box, puts the box into his front pocket. "Thanks, Doctor."

"You're welcome, Leonard." She links her arm with his. "Come on. I'll show you around."

She introduces him to scientists and assistants, shows him the computers and other machinery around the lab. She takes particular pleasure in showing him the file room. The metal cabinets are huge, and there's rows and rows of them. For a moment, August stops thinking about his situation and finds himself amazed that all the information stored in this room is barely a breadcrumb compared to the amount of information that he has access to on his Lens. The idea of information being a physical thing—something he can hold and touch—is strange to him, like Holden's books.

Back out in the main room, she smiles at him. "So. What do you think?"

"To be honest, it's smaller than I thought it would be."

"We only bring the most fascinating subjects here. Not usually more than ten at a time. Hammond is like..." She thinks for a moment. "A filter."

"How long do you keep them here?"

"As long as they're interesting. A few weeks, months, a year."

August nods. "Okay."

A man walks over to Kovich. He has gray hair, light eyes, and a certain dignity to him that reminds him of Holden—until he gets close and August sees that it isn't dignity at all, but superiority, cold condescension. He has empty, icy eyes, not like Holden at all.

"Hello, Mara," he says to Kovich. He has a slight accent that August can't place. "New friend?"

He can tell Kovich is made uncomfortable by this man, but she hides it well. "Rhys, this is John Leonard. My *bodyguard*," she says with a quick roll of her eyes. "John, Rhys Weir, our resident Dr. Frankenstein."

Weir smiles at Kovich. "I'm flattered." He extends his hand to August. It's soft and strangely warm. "Thank you for keeping our dear Mara safe."

"My pleasure, Dr. Weir. Good to meet you."

"You might change your mind about that." He smiles again. "Most people do."

August doesn't know what to say to that.

Weir turns back to Kovich. "Mara, I wanted to ask you if I could raise Thirty-One's drug doses."

"You don't need my permission for that."

He hands her his clipboard. "Actually, I do. Thirty-One keeps getting accustomed to the doses. I need you to sign this so I can raise the levels past the maximum recommended."

"I've never had to do that before." She scans the form, pen in hand.

Weir looks pleased. "Thirty-One is fiercely resilient, amazingly adaptable." He looks at August, a sort of sparkle in his eyes. "He's my favorite. My special project."

Kovich signs it, hands it back to him. "Be careful, Rhys. I mean it."

"Always." Weir gives her a nod, a final smile, and walks away. He goes through a door that August assumed was a closet or supply room. Kovich didn't show it to him, and he thought she showed him everything.

"That section of the lab is Rhys' little lair," Kovich says when she sees him looking. "His experiments are..." she searches for the right word, "different. It's also where we keep—" She stops herself. "Well. That's need-to-know, and you don't, not just yet."

Kovich introduces August to a few more people, then the tour is over and her day begins.

August's responsibilities are simple, singular: follow Kovich wherever she goes, keep her out of harm's way, keep an eye out for trouble. He'll work five days a week, pick her up in the morning, stay with her all day, drive her home. At night and on weekends, two other bodyguards will take over. Unless Kovich decides to work on a Saturday or Sunday, which she says she rarely does, August will be free every weekend.

The first week in his new job, he spends most of his time at Hammond while Kovich wraps up her work there, giving instructions to her colleagues. She'll return to the prison from time to time, but Freedom Laboratories is her home now.

The day and a half he spends at Freedom makes August wonder how he'll stand being there five days a week.

He's present during only one experiment. But he knows there will be more.

His only comfort is knowing that on the weekends, he'll be home with the insane people he calls his friends, and more importantly, with Eden—Eden, who, without even trying, has become the best part of his life.

Chapter 18

HAWK LANDS on the ground in front of Damian, his wings slowing his descent like parachutes.

"Fuck me," Damian mutters, stubbing his cigarette into the grass.

"Right here, right now?" Hawk smiles. "I have no objections."

"Christ." He taps out another cigarette.

"Chain-smoking?"

"What?"

"That's your fifth one."

Damian looks up at the sky, then glares at him. "You been watching me?"

"I couldn't help myself." He walks up to him. "Any left?"

Damian tosses him the pack. The lighter is inside.

"Many thanks." Hawk lights one, hands them back. "May I?" He gestures to the ground beside Damian, who shrugs.

Hawk likes the way Damian's shoulders rise and fall, how he can just make out the shape of his upper body through his shirt. He shakes his head as he sits. Such a gorgeous body, and it will only ever be enjoyed by women, he thinks jealously, though he doesn't have anything against women himself. Beauty is universal. Layla and Eden are a pleasure to look at. Adair Holden is handsome in his way. And Leonard is just gorgeous, with his wavy blond hair and caramel eyes.

"I'm a lucky man." Hawk raises the cigarette to his lips.

Damian looks over at him, eyebrow raised.

"I'm surrounded by gorgeous people on all sides. How many men can say that?"

Damian ashes his cigarette. "You are way too fucking cheerful to live in this house."

Hawk laughs.

They sit in silence for a few minutes. Hawk can sense another cold front coming in. The sun is high in the sky, a muted glow, hidden behind clouds and smog. This little knoll that dips down toward the forest is worn in patches; cigarette butts are scattered throughout the surrounding grass.

Hawk looks at Damian. "This is your place."

He's lighting another cigarette, speaks through his teeth. "What the fuck are you talking about?"

"You sit here often."

"So what?"

"Just an observation."

The cigarette catches. Damian takes a deep breath, holds it a moment before speaking. "Here's an observation." Smoke trails between his lips. "I've noticed that you haven't told any of us what you were in for."

"Ah." Hawk takes a drag. "I'm not sure if I can trust you with my secrets yet, Damian Grace, lovely as you are. Another time, perhaps."

"I can hardly wait."

He wants to ask Damian why he sits out here and why he chain-smokes. But he knows Damian won't tell him. He may not know himself. Hawk could look inside his mind, find out on his own. It's tempting, but one of his few moral principles is to never read someone's mind unless they've given him permission.

"Thanks for the cigarette." He stands.

Damian smokes silently, as if he hasn't heard Hawk.

"And the stimulating conversation."

He looks up at him coldly, eyes like black ice.

Hawk sighs. "I could look into those eyes all day."

"Fuck off."

"As you wish."

He takes to the air again, and from high above he watches Damian smoke his last cigarette, then dust off the back of his pants as he stands. He looks up, squints. Hawk knows he's only a speck of black in the sky, that Damian can't possibly see him clearly, but it seems he can see well enough to give Hawk the finger.

Hawk laughs, watches until Damian is inside the house. Then he flies farther, descends to coast over the tops of the trees. Through the sparse, dead branches he sees Eden, breather on, sitting on the ground, her back against a tree. He dives, and she sees him when he's about halfway to the ground.

"My love, what are you doing out here all by yourself?"

She smiles through the clear mask. "Thinking."

"Do you want to be alone?"

She shakes her head, and he sits by her.

"I was just having a cigarette with Damian."

"He must've loved that."

"Honestly," he leans his head down to hers, "I think he's flattered. Truly."

She looks at the tree ahead of her. A breeze blows across the forest floor, stirring the leaves and pine needles. "The night Liam died, I came out here."

The wind takes her words away almost before he hears them. "Why?"

"To scream."

She says this without any emotion in her voice. But he can see it in his mind, her by this tree among the dead leaves, alone in the cold. He wishes he could have been there for her, wishes he could say something to comfort her now.

"When I came back, Damian was in the living room. It was dark. He didn't think I saw him, but I did." She looks up at him. "He was waiting for me. And I think he would've come looking for me if I hadn't come back."

This makes Hawk smile. "Such an enigma." He lies back on the soft earth, his wings protecting his bare back from the damp coldness of it. He's surprised, but pleased, when Eden lies down too, and rests her head on his thigh, looking up through the trees like he is.

"August will be home in a few hours," she says.

"Yes. I'll be happy to see him. Won't you?"

"I'm always happy to see him."

"Do you love him?"

"Of course."

"You know what I mean."

She holds her breath for a moment, lets it out slowly. "I don't know. Sometimes. I don't know."

"He loves you."

He feels her nod. "I know." She sighs. "I think I'm supposed to be alone. Liam is gone."

"No one needs to be alone, Eden. There are far too many people on this horrible little planet for that to be the case."

"I don't *need* to be alone. I just think I'm supposed to be."

"I respectfully disagree."

The birds chatter in the cold sunlight. He can see them in the branches above, little sparrows puffed up like tennis balls against the chill.

"I hate being alone," Eden says quietly.

He leans up on his elbows to look at her. "Then don't be."

☙

"August?"

His head spins as he turns to her. He's glad he's sitting

down. "Hey, there she is." It's dark. She's a shadow, backlit by the light spilling onto the porch through the front door, but as usual her eyes are like stars peeking through the darkness.

"Aren't you cold?" she asks him.

He should be. Maybe he is. He shrugs. "I'm cool. You going to keep me company?"

He thinks she'll take the chair next to him, but she sits on the floor beside his leg, rests her head against his thigh. "You're sad."

"Who, me? What have I got to be sad about?" He lifts his bottle. "Good beer. Comfy chair. Sexy girl. I'm the happiest guy... in the world..." Every word draws more and more energy from him, so that by the end of it he's choked up and his last words trail away. Whatever has been giving him the strength to lie disappears.

Eden wraps her arms around his lower leg, kisses his thigh where her head is resting. "You're so brave."

He means to laugh, but it comes out more like a stifled sob. He pinches the bridge of his nose, as if that will help somehow; it doesn't. "Oh, Eden..." He gives his head a quick shake, tries to keep back everything he's been hiding. "All I could think about was you when I was there." He absently puts his hand on the back of her head to touch her soft, silky hair, closes his eyes. It feels so good to touch her. "God, I'm drunk." He finishes the beer, tilts his head back, rests it on the top of the chair. "They're crazy people, man." He knows he's mumbling, wonders if he's even understandable. "All of them. I can't wait to kill them all." August isn't a killer by nature, like Liam or Damian, but as the days go by, he's starting to understand the urge.

"You're good, August." Eden holds him tightly while he strokes her hair. "You're wonderful."

"I just told you I'm looking forward to killing people."

She looks back at him. "So am I."

He moves her hair behind her ear. "Can I see your fangs?"

She bites her lower lip so the fangs come down over it. He stops short of touching one with his thumb.

"They're so cool. *You're* so cool." He smiles. "You are so cool, Eden. And sexy and funny and I want another beer." She moves to the side as he stands. "To the kitchen," he points.

"I would've gotten it for you."

He holds the door open for her. "I've got two legs. I'm not Damian."

"I heard my name." Damian is in the living room watching Cube.

"I was just saying how much I admire you." August forgets about going to the kitchen, walks in, slumps down on the couch beside him. He doesn't realize Eden hasn't followed until she comes back with three open beers in her hands. "Ah, shit." He takes the one she offers him. "You did the slave thing."

"Embrace the slave thing, Gus. I have." Damian takes his beer from Eden, doesn't even look at her.

"That's because you're a lazy prick." August swallows back a deep gulp, drains almost half the bottle.

The three of them sit and drink in silence. August can't follow whatever Damian is watching, so he watches Eden instead, watches her arm as she lifts her bottle, the way she puts it to her lips—her lips in general—her throat as she swallows. He thinks he'll go crazy when she flicks her tongue out to lick a few stray drops from her lip.

"Do I need to leave the room?" Damian glares darkly at August.

August blinks. "What?"

"Either take her upstairs and fuck her, or finish your beer and go to bed."

"You seem unusually grumpy tonight, my friend." August puts a hand on his shoulder. "Tell Uncle Gus what's wrong."

"I'm going to smother you with this pillow."

"Hey, man. Two days, and I'm gone and out of your fur."

Damian looks back at the Cube. "Take that fucking parrot with you."

"Hawk? What's wrong with him?"

"He keeps looking at my ass."

August sits back, shrugs. "Well, you've got a nice ass, man." He looks at Eden.

She nods. "It's true."

"What the fuck have you done to her, Gus? She used to be quiet." He turns to Eden. "Shut up and get me some chips."

She leaves without a word.

"Dude! Why do you have to be such a prick?"

Damian ignores him. Eden comes back a moment later with a bowl full of potato chips.

"Oh! I got it." August punches Damian's arm lightly. "I got it. The badittude, the extra prickiness." He looks at Eden, winks. "I got it." He puts his hand to one side of his mouth, whispers loudly, "Someone isn't getting any." He looks at Damian, is about to say, "Well, neither am I," but before he has the chance, Damian swings his fist into August's stomach. "Oh... fuck..." He drops the bottle, slides off the couch onto his knees, wraps his arms around him- self. "What the... *hell*... Damian?"

Damian gets up and leaves the room.

Eden is beside him, holding his arm. "Are you okay?"

"What the fuck was *that*?" It hurts so much he's afraid Damian has ruptured his spleen or something.

"He's been in a really bad mood. I mean, more than usual."

"Fucking Layla," August says through clenched teeth. "Or not, in this case."

She's trying not to smile. "Can I do anything?"

"Go upstairs and bite him."

She laughs a little. "Let me help you up."

"No, no, I'm good. I think I'll just…" He moves his legs so that he's sitting instead of kneeling, leans his back against the couch. "I'm good right here."

She sits next to him.

"From crazy to crazy," August says. "I can't catch a break. This fucking house." He shakes his head. "Hey, you want to go to a hotel?"

Her eyebrows go up.

"That came out wrong. Unless…"

Her expression doesn't change.

"Okay, yes, that absolutely came out wrong. I just meant, do you want to get out of here?"

"And go where?"

"Jesus, I don't know. Anywhere. There's a really nice tree half a mile from here, real popular with the locals."

She starts to laugh.

"Squirrels, chipmunks, raccoons—they all say it's the place to be on a Friday night."

She covers her mouth the more she laughs.

"Don't. Let me see your smile. Come on." He takes her wrist, gently pulls her hand down.

"You're funny," she says.

"Funny looking."

"No, just funny. You're very handsome."

He raises his eyebrows, surprised. "Yeah?"

"You know you are."

"Yeah, I know. But I didn't think you did."

"Well, I do."

He should kiss her, he thinks. But he thought that once before and look how that turned out. He sighs. "Hey, I don't want you to do the slave thing, but…"

"But you want another beer and you can't stand up?"

"I love you."

She gets up. "I'll be right back."

He watches her walk away, wishes she'd said it back. It wouldn't have meant anything, but... it would have been nice.

❧

"Richard, this is impossible. They take away my Lens. They won't even let me use an old iPad to take notes. They gave me a notebook. An actual notebook. With *paper*. I can't remember the last time I used a pen."

"But you have those notes?"

"No," Lena says. "They take those too, and file them for me to look at next time. They have *filing* cabinets. A room full of filing cabinets."

"Filing cabinets? Did they use paper files at Hammond?"

"Not that I'm aware of."

"Strange." Richard sighs, and she hears it.

"I'm sorry," Lena says. Her voice sounds lonely and defeated on the other side of the Burner Lens. They can't use their own Lenses because, without a doubt, someone would be listening; if not to Lena, then definitely to Richard.

"You have nothing to be sorry for."

"I'll think of something."

"Well, what's important is that you're there."

There's a tight silence on the other end, then, "Richard. It's horrible. It's worse than Hammond."

"Lena, if this—"

"No, I can do it. It's just a lot." She takes a deep breath.

"Do you know any of their names? There must be someone who's missing them. Family, friends."

"I don't think so. My guess is that they've chosen prisoners who never got blinks or visitors. They don't use names here, only numbers. I can describe them to you as I meet them."

Richard nods. "Yes, that would be helpful."

He links the Burner Lens to his tableface, listens as Lena describes a man she knows only as Twenty-Seven, watches as the computer inputs the information and creates an approximation of his face.

He's still looking at the lifeless rendering long after he's said goodbye to her.

※

The man finally faints.

August watches as his eyes roll back and his body goes limp. His bindings prevent him from sliding off the still-moving treadmill. The lab assistants quickly turn off the machine. It takes three of them to lift the man, identified only as Thirty-Seven, and put him into a chair. They all remove their HushPlugs and pocket them.

Expressionless, the doctors, Hoffmann and Lennet, take notes, listening as the assistants rattle off different instrument readings. Kovich consults her own clipboard, speaks quietly to them.

They put him on that treadmill an hour ago. A man who was obviously in good shape once, but is weak and thin now, Thirty-Seven was exhausted after ten minutes. Fifty minutes later, he passed out.

August doesn't know what the point of this test was, and it's not his place to ask. His only function is to make sure that nothing happens to Kovich, not that there's even a remote chance of Thirty-Seven causing her any harm.

He wonders what the man's name is. He looks at him, red-faced, covered in sweat. There are thick, wide bandages on both of his arms, the result of some other experiment. He has gills on his neck and bluish skin that turns different shades depending on the light. His eyes are more round than almond shaped, fish-like and a bright green. August tried not to look into those eyes, but once today, he unintentionally caught the man's gaze, and the aching despair he saw there was agony. But worse than the despair, so much worse, was the unspoken plea for help. He wanted to tell Thirty-Seven, like he wants to tell all of them, *It's coming. Help is coming.*

But he can't. These people are so heavily drugged at times that they often talk to themselves, talk in their dreams; it's too much of a risk to give them hope.

He's watching Hoffmann fill a syringe, approach the man. The lab assistants force Thirty-Seven's arm to lie straight, and he doesn't resist. As the needle goes in, Kovich steps up to August, gives him a smile. "All right," she says. "Lunch?"

❧

August brings her a second cup of coffee.

She looks surprised. "Oh. Thank you." She catches herself, masks her gratitude. "I didn't take you for the kiss-ass type."

"Just the friendly type, ma'am."

"Stop calling me ma'am. My grandmother was ma'am."

"Sorry ma—Doctor."

"Better," she says. "I'll beat it out of you."

He smiles, raises his mug to this woman he hates. "I promise to do my very best." He drinks the bitter coffee.

Kovich reads over a file while she eats her lunch. He's grateful for the quiet. Then she looks up suddenly. "Question. Why don't you wear your HushPlugs?"

"I'm sorry?"

"Your HushPlugs. Why don't you wear them?"

He shrugs. "I like being fully aware of my surroundings."

She nods, looks down at her file again. "I definitely picked the right man for the job."

"Thank you, ma'am."

She glares at him.

"Doctor."

She raises an eyebrow. "Can't take the Army out of the boy, huh?"

"Guess not."

The door to the lounge opens. "Oh, excuse me," says a woman, looking up from her clipboard. "Am I interrupting?"

"No, come in, Lena. John, this is Dr. Lena Marsh. Dr. Marsh is our *doctor* doctor here at the lab."

"Hi," Dr. Marsh says. She's pretty, but has a mousy sort of presence, like she wants to be as small and invisible as possible. The glasses don't help.

August stands, shakes her hand. "Nice to meet you, *Doctor Doctor Marsh.*"

She smiles a little, takes his hand. "You too."

"John is a bodyguard who thinks he's a comedian, Lena," Kovich says. Then to August, "And Lena is a physician, not a scientist. We keep her around for when things go wrong. John is a Hammond transplant too, Lena."

Marsh nods. "I think I remember seeing you at the prison."

"You should've come over and said hi."

"Oh." She blushes a little. "I'm sorry."

"No worries."

"Everything all right?" Kovich asks Marsh.

"I was just coming in for a coffee, but I did want to talk to you about Thirty-One. I know he isn't really my business—I've never even seen him—but I heard that you authorized an increase of his drug levels beyond the recommended dosage."

August listens without looking interested. Thirty-One. Weir mentioned him before—his "special project," he called him. August still hasn't seen this mysterious subject or been in Weir's lab. There has to be more than just one prisoner in there.

"Yes. What about it?"

Marsh looks nervous. "Well, the drugs are extremely potent. Raising them like that? I don't know if a person, even a dysmorphic person, could handle those levels for very long. But like I said, I don't really know anything about that subject."

Kovich nods, stands. "Come to my office when you're done and we'll talk."

Marsh nods. "Thank you." She looks at August again before he follows Kovich out. "Nice to meet you."

"Same here, Doctor."

Outside the lounge, Kovich sighs again. "God, is it six o'clock yet?"

&

Dairen is at work. Richard is at a fundraising meeting. Most of the residents are at their own jobs, or in class, not that any of them would think it strange to see Sierra go into Richard's office.

It felt wrong to eavesdrop on Richard. It feels wrong to do what she's doing now, going through the most recent activity in his tableface.

She finds a computer-generated image of a man's face: lizard-like eyes, scales lining the sides of his neck and the back of his head. Next to the image, Richard has noted: *six foot four; one hundred seventy pounds; forty years old; chameleon; Russian.*

She copies his remarks into her little notebook, describes the computer drawing. She writes "Lena Marsh," because that has to be the Lena to whom Richard was speaking—the doctor in Hammond who brought them the information about Rico Martinez. She was there when he was killed.

She looks back at her notes to review Richard's side of the conversation, the only part she could hear. *"Filing cabinets? Did they use paper files at Hammond?"*

Lena must be working in a different lab, one that's associated with Hammond, but not Hammond. That has to be it.

Why hasn't Richard said anything about this?

But she knows the answer. It's the same reason he never told either of them about Adair Holden: to protect them, to keep them from harm.

What will Adair Holden do with this information? Will he find the lab somehow and destroy it? Free the prisoners, like he did at Hammond?

People died at Hammond. If what she's found leads to something bigger, she could be responsible for more deaths. But if she does nothing, she'll be responsible for the suffering, and possible deaths, of those people in this phantom laboratory.

Peace is an outcome, not a solution. Change comes first, and change can be violent. That's where people like me come in.

People like me.

Is Sierra like Adair Holden, a fighter? Or is she like Richard, trying to do the right thing the right way?

She looks down at her scribbled notes and her eyes catch the flat, computer-rendered gaze of the mysterious prisoner. And it's as if this man she's never met is saying, *You know who you are.*

Sierra closes down the tableface, gets up, leaves the room, pulls the Burner Lens from her pocket. She blinks and waits.

Chapter 19

AUGUST SHAKES the rain off of himself, steps into his apartment. But before he can close the door or tell the lights to turn on, he feels an arm encircle him and pull tight against his throat. He's shoved further into the room, the door slamming behind him.

"It's John, right?" The voice is rough, like sandpaper, with a thick London accent, so similar to Liam's that, for a second, he's more disconcerted by that than by the arm that's choking him to death.

He slams the man back against the wall, elbows him as hard as he can. The hold loosens. August steps away, coughing, manages to say, "Lights, on!"

They illuminate the room just in time for him to see the man leap forward to tackle him. He's stronger than August, stronger than Damian. It's like being trapped under a car.

That solid, tree limb of an arm presses down on his windpipe again. His vision sparkles red and green, like Christmas lights. He tries kneeing the man in the gut. It has no effect.

Get off me, he thinks at the man. *Stand up! Stand up!*

The arm lifts away. The man stands, frowns. He shakes his head, like there's water in his ears.

August scrambles to his feet, unholsters his gun, aims it.

"What the fuck did you just do?" The man rubs his head.

"I believe I just pulled a gun on you." He forces the words through the ache in his throat.

"No." The man glares at him, understanding in his dark eyes. "You fucked with my mind. You're d-form."

August's arm burns. He's going to have to kill this guy, whoever he is. And he's never killed anyone before. What will he do with the body? How can he possibly get rid of it? The man is a giant—stocky, built like a house. He's got to weigh at least three hundred pounds, all muscle. And he's d-form.

He's *d-form*.

August's indecision costs him his advantage. The man lunges at him, knocks the gun from his hand, plows his fist into August's stomach. August thinks he'll throw up. Then he's being lifted off the floor by his shirt and shoved against the wall. He feels it wobble behind him.

"Now, what's a d-form doing playing bodyguard for Kovich, eh?" He shoves him again. "Looks like you and me need to have a talk, John. A nice little chat." He searches August for more weapons with his free hand. August's feet aren't touching the floor. "We're going to sit right over there and chat. You going to be a good boy, John? Or do I need to tie you up?"

"I'm good," August strains to say.

"Try that telepathic shit again, I'll break your sodding neck. Pop your head off like a bloody champagne cork." He throws him onto the couch. The pain in August's gut is so bad he can't sit up straight.

"All right now, Johnny boy." The man sits in the chair across from him. His hair is black and his eyes are navy blue where they should be white; he has swirling green irises, encircled by a thin silver line, like a satellite image of a hurricane, his pupil the eye of the storm. He's tall, maybe six-five, with thick, muscular arms, a broad chest and shoulders. "Let's just skip the part about you being a traitor to your own kind. That's between you and your god. There's one thing I want from you and one thing only."

"What's that?"

"Your thumbs."

August's heart stops.

The man leans forward, his smile like a reptile's upturned mouth, sharp and cold. "And we can do this one of two ways. You can come with me, or..." He reaches out, grabs August's wrists; the bones scrape together. "I can just take them and put them in my pocket. Don't make much difference to me."

This guy could pop August's hands off with one quick pull. "I kind of like them where they are." The man lets go. August wraps his arms around his stomach. "Mind if I ask... what you need them for?"

"I want to see where you work, John. Call it a homecoming." There's that smile again.

A homecoming? August wonders what he means. "I'm assuming it's my prints you want."

"You assume correctly."

"Why do you want to get into the lab?"

The man's bright, spiraling eyes take August in. He seems to consider, then come to a decision. "Guess there's no harm in telling." He leans back in the chair, comfortable, unnervingly relaxed. "Let's just say I spent a little time in the old lab and it weren't exactly a holiday."

"They let you go?"

The man smiles thinly. "Got myself out, actually. They repair the damage yet?"

August is lost for words. Nobody told him about a breakout. It's something he should know. Why has Kovich kept this from him?

His confusion must show on his face because the man says, "Don't tell me you don't know the story of Twenty-Five. I'm kind of hurt."

"That was your number? Twenty-Five?"

"It was indeed."

August has heard of d-forms who are stronger than average. This man looks like he could take out every person in the lab, guards included, with one swipe of his big, muscular arm. Maybe he did. "You escaped? How?"

A shrug is his answer.

August breathes faster. "Right. So, what's your plan? I get you into the lab and then what? You're going to take the place all by yourself?"

"Aw. You're not worried about me, now, are you, John?"

"You'll never get through security. My prints aren't enough."

"Retinalocks, eh? Well, good thing for me you've got two eyes to go with your two thumbs. Mind if I borrow them as well? Promise I'll give 'em back."

August's throat is thick. This one, vengeful motherfucker is going to ruin everything. "You won't make it. I'm telling you, you won't make it, not without help."

The man gives a short laugh. "You offering?"

August stares at him, tries to think. And, of all things, his mind brings up a memory of Layla. Maybe it's because that was the last time someone shoved him down onto a couch.

She never showed any interest in him until after she hooked up with Holden; just came over to his apartment one night, and suddenly he was on his couch and she was on his lap, kissing him like no one ever had. He was too drunk to even think about what he was doing until she went for his belt.

"Whoa, whoa, whoa. Hang on a minute."

She raised her eyebrow, annoyed, sat back on his knees. "What?"

"Just... just give me a minute, okay?"

She crossed her arms.

"*Okay?*"

She rolled her eyes, waited while he examined his alcohol-soaked conscience.

He respected Holden, was kind of scared of Damian. Holden was the first person he'd ever met who'd treated him like a human being, and Damian—Damian was just fucking scary. This would be very wrong.

But, goddamn—it was Layla. He grimaced, bit his lip, looked up at her.

"Jesus Christ, August!" she said. "Just make a fucking decision!"

Make a fucking decision. Just make a fucking decision, August.

"Yes," he says.

The man gives him a look. "'Yes' what?"

"Yes, I'm offering to help you."

The man's face darkens, and in the blink of an eye, he gets a hold of August's arm again. "I'll just take them with me." He wraps one hand around August's fingers, the other just below his wrist, ready to snap his hand off at the joint.

"No, no, no!" August tries to pull his arm back, but it only makes the pain worse. "You don't know what the fuck you're doing! You have no idea what's going on!" The man pulls his wrist hard in both directions. August cries out, tries to loosen the man's fingers with his free hand, but it's pointless. He feels sweat prickling on his forehead, gathering above his lip. He clenches his teeth. "I get it, okay? I get it. They fucked you up. You want your vengeance-is-mine moment. But there are other people trapped in there, just like you. We're going to get them out. But they'll never see the light of day again if you march in there on your own. They'll kill you. They'll kill me. And all those people will be fuck- ing guinea pigs until they die. Believe me! This is way bigger than your personal fucking vendetta!"

The man eyes him. "Who's 'we'?"

"I can't tell you that."

Fire shoots up his arm. His tendons scream. "Jesus, fuck!"

"*Who's we?*"

August grits his teeth, shakes his head. "No." His eyes water. The man's face becomes blurry. He pulls harder. August screams, catches himself, tries to swallow it back. He pictures Holden and Eden and Damian and Layla. "No," he gasps, "no."

And like a rubber band stretched and released, August's arm is free. He clutches at his wrist, shudders with pain. "Jesus, *fuck...*" he hisses, trying to breathe through the spikes and knives that slice up and down his arm.

"Okay." The man sits back. "Figure a guy who's willing to lose a hand for his mates is probably telling the truth. I believe you."

"Oh, that's a fucking relief."

"Hey, I let you keep your hand, didn't I?"

"Charming *and* generous." It's like someone is scraping a comb over the nerves in his arm.

"Want me to massage it for you?"

August moves quickly to the other side of the couch. "You just—keep your hands to yourself."

The man shrugs. "Just trying to be friendly." He watches August for a moment. "So what now, John Leonard? I'm not leaving till I get some answers." He sits back, completely at home in the big chair as if it were his own.

"Am I allowed to ask a question?"

The man opens his hands in a conciliatory gesture.

"How did you get out of the lab?"

His eyes shift slightly. "Just woke up one day, got my bearings, made a run for it." He shrugs. He's not telling the whole truth. "I got away all right, but I couldn't remember where I'd come from. Took a while, but it finally came back to me."

"How long were you there?"

"About five months, I reckon." He nods to August's hand. "How's the old wrist, then?"

"I'll live." He lies back against the cushions, exhausted. He's at a complete loss as to what to do. He needs to talk to Holden. "I need to blink someone."

"I don't think so, mate."

"If you want answers, I need to talk to someone."

"No bloody way."

August puts his head in his hand. "So, what? Are we just going to sit here and stare at each other?"

"That's up to you, John. But let me ask you something. Before the lab, I was in Hammond with this bloke, good guy. But he was prime lab material. Was only a matter of time for him."

"What's he look like?"

"Big fella with wings, brown. Arab or something. Iran or Afghanistan. One of those places. And clawed feet. He had clawed feet, like a bird."

August lifts his head up slowly, gapes at him.

"What? What'd I say?"

"You're shitting me."

The man frowns. "Don't follow you, mate."

"You are *shitting* me!"

"What are you on about?"

"Hawk. He was in Hammond with you. Hawk."

The man's eyes fill with worry. "You know him? He's there? Is he all right? How bad's he got it?"

August laughs. "Man, this is too fucking much." He stands up. "Jesus Christ." He turns toward his room.

"Oi! Where do you think you're going?" He hears the man get up and follow him.

"I've got to pack a bag. We're going away for the weekend."

"You what?"

At the door of his bedroom, he turns. "And it's August, by the way."

The man looks at him like he's crazy. "It's October."

August bursts out laughing again, tells the room's lights to turn on. "God, I can't wait to tell Eden all this."

"Who the fuck is Eden?" The man catches up with him, puts a hand on his arm.

"Hey! Hands!"

"What the fuck are you on about, John?"

August steps away from him, pulls his bag out from under the bed, unzips it, looks at the man again. "My name is August Wright. I work for Adair Holden and we're going to tear Freedom Labs to the fucking ground. You want in?"

The man is speechless. His eyes flit back and forth. He runs his hand down his face, shakes his head, starts to grin. "Well, fuck me." His smile is contagious, and in one moment he's gone from being scary to likeable. He meets August's eyes. "August, is it?"

He nods. "August Wright."

The man extends his hand, and August forgets to be afraid as he takes it. "Mark. Wayland Mark."

❧

Wayland lets August take away his thoughts of the journey without a fuss. He understands why he needs to do it; doesn't like it, but he understands.

He doesn't trust telepaths, he told August. "Nothing personal."

"What about Hawk?" August asked him.

"He's why I don't trust them."

Which is not entirely true, but it's close enough. Hawk told him how to recognize telepathy, what it feels like to have someone else hanging about inside your mind. He never put that knowledge to practical use until tonight.

Throughout the drive, he's felt August pull out his thoughts of the journey like playing cards from a deck and fling them away, one by one.

At the moment, August is yelling into his Lens. It's hard to follow the conversation. The short-term memory loss is making him dizzy.

"Just put Holden on, goddammit! Why are you all sharing the same fucking Lens? No! I don't want to talk to—Damian... Okay... yeah. Yeah I got it. You're going to kill me. Can I talk to Holden first?... Thank you. Jesus." August knocks his head back against the headrest several times.

Wayland woke up this morning to the sound of a voice that wasn't speaking—not out loud, anyway. He almost always wakes up to that Voice. The Voice who tortured him, told him lies; frightened him in a way he never thought anything could. They're only dreams. But it was all real once.

And this is what he's really after in the lab—that Voice... and one other. Both without faces and only one with a name. The nameless Voice that tried to crush his soul, and would have—if the other voice hadn't saved him.

He clutches his head. "Ah, Jesus, can you stop now? I've got no idea where the fuck I am. I'm officially lost, all right?"

August ignores him, is still on his Lens. "Yeah. I know... I appreciate that. I—" he sighs, "I've got that covered—Hey, who knows that better than me? I'm the one locked in that fucking hellhole all day!" He shakes his head. "I'm sorry, Adair. I'm sorry—No, I shouldn't have—" He's quiet for a time, listening, nodding. "Okay. Thanks—Oh, hey, wait. Is Eden there?" He looks disappointed. "No. Nothing... I'll see her when we get there... About half an hour... All right. Hey, I'm really sorry I... Okay. See you soon." He blinks off, removes his Lens, rubs his eyes. "You've got the all clear."

"Do I get to meet the whole gang and all?"

"Oh, you bet. And they just can't wait to meet you."

"Happy family, then?"

"The happiest."

"Hey, that gorgeous girl on the news. The one who took down Corbin. Monroe, is it? She's not single, is she?"

"Only when she wants to be."

"Ah." Wayland watches the traffic and trees go by for a moment, then looks at August. "You know, I'm having a really weird day."

"You and me both, man."

They're far upstate now, a few houses here and there, no streetlights. It's almost totally dark. But the ever-present smog is too thick to see many stars, even all the way out here.

A thought occurs to him. "So you're all right, going back and forth like this? Not worried about someone following you? Tracking you?"

"Nah, I'm good. We've got the best tracker blockers. Plus, Kovich trusts me. I mean, really trusts me. So they leave me alone." He stretches his arms out, yawning.

"Well, that's bloody impressive."

August shrugs. "It is what it is."

Suddenly, Wayland's mind feels whole again, closed off. August has stopped taking his thoughts away. He breathes a sigh of relief. "Thanks, mate."

"I figure you're pretty lost at this point."

"Completely." Wayland relaxes, leans back against the headrest. His eyes get heavy. He closes them. Only for a moment, he tells himself. Just for a moment...

... but then he hears a whisper in the dark.

Your name is Wayland Mark.

You're beautiful and you're strong.

Your name is Wayland Mark.

You're beautiful and you're strong.

In his dreams, he wakes up. He wakes up and finds her and

takes her away from this place. He hears her voice in his dreams. He hears her when he is almost awake. But he never wakes up.

Your name is Wayland Mark.

He's learned to listen for her when he can't remember who he is, when he can't remember his name. Even when she doesn't speak to him, he can *feel* her reminding him.

He doesn't even know who *she* is. She's told him her name, but he can't remember.

You're beautiful and you're strong.

In this dream, his mouth is full of cotton as he tries to open it. His arms are strapped down tightly, but not tightly enough. He snaps free and his hands pulse with the return of blood. He touches his mouth. His lips are dry. He tries to open his eyes. Something struggles against him to keep them closed.

You're beautiful and you're strong.

In this dream, he forces his eyes to open, and the light above him is agony. When was the last time he opened his eyes? He can't remember. There are needles in his arms and tubes attached to the needles. He tears them out and it hurts. His vision is blurry. There are machines humming and loud beeps and shining metal objects he can't make out. He rubs his eyes when they start to water. His legs wobble underneath him when he stands. There's a pain in his head like nothing he's ever known.

And then, there's a voice. A startled, frightened voice. This voice is not *the* Voice, and it's not *her* voice either. Neither of those voices was ever filled with fear. But this voice... is terrified. This voice screams for help.

He needs to shut it up. He needs to. And he needs to find *her*. Where is she?

Wayland charges at the owner of the frightened voice. He knows he has killed it when it stops screaming. Another and another and another and suddenly, the whole world is full of different voices: female voices, male voices, high, low, growling, screaming voices. How can he find her if he can't hear her?

He is knocking things over, destroying whatever he comes in contact with. If he could remember her name, he would call to her—

"Hey."

Wayland jerks awake. Whose voice is he hearing now? He turns and sees August looking at him, and remembers where he is and who he's with.

"Nice nap?"

Wayland focuses on slowing his breathing. "Sorry, mate. Didn't mean to fall asleep."

August eyes him. "You okay?"

Wayland nods. "Yeah. Fine. Had a weird a dream is all."

"Well, your reality is about to get a whole lot weirder. We're almost there."

In less than half an hour, August pulls onto a dirt road that Wayland wouldn't have seen if he'd been the one driving—it's well hidden among the trees. August blinks again, tells his people that he's pulling up. The road winds for a bit, then opens up onto a medium-sized house. There are a few lights on, a porch, and a detached garage. It's centered in a small clearing, surrounded on all sides by forest.

"Not exactly what you'd expect terrorists to live in," Wayland says.

"Yeah, we thought about a cave, but our desire for indoor plumbing won out."

Wayland nods to the porch. "Who's the babe? Didn't see her on the Cube."

He sees a slight smile on August's face. "That's Eden." The smile starts to fade. "But don't bother."

"My mistake, mate. She yours, then?"

They pull into the garage. "No. But she's spoken for."

∾

Eden watches them come up to the house, smiles when she looks at August. As they climb the steps onto the porch, he says, "Eden, meet Wayland Mark. Wayland, Eden."

Her smile vanishes. She stares at Wayland as he shakes her hand. When he pulls away, she doesn't let go. Wayland looks back at August, winks. "The ladies love me."

He starts to pull away again, but she grips his hand. She doesn't speak, puts her other hand on his. Her eyes fill with tears.

"Hey." Wayland frowns. "Now you're making me nervous, darling."

When she still won't say anything, August steps closer. "Eden?"

Wayland looks at him, lowers his voice, says out of the corner of his mouth, "Is she... you know? *All right*?"

"You're Wayland Mark."

Wayland freezes at the sound of Eden's voice. His face changes. He turns his head slowly back to her. He can't speak for a moment. Then, very quietly, he says, "Jaida?"

Her tears spill over. "Yes!" She kisses his hand. "Yes. Yes. You're Wayland Mark!"

He looks down at her hand, as if to make sure it's really there. "You can't be here," he whispers. "How are you here?" He raises his other hand, touches her face slowly, carefully, as though she were made of glass. "I was coming to save you."

"You did save me. That day. You saved me."

He shakes his head. "I couldn't find you. I couldn't find you."

"I got out."

Disbelief fills his spiral green eyes. "How?"

Her smile makes her eyes sparkle; she's more alive than August has ever seen her. "You punched a hole in my wall."

Wayland's laugh is shaky. "Really?"

"Yes."

There are tears in Wayland's eyes now, too—this giant who, four hours ago, was ready to pull off August's hands. He laughs again, louder this time, puts his hands on her shoulders, looks her up and down. "Look at you. You're..." He hastily wipes a tear away as it falls. "You're shorter than I thought you'd be."

Eden throws her arms around him. He holds her tight, and they both laugh and cry and laugh.

It's such a pretty sound, her laugh. August realizes he's never heard it before, not like this. "You guys going to share with the rest of the class?" he asks.

Wayland wipes his eyes with the back of his hand, claps his other one heavily on August's shoulder. "I'm really, really sorry about your wrist, mate."

"Forgiven. What the fuck is going on?"

Wayland doesn't answer, and Eden doesn't seem to hear. She only has eyes for Wayland. "Come inside and meet everyone!" She takes Wayland's hand, opens the door. "And I'll make you something to eat and... oh, whatever you want!"

"Hey, what about me?" August calls as the door closes behind them. He opens his arms, looks up at the ceiling. "I fucking hate my life."

Then Eden is running out onto the porch again, has her arms around him before he can think. "Thank you, thank you, thank you!"

"Um... you're welcome?"

It happens so fast. She kisses him on the lips, then runs back inside.

"Hey!" He's still standing there with his arms open. "Could you do that again? I wasn't ready!"

"Come on!" she calls back.

He stays on the porch. He can hear her introducing Wayland. And he's jealous—jealous of how excited she sounds, of how happy seeing Wayland has made her. Because all August wants in the whole world is for Eden to be just as excited and happy to see him.

♋

"I think I was dreaming, hallucinating or something. I don't know," Wayland is saying. He's sitting next to Eden at the table; they're holding hands. "Something happened, anyway. I was always sort of half-awake. But this time, I woke up all the way, and tried to get out, but I was so bloody drugged. Suppose they got me back down again. I don't remember. Don't remember seeing anyone or hearing anyone, just myself, you know? Screaming? Then it was quiet for a bit, and then I hear this voice, right, telling me to fight, you know? To live." He looks at Eden. "Never saw her face. Didn't ever think I would." Eden can't take her eyes from Wayland. "And you have to understand. In that place, up until then, I'd only ever heard one voice. *The* Voice. He would talk while he—" Wayland swallows quickly; he seems to disappear for a moment into some dark place, his voice becoming distant. "He'd just talk and talk. And I thought... I don't know. I started to think we were the only two people left in the world. That it was just me and him."

A shadow passes over Eden's eyes and she squeezes Wayland's hand.

He looks at her. "But then, there you were." His voice breaks slightly.

She smiles up at him, but her eyes are filled with sad remembrance.

He puts his other hand over hers, then turns to Holden. "You can't know what it was like, after all that time alone, stuck with this... invisible psycho in my head... and then hearing Jaida..." He shakes his head. "And after that, when the Voice would talk to me, he didn't have..." he searches for the right word, "... *power* over me anymore, I suppose. Because I knew Jaida was there. So I fought the drugs; I fought him. Never saw him, though." There's a dark, hateful look in his face, and August knows that if Wayland were to ever find this "Voice," he wouldn't hesitate to tear him apart. "Anyway. The day I woke up, after they got me down again, I heard her, and I knew I could do it, just bust out, get away. Took a little while, but I did it. I was so out of it, though." He looks at Eden again, a tortured expression on his face. "I tried to find you..."

"It doesn't matter," Eden says.

But August can see that Wayland's guilt hasn't been assuaged by finding Eden—Jaida—alive.

"How did you speak to him?" Layla asks, eyebrow raised.

Eden lowers her eyes to the table. "I was with the Voice, too. For a long time. Then I woke up in this little room one day... made of concrete and cement. There were no windows, just this light..." She starts to scratch at the table. August can tell she's shaking her leg underneath. "I started hearing voices. I thought I was going crazy, but they were coming from this one vent near the ceiling."

"Jesus," Damian says. "You and vents."

Holden gives him a look.

Damian shrugs. "I'm just saying."

"Go ahead, Eden," Holden says, his voice kind and encouraging.

She nods quickly. "So, I could hear the Voice talking to someone else. He called him Wayland Mark sometimes, but he would usually call him Twenty-Five."

August sees Wayland flinch slightly.

Eden looks up at him. "I'm sorry."

He pats her hand. "It's all right, love. But that's what happened, yeah. He made me afraid to say my name. Punished me for it, you know? It got so that if he ever did call me Wayland, I'd correct him, tell him I was Twenty-Five."

Eden digs her nails into the table. "And I... I just listened. I don't know how long. Days, maybe? Weeks? It was like I was frozen or something. Like I was dreaming. I'd just sit there and listen. And sometimes you would scream..."

August sees a tear fall onto the table. "Eden..." But he's not close enough to reach out and touch her.

"And I..." She shakes her head. "I just sat there... while he *tortured* you."

"Don't do this to yourself, Jaida. Please," Wayland says.

They wait for her to go on, but she doesn't. Holden sits quietly, patiently. Layla gives Damian a look, but Damian has his eyes on Eden.

"Finish it." His voice is firm, but quiet.

She lifts her head, meets his unwavering gaze.

"Finish it."

"Fuck off, Damian. Jesus." August glares at him.

"No, it's okay." Eden wipes her eyes quickly. Her voice is stronger now. "It's like Wayland said. One day, I heard him scream, but it was different—not like pain—and I heard other people shouting and screaming, too. They were saying, 'Get him down, get him down.' And it was all different suddenly—all those other voices. And it was like... I woke up, too." She looks at Wayland. "I thought they were going to kill you." She shakes her head. "But then it got quiet. And... I don't know. I just... I started shouting up into the vent. I just thought maybe if you were still there and you could hear me... maybe it would help."

"How come nobody else heard you?" Layla asks, frowning.

"I don't know."

"They don't use cameras, Layla. I told you that." August is tired of her attitude, her skepticism. "If nobody was in the room, nobody would have heard her."

"Well, *I* heard her." Wayland lifts her hand and kisses it.

August tenses when he sees this. Layla catches his eye, and she's smirking at him, letting him know how pathetic she thinks he is. He hates her for it, but knows she's right.

"Did you ever see the Voice, Eden?" Holden asks. "He could still be at the lab. August might know who he is if you can describe him."

"No." Eden shakes her head sadly. "But I'd recognize his voice in a crowd of thousands."

"So would I." There's a long moment of silence, then Wayland says, "Well, that's it, I reckon."

Holden looks to Wayland. "You were going back for her."

"Yeah. That and other things."

"Well," Holden says, "Eden is here, and we," he gestures to Damian, Layla, and August, "are taking care of the 'other things.' The question is, will you help us or go your own way? We've worked too hard—*August* has worked too hard. We can't be against each other, not when we have the same goals."

Wayland raises his hands. "Mr. Holden, I am at your service, no holds barred. If I'd known about all this, I never would've tried to pull John's—August's hands off."

"You couldn't have taken just one?" Damian asks.

August turns to him. "Thanks."

Damian gives him a nod and a half smile, then looks at Eden, taps his empty beer bottle on the table.

She stands to get him another. August sees how Wayland looks at Damian, and how Damian is giving Wayland the same dark smile he gave August when he first met Eden.

Holden either pretends not to notice or doesn't care. Layla sits quietly beside him, her suspicion, like all of her emotions, clear as day on her face. "Why didn't you tell us any of this, *Jaida*?"

Eden doesn't answer.

"Should we call you that?" August tries to catch her eye. He doesn't give a shit why she didn't tell them, and he wants her to know that.

"No," is the only answer she'll give.

"Why not?" Layla asks.

Holden puts a hand on Layla's arm. "Eden. You can tell us in your own time or not at all."

"Oh, God," Layla mutters, pulling her arm out from under Holden's hand.

Holden ignores her, looks at Wayland again. "Wayland. Please call me Adair." He stands and extends his hand. "You're welcome to join our bizarre little family here. Very welcome."

Wayland rises also and shakes Holden's hand enthusiastically. "Thank you."

"Dair, we don't even know him!" Layla says.

"Hawk knows him."

"Yeah, according to *him*!" She gestures to Wayland. "Where the fuck is Hawk? I want to hear it from him."

Holden sighs. "Eden knows him."

Layla's face darkens, her bright aquamarine eyes more like smoldering embers than jewels. "Right. How could I forget?" She pushes her chair out, stands, leaves the room.

Damian watches her go, then looks at Wayland. "I don't think she likes you, big guy."

Wayland sits back down. "Can't be loved by everyone."

"No, you can't." Damian takes his beer when Eden hands it to him.

"Ignore him, Wayland," August says. "Damian hates everybody. I'd be worried if he liked you."

"Boys," Holden says, his face turned in the direction of Layla's exit. Then he looks at Wayland. "Excuse me. I'll be a moment."

"Yeah, sure. No worries."

Before he steps into the hall, Holden says, "I'm very glad to meet you, Wayland. Eden's very special to me."

"You're not alone in that." Wayland puts his hand on Eden's again as she sits beside him. August clenches his teeth. He's starting to hate Wayland fucking Mark.

When Holden is gone, Wayland turns to August, is about to speak, when the sound of the front door opening and the click-clack of Hawk's talons reach them. "I hope you've saved some food for me," he calls, stepping into the kitchen. He freezes. "Oh my God..."

Wayland stands, a huge grin on his face.

"I'm dreaming," Hawk says.

"Shitty kind of dream, mate."

"What are you doing here?" He moves around the table, throws his arms around Wayland, laughing loudly. He pulls away, holds Wayland's face in his hands and shakes him. "What the fuck are you *doing* here? Leonard!" He turns to August. "Did you find my friend?"

"Uh... he found me."

"Had a bit of a... misunderstanding at first," Wayland says.

August looks away from them. Eden has slipped unnoticed back to the stove, and he watches her silently prepare a plate for Hawk, a quiet, peaceful look on her face, in her smile. He catches her eye. And for a brief moment, that smile is for him.

"What did you do to my friend, Wayland?" Hawk asks.

"Nothing permanent."

"But it's all been resolved, yes?"

August reluctantly turns his attention back to Hawk. "I'll let you know when the bruises fade."

Hawk puts his hand on Wayland's arm, looks at August. "You must be friends. I love you both too much to take sides."

"Jesus Christ." Damian gets up and leaves.

"I don't have to be friends with him, do I?" Wayland asks.

Hawk smiles, pulls out a chair and sits. "Damian Grace is an acquired taste, my friend."

Wayland raises an eyebrow, takes his seat again. "Doesn't seem your type, mate."

"Did you *look* at him?"

"Probably not as closely as you have."

Hawk laughs. "Oh, God! This is brilliant!" Eden puts a plate on the table in front of him, and Hawk grabs her hand and kisses it. Jealousy pulses through August's chest again. It seems that everyone can openly show their affection for Eden, and receive it in kind, except for him. "This, Wayland," Hawk says, "is the one who's really stolen my heart—well, besides Leonard, of course. You'll love her."

"Way ahead of you, mate."

"We've met before," Eden says.

"Really?"

Wayland gives Hawk the short version of their story. August watches Eden as he tells it again. Her eyes are still full of surprise, disbelief, joy. He can't be mad at her, shouldn't be jealous. If he really loves her, he should be happy for her, shouldn't he? He stands up without thinking, and they all look at him.

"Leonard?" Hawk sounds concerned.

"I'm just... going outside. Fresh air. I'm fine."

As he leaves the kitchen and steps out onto the porch he hears Hawk say, "Poor Leonard. He wants you all to himself, Eden."

℃

When he hears the front door open, he's not expecting it to be Holden.

"She's never who you think she is," he says as he sits on the step next to August.

August frowns. "What?"

"Eden."

"Oh." He thought he was talking about Layla. "Yeah. Well, I like a good mystery."

Holden rubs his hands together against the cold. "When I first saw her, she could barely speak. She was practically starving. Layla disliked her instantly, of course."

August smirks. "Of course. I think you're the only person she ever liked right off the bat."

Holden smiles slightly. "Yes. Well." He leans forward, looks out into the dark. "She wouldn't tell us her name. Or couldn't. I don't know. So I gave her one."

"Layla told me." Saying that, August wonders, not for the first time, if Holden knows about him and Layla. If he does, he's never given any indication. He either lives in blissful ignorance or is the most patient man August has ever met. Or could he just love Layla so much that he doesn't care what she does? Is it possible to love someone that much? To just take them as they are and never expect them to change for you?

Holden goes on. "I remember telling Liam that Eden was vulnerable. I was trying to——" He shakes his head. "I asked him to leave her alone. For her sake."

August can see that Holden regrets this, sees the pained expression of guilt on his face. "I would've done the same thing, Adair. I know what he—well, you know."

"Better than anyone."

"Yeah. So... don't feel bad, you know?"

"You didn't see him," Holden says. "You didn't see his face.

That day, just before we left for Hammond. I came around the back of the house to go to the car. They were sitting right here. She had her head on his shoulder and he was holding her hand. He wasn't wearing his gloves." He pauses. "And I was so angry. I could hardly speak. In the car, he told me that she said she loved him and I was..." he sighs, "so angry, August. I was so angry. But I asked him if he loved her. He looked me right in the eye, right at me, and told me that he did. And I believed him. I'd never, ever seen his eyes like that."

August shakes his head with a smile. "Liam in love. Who'd have thought?"

It's quiet then. He listens to the sound of the wind in the dead, empty branches. He can hear Hawk and Wayland talking, can't make out what they're saying. He hears Eden's soft voice in reply. He thinks of the last time he saw Liam, so many months ago, finds himself wishing he had that image of Liam's face, happy. He can't picture it.

He looks at Holden. "You miss him?"

"I do," he says, without hesitation. "I never did right by him. I was too angry, too... I always thought... I thought there'd be time. He was still so young..."

"You were there for him, Adair. If it wasn't for you, he'd still be in prison. You know that."

"He had us both to thank for that, I think."

"Yeah, maybe, but... I wouldn't have done it if it weren't for you."

"Well." Holden is quiet for some time, then, "But he was the same man when he got out—only older and angrier. With Eden, I started to think, maybe there was a chance for him." He runs his hand down his face. "God, he was so surprised."

"Surprised?"

He looks at August. He seems old, suddenly, and so sad. It

hurts to see him like this. "When those bullets hit him. He looked at me... as if he thought I could explain it or fix it. He looked down at his chest." Holden puts a hand on his own chest. "Then he fell. And when I lifted the goggles away, his eyes were just... surprised."

He's never heard Holden talk like this, doesn't know how to respond, doesn't know why he's chosen this moment to open up to someone, whether he even meant to. It makes him wonder what he tells Layla, what secrets she knows about him that the rest of them never will.

"I couldn't watch it," August says. "That vid. The part where Liam... I couldn't watch it. Eden watches it. She says... she needs to be reminded that he's dead."

"I know."

He feels that heavy sadness in his chest that's becoming too familiar. "I miss him too. I really do. But—" He hesitates, considers his words. "I think it would have taken a lot more than Eden to..."

"Save him?"

August looks down at the step. "Something like that."

Holden doesn't say anything for a time. Then he nods slowly. "Well, in any case," he reaches up for the railing, pulls himself up, "I have since discovered that Eden is probably the least vulnerable person I know."

August nods. "I'll drink to that."

"You'll drink to anything," he says with a chastising smile.

"I'll drink to that, too."

Holden opens the door, pauses before stepping through, takes a breath. "August, I know what I've asked you to do is probably the hardest thing you've ever done in your life."

August starts to lie automatically.

"Thank you," Holden cuts him off.

It feels like there are rocks in his throat. He wants to tell him that, no, he's fine, no problem, thick skin and all that other bullshit. But he swallows, nods, and all he can say is, "It's really bad, man."

"I'm sorry. I wish I could be there with you."

"No, you don't." This comes out more harshly than August means it to. He clears his throat. "Look, just... promise me you're going to turn it to dust and it's all good."

"There will be nothing left. I promise."

"Then I'm fine."

Holden looks at him a moment longer, then turns and says, "Goodnight," as he steps inside.

August doesn't say it back. He can't remember what it means to have a good night; what it feels like to wake up and not be haunted by the nightmares he hopes he's left behind, only to go to Freedom Laboratories and be reminded that all of them are real.

❦

After a while, Hawk leaves them to talk, and he's alone with Jaida for the first time. Everything is so surreal, and he's sure he's never been happier in his life.

"So. August tells me you're spoken for." Wayland smiles. "Always had a hope I'd sweep you off your feet, ride off into the sunset with you. I'm not much of a horseman, though. Who's the lucky guy, then?"

Jaida's beautiful eyes grow sad. In all of his dreams about her, he never imagined eyes like those. "He died. At Hammond."

He thinks for a moment. "The bloke who took the bullets?"

She nods.

"Jesus, Jaida. I'm sorry."

"Thank you."

He remembers seeing it on the news. He'd never seen anyone move that fast. "Brave guy."

"Yes."

"Like to think I could do something like that."

"I know you could." She touches his arm. "I can't tell you how happy I am to see you. Really see you. I never thought..."

He puts his hand over hers. "Feeling's mutual, love. Don't, now." He wipes her tear away with his thumb. "You'll get me going again. Already embarrassed myself enough tonight."

She kisses his hand, like she did on the porch. "You'll stay, won't you? Here with us?"

He sighs, squeezes her hand. "I can't. Reckon I'll have to at some point. But I got to enjoy my freedom while I can. You understand, yeah?"

She nods.

"Why don't you come back with me, eh? Get out of here for a while? I'm not too keen on how those two talk to you. Was about to hit that one fucking bastard. What's it? Damian."

"He'll grow on you."

"Yeah. Like a bloody cancer."

She smiles. "There's so much more to them than they show."

"I'll take your word for it." He pats her hand. "So, what do you say? Come stay with me for a bit?"

"I can't."

He wants to ask her why; tell her that those idiots can look after themselves for a week; that she's better than some kind of fucking indentured servant. Before he can get the words out, though, she says, "I love them. I need to be with them. This is my home. They're my home."

He shakes his head, smiling. "You really are an angel."

"And besides, I wouldn't leave Adair for the world."

"Yeah. I get that. I'm all in, too. Together again, eh?"

"And this time I know what you look like."

The impossibility of all that's happened tonight overcomes him again, and he covers his face with his hand and laughs. "Oh man, I just can't fucking believe this. You sitting next to me. Hawk. It's too fucking wild. Almost makes me believe in God. I'm not dreaming, am I?"

"Not unless I am, too."

He laughs again. "No, I know I'm not. 'Cause, for some fucking reason, I thought you were a blonde."

"Really?"

"Yeah. Who the fuck knows, eh?" He rolls his eyes. "So tell me about you. All I know so far is that you saved my life and you're not a blonde."

"What do you want to know?"

"Oh, Jesus, everything. Start with the name change and work your way back."

Jaida's face shadows; the smile fades.

He takes her hand in both of his. "Oh, darling, no. Never mind. Doesn't matter. I didn't mean to upset you—"

"I didn't have a number," she says quickly, quietly. "At the lab. I didn't have a number."

"Why not?"

She cups the side of her neck, just under her ear. "The Voice said I was... *special*, that I was more than a number. So he called me by my name." She looks up at him; her eyes catch the light. "When Adair and Layla found me and asked me my name, I didn't tell them. I didn't want to hear anyone say it ever again. Adair told me that, until I felt I could tell them, he would call me Eden. I liked that. So..."

"Fuck, I'm sorry. I didn't know."

"Oh, no." She puts her hand on his arm. "No. Today, when you called me Jaida—I felt so happy. It was my name when we found each other, and in your voice, it sounds beautiful. Please don't call me anything else."

"You sure?"

"Yes."

He breathes a laugh. "Just as well. Knowing me, I'd fuck it up every bloody time. But if you change your mind—"

"I won't."

They sit in silence for a moment. Wayland takes her in again—the eyes, the skin, the fangs. She's nothing like he imagined. He's glad of it. "Can I ask you something?"

"Of course."

"Are you telepathic?"

He sees her tense. "Why?"

"I don't know. Nothing. Never mind."

"No. Tell me."

"Well, it's just..." He hasn't really thought this through, hasn't been able to put into words, even to himself, what he's thinking. He wishes he hadn't said anything. "It's just that... sometimes, when I heard you... it wasn't like hearing. It was like I *felt* you talking or—I don't know." He shakes his head. "Nah, it doesn't matter. Forget it."

She turns away from him, is quiet for so long, he doesn't think she'll say anything. Then she takes a slow breath, speaks quietly. "I only called out to you once."

He frowns. "What?" He heard her voice a hundred times at least; he's sure.

She finally looks at him. The hold her eyes have on his is like something physical; he couldn't look away even if he wanted to. "I'm empathic."

"Empathic?"

"I feel... what other people feel—like they're my own emotions. And I can..." she hesitates, "change them... or take them away..."

Wayland just stares at her. "I don't... I don't understand."

"When you heard me, I felt what you felt, how my voice made you feel. And after that, whenever things got bad, I would—it's so hard to explain—I would... bring those feelings up and sort of... put them on top of whatever else you were feeling. It was the only way I could help you."

He told August he didn't trust telepaths. He's never heard of empaths. Changing thoughts is disturbing enough, but changing a person's feelings? Taking away those feelings? He doesn't mean to, but he lets Jaida's hand go and looks away from her.

"Wayland, please," she says. "I've never told anyone. Not even Adair."

And he's angry. He doesn't want to know this. "Why are you telling me?"

"Because... when I felt you—it saved me. *You* saved me. I didn't even realize it at first. I was dying in that room, and every time I fell asleep and woke up again, all I could think was, Why am I still alive? What's keeping me here? And then, I *heard* you. I *felt* you. I'd been feeling you the whole time. And I hadn't felt anyone..." she shivers and her voice shakes, "for so long... Only emptiness... It was like being in a dark room for so long you forget what light is."

"What about the Voice? What did he... *feel* like?" He says this too harshly, regrets it, but stops himself from apologizing.

"Nothing," she says, a cold, faraway look in her eyes. "He felt like nothing. He *was* the emptiness. He was the dark room."

He's not following her. She's frightening him with all her talk of feeling people, of emptiness and dark rooms. It doesn't make sense. "But I *heard* you. I heard your voice. You spoke to me. Over and over."

She looks at him again. "I only spoke to you once. After that

I just kept the feelings you had when you heard me at the surface for as long as I could. Maybe that made you remember my voice and you thought you were actually hearing me. What I made you feel—they were your own emotions. I just made them stronger and took away—" her voice breaks, "—your sadness."

"My sadness?" And it's like water rushes over him, washing away every thought he has, because he finally understands what she's trying to tell him and what it really means. He looks at her in awe. "You feel *everything*? In all of us? All the time?"

"Yes."

"How—" He shakes his head. "How can you stand it?"

"It's who I am."

"Jaida—"

She rests her hand against his cheek. "You felt strong and loved when I spoke to you. You felt hopeful. And I made you feel that way again and again and you got stronger. And then..."

"I woke up."

"Yes."

He hides his face in his hands. "And I left you behind."

She puts her head on his shoulder, and he lifts his arm from between them so he can hold her. She hugs him around his waist. "I would never hurt you, Wayland. I wanted you to live. People can die of despair."

"God, Jaida, you've been through enough, haven't you? To have to feel all the shit I've felt? And everyone here? We're all about as fucked up as people can be, aren't we? And you taking it all in? Can't you turn it off? Give yourself a break?"

She doesn't answer, just holds him more tightly.

"I'm sorry I got angry," he says.

"Don't be." He feels her take a deep breath. "Just promise me something?"

"Anything, love. Anything."

"Don't tell them? I can do more good for them if they don't know."

He thinks he understands. If his reaction to what she's told him is anything to go by, then he's pretty sure it wouldn't go over well with the others either. "Yeah. Okay."

"I told you because you asked, and I didn't want to lie to you."

"Hey," he says. "Look at me, Jaida."

She lets go, raises her face to his.

"We've got a bond, you and me. I wouldn't break it for the world."

She touches his face again. "I love you, Wayland Mark. You're beautiful and you're strong. You really are."

She hugs him again, and he feels happy, doesn't care if it's coming from her or if he really feels it. He rests his chin on top of her head. "Say that again for me, would you, darling?"

❧

"August?"

He looks up, takes the Bolts out of his ears. "Cube, pause." The images freeze.

Eden stands half in the hall, half in the living room, her feet straddling the hardwood floor and the rug. "Sorry to bother you."

"No, it's fine. What's up?"

"I just wanted to thank you again."

"I didn't really do anything, you know. I mean, I got the shit kicked out of me, but that's not hard."

"I'm still grateful."

"Okay. Well... you're welcome then, I guess."

She nods, seems about to leave, but instead says, "I'm sorry if I acted a little... crazy earlier. You must've thought I'd lost it out on the porch."

She's trying to explain the kiss, trying to tell him without telling him that it didn't mean anything; just a heat-of-the-moment kind of thing. August wishes she'd just go away, but only shrugs. "Hey, it's been a crazy kind of day."

Eden smiles. "Yeah." She puts her hands in her pockets. "Okay, well, goodnight." She starts to turn.

"Did he make you laugh?" The words are out of his mouth before he even realizes he's going to say them.

She turns back. "Who?"

"Liam."

"Why?"

"I never heard you laugh before today. I mean, not really. Not like that. And I was just wondering—" August shakes his head. "Nothing. Never mind. I'm tired and I drank too much, which is so rare for me. Cube, resume."

"Cube, off." Eden comes over, sits down next to him. "What do you want to know?"

He wishes he hadn't said anything, just let her leave. "I don't know. Never mind."

"August."

He leans forward, rests his elbows on his knees. "It's just... I knew Liam for a long time. And he wasn't... No, never mind. I'm drunk."

"I know the kind of man he was, August."

He looks at her, at her gorgeous face and deep, honest eyes. "I don't know if you do."

She lifts her hand to touch his face. "He was beautiful, like you."

August closes his eyes. "Your hand is so cold."

She pulls back.

"No, no." He takes both of her hands and rubs her fingers. "No."

She watches his hands. "I can't explain it. There was so much more to him than anyone knew. But I waited too long... I wanted him to understand that I loved him... That I... *saw* him."

He holds her hands, keeps his eyes down. "Do you see me?"

"Yes."

He looks up at her, sits still. "I want to kiss you."

"I know."

"So... I'm going to. Okay?"

She doesn't move.

In a way, he gets her and Liam. Especially Liam. August saw the way women looked at him whenever they were at a bar, or just walking down the street. Everything about Liam was wrong—the pale skin, the scar, the eyes. So, to have someone look at him and love him—he gets that. But he saw Liam at his worst too many times. And he wonders if it's better for Eden to have lost him before seeing that side of him herself.

But as he kisses her, he thinks that it would be impossible for anyone, even Liam, to do anything to Eden except love her. Because as she kisses him back, she gives him something, some part of herself or... something. He doesn't know. But it makes him feel so sorry for Liam—he finally got what he'd always wanted and then he died. But at least he got it, August thinks. Maybe he should feel happy for him instead.

He pulls back slightly because he wants to see her face. "Your tongue is really... interesting."

She gives him an odd look. "Is that good or bad?"

"I'm pretty sure it's good. But I think I need to explore the issue a little further to form a final opinion. It might take a while." He presses her down onto the couch and she lets him, running her fingers through his hair as he kisses her again and she kisses him back. "Yeah, I'm still not sure."

Someone is walking around upstairs, but he doesn't care. And Eden doesn't seem to either. He can taste wine on her tongue.

"Hey, you're not drunk, are you? Because I'll be sad if you don't remember all this in the morning."

"All what?"

He kisses her neck. "Everything we're going to do upstairs. I'm going to keep you up pretty late."

"I'm not drunk."

"Do you want to be?"

"No. I just want you."

He kisses her again, slips his hand under her shirt. God, she's so soft. "I *am* kind of drunk, but I have no problem with you taking advantage of me." He kisses her neck again. Her skin is cold. She tilts her head back, and he kisses her throat and collarbone. "You have no idea how long I've wanted to do this."

"I think I have some idea." Her voice is a breathless whisper.

He moves down the couch so he can kiss her stomach. "Every time I come here, you drive me fucking crazy. You know that, right? You know you drive me crazy."

"I don't mean to."

"You don't even have to try." He pushes her shirt higher.

"August."

The tone of her voice makes him stop and look up at her.

"He did make me laugh."

He sits up, looks down at her beautiful face and her dark, silky hair spread across the pillow. He pulls the ends of her shirt down to cover her stomach. "You love him."

"Yes."

"That's not going to change."

"No."

He sighs, falls back against the cushions. "We can stop."

She kneels next to him. She kisses his neck and then he feels her tongue.

"Jesus, Eden. Don't do that if you're about to say goodnight to me."

"What happened to going upstairs?"

He turns his face to hers. "If we make it to my room, I'm not going to let you leave."

She stands up, offers him her hand. "I won't want to."

She loves Liam. She wants Liam. She wouldn't look twice at him if Liam were here.

But Liam isn't here. Liam is dead.

August takes her hand. "Come here." And he pulls her gently onto his lap. He wraps his arms around her and she rests against him. "I'm really sorry about Liam. I'm so sorry." And he means it. He kisses her forehead.

"Thank you."

"But you've got to know. I care about you. I'll be good to you."

"You're already good to me."

"Okay. Then I'll be really, really good to you."

She lifts her head and kisses him. "I'll be really, really good to you, too."

☙

Eden's back is to him. As the sun rises, it lights up her long hair and he sees that it's not black, but a very dark green. It's strange that he's never noticed that before. He weaves the ends of it between his fingers, moves it aside, kisses her bare back, her shoulder, her neck. She takes a deep breath, turns around.

"Hi." August touches her face.

"Hi." She smiles. "It's so early."

"I know. I want to get up before everybody else and have breakfast with you."

"What would you like?"

"I would like you to relax and let me cook."

"Seriously?"

"Don't look at me like that. I can be domestic."

"Okay."

"I hear the doubt in your voice and I don't appreciate it. Have I told you how beautiful your eyes are?"

"Several times."

"What about your lips?"

"I think so."

He climbs out of the bed to dress. "Oh, and I've decided that your tongue is fucking incredible, by the way."

As he reaches for his pants, she says, "What are you doing?"

"Getting dressed."

"Why?"

"I generally don't make a habit of walking around naked."

She holds her hand out to him. "Come back."

"Breakfast."

She shakes her head.

"You're killing me, Eden. I have to leave soon."

Her eyes fall. "You have to?"

"You know I do. I don't want to. I gotta take Wayland back."

She sighs, looks out the window, then smiles again, turns back. "Ten minutes?"

"You got a stopwatch?"

"Please, August. I want to feel you again."

He sits on the bed, sighs, takes her hand. "This is going to sound pervy—but, I've imagined you naked so many times—"

"That does sound pervy."

"Hey, come on. Let me finish embarrassing myself."

"Okay."

He takes a breath. "I've dreamed about you. But you, the real thing, when I saw you last night, you're—" He pulls back the sheet to look at her. "None of my fantasies ever got close. You're perfect."

She runs her fingers down his bare arm, over his thigh. "Ten minutes?"

He smiles.

☙

Damian walks into the kitchen as they're finishing their breakfast. He ignores them, starts to pour a cup of coffee, stops mid-pour. "Oh my God." He laughs, looking over at August.

"What?"

"You're shitting me." He shakes his head, finishes pouring. "Just when I thought this house couldn't get any more incestuous."

"What's your fucking problem, Damian?"

He smiles. "Jesus, Gus. First Layla, now her? You're the only one of us that gets to leave the house on a regular basis, and you come back here to get your rocks off? I was just kidding when I told you to fuck her."

August's gut twists into knots. He looks at Eden. She's watching Damian, her face a mask. "He doesn't know what the fuck he's talking about." He doesn't want to lie to her, but this is something he should tell Eden himself, something he would have... eventually. But not now. Definitely not now.

"Eden. The only one of us Layla *hasn't* fucked is you, but I wouldn't put it past her." Damian drinks his coffee. "I'll say this, Gus. You're a braver man than I am. I mean, she's pretty and all, but any bitch crazy enough to fuck Aldrich by choice, I don't want to touch with a ten-foot pole."

August jumps out of his chair so fast he knocks it over. "Shut your fucking mouth, Damian!"

Damian slowly lowers his mug. The steam rises in front of his face. "I know you didn't just say that to me, August."

He feels like his head might explode, like his chest is filling with thick, hot lead. August isn't a fighter; he's a talker. He's talked his way through life to survive it. His weapons are his mind and his lies. But Damian has known him too long for his telepathy to have much effect on him, and he always knows when someone is lying.

It strikes August then that he hates Damian. He *hates* him. He never has before. It never occurred to him that he ever would. But he does. Seeing how he treats Eden, the things he says to her...

There's a knife on the table and August grabs it.

Damian's dark smile invites him forward. "Try it."

Suddenly, Eden is standing between them. She pushes August's wrist down.

He meets her eyes. "Eden..."

She turns away from him. "What would you like for breakfast, Damian? And I'll wear gloves if you don't want me touching your food."

Her voice is so quiet, so devoid of feeling.

"The usual." He walks past her, sits at the table. "And more coffee."

August watches Eden get the pot from the counter, watches her top off Damian's coffee. Damian winks at him as she does.

He throws the knife down onto the table. Damian doesn't even flinch, and August hears that taunting laugh as he storms out of the room.

He grabs his bag, shouts up the steps to Wayland.

"Down in a minute, mate!"

Outside, he throws the bag into the trunk, slams it shut. At the driver's door, he presses his thumb against the printlock so hard, the car gets confused. "Print not recognized."

"You stupid, fucking piece of shit." He punches the door.

"Print not recognized."

"Oh my fucking God—"

"August!"

Eden runs down the steps to him. "What are you doing? Look at your hand!"

He's bleeding. There's blood on the door. "Fuck."

She takes his hand. "August..." She circles her finger around the cut. "Were you just going to leave?"

"I didn't think you'd want to talk to me."

She frowns. "Why? Because of Layla? I don't care about that."

He stares at her for a moment, confused. "But—"

"It doesn't matter."

"I want to say it was a long time ago—"

She puts her hand on his chest, repeats slowly and assuredly, "It doesn't matter."

He looks down at her hand, there over his heart—a heart he lost to her a long time ago, maybe even when he first met her. He puts his own hand over hers. He hates that he has to leave. Nothing seems to matter now except being here with her. The lab and the subjects and Kovich are far away, amorphous. He looks toward the house. "I don't want to leave you here with Damian."

"Damian would never hurt me."

"He hurts you every time he opens his mouth."

She touches his cheek to turn his head back to her. "No. He doesn't." She kisses him.

He keeps his eyes closed, even after she's pulled away. "Why are you so good to me?"

"How could I not be?"

He feels stupid, useless, kicks at the dirt. This isn't how he wanted to say goodbye to her. "Adair said that Marlowe got in contact."

She nods. "I'm meeting with her in a few days."

He feels a flicker of panic. He knew this was coming, but… "Will you be okay? I mean…" What if something happens to her? What if Marlowe forgets to turn her tracker-blocker on and they get caught and they take Eden away…?

"August, I'll be fine." Her smile, her voice, almost soothe him.

"I don't like it."

"I do. I told you I wanted to meet her."

"Yeah… but still. Please be careful."

She nods. "I will."

He runs his fingers roughly through his hair. "Oh, man. This fucking sucks." He can't think of anything else to say except, "I'll be back in a week."

"I'll be here. Please don't worry about me. Just think of me, okay?"

"I'm pretty sure that's all I'll be thinking about."

She smiles. "What about this?"

His hand is throbbing. "I'll take care of it later. I don't want to go back inside." He looks over at the car, at his blood on the door, then back at the house, at the window of his room. "I meant what I said last night, you know. I'll be good to you."

She kisses him again. "I meant it too."

Chapter 20

DISAPPEARED, THEY SAID. Marlowe's car disappeared. They've been keeping track of her movements virtually, watching her by way of the standard built-in tracker in her car. It's been a dull surveillance. She doesn't drive much, and when she does, it's to the store and back or something equally mundane. Then, all of a sudden, she vanished. Her car was in the driveway and then it wasn't. Either her tracker malfunctioned—which is just as likely as not—or...

She has a tracker-blocker.

He sent one of his people to see if the car was there, and it wasn't. He called for any car in the nearby area to keep an eye out for her. So far, nothing. A tracker-blocker, then: illegal, expensive. Where the fuck did she get one of those?

He wanted to put a decent tracker on her car, one that couldn't be blocked. The trackers that car companies are legally obligated to build into every make and model are all right, but he wanted one of his own, a more dependable version, impervious to blockers. He couldn't get the permission, though.

"Motherfucker." He stares down at his tableface, at the representation of Corbin's shelter where Marlowe's car should be parked. He waits for the dot that symbolizes her to reappear; it doesn't. "Motherfucker."

He thinks of how she shook his hand after he interrogated her; how she smiled a little because she knew she'd won, had beat him at his own game.

He wonders if she's smiling now.

ᘒ

A tableface ad blinks up at her as she waits in the diner—pics and vids of smiling scientists, lecture halls, and sparkling laboratories.

Freedom Pharmaceuticals: Fighting for Your *Life.*

"Sierra?"

She jumps, looks up from the table. The woman is short, lean; she has pale green skin and snake scales, like henna, rising up either side of her neck, behind her ears, and coming down her forehead through to just under her eyes, ending in small triangles. And her eyes—they're a glowing yellow, with black slit pupils and no lids. "Are you...?"

The woman nods and smiles, sits across from her. "My name is Eden."

"Nice to meet you," Sierra says automatically.

"Is it?"

The question catches her off guard. She doesn't know what to say. "I—"

Eden smiles again. Sierra sees fangs. "I mean you look nervous."

"Oh." Sierra shifts uncomfortably. "I am."

"It's okay."

Sierra wonders if she can really do this, wonders how she got here—from a morning talk show, to a field of chaos, to a prison with a terrorist, to this diner with this woman.

"You're all right, Sierra. You're doing everything right."

The woman's eyes are like magnets. They draw Sierra in, make her forget her fear. She nods. "Okay. Okay. I'm fine. I just—I never saw myself here. I mean, in this mindset. Everything's—different now."

Eden tilts her head, seems to look into her, and it makes Sierra wonder if she's telepathic. She doesn't sense an intrusion into her mind, but something feels strange.

"I want to thank you," Eden says.

"For what?"

"For visiting him. That was brave."

Sierra doesn't feel brave. Her head hurts; her mouth is dry. "I didn't go for *him*... exactly. Not at first."

"I know. But you went. You're very brave."

Sierra likes this woman. She feels safe with her, suddenly, like she isn't doing anything wrong; like she isn't going behind Richard's back; like she didn't lie to Dairen about where she was going today.

"So, do you have something for me?"

Sierra hesitates for only a second before taking out the folded pages and passing them to Eden under the table.

Eden doesn't look at them, just puts them in her pocket.

The chatter in the diner, the clinking of utensils on plates, fill the silence between them. The light from the sporadic tableface ads reflects off Eden's eyes.

Oh Baby 02 Bar—Breathe Easy, Drink Hard

Escape the Smog at Adirondack Park—The Air's Just Fresher Here

When Eden doesn't say anything else, Sierra asks, "Is that it?"

"Are you kidding?" Eden's smile is back. "I'm starving."

They talk over their meal, and soon Sierra is as comfortable with Eden as she is with any other friend.

It's only after they part ways and Sierra is nearly home that she realizes how much she told Eden about herself and how very little Eden revealed in return.

↜↝

"What happened?"

Eden closes the door. "Nothing."

Damian starts the car. "I've been waiting for over an hour."

"I was hungry."

He glares at her. "I'm not your fucking chauffeur."

"You are today." She holds up a bag. "I got you a burger and fries."

"Oh, good. I'm glad you let her know there were two of us."

"Fine." She lowers her arm. "I'll warm it up for my lunch tomorrow."

He grabs the bag. "Give me that." He takes out a fry. "You're ballsy all of a sudden."

She sighs. "Sorry."

"No, it's kind of hot."

She looks at him with wide eyes.

He takes a bite of the burger. "What? I can't change my mind about things?" He swallows, smiles, puts the burger back in the bag, moves it to the side. He opens his arms, nods down to his lap. "What do you say? Right here, right now. It's a long ride."

"Not long enough for me."

She sounds like Layla, and this both amuses and disturbs him. He raises an eyebrow. "Come on. Gus can't be that good."

She looks out the window, says nothing.

"I know you're not talking about Aldrich."

She still doesn't say anything.

He watches her. "Didn't take you long to get over him."

She tenses, turns to him. "I'll never get over him. You know that."

He remembers coming home after Hammond, how he held her arm and told her not to fall apart, that no one would care if she cried. He remembers her screams echoing through the forest, growing weaker and weaker until she had no choice but to come back. He waited for her in the dark that night. He waits for her now.

And after a few moments' silence, she says, "I can't be alone again, Damian."

It's like she's pleading with him, as if it matters to her what he thinks, as if she needs him to understand.

Eden reads him easily, and he hates that his thoughts are so obvious. "I know it would be different for you if you lost Layla. But I *can't* be alone."

A searing chill runs through him. He doesn't want to think about what life would be like without Layla. It came too close to being a reality once, and he's never going to let that happen again. He pushes these thoughts away, pushes Eden away. "Come on," he says. "Aldrich versus Gus."

She narrows her lidless eyes, lifts her mouth in a smile that barely reveals one of her fangs, and he's struck again by just how much she reminds him of himself sometimes. "If you really want to know what August is like in bed, why don't you just ask Layla?"

He wasn't expecting that. "What the fuck did you say?"

"What are you going to do? Throw me out of the car?"

"I'm thinking about it."

She looks straight ahead. "I could bite you faster than you could open the door."

His anger cools and he can't help smiling, but he doesn't let her see. He tosses the bag into her lap. "Have a fucking fry and shut the fuck up."

They pass the food back and forth until it's gone, don't speak for the rest of the trip.

They don't have to.

೮ಾ

They've opened her skull.

But at least she's asleep, he thinks.

She sits upright on an inclined, metal operating table, hands strapped to the arms, legs likewise at the bottom. A cool light fills the room. Dr. Hoffmann wears a headlamp along with his other surgical gear. He works in tandem with a botdoc, the robot's long, multi-jointed arm helping him through whatever procedure he's engaged in. Several assistants are with him, but August, Kovich, and other scientists watch through the large glass window in the observation room.

Hoffmann narrates his work in a flat monotone, explaining to them what he's doing. August can't really follow the medical jargon. He tries to think of something else, tries to pretend he isn't seeing what he's seeing. He wishes he could lie to himself as well as he does to everyone else.

He sees her brain. They poke small instruments into the myriad folds, watch the various monitors; one of the assistants takes notes. Sometimes the woman on the table twitches, and August is terrified she's woken up. But they're only reflexes, not conscious movements.

He can *see* her *brain.*

It scares him, not because of the blood or the carefully carved away skull that reminds him too much of the top of a jack-o'-lantern. No. It's the organ itself: the center of everything—of memory, pain, emotion—everything that makes a person a person. And he wonders, is that all she is? Is that all *he* is? Tangled muscle and blood? Is that who August is? Is that *where* he is?

He feels a hollowness in his stomach, in his heart. He makes himself think of Eden. There's a certain peace there, because he knows without a doubt that she is more—she's more than that meat-like organ he can't stop looking at.

But his peace is broken and the cold fear returns when Hoffmann nods to an assistant. "All right. Wake her up."

❧

"I can't just let you use the Feed, Wynne."

Aaron Lee stands in Jamie's office at the Department of Dysmorphic Affairs and Terrorism's headquarters in Washington, DC—the office Jamie calls "the fishbowl." It has glass on all sides. He can see into the hallway and into the offices to his right, left, and behind him. It was designed, he was told, to allow light to come into every office. This would heighten people's moods and better morale. The idea made him laugh then; it just annoys him now. But, he supposes, it makes no real difference. He's come to see the fishbowl as a visual representation of his generation's complete lack of privacy, the absence of which is paramount to maintaining national security and anticipating domestic terrorism, or so they say.

There are digital cams all over the country—traffic cams, private and public security cams, and likewise private and public tablefaces, wallfaces, Lenses. All of their footage is collected, sent to, and held in one place in an invisible storage compartment made possible by the great god Internet, and simply called: The Feed. Jamie doesn't pretend to understand the intricacies of it, but he doesn't care. That's Lee's job. He just needs access to it. No permission is needed to collect the footage itself, but looking at it, searching through it—that's where things get sticky.

He leans back in his chair behind the stern, utilitarian desk that is the defining object of his office; that, and the chair across from it. He has no PhotoCubes, no comfortable couch to sit on when he needs a break. Nothing. This isn't his home, and he won't add anything to it that might make it seem that way.

He looks up at his friend and fellow DDAT employee; not an agent, like he is, but an information specialist. "Come on, Lee."

"Do you have the eWork?" Lee asks. "No. You don't."

"No, I don't. I'm not going to use any information you give me to make an arrest."

"I don't care." Lee starts to turn away.

Jamie gets up, quickly moves around the desk. He puts a hand on Lee's shoulder. "I had a tail on this girl and she just disappeared. I've got to know where she went."

"And I've got to have eForms, fingerprinted, dated."

"Lee. Come on. Pretty please?"

Lee closes his eyes. He sighs. "Who is she?"

Jamie sends a pic to Lee's Lens.

"Sierra Marlowe? Are you serious?"

"As always."

"Goddammit."

He pats Lee on the back. "Thanks, pal."

Lee slouches in the doorway, then turns to Jamie. "I hate you. You know that, right?"

Jamie laughs.

❧

"I recognize the description. It's Twenty-Seven." August hands the note back to him.

Adair stares at the papers laid out on the table, is filled with the same painful incredulity he felt when he first read the notes Sierra gave Eden earlier in the week.

Richard knows about the lab. He knows. How long has he known? How can he have sat on this information and done nothing? But the answer is obvious. Richard always wanted to do the right thing the right way, work within the boundaries of law and bureaucracy.

He's brought back to thirteen years ago: Richard, settling for Francis Harold's joke of a sentence because there was "nothing else they could do." Well, Adair found something else, and he did it. He would do it again.

"What's the point of Corbin having someone in the lab if he's not going to fucking do anything?" Layla picks up one of the notes, the one about Richard's mole, Lena Marsh. She stares at it in disgust, puts it down again like it's something toxic.

Adair takes it; his eyes move over the words. "Evidence..." he says, almost to himself. "He's looking for evidence. Like he did with Martinez."

"Well, he won't get it." August sits back. "No Lenses, no cameras, no holowatches. If Corbin goes after Freedom with only Marsh's eyewitness testimony, they'll crush her. Hell, they'll probably kill her."

"No," Adair says quietly. "No. He'll get his evidence. We'll get it for him."

Damian frowns. "What?"

"We'll take the files."

"There are thousands of files," August says.

"We don't need all of them. A few large bags. I can put as many files in as possible. It won't take long. The rest of you will free the prisoners."

"Why, Dair? Who cares about all this? Who gives a fuck about Corbin?"

"We've just been given an opportunity to make this more than just a destructive act. Aren't the files signed and printed?"

August nods. "Every one. But if we do this, it'll make it look like Corbin was involved. He'll lose credibility. It could get him thrown in prison or worse."

Adair presses his fingers against the notes. "What about our eyewitness? What if Dr. Lena Marsh was able to steal some files before the building was destroyed or has been gradually smuggling out a few at a time? It's not beyond the realm of possibility. It'll be shaky at first, but they'll never find a connection between her and us, because there isn't one."

Layla looks at Adair, understanding in her eyes. "It'll make you look like a hero, not a terrorist."

He takes her hand. "I don't know about a hero, but it will certainly make us look a bit less like psychopaths."

"Don't count on it," Damian mutters.

Adair looks to August. "What do you think?"

"I'll talk to her," August says, "feel her out. Make sure she's really on the side of the psychopaths."

"All right. Find out as much as you can. Get her to trust you."

August gives him a bitter smile. "That's my specialty."

❧

Layla turns the knob on the door, is surprised to find it locked. She knocks lightly, waits, knocks again.

She hears him walking, unlatching the door. His eyes widen when he sees her.

"Hi," she says.

August is wearing shorts and nothing else. His face is flushed, his hair tousled. He looks to the side, back at her. "I—um—what—what do you want?"

She gives him a look. "To borrow a cup of sugar. What do you think?"

He looks away from her again, runs his fingers through his hair. "I'm not—uh—it's kind of—"

She kisses him, walks him back into the room.

He puts his hands on her shoulders, pushes away from her. "Layla."

She catches movement to her right, turns, sees Eden's yellow eyes looking at her from August's bed. Layla looks back at him. "Are you serious?"

"Layla—"

She puts her hands up. "It's fine." Her face feels hot.

Eden watches her. She doesn't seem surprised, or even offended, to see her there. Layla turns back into the hallway, hears August's door close; he's followed her and she feels his hand take her arm.

"Layla."

"It's fine." She smiles, shrugs. "I was just bored. It was between you and a movie."

"Layla—"

"What is it? A tongue fetish or something?"

He lets go. "No."

"Then what?"

He looks into her eyes, then quickly away.

Layla covers her mouth, pretends to hold back a laugh. "You're not—oh my God. With *her*? August! You're breaking my heart."

When he meets her eyes again there's an anger there that she's not used to seeing. "Just go, okay?"

She feels that heat in her face again. A spiral of fury winds its way through her chest. "You do know who her last boyfriend was, right?" She leans in close to him, puts a hand on his arm. His fists tighten at his sides. "You're second to Liam," she whispers, lets him go, walks backward down the hall. "Think about that." She turns and keeps going.

She stops after she hears him go back into his room, breathes as slowly as she can. The wood floor under her feet feels like wet ice. She looks over her shoulder, half expecting Eden to be standing behind her, staring at her again with those flat yellow eyes, seeing everything and saying nothing.

Layla puts a hand on her throat, gives her head a quick shake, fixes her hair, adjusts her clothes. She walks down to the other side of the house.

Damian's door is never locked.

⌘

"Man, Gus must've really pissed you off." Damian puts his arms behind his head, leans back into the pillows, watches her, standing at the open window.

Layla is beautiful naked. Her iridescent skin catches the moonlight. Her wings shimmer when she moves her arms, and her feathers lift and fall in the light breeze. She turns to him. "What does August have to do with anything?"

"Don't play dumb. I've known you too long."

"Maybe I just missed you."

"Maybe. But you only come to me when you're angry."

"No I don't."

He smiles. "I have the scratches on my back to prove it."

She gives him a look. "Aw, poor baby. Did I hurt you?"

"Only the way I like."

"You're sick."

"*You're* here."

Layla faces the window again. "Touché."

He watches her a moment longer, then, "If you're planning on staying up to watch the sun rise, I'm going to sleep."

"This window faces west."

"You're going to have a long wait then." He closes his eyes, breathes in the scent of her all around him, on the pillows, on the sheets... on his skin, and he allows himself to fall away into his own satisfaction for a moment.

"He's sleeping with Eden," she says in a low, quiet voice.

Eyes still closed, he mumbles, "And I'm d-form. Any other news?"

"You knew?"

He sighs, the moment gone. "Hell yes, I knew." He looks at her. "You didn't?"

Her shoulders fall.

Damian laughs. "You're such a whore, Layla."

She spins around. "What the fuck did you say?"

He sits up. "You're a fucking attention whore. You need everybody's eyes on you. You even got pissed when Aldrich started stalking Eden. Didn't want those rat eyes looking at anyone else."

"Fuck you."

"Fine with me. I'm not tired."

She takes two quick strides to the bed. He catches her arm before she slaps him.

"See?" he laughs, pulling her in. "Angry." He wraps his arms around her waist. She's cold from standing by the window. "Take it out on me, *hummingbird*."

"I'm going to scratch your eyes out!"

"Keep talking." He pulls her onto the bed, flips her onto her stomach, pins her arms behind her.

"Stop it!"

"Or what?"

"I'll scream!"

He covers her mouth with his other hand. She sinks her teeth into it. He hisses, pulls back. Pain shivers up his arm. She gets out from under him. He shakes his hand out. "You bit me."

"It's not the first time."

He looks at his hand, at her teeth marks. He smiles. "That's a good one."

"Only the best for you." Layla wraps herself up in the quilt, rests her chin on her knees. She looks younger that way, like when he first knew her.

He traces the bite mark with his finger, the indentations in his skin already going away. He wishes they wouldn't. Then he looks at Layla and sees what he always does when she's dropped her guard—the sadness of perpetual dissatisfaction.

"Come here," he says.

"No. I'm tired."

"Come. Here."

She gives him an exasperated look. "Damian, I've got nothing left. My whole body hurts."

"I want to try something different."

"I'm not in the mood to experiment. Besides, between the two of us, I think we've thought of everything."

Damian pulls the sheet back. "I want to hold you."

Her eyes widen, and it almost makes him laugh. "You want to *what*?"

"Hold you."

Weariness turns to suspicion. "Why?"

"Why not? Let's pretend we're normal people and we love each other." He pats the space beside him. "Come on."

Frowning, Layla moves over and lies on her side next to him. He pulls the covers up, kisses her back, puts his arm around her, rubs his thumb up and down her stomach. Her silken feathers brush his face.

"This is weird," she says after a minute.

"I think it's nice."

His eyes feel heavy, but he's not ready to sleep. He knows she won't be here when he wakes up.

It's quiet, almost peaceful. He holds her for what feels like a long time. He begins to wonder if she's fallen asleep, which would be a first, when her fingers softly stroke his arm. "Damian?"

"What?"

"You don't love me."

It's not a question, so he doesn't have to answer it, doesn't have to lie. He pulls her tight, kisses the base of her neck. "I love to fuck you."

She relaxes, takes a breath. "This is kind of nice."

❧

When Damian is asleep, Layla moves slowly out from under his arm. The floor is freezing under her bare feet. She gathers her clothes. It's quiet in the hall as she walks back to her room.

Her side of the bed is cold. She shivers, moves closer to Dair but doesn't touch him. His back is to her.

"I'm awake," he says.

And she's so glad that he is. She wraps her arm around him, hugs him close, presses her body against his. "I tried to be quiet. I'm sorry."

"I'm not." She can hear a smile in his voice. He takes her hand, kisses it.

And she says the words that have only ever been meant for Adair. "I love you."

"I know you do, my beautiful girl." He kisses her hand again.

"I love you, I love you." She kisses his back through his shirt. "Are you mine, Dair?"

"Forever and always, my hummingbird."

He turns onto his back and she lays her head on his chest, holds him around his waist. She listens to his heartbeat, closes her eyes. He's so warm. And he's hers. All hers.

Forever and always.

❧

She falls asleep on his chest. He listens to her breathe, focuses on how perfectly her body fits against his. He reaches down to pull the covers up over her bare shoulder. She sighs, but doesn't wake. He closes his eyes.

When Layla first came to him, he didn't understand.

She was beautiful. He was naturally attracted to her. He cared for her. But he didn't know that he loved her. He was past love, he thought; not past the need, perhaps, but past the possibility. He was over sixty by then, only getting older.

And, of course, there was Damian.

He never flirted with her, never made any advances. When he first met her, he told her that her features were striking and that she had a beautiful name. She liked that; he remembers how she smiled. And while they grew close and enjoyed each other's company, he never expected anything from her. It was she who decided, for reasons all her own—and to his disbelief and joy—to come to his room one night and never leave.

Adair is more than twice Layla's age, but that night she showed him that age has nothing to do with sex when love is involved. And he does love her with all his soul, and knows that she loves him.

The next morning at breakfast, Damian winked at him, smiled, like they shared a secret. And, in a way, they do. Layla is a secret. She is a lust-filled, rage-driven, insatiable mystery.

When Layla first came to him, he didn't understand, and he still doesn't. But she has his heart, and no matter where she goes or who she's with, she always will.

Chapter 21

D R. MARSH? Are you all right?"

She's facing her car, turns around quickly, startled, her hand on her stomach. "What—? How long have you been standing there?"

August looks behind him, back at her. "I just pulled up. I forgot to pick up my Lens at the desk."

"Oh." She smoothes the front of her jacket. "I was just leaving... Goodnight." She turns, presses her thumb into the printlock.

He steps forward. "Hey, I didn't mean to scare you." She looks back at him. "You just seemed upset. Are you okay?"

"I'm fine." She opens the door.

He waits a moment, then, "It gets to me, too."

Marsh turns sharply. "Excuse me?" She's nervous, suspicious. He doesn't blame her.

"This place," he says. "It gets to you, right?" It's easy for him to seem sincere now. He's actually telling the truth for a change. "I mean, I know they're just d-forms—I mean, dysmorphics—but—" He puts his hands into his pockets, giving her the impression that he's opened up to her and now regrets his words, is shutting down. "Never mind. I'm tired. Long day, you know?" He smiles nervously, unconvincingly. "Well, goodnight. Sorry to bother you."

August walks toward the building. He hears her door close, stops himself from looking back to see if she's gotten in or not.

"John?" she calls after him.

And just like that, he's got her. He stops, turns around.

"It's John, right?"

"Yeah. John Leonard."

She gives him a small, hesitant smile. "John. You weren't bothering me. I—" She pushes her hair back. "You know, long day, like you said. I'm sorry."

"No worries, Doctor."

"Lena. After hours I'm just Lena."

"Okay. No worries, Lena."

There's a short silence, then, "Good. Okay. Well—"

"Have you eaten?"

She blinks. "What? No. I haven't."

He shifts his weight from one foot to the other. "I don't feel like going home yet." And he's back to lying. All he wants to do is go home, have a drink, pretend he doesn't have to come back here tomorrow. "You want to grab dinner?"

"Um..." She looks unsure, but he's already broken into the suggestible part of her mind, making her think she can trust him. "Okay. Yeah. That'd be nice."

He lets her choose the place, a nearby restaurant, follows her car there. They make small talk while they order and wait for their food. Her mind relaxes each time he makes her smile or laugh.

When the food arrives, it gets quiet between them, the sounds of other people eating and talking, watching something on a table-face, filling the silence.

Lena eats slowly. Then she stops, lightly taps her fork on her plate. "I'm a doctor, you know?"

He nods.

"I'm not... a scientist. I don't just take things apart. I'm supposed to..." She spins the fork in a circle, shrugs. "Put them back together." She goes back to pretending to eat.

"So... why are you working at Freedom?"

She looks embarrassed. "It pays well. And it gives me an opportunity to work with dysmorphic humans. There isn't enough known about them, not medically, and sometimes dysmorphic anatomy is very different from a normal human's..." She trails off.

She's not lying, not really. He figures that those were her reasons for working at Hammond Prison before the death of Rico Martinez; before she started working for Richard Corbin. And he's impressed. He knows why she's really at Freedom, but if he didn't, he would believe that money and knowledge were her only motivations. He *did* believe it. It never occurred to him that this shy, quiet woman was anything but what she appeared to be. And unless she's dysmorphic, too—and he seriously doubts she is, because wouldn't Marlowe know that?—Lena Marsh is as good a liar as he is. And that's saying something.

"So, that's basically it," she finishes. "What about you?"

"Oh, you know. I was working at Hammond. Kovich offered me the bodyguard job after the breakout. More money, less work."

"Did you know what you were walking into?"

"I thought I did. I saw some of the lab at the prison, you know, but," he shakes his head, "it's nothing like Freedom."

"Kind of an ironic name, isn't it?"

August half smiles. "A little." He moves his food around on his plate. "You mind if I ask why you were upset earlier?"

She looks up at him, then quickly away.

"You don't have to tell me."

"No. I—" She clears her throat. "I'm just getting tired, I guess."

"Maybe you should take a vacation or... a weekend away or something."

She smirks. "Do you have a house in the country you haven't told me about?"

August smiles. "I wish."

As they finish eating, August tells his usual lies when she asks him about his background—born in the Midwest, average upbringing, military.

"Do you have any family?"

He shakes his head. Although, he thinks his mother is probably out there somewhere, alive just to spite the living. "I'm on my own," he tells her.

"Same here." She hands her plate to the busboy when he comes over to see if she's finished; August does the same. "How is it, working for Dr. Kovich?" she asks when he's gone.

"Fine, I guess. It's a job."

She leans in, lowers her voice. "Can I ask you something?"

"Go for it."

"What's with the shoes?"

He laughs loudly and she shushes him. "What?" he says. "She's not here."

"I know." Lena grimaces. "I just always feel..."

"Watched?"

She nods.

"Me too."

Lena sits back. "I shouldn't be talking to you."

"Hey, I *work* for Kovich; she doesn't own me. I've got one job: keep her alive. It's not as hard as you'd think. Other than that?" He shrugs. "I mean, you're not planning on blowing up the place, are you?"

Her eyes widen. "No!"

"I'm kidding. Sorry. Bad joke."

She looks behind him at the door, then taps the tableface to call up their bill.

He's losing her. He tries to ease her mind. At the same time, he asks, "You still want to know about the shoes?"

Lena looks warily at him, but smiles slightly.

"A pledge of trust between friends?" he says.

"Are we friends?"

"Yeah. Why not?"

She bites her lip.

"You want to hear it or not?"

Lena looks into his eyes.

You can trust me. You can trust me, he thinks at her; and soon, he feels the thought sinking into her mind like a stone settling to the bottom of the sea.

"Yeah. Tell me."

"Friends?" He extends his hand.

"Friends," she says, taking it, smiling in earnest for the first time that night.

☙

"I've decided that Sierra Marlowe is the most boring person I've never met." Lee puts a Cube unceremoniously onto Jamie's desk and shows him the various stills he's collected of Sierra Marlowe. He tells him that the computers went through a month's worth of footage from hundreds of traffic and security cams within a fifty-mile radius to find faces that matched hers. "She goes to the green market twice a week." There's an image of Marlowe picking out apples from a stand at a farmer's market.

"They still have those?"

"Apparently." The next pic is of Marlowe sitting at a table with her boyfriend, Dairen Corbin. "She likes to have lunch at a place called The Rose. Fascinating, huh?"

"I get it, Lee. Let me look for myself, okay?"

"Oh, please, knock yourself out." Lee slumps down in the chair across from Jamie's desk. "I hope you get as bored as I did."

Jamie scrutinizes each captured image. He points. "There we go. This is the day."

Lee sits up straight. "Okay, there is one interesting thing about this pic."

"I see it," Jamie says. It's a pic of Marlowe through the window of a diner. "Whoever she's sitting with is wearing a cam collar." The face is obscured, impossible to see.

"Look at Marlowe's neck."

Jamie does. "She's wearing a collar, too. Why can I see her face?"

Lee shrugs. "It must've malfunctioned. It's a delicate piece of technology."

"Who's she sitting with?" Jamie can see that the woman's hands are slightly green, but there are no other distinguishing features. "Fuck." He stares and stares, and then, "Oh. Oh yeah. I'm good. I'm really good."

"What?" Lee frowns.

"There, right there." He points at the napkin holder, makes the Cube zoom in on it.

"Oh my God." Lee shakes his head. "I didn't see it. Fuck me."

Part of a face is reflected in the metal napkin holder's surface: one yellow snake eye, half a nose, and half a smile, revealing one, sharp-looking fang. "Who the fuck is this? Can you—"

"No!" Lee jumps up from the chair. "No. Not this time. Not without the eWork. You're killing me, Wynne."

Jamie won't be able to get the proper authorization to use the Feed, not with this. A lot of people wear cam collars for the same reason they use tracker-blockers, even though they're both illegal. They desire what is ultimately impossible to attain: privacy. And besides, technically speaking, he's never seen these pics—or at least, he wasn't meant to. "Lee, come on. Just do a search for this woman's face, see what you come up with."

"Jamie." Lee puts up his hands. "You're testing our friendship here. I'm serious." And he is serious. Lee never calls him by his first name.

So Jamie backs off. "Okay. Okay."

"I'm sorry—"

"No, really. It's okay. I'm the one who's sorry." He stands, extends his hand. "I really am."

Lee hesitates, then takes it.

"But if you have a change of heart—"

He yanks his hand away. "Fuck off, Wynne!"

"I'm kidding! I'm kidding!" He goes around the desk, pats Lee on the back. "Come on, let me buy you a drink."

☙

It's the end of the week, almost the end of the day. August thinks he'll go mad waiting for the endless hours to just fucking end.

He's staring at the clock when a red light flashes over the door to Weir's lab, followed by a screeching alarm.

Kovich puts her hand on his arm, pulls. "Come on!"

He follows her across the wide room. As soon as Kovich gets past the door's security, August hears screaming—a deep, ragged cry. An animal sound. They run, turn a corner. The screaming grows louder and louder. It's worse than anything he's ever heard in this place.

The glass doors are already open. The d-form on the table is thrashing madly. His scarred back is to August. There are nurses and doctors sprawled out all over the floor, unconscious or cradling wounds; August is sure at least one of them is dead. They're trying to pin the man down to inject a sedative. He punches one of them in the face. Blood splatters in an arc across the wall behind her as she falls. They prod him, but he doesn't seem to feel it. He spits and screams, no words, just sounds that bore into August's brain like a drill. He wants to cover his ears.

The man turns around. August sees his face. The world stops.

He's skeletally thin. His hair has been shaved off. He's missing an eye.

But there's no mistaking that scar.

"John!" Kovich screams. She has a syringe in her hand.

August moves instinctively, grabs Liam's arms, holds him down. Liam looks up at him, his purple-red eye rolling back into his head. His other, empty socket is infinitely deep, abyssal. He has tears on his wrists where he broke through the restraints. *You don't know me,* August thinks at him frantically. *You don't know me!*

They get the needle in, and a moment later, Liam's eyelids flutter closed.

The silence in the room is a physical presence. Kovich is breathing fast. "God, you're strong," she says to August between breaths.

Weir stands nearby, arms crossed, watching everything as if it's all a demonstration for his benefit. "We got one syringe in him before you came in," he tells Kovich. "Otherwise, Thirty-One here would have thrown our dear Mr. Leonard across the room, like he did poor Dr. Hughes." He gestures to a man on the floor. He's not moving.

"Jesus, Rhys!" Kovich hurries over to Hughes, kneels, presses her fingers to his throat. But it's obvious that he's dead. "I think his neck is broken."

Weir stands over Liam. He smiles, speaks with a kind of affection that makes August sick. "Incredible spirit, this one has." He touches Liam's shoulder. August wants to push him away, hit him, beat him to death. "What on earth does he have to live for that he fights so hard?"

"Rhys!" Kovich is still kneeling on the floor, tending to another colleague's head wound.

"Yes, I know." Weir goes to a digicom on the wall, speaks into it. August isn't listening. Liam will have new scars, he thinks, looking at his bloody, torn wrists. His whole life's history is carved into his skin.

August backs up against the wall, looks at the ceiling. There's a light above Liam's bed, right over his head. It's blindingly bright. His stomach drops. They must use that light to torture him, he realizes, remembering Liam's thick black goggles, what Eden said about why he liked Worlds. August stares into that light until his eyes water, until they burn.

Other people come into the room with gurneys and medical supplies. Lena is with them, asks if he's all right. He tells her he's fine. Kovich leaves, and he's forced to follow her, forced to do his job, forced to be not-August, to react to what he's just seen as John Leonard.

"Rhys is an idiot!" She tears off her gloves as she walks, throws them onto the hall floor. "These fucking chances he takes. He's going to get someone—" She freezes, covers her mouth with her shaking hand. "Oh my God." She looks up at August. "Oh my God." She leans back against the wall, slides down to the floor.

"Doctor?"

"I'm fine. I'm fine. Just let me—" She hides behind her hands. "I'm fine."

August stands near her, trying not to think of anything at all, trying to bury himself as deeply into his lies as possible, to forget who he is. When Kovich doesn't get up, just stares straight ahead, her hand over her mouth, he sits down on the floor next to her. *I am not August. I am not August.* "He looked familiar."

"He should. He was all over the Cube after Hammond." She lowers her hand. "That's Liam Aldrich, one of Adair Holden's people."

August swallows. "I thought he was dead."

"So does everyone else. So keep it to yourself." She looks at him. "He should be dead. What am I talking about? He *was* dead.

For ten minutes." She shakes her head. "We revived his body for the organs. You can imagine our surprise when his eyes opened and he started breathing on his own and cursing at us."

August almost smiles. Of course that's how Liam would claw his way back from death—screaming and cursing at the ones who saved him.

"It turns out Aldrich can go without oxygen for just over fifteen minutes. Lucky him."

"Yeah." He doesn't want to think about what experiments they might have done to Liam to discover that.

The hallway feels so narrow suddenly; it scares him, and he's too aware of how deeply underground they are, can almost feel the weight of all that steel and concrete above his head. He looks up at the ceiling.

"He hasn't given up a damn thing. Not one useful piece of information." Kovich says this with something like admiration. "I've never seen anyone stand up to Rhys like that. Not even Kelley Pierce."

"The bomber? He was here?"

She nods. "He fought hard, but not like Aldrich. Weir got to him eventually. He gave away three DCo cells in the tri-state area, but he didn't know where Bryce was."

August remembers the big DCo bust a year ago. Twelve people arrested, one shot while trying to escape. "What happened to Pierce?"

"He went back to Hammond after Weir was finished with him. He was one of the prisoners who escaped actually." She crosses her arms. "But Aldrich? We can keep him as long as we want. You get carte blanche with a dead man."

"What?"

"We had to be careful with Pierce and Adair Holden. Everyone was watching us. We couldn't just take them out of gen pop, not with so many eyes on us. When people forgot about Pierce, he was ours to do with as we pleased, but we couldn't keep him forever. People didn't get a chance to forget about Holden before he escaped. But Aldrich? Everyone thinks he's dead. Carte blanche."

"Carte blanche..." August murmurs. Blank paper. Empty paper. Empty... like Liam's eye socket. That's all Liam is to Kovich: blank paper. Upon which she and Weir can scribble and scribble and scribble until it tears.

They sit together in silence. Kovich rubs her hands up and down her arms, shudders. "Sometimes this is too much."

He waits, watches her.

"Once you get enough death threats, you'd think you'd get used to it after a while. But you don't. Especially when someone's actually tried." He can see a hint of embarrassment in her eyes, revealing a vulnerability he would never have expected from her. "John..."

"What is it?"

She looks down at her hands. "I haven't told you something. And I wasn't going to. No one likes to talk about their fatal mistakes."

"Fatal mistakes?"

And she tells him what he already knows: about Wayland and how he escaped; that Weir's thoughtless behavior and risky experiments were to blame, as they had been for Rico Martinez's death and what just happened with Liam. She tells him about Eden; how Eden bit her and how she lived through it; how Eden's eyes frightened her more than the venom; that she believed, if Eden had had the strength, she would have literally torn her to pieces. She shows him her scar, two small white bumps on the side of her neck, paler than the rest of her skin.

"Rhys thinks she might be alive. Can you believe that? He thinks somehow she came across Adair Holden and helped him escape." Her tone is only a little dismissive. Part of her must be terrified by this possibility, and this gives him some comfort, but not nearly enough.

"You're safe," August tells her. "If she's alive, she won't get anywhere near you. I promise."

Again, that sickening vulnerability fills her face. She doesn't say anything, just looks at him. And he can see that she believes him, that she trusts him.

He was only a few hours away from the end of his day and then only four more from Eden.

Why did this have to happen before he left? Why did he have to see this?

Why does he have to know?

And he hates himself. He's just seen Liam, his friend, Liam, strapped to a slab, starved, missing an eye, and all he can think about is how it affects *him*.

Later, in his car, he looks blindly out of the windshield for a long time, then he beats his hands on the steering wheel and screams.

✦

When he pulls up the driveway, he sees Eden waiting for him on the steps. She stands, a beautiful smile on her face. He pulls into the garage, stares at the wheel. He wants to back out, turn around, drive away—from her, from Holden, from all of them.

He wants to get out of this car as fast as he can and run to her.

He jumps when she taps on the window.

"Are you planning on getting out any time soon?"

August forces a smile, opens his door. He takes his time, standing slowly, pretends to look for something on the floor, anything to avoid her eyes.

But after he closes the door, she kisses him. He doesn't know what to do except kiss her back.

Then he thinks of Liam, of the gaping hole in his face, how he screamed.

He takes Eden's shoulders, gently pushes her away.

"What is it?" She touches his face. "What's wrong?"

Why is she so beautiful? Why is she so perfect? "I have to tell you something."

She waits, but the words stick in his throat.

"Are you okay?"

All week, every day and every night, he thinks of her, of her smiling face, of how her hair spills over the pillow behind her head, of how she touches him, of how she feels; and of how *he* feels, how happy he is during and after, how the pleasure doesn't end when it's over, doesn't leave him empty and lonely. A thousand one-night stands are nothing next to that brightness and heat that fill him when he holds her afterward and she falls asleep on his chest and is still there in the morning, wanting him again.

"I—" Again he loses the words. Again he holds back.

"August, you're scaring me. What is it?"

He speaks in a rush. "I love you."

But those aren't the words. Those aren't the right words.

She breathes out a quiet, relieved laugh. "I thought you were going to tell me something terrible."

He kisses her. "I love you." He runs his fingers through her hair. "I *love* you." But they're still not right; they're still the wrong words.

Eden pulls back, holds his arms, looks at him, into his eyes, into *him*. "I love you," she says, for the first time.

And there's such gravity in her words. They're serious, certain, unyielding. She's sure. She's *sure* that she loves him. And he's sure that she's only ever said those words when she meant them, not carelessly, like the rest of the world does.

He's wanted her to say them for so long, and now it's too late. "Eden, I've never loved anyone. And no one's ever loved me."

"I'm here." She puts her arms around him, holds him tight. "I love you."

He hides his face in the curve of her neck, holds her like that until he's sure he won't cry; until he's sure that he can keep going without breaking down and telling her everything.

Until he is as committed to this lie as he is to all the others.

pre-order your copy of

FREEDOM

Book 2 of *The Deformed*

coming May 2024

go to abigailmccue.com for more details

Acknowledgements

I'm happy to have this opportunity to officially thank the many people who helped make *The Deformed* a reality.

Thank you Tim Reynolds for believing in me and pushing me no matter how hard I fought you. And thank you for your beautiful performance of the audiobook, as well as for the incredible cover art and book design. You're my own personal Renaissance Man! I love you eternally!

Thank you Antonia Jenkins and Pamela Smith, my first audience, for reading the original draft, giving me your honest opinions, and then reading the final draft. It's a long damn book and I'm more than grateful for your patience and insights.

Thank you David Gatewood a million times over for your masterful editing and especially for challenging me to be my best.

Thank you Morgan O'kane and Zeke Healy. Your music and joy inspired me to pursue my dream of being an author.

And a very special thanks to Uncle Kimo, and my late aunt Aunt Leslie, for sharing your home with me so I could put the finishing touches on the first draft in the peace and quiet of the Shenandoah Valley.

And finally, thank you to all the people who donated to my GoFundMe Campaign, listed below. Every dollar helped with the costs of publishing, and I was honored that so many of you thought I was worth investing in.

You're a wonderful bunch of people!

GoFundMe Heroes!

Rachel Arnsdorf
Kim Brown
John Cheary
Celeste Ciulla
Cynthia Cruey
Amanda Cobb
Cynthia Darlow
Kevin Fecu
Richard Ferrone
Lara Franicevic
Andrea Gallo
Danny Gray
Thomas Hampton
Paul Hecht
Jenny Ikeda
Natalie Imlay
Timothy Imlay
Michael Ingram
Liz Irwin
Antonia Jenkins
Janice Jenkins
Tracy Liberatore
Dylan Lorenz
Susan Lyons

Nick Malizia
Jefferson Mayes
Deborah McCue
Katie McCue
Mary Ellen McCue
Carol Monda
Trisica Monroe
Domhnall Murphy
Jennifer O'Donnell
Kimo O'Connor
William Ortiz
Tina Prause
Ruth Reynolds
Barbara Rosenblat
Brad Ruderman
Colette Shepard
Ellen Shepard
Pamela Smith
Henry Strozier
Deirdre Synan
Jill Tanner
Mark Turetsky
Ken Vallario
Nancy Wu

About the Author

Abigail McCue is a professional in the creative field, with a passion for storytelling. Her exploration of other worlds, character-driven science fiction, and villains, in particular, has been a driving force in her life since she was a teenager. Complicated, mysterious and curious, to her a villain's choice is more nuanced, their motivation often tragic and compelling. In *The Deformed*, she abandons good and evil in the traditional sense, in favor what it really means to be human—by exposing the heroes and villains that exist in everyone of us.

Abigail writes longhand and dictates to a computer using a program that doesn't understand swear words. It keeps things interesting. In addition to writing novels, she is a longtime audiobook producer living in the Hudson Valley with her husband and fellow producer, Tim Gerard Reynolds—who is the voice for the audiobook version of *The Deformed*.

For more information, visit abigailmccue.com

9 780999 328415